# BLACK
## *Tuesday*

# Nomi Prins

# CONTENTS

Other Books by Nomi Prins

*It Takes a Pillage*

*Jacked*

*Other People's Money*

*The Trail* (under pseudonym Natalia Prentice)

**"There will never be another crash like this again."**

John Maynard Keynes

Black Tuesday

# PROLOGUE:
## The Crash

# WALL STREET

## October 29, 1929

Leila's nerves bristled at the sound of shouting men. Their voices seeped through the diner's bay windows.

Raspy voices. Fearful voices. Angry voices. They transported her back to the time in her childhood when the strains of men yelling meant brutality and death. An image of her grade-school teacher stricken by the swords of Cossacks, followed by one of her brother being beaten to death and another of her mother's bruised face, bombarded her mind. She winced at the memory. She had come so far, to a new world and a fresh life, but the violence of her past lingered, impervious to the passage of time or change in geography.

The floor rumbled as the men stomped by, as if at any moment it would give way and pull her down beneath it. Her eyes darted around the tiny diner. Customers consumed their evening coffee, nailed to their seats with the sluggishness and desperation of men drinking their final cups. Their hesitation confounded her. Usually, their bravado filled her diner. But tonight, in contrast to the commotion outside, they sat silent and scared. Not of the kind of violence that men could unleash on each other, but of the amount of money they had lost, and could still lose.

The stock market crash had killed their confidence. Money was as treacherous a weapon as a shotgun, or a sword.

"Okay, boys. It's six o'clock. Closing time!" she announced for the second time. She considered pushing them out, despite her diminutive frame. But reluctantly, they began to move, grumbling as they gathered their derbies and coats. "What'll I tell my wife?" "How will I face my family?" "Is everything gone?"

She had no response for them. She could tell them that anything could change in an instant, but it didn't seem like something they'd want to hear.

She thought about her behavior less than twenty-four hours ago. The passion she had never felt with her boyfriend, Nelson, had flowed so easily in her union with Roderick, a man who would never – could never – be hers. How can you want someone so much, and hate him so much at the same time? *Damn you, Roderick.* Last night played tricks with her heart; the moments that had transpired in the diner teased her. She didn't feel safe here anymore.

"Wish me luck, Leila," said a night watchman. "It's a goddamn mess out there."

*You don't know the half of it,* she thought. She nodded and sent a quick smile his way, then cleared the last of the china plates from the countertop. Before she could stop it, a coffee mug flew from her grasp. It shattered in bone-white fragments across the tiled floor. *That* tiled floor. She bent to her knees to scoop up the shards. *Don't think about that now,* she chastised herself. *Do what you should have done last night. Go home. Help your uncle. Leave before things get worse.*

Quickly finishing up, she grabbed her woolen wrap and stepped outside. She grazed the pavement, caught off-balance by a flock of men oblivious to anyone in their path. The stock market had made fools of them all, and they only had themselves to blame. No, she realized, that wasn't exactly true. The thought ignited a flicker of loneliness, which was odd because she would have expected anger instead.

She bolted the door shut, then smoothed her skirt, tucked some loose strands of her raven hair behind her ear, and faced the seething street.

"Banks run out of dough! Get your paper!" cried Peter, the paperboy, in his high-pitched alto. He was standing beneath the diner's red-and-white checkered awning waving papers about. Coins from the gloved hands of pale-faced men pelted his tin pail like hail.

Leila emitted a tense yawn. She had woken up well before dawn, but the questions in her head drained her more than the lack of sleep. Why had she been so eager to betray Nelson? Why hadn't she warned her uncle with what she knew? Why had Roderick left so abruptly last night? When would she see him again?

The stench of sweat, cigars, and autumn's damp chill stuck in her nostrils. Her ever-present impulse to run was hindered as she waded through crumpled newspapers and hills of discarded ticker tape. The sharp edges of anonymous briefcases speared her stockings.

*I need to get out of here.*

Before her, the street was triangulated amongst the New York Stock Exchange – marked by majestic limestone pillars and a crown of Grecian sculptures, the Federal Hall – guarded by a statue of George Washington, and the three-story beige façade of the Morgan Bank. Waves of men surged onto the front steps of the Exchange, their bowler hats thumping and their fists pumping. They were shouting, "Thieves! Bastards! Give us our money!"

The topmost windows of the Morgan bank seemed to twinkle brighter than usual in contrast to the stark fortress beneath them. Several guards defended the bank's revolving doors from livid shareholders. Leila thought about Roderick's confession as she watched them rush the guards, and wondered what would happen if they were not held back. What if they had pistols or knives? What were they capable of doing in their moment of anguish and blame seeking? She wondered what the Morgan partners were doing inside.

From the corner of her eye, Leila saw a dark form plunge from the top of the bank. It took a split second for her to register that the form was a body. It crashed onto the roof of a black Cadillac Coupe, scarcely ten feet in front of her, with a hollow crunch; its limbs splayed out in four different directions. The windshield glass sprayed onto the sidewalk like a cascade of water. Too late, someone yelled, "Watch out!"

Almost instantly, the crowd spread away from the car. Gravity pulled the body from the sloped roof. It smacked onto the sidewalk. Leila stood paralyzed, her gaze transfixed to the landing spot. Her feet were stone; her breath lodged in her throat.

On the lamp-lit corner of Wall Street, with the buzz of the shareholders emanating from the steps of the New York Stock Exchange across the street, Leila clutched at the nausea careening through her stomach. Her eyes gradually moved to the inert body, while her ears captured questions flying around her.

"Did you see that?" cried a heavily bearded man.

"Who is he?" a lone female voice rang out.

"Is he still alive?" a man shouted from behind her.

A trickle of crimson seeped from beneath the head of the sandy-brown-haired man. He had landed facedown without the courtesy of a hat to mask the carnage, or perhaps it had flown away during the drop. Leila trembled at the thought of what the crash must have done to his features. Part of her wanted to flee; part of her wanted to help.

The trail of fresh blood gathered force, streaming towards the gutter, soaking the sheets of newspaper and smothering the feverish black headlines. More onlookers gathered, bumping Leila aside. A handful of guards who had been stationed by the Morgan doors erupted onto the scene. A group of Wall Street policemen streaked past her to join them.

"Give him room!" yelled a stout officer, as his partners pushed the crowd away with their batons. "Move back! *Everyone.* Move... back!"

A taller officer brushed away pieces of sparkling glass with his boot. He knelt by the body, fingers to the man's throat, feeling for a pulse. Another policeman knelt down and traced a heavy, white chalk outline a few inches from the body.

From out of nowhere, two Packard ambulances barreled down the street, their engines roaring and siren bells blaring in two-tone spurts. Emergency medical workers leapt from one ambulance, peeled open its back doors, and extracted a stretcher. The portly police officer stopped them a few feet shy of the man.

Leila strained to hear him say, "There's nothing you can do for him now." The finality in his voice made her want to assist. Maybe there *was* something she could do. She inched closer.

"We need to see," argued one of the medical attendants.

"There isn't anything to see here," said another police officer.

*What an absurd thing to say*, thought Leila.

Leila caught snippets of voices from people hungry for gossip. She heard someone say, "I hope it's not Andrew. I'd jump too if I lost as much as he did today." She hoped so, too. Andrew was a trader at Morgan, a sweet boy who had come to work on Wall Street to help his family keep their farm.

As employees streamed from the doors of the bank, Leila got the impression that the news had taken almost no time to spread inside. She wondered if they already knew who he was. One of the officers dug into the man's breast pocket fumbling for a wallet, but there was none. Whoever he was, he had left his credentials behind.

"It's like the bomb! The Morgan bomb in 1920!" cackled a toothless fruit vendor.

A stocky officer with thick arms and even thicker eyebrows scanned the crowd, using his nightstick as a guide. "Did anyone see which window he jumped from?" he asked.

His gaze fell upon Leila. She stepped another foot closer to the body.

"You, Miss. Did you see which window he came from?" the officer asked Leila.

"No," she trembled, "I saw a shadow and then he... he was on the car, and then the ground."

"Anyone else? Anyone?" the policeman called out. "Did anyone see *anything*?"

Leila stared at the blank faces around her. No. No one had looked up. *No one cared.* They were all consumed with their own problems. Not just bankers, but tailors, cabbies, and tradesmen had lost their fortunes and futures, and they had no idea why.

Leila let herself glance more directly at the body. His clothes were well pressed, the seams finely tailored, and his shoes... his tan English-imported shoes. Her heart skipped a beat.

Wait a minute. She knew those shoes. *No. No. No! No!* Dizziness filled her head. She swayed from the internal impact. She took two steps backwards and tripped over her own feet.

"Watch it lady!" a young man exclaimed.

"Oh my God!" Leila cried out. She slammed to her knees and covered her mouth with shaking hands. Her fingertips lost all sensation.

*No, no. It can't be!*

She knew exactly who that man was.

# PART I:

## The Build-up

# 1.

# *March 3, 1929*

*Dear Mama,*

*I can't believe it's been five years since I came to America. Sometimes I feel like you will never be able to come over from Kiev and join us, but I know that one day, you will. Uncle Joseph says that people are coming down from Canada. He is looking into it.*

*Guess what? I have a new job! At a diner called the Morning Spot – it's on Wall Street, where all the giant banks are. Men go there to make money and trade shares of stock at a place called the New York Stock Exchange. I know I promised to help Uncle Joseph at his contracting office – I can't tell you what a mess his paperwork is – but he said I could work for him on the weekends. I'm not going to be a waitress either, Mama, I'm going to be a manager. Imagine that!*

*Aunt Rosa says hello. I'm afraid she's not walking as well as she used to, but her spirits remain high. The twins are working hard at the docks at the Fulton Street fish market. I almost never see them. Jonathan is always making jokes and playing with Rachel when he can. Joshua keeps pretty much to himself.*

*He has a bit of a temper. Rachel just got an "A" on
her English paper. I told her she would have to help
me with English from now on. You should have seen
the look in her eyes.*

*I love you and miss you.*

*Leila*

*P.S. I have fourteen dollars saved since January
for your journey.*

\* \* \*

Leila posted the letter on her way to the Third Avenue
El, a weekly ritual. But, on just her second day, she couldn't
calm rising doubts about her decision to take the job. The
money would come in handy, of course, but something about
the area chilled her from the inside. It warned her that she
was an unwelcome guest granted temporary visiting rights
amongst the regular crowd.

Yesterday, the rackety train that transported her to Wall
Street from her Orchard Street tenement derailed mid-
way, so she spent an hour trapped in an airless car whose
wooden seats reeked of sour clothes and raw chicken.
Dodging to avoid a stout Italian sausage peddler barreling
at her with a fully-stocked cart of steaming breakfast links,
she snagged her finest – well, she only had two – dress
on the stairway railing leaving the El. On top of that,
her customers reminded her of misbehaved toddlers,
with monogrammed wallets and silk-brimmed hats. As
she knotted and tucked an escaped thread into the new
hole in her dress, she noted the taut faces of the laborers
and clerks sharing her car, and replayed in her mind the
conversations that had brought her here.

Last week, as the sun beamed early light between the
arrays of vendors positioning their wares, Leila was running

late. She had promised her Uncle Joseph she'd be at his Forsyth Street office by seven o'clock. An ace contractor, her mother's oldest brother was lost when it came to reports and figures.

At ten past seven, she dashed along Houston Street and ducked into the Morning Spot diner to purchase her uncle's coffee. She was awaiting her order, her mouth watering at the cinnamon scent wafting from the coffeecakes, when Moishe, the owner, ambushed her.

"Leila, my dear!" he called out, dropping a breakfast order eight tables away. He waddled towards her, his baker's apron fluttering, and took her hands in his. Leila could already tell that she would not be the only one in his diner involved in the conversation. The garlic breath of Otto, the pensive shoe-cutter, and Jacek, the Polish electrician that worked with her uncle, beat at her back. She saw Clara, the local beauty, come up from behind Moishe – her slender frame towering over him, her caramel curls bouncing. Leila laughed inwardly at the concern of this extended family; they acted as though her decision would alter their lives, too.

"You'll be perfect there, Leila," he persisted. "That beautiful long hair, not bobbed like all those *nafkas* uptown, and those sparkling brown eyes – my Wall Street customers will fall in love with you. Who knows, maybe you'll find a nice, rich husband in the mix."

"I have a boyfriend," she reminded him.

"Like I said, a nice rich husband."

"Moishe, your offer much appreciated, but I don't know anything about being a waitress," she told him. *IS much appreciated*, she mentally corrected herself. *IS. And I don't want to be a waitress.*

Since arriving in America, she had strived to educate herself, even as she abandoned school for working with her uncle. She'd spent hours on the second floor of the Seward

Library reading the simplest children's books, carefully writing down all the new words in her notebook until she could spell and remember them before moving on to more complicated works. *IS much appreciated.*

She began dating an Irishman to escape the suitors of her own heritage. She aspired to be more than a waitress, more than a Russian immigrant. She longed to make her Mama proud and even though her Papa was no longer around, she wanted him to know – somehow – that she strived for a better life, as he once had.

"Who said anything about being just a waitress? You'll be the boss too, do the books, and be the hostess; it'll be like you're me, except downtown. What more can you want? Just try it for a couple months," Moishe beseeched, his fleshy hands active.

"Nelson is convinced that all bankers are devils," Leila rebuked, mostly because she felt she should. But did she really believe that? She believed the Cossacks were devils and they weren't bankers.

Giving it more thought, she grew increasingly excited at the opportunity Moishe was presenting her.

"Your boyfriend needs to be more accepting of others," said Moishe. "This is America. We're all here to prosper. So what if some prosper faster than others?"

"Some would say they are stealing from others," Leila replied.

"Stealing, schmealing," Moishe dismissed, "we all need to drink coffee and eat eggs. Now what do you say? Help out an old man."

"You're not old," smiled Leila. "You're barely forty. Okay, maybe you are old!"

Leila knew her objections were silly. Her Tanta Rosa's health was rapidly declining. The twins were struggling. Her uncle could barely pay her a wage that allowed for living expenses, let alone saving enough to secure her mother's voyage from Russia or buying her little sister, Rachel, books she could keep, instead of borrow. And who knew, working downtown might be just the ticket out she'd been hoping for.

She eyed the eager faces around her.

"Think about it," begged Moishe. "It could change your life."

"He's right, you know," agreed Jacek. "Your uncle will be fine without you."

"I hear the men there are *very* handsome," Clara added with a wink.

Throughout the day, as Leila processed paperwork in Joseph's simple office, she mulled over Moishe's offer with a mix of guilt and eagerness. That evening, her head crammed with numbers from the day's accounting, she ambled south from Houston Street along Orchard Street. She passed broken sidewalks piled high with garbage waiting for the trash truck that came once a week – if it didn't break down. She caught herself longing for a world that didn't stink of fish heads, brine and the sewer.

She bumped into a group of laborers piling out of a bootleg beer saloon. The men were belligerent, poking their fingers into each other's chests as they each schemed about how to change their conditions; if only they could overthrow the rich. She wanted to believe them, but she couldn't. With every step, she realized that this world wasn't going to change. It was choking her. She would do anything not to be caught in it forever.

That night, she lay awake for hours staring at a ridge of plaster that divided the ceiling into halves. The soft snores of her aunt and little sister pervaded the room they all shared. She thought of how much money she could save to transport her mother to America. She considered heading for Hollywood one day, with its sun and space and glamour.

As the minutes ticked by, Leila thought of life back in the old country and about how far she had come. She missed her father and brother, Adam, now dead for ten years, murdered at the hands of a pack of wild, drunken Cossacks. She shuddered at the memories of hiding from them, huddled with her baby sister in their family's cellar, barely staving off hunger and rats. If it hadn't been for the nuns who had found them a few days later, she didn't know if they would have ever survived or seen her mother again. After all she had been through, she knew she couldn't walk away from an opportunity for something better.

The next morning, it was she that cornered Moishe in the diner.

"I'll take it! I'll take the job!" she exclaimed.

"That's wonderful!" Moishe responded. "You won't regret it."

So far, she found herself regretting it deeply. On her first day, she discovered that a few of the more aggressive customers liked to occupy the table by the cash register where they could brush up against her buttocks as she walked by. With each graze, she had an urge to tell them exactly what she thought of their brutish manners and smack their roaming hands, but since she had committed to this job she just smiled and held her tongue.

Leila surveyed the modest eatery – thin as a Pullman railroad car, with eight small wooden tables running along the wall opposite the counter. She recalled her mother's advice: *from responsibility comes possibility,* and resolved to make the diner her own.

She dusted the tabletops and the carved wooden benches fashioned from old church pews. Upon the tables, she arranged the bottles of Heinz Ketchup, Del Monte Mustard, and Lea & Perrins Worcestershire sauce – garnishes for the newest fad: hamburgers. The whole place stunk of beef no matter how much she cleaned it. She lined up the aluminum salt, pepper, and sugar shakers, and wiped down the counter that seated ten comfortably, though during rush periods, thirty men fought for space at its swivel stools.

By nine a.m., the place buzzed with impatient customers. With the exception of Ellen O'Malley, the head chambermaid at the inn next door, they were all men. Most of them worked at the banks, the brokerage houses, or the New York Stock Exchange. Some, like the cobblers and tailors, provided services for the wealthier types.

Leila wiped her hands on her white cotton apron, straightened her skirt, and tried to think about whatever these men were thinking about so she could engage them in conversation and maybe larger orders. The door jingled. Three suited men arguing about the price of Standard Oil stock entered. Leila marched over.

"Welcome to the Morning Spot!" she chirped.

"Hey Miss, where's my coffee?" called a patron sporting a dark grey and black striped trilbies hat and a brown three-piece flannel suit.

"Coming right up," she said as she finished seating the incoming men. She handed another customer a menu and grabbed the coffee pot from behind the counter.

"How about today?" he complained.

*How about I pour it on your lap?* she thought crossly.

"Miss, I need the bill; I'm going to be late for the market's open!" yelled another man with salt-and-pepper muttonchops, his balding head a shiny red.

"Certainly, won't be a moment," she smiled.

Leila glanced over at Nan, the other waitress, who was immersed in an argument over whether a patron's eggs were overcooked or not. Four more customers rushed in for their fix.

"Morning gentlemen, can I help you?" she asked, tucking some errant hairs beneath the white paper waitress hat that sat upon her head like a nurse's cap.

"Yes, you may," said a tall newcomer with a deep, dulcet voice. He sauntered past the cluster of men; his assertive posture captured her attention and made her heart leap. He stood there inspecting the place as if he were about to take it over. Others seemed to notice and parted for him. He assumed a counter stool without waiting to be seated.

"Miss, the BILL?!" called the muttonchops man.

"Here you go," she replied, absently scribbling the 15-cent tally on her pad and tearing the slip as she continued to observe this quietly commanding customer.

He was tapping his fingers on the countertop, concentrating on *The New York Times.*

"May I help you?" she asked. She felt a rush of heat invade her cheeks.

"One coffee – black," he said, reaching into his pants pocket for some change.

"Of course, sir," Leila replied. "Right avay – away!" she corrected. She cursed herself silently for her mispronunciation. As hard as she practiced, her nerves sometimes had an accent of their own. *Stop staring at him,* she scolded inwardly. She peeled her gaze away from the man's clean-shaven face and strong jaw, quickly pouring a mug of freshly brewed coffee and handing it to him.

"Here you are," she smiled brightly. She hoped he would say something, anything, to her.

He plunked down twenty cents, grabbed the handle and saucer, and sipped.

"You're welcome," she said.

He reached into the breast pocket of his charcoal suit, extracted a silver-mounted leather hipflask, unscrewed it beneath the counter top, and poured a generous shot into his cup. She couldn't help but stare at him.

"Medicine," he explained, when he looked up.

"Of course," she replied.

Prohibition might be the rule of the land, but he was not the only man that took his coffee with a side of "medicine."

He gulped the mixture, then returned to his paper, studying stock quotes from the previous day as if he was committing them to memory. Delicate lines framed his eyes, though the rest of his skin seemed too young to match. When he was done, he dabbed the corners of his lips with his napkin, swiveled his stool around and headed for the door.

"Have a nice day, sir," Leila called to his back.

As the door jangled, she realized it wasn't his indifference that mesmerized her – or his broad frame – but his calm intensity. He seemed compelled to fight some internal battle, alone. She recognized a need to burrow away from a world in which he didn't quite belong; she knew that desire all too well. Leila wondered what he was hiding from.

She couldn't wait to see him again.

# 2.

# March 24, 1929

*Dear Mama,*

*Another winter is gone. The mornings are warmer and tiny buds are sprouting on the trees of Orchard Street. I am enjoying my job much more. At first, I thought all the men that came into the diner were rude and boring. But, there is this one man. I don't know his name. He is very handsome and quiet. He comes in to read the morning paper every day at nine o'clock. He doesn't talk to the others, but they all seem to know him. I realize I am with Nelson two years now, but he has become so angry all the time, always ready to start a fight, and for some reason this stranger makes my heart blush. Did I tell you how handsome he is? And tall. Like a movie star.*

*I've started to read the business papers myself, too. If I'm going to be a good manager, I need to know what my customers are thinking about, right Mama? Mostly I talk to them about the markets, but sometimes we talk about their lives at home, the girls they are about to marry, the children that are growing up too quickly. Someone told me that the Morning*

*Spot is the only sane place here in the thick of this busy, crazy financial district.*

*I love you and miss you.*

*Leila*

*P.S. I made eight extra dollars at the diner this month for your journey.*

\* \* \*

Each morning, the stranger swigged his alcohol-laced beverage while hunkered over the counter. He would scan the market pages and leave exactly fifteen minutes later. Leila learned that this was an hour before the stock market opened. She began to anticipate his arrival with a growing awareness of his slightest movements: from the degree of erectness of his shoulders, to the small tick that flickered beneath the center of his right cheek when a particular stock seemed to jump up at him. And despite no discernible communication having taken place, her infatuation hijacked her moods. When will he talk to me? Does he think I'm pretty? Will he think I'm smart? Why do I care so?

After three weeks, she could no longer stand the ups and downs of this silent anticipation. On a Sunday night, after helping Rachel with her arithmetic lessons at the wobbly table that served as desk and dining area, she enlisted the advice of her best friend, Rivkah. Rivkah was a curvaceous Hungarian girl who had arrived in America when she was eight and had no trace of the foreigner's accent that plagued Leila.

"I don't know what it is," she told Rivkah, as the two girls huddled on the second step of the front stoop of her tenement. They were smoking the latest brand of *Lucky Strikes* – mauve cigarettes, slender and "feminine," as the ads described them. Every so often, they rose to allow neighbors weighed down with groceries to sidle past. In the distance, the rattle of the El echoed through the narrow streets.

Across the street, behind the fire escapes that crisscrossed the red-brick tenement facades, one family that had saved their pennies to purchase the latest Edison radio, or bought it on credit – no one was sure – gathered in their living room. The notes of their jazz music program filled the street with a soft melody.

Leila continued, "I have so many things to worry about. And a boyfriend who wants to marry me. *Why* can't I stop thinking about him?"

"Crush," concluded Rivkah, like a boardwalk gypsy. "Maybe you're a little bored with Nelson. It happens. So, you think he likes you and is too shy to say anything yet?"

"He does not seem like the shy type, more like – busy. But there's something about him. All the other men come in and boast to each other; he's more... serious."

"Well, why don't you wear a shorter skirt or something? I've been meaning to tell you, it will be much better for your tips if you go more modern. Add color. Plum is in."

Rivkah, a plump girl with unruly ginger hair that made her appear more Gaelic than Eastern European, had no qualms with upward-creeping hem lines, which puzzled Leila, as she couldn't help but notice her friend's knees resembled a pair of raw potatoes.

"Believe me, Rivkah, the men down there are free enough with their hands. I do not want to encourage them." Leila didn't really like her legs. She wished they were longer and thinner, shapely like the blondes in the *Lucky Strike* ads.

"I still think you'd make more money if you weren't such a prude," Rivkah retorted. "Anyway, so here's what I'm thinking – why don't you just, you know, talk to him?"

Leila sighed. "Because I don't know what to say." The El rumbled again, as if angry that its cars were emptier because it was Sunday. "I don't want him to think I'm some dumb immigrant. What if he just wants to drink his coffee in peace?"

"Flirt a little. Say something about the markets, or whatever they talk about down there," advised Rivkah, blowing rose-gray smoke puffs into the dark air. "Men aren't hard to figure out. They like when you pretend to be interested in the same things they are. How do you think I got your cousin, Joshua, to notice me? I said something about salmon being scarce this season. What do I know about salmon?"

Leila laughed, "Joshua is three years younger than you are – you're scandalous!"

"Who cares," replied Rivkah, "he's adorable. How old is your new boyfriend?"

"He's not my boyfriend," Leila corrected. She flicked some ash onto the sidewalk. "I don't know, he's older. Thirty maybe?"

"A rich older man – I must tell Moishe. He'll be so pleased," she teased.

"Don't you dare!" said Leila. She was sorry she'd mentioned him. Rivkah had better keep this conversation to herself. "It's nothing, just like you said – a little crush." The two burst into a fit of giggles.

"What are you lovely lasses laughing about?" asked a young man with a warm Irish brogue, sporting suspenders over black trousers. In the evening shadows of the dim cast-iron streetlight, Nelson O'Leary's cobalt eyes complemented the sparkle in his grin.

"Nothing," they told him simultaneously.

Leila sprung up. His lips sought hers, but she turned away, offering her cheek.

"I don't believe you," he said, circling her waist with a muscular arm. "But, I'm not going to get into a lather over it – do you know why?"

"I have no idea," said Leila, squirming slightly. She wondered why the firmness of his grasp suddenly seemed so unwelcome.

"Don't look at me," said Rivkah, palms raised.

"It's opening night at Yankee Stadium!" Nelson exclaimed. "With all the bad news coming on the construction front – people losing work left and right – I'm looking forward to some home runs! That's why."

"What bad news?" asked Rivkah.

Leila's face fell. That kind of question had the effect of sending Nelson into a tirade against the upper class. Lately, his temper flared at the slightest provocation. It scared her. She tried to deflect what could otherwise be a rough conversation. "Well, if you hear my customers talk, things have never been better."

"That's because those idiots think that their markets represent the real world," he scorned, "but unions are getting busted. People can't find jobs. Fords are barely selling. Leila wake up; things are getting worse all around you."

"Don't act like I'm stupid," Leila snapped. "I didn't mean that things are like the bankers say. I mean, I do live – here," she gestured to the hanging clotheslines dotting Orchard Street. "And Uncle Joseph was just saying that steel production was declining, which was pushing prices of material up, and pinching his business. But—"

"See, that's what I mean," interrupted Nelson. "More people are in dire straits than ever and Hoover is talking about prosperity like he's never been to Orchard Street, though he's sure been to Wall Street. You know, you're in an ideal spot to spy on those capitalists down there. What do you say Leila, you want to be the next Emma Goldman?"

"I barely have time to keep up with food orders, let alone be a spy," she retorted, nervously shifting her feet. She was used to deflecting Nelson's dramatic ideas, his grand visions of uprisings of the poor, and how the masses were going to overrun Wall Street one day. She didn't have the same faith. Masses did nothing while her Papa and brother and many other families were slaughtered in Kiev; they feared for their own lives.

"You mark my words, Leila, things are going to get bad – even for those Wall Street bastards – it's just a matter of time."

She saw him form a fist. Maybe he was right, but his anger propelled her out of his grip. "Are you staying for dinner? Tanta Rosa has been asking about you. She's preparing brisket in your Honor." She smiled prettily.

"Sure! Rosa's brisket could cure the world's ills. Besides, I promised to fix her chair. She said the wobbling hurts her back, poor thing," he said, raising his tool bag. "I'm going to take care of it right now. Are you coming up?"

Leila bowed her head slightly, "Yes, I was just giving Rivkah some – female advice. I will be right there, okay?"

"Sure thing," he replied, with a wink. "Good luck, Rivkah. He's a lucky guy."

"Oh, it's not for me, it's—" Rivkah began before getting stymied by Leila's glare, "uh, thank you Nelson. Never can get enough of Leila's wisdom."

Once he was out of earshot, Leila said, "I wish he'd stop getting so worked up."

"Don't worry about it too much," said Rivkah. "They all get that way, sometimes. He's probably just having a tough time with his job. He'll be okay."

"I hope so," replied Leila. "He's been acting strange since his brother was involved with the White Hand Gang. I don't want to see him in any trouble."

Rosa's brisket was indeed a masterpiece. Yet after dinner, as Nelson helped Leila clean up the kitchen, she couldn't keep her mind from roaming. She wondered what the stranger was doing tonight, and if he had a sweetheart with him.

Nelson kneaded Leila's shoulders while she washed plates in the cold suds of the roll rim sink. He trailed the side of her neck with his lips and asked her to come over to his apartment on Ludlow Street. She knew what he had in mind; it was one of their Sunday night rituals, though of late, it was more like every other Sunday night. It was impossible to be intimate in this cramped apartment, but Nelson's roommates worked on the George Washington bridge Sunday nights. She had lost her innocence to him there on the night they broke ground. Tonight, his kiss invaded her skin like a trespasser.

"I must be at work early," she told him, surprised by her own skittishness.

"Earlier than last Monday?" he asked.

"Yes, it's – I have early delivery of milk bottles that I must attend to." She felt horrible. It was the second lie she had told him today. She wished he would stop searching her face with his inquisitive eyes, waiting for her to change her mind.

"Next week. Or maybe later this week?" she offered, to make him feel better.

"Sure, Leila," he leaned down to kiss her. This time she let him, but the gesture produced little more than friendly warmth. Thoughts of the stranger flitted through her mind; of his fine-pressed suits that represented a finer life, of his hazel eyes that carried some dark secret in their forest-green flecks. Could he be causing this feeling of distance between her and Nelson? Or had they already begun drifting apart, and the stranger had merely floated into the opening space?

Monday morning brought a worried group of bankers into the Morning Spot. Investors in oil companies were selling all of their stock. Leila watched the men's legs fidget more than usual in the cramped booths; their faces taut and conversations terse. Leila was as anxious as her customers, not because of the market, but because it had kept the stranger from coming in. *So much for the conversations we were going to have.*

The next morning, she didn't quite start a conversation with him, but she did manage to eavesdrop on one. Seated in his usual spot, dressed in a dark-brown suit with a white handkerchief peeking from its front pocket, he focused on the paper, oblivious to the animated talk around him, imbibing his spiked coffee.

"People on margin are getting hit," said Oliver, the man with the muttonchops – now a regular – chewing his toast. He glanced around to see whom he could engage in his monologue. "All these guys who put 10 percent down and borrowed the other 90 percent from banks to bet on stocks – they have no money to pay them back. It's bad."

"I'm in that boat," added the local tailor. He usually spent his lunch hour at the Morning Spot, complaining about the dismissive behavior of the high-hats that bought his suits. Today, he was in the diner earlier than usual, downing his eggs with the very men he despised. "I don't have any extra money to pay my broker, so I have to sell my stock to come up with it, but prices keep dropping so it's not worth as much. It's like following a damn dime down a drain. I'd rather just borrow money until things turn around."

"It's called a credit crunch," boasted a young broker, proud of his fancy phrases. "Everyone's trying to borrow money, so rates jumped to twenty percent."

"That's why I can't afford to borrow any more," lamented the tailor.

"Think it's all going to come crashing down?" asked another customer timidly. Leila noticed they all directed their comments and questions to the man who made her insides flutter. Who *was* he?

"It'll be fine," he said calmly. "Charles Mitchell, the head of National City Bank, is putting $25 million into the market to give it a boost. You'll see, tomorrow things will bounce right back." He plunked a few dimes on the counter. Before he turned towards the door, he shot Leila a glance. She smiled back, cocking her head slightly.

The next morning, she awoke extra early. She spent twenty minutes in the dark at the small vanity table, brushing her hair. She lined her eyes with a coal pencil she had borrowed from Rivkah. She applied a crimson lipstick before she bounded off for the diner.

The stranger's words proved true. The markets did jump back. Brokers drank quickly, and skipped toward their offices to pick up buy orders. But far more important to Leila, he surprised her with two small words after she brought him his coffee.

"Thank you," he said, his bold eyes catching and holding hers.

She nodded brusquely before rushing to a customer a few seats down. *Stay calm*, she cautioned herself.

A few moments later, he called over to her: "Miss. I'll take another."

She approved his request with her eyes, her mind forgetting all the other customers at the counter. She poured him a second cup, using both hands to steady each other.

Again he went through the process of adding to the mug from his flask, two shots this time. She could no longer resist. She didn't even know where her shyness around him came from. "Hard morning?" she asked softly.

"Hard night," he replied.

"Oh, I'm sorry to hear that," she said. She wondered what could possibly be so hard for someone like him. She caught herself. *You don't know anything about his life.*

"Things are much better now," he said. She felt his eyes roam her body. She liked the tingly sensation it invoked in her. She snuck a glance at his full, slightly parted lips.

"So, is Charlie Mitchell hero now?" she asked. *A hero. A.*

He looked surprised, but impressed. His shoulders drew back as his neck extended, revealing a sharp Adam's apple. "Well yes, *Charles* certainly is. For now."

"He put enough money into market to bring call rates down to eight percent from twenty percent, is that right?" She wasn't exactly sure what call rates were.

"That's right," he said. A twinkle escaped his eyes. "By giving the market money, there's more around for people to borrow, so they get charged less to borrow it."

She failed to mask her confusion. "I'm sorry, I – so how is that exactly?"

He checked his golden pocket watch. "I'm going to be late," he said.

"Oh," she said, crestfallen. "I understand. Another time."

He relented. "Okay. Say you don't get your ground beef delivery one morning, and you only have a little left from the night before."

"You charge more for what you have left?" she offered, eager to impress.

"Let me finish," he said with a schoolmaster's tone that made Leila want to crawl behind the counter. "Say everyone wants a hamburger. One guy offers to pay $3 for one. The other guys either can't afford that much or you run out of meat. Either way, unless you get new meat, people stop coming for hamburgers. Once you do, problem solved."

"New meat. Yes. Oh, I see," she said. "Mitchell – Charles – putting in money was like me getting a new batch of ground beef. It put things back to normal again."

"Exactly," he replied. "It really is easy to fix these things."

He spoke so assuredly, but she had her doubts. Nothing was ever that easy. As she racked her brain for more dialogue, he tipped his hat and took a step toward the door. He paused and walked back toward her. "My name's Roderick," he introduced himself. He removed his glove.

"Leila." She slipped her hand into his. It felt smooth, not calloused like Nelson's.

"That's a lovely name," he said, flashing a smile. "For a lovely woman."

"Thank you," she said, a thrill racing through her. "Nice to meet you."

She was startled by the intensity of her physical reaction. She had merely gripped his hand. And yet it seemed as if she had just disrobed, right in front of him. Her other customers faded into the wood and chrome of the diner.

"Likewise, Leila," Roderick replied. His hazel eyes locked with hers. She felt a steady heat in the firmness of his grasp. She desperately wanted to keep her hand in his all day. Then in a matter of seconds it was over, and he was gone.

# 3.

# *April 7, 1929*

*Dear Mama,*

*I don't want to upset you, but Tanta Rosa's health is really going downhill. I never know what to expect anymore when I come home from work. Some days she can stand, others she can barely move. The doctors around here haven't been able to change much. They say she should rest, eat well, and take this drug called Phenobarbital to keep her muscle spasms away. I'm afraid none of this is helping. Something called multiple sclerosis is attacking her nerves. It makes me want to cry, but she is so brave I would never let myself do that in front of her. Yesterday, Joshua got so mad at the sight of her falling against the kitchen wall, he threw a chair across the salon and stormed out of the apartment. I don't know how to help her. If you have any ideas, please write me.*

*Besides that, Rachel has a crush on a boy at school. Her first one. She asked me about my first crush, and I changed the subject. I can't bear to think about what happened to Isaac and Adam and Papa. It's still so hard. Sometimes, it feels like the Cossacks will be following me forever. I know that's silly. I hope you are staying safe. The man at my diner, his name is Roderick. I think he likes me. I don't know what to do about Nelson. I think he's more interested in his union meetings nowadays anyway.*

*I love you and miss you,*
*Leila*
*P.S. I saved another four dollars this week.*

\* \* \*

Leila hovered in the kitchen entranceway observing her aunt doing the washing in the soup-stone wall tub. Her thin arms trembled as she squeezed the excess water from the twins' socks and hung them over the back of a nearby oak chair – "the laundry throne" as dubbed by Rachel. Such determination drove her, Leila noted with pride. This disease was coming with a vicious force, yet she would not succumb.

Leila recalled how her mother's older sister, Rosa, received her and Rachel so tenderly, opening her apartment and her heart. The twins, three years younger than Leila, were not immediately thrilled with their older cousin and her talkative little sister invading their home, but soon bonded like brothers. Jonathan reminded her a little of Adam, not in looks since he was a fair-haired boy, but in playfulness. Joshua was more broody. Leila still wondered how they all managed to fit into the cramped space.

Everyone slept in shifts and shared a hallway washroom with leaky pipes, icy water, and cracked tiles, with two other apartments. The twins awoke from their shared mattress in the salon to greet each day's catch well before sunrise. Leila left for work several hours before they returned, and Rachel got up last, eating breakfast with Tanta Rosa before heading to school. During the day, if Rosa didn't have visitors, she stayed alone.

For years, Rosa worked as a seamstress for a tailor in the apartment two flights below, sewing dresses for the bourgeois ladies uptown by a cloudy window that never provided enough light or air. When her illness spread, the tailor replaced her with a young Polish woman, and Leila joined the twins in helping to pay more for doctors and rent.

Rosa, once so spry, now had to walk gingerly, making her way the few steps from the bedroom to the kitchen by planting both hands on the mustard-seed wall and inching sideways. As it had become too difficult to traverse the five flights of stairs, the twins, Leila, and Rachel familiarized themselves with the spots Rosa preferred to buy her meat, fruits, and vegetables, haggling with the pushcart vendors on Hester Street in her place.

"Tanta, can I help you with that?" Leila asked. It was the least she could do.

"No thank you, dear. I'm almost done. I was just thinking, there's a new show starting tonight," Rosa said, wringing the suds out of Rachel's school-dress. "I miss taking my favorite girls to the theatre."

Leila had no interest in Yiddish theatre. The new Hollywood talkies at the Loews-Canal cinema thrilled her more. She had seen *The Jazz Singer* with Nelson there two years ago, and many films since. The plush velvet seats, majestic maroon curtains, and smell of popped corn transported her away from her daily life as much as the stories.

"You'll be there again, Tanta," Leila said. "Next time you're in remission, all three of us girls will go. Rachel loves Sophie Tucker."

The lines on Rosa's brow danced as she chuckled, "Have you seen Rachel's latest impersonation of Molly Picon? Our girl's going to be a world-class comedian someday."

"You see, you don't need to go to the theatre – Rachel brings it to you."

"Yes, that she does, but I miss the outings; how we'd all go together, gather at Moishe's after the show.   Regular Broadway critics we were."  She sighed.

"You've got a critique or two left, Tanta.  We just need another good remission, and then…"  Leila's voice faltered.  She was afraid to finish that sentence.

"And what if there isn't another?" her aunt asked with uncharacteristic pessimism.

Leila eyed her aunt's hollow cheekbones and defiant limbs, the silver streaks in the wiry raven hair that she wore braided down her back.  She felt her throat constrict.

"Listen to me go on," said Rosa, with a labored flick of her wrist.  "Of course things will be fine.  Enough with this *tsuris*.  How are things with you and Nelson?"

"Fine," answered Leila.

"That's all?  Just fine?"

"I don't know, I wish he could be happier.  He's always on about how miserable things are or fighting about something, ever since his brother was shot.  I'm afraid he may join the gangs again.  I guess I'm tired of it."

*I'm tired of not being the fighter he thinks I should be.*

Rosa nodded and swayed her body back and forth.  Her eyes closed, as they transported her to the internal movie of her past.  "He's a good man.  With a loyal heart.  You should try to see where he is coming from."

*Should.  Should.  Should.*

Rosa's words made Leila feel inadequate.  She could not help but think of the stranger at the Morning Spot.  Did he have any warmth?  Any goodness?  She knew nothing about him, and yet he had somehow burrowed into her heart.

"I know," replied Leila, "but that won't make him easier to deal with."

"You remember what I told you when you first came here – a young girl of fourteen, not knowing a word of English?" she asked.

"I do, Tanta." Leila braced herself for a speech she'd heard many times before. It was her duty to listen diligently, but her heart impelled her to flee. She loved her aunt with all her being, but that love imposed a burden that she wished she could shake.

"I told you that in order to succeed in America, you must find your purpose. And always help those less fortunate than you."

"Which is exactly what Nelson strives to do every day, I know. It's just that you and he have such courage and patience. I wish I did. Instead, I just want to get out of here—," Leila stopped herself, but Rosa seemed to understand exactly what she meant.

"Sometimes you don't find your cause, Leila," said her aunt with a little smile. "Your cause finds you. There is a fight buried in all of us. You remember the Factory."

Leila nodded, "Of course I do." The Triangle Shirtwaist Factory was her aunt's Pogrom.

"When the Ladies Garment Workers Union called a strike, I walked off even though I was terrified of losing my job. But that strike gave me such a feeling of elation. I mattered," Rosa's hand clenched at the recollection. Then as abruptly as it tightened, her fist crumpled to the frilly tablecloth, landing on a spot seared by Joshua's cigarette.

"Then there was the fire itself," Leila prompted, to propel her aunt's memory.

"Yes," said Rosa, "it was March 25, 1911. I will never forget the day. The entire loft burst into flames. Fire poured through the stairwells and elevators. Two dozen women rushed to fire escapes and plummeted to their deaths," her eyes moistened.

Leila sat patiently. The Factory owners were no better than the Cossacks to her. The life of every immigrant was tinged with vicious, needless deaths.  Her aunt's life was miraculously spared eight years before hers was.

"Hundreds of people gathered outside the building, watching.  Oh how the fire engines charged through the streets!  The firemen saw workers yelling and screaming for their lives.  But the fire truck ladder only reached the 6th floor, and management had locked the fire doors from the outside so women couldn't use the emergency exits."

"Bastards!" exclaimed Leila.

"It was a miracle I had run downstairs to get those brass buttons," she continued.  "They saved my life.  But others, they were not so lucky; so many workers jumped to their deaths.  Hundreds perished, most of them young women, like you – like I once was."  Rosa paused.  "The Triangle owners were tried for manslaughter, but acquitted."

"They should have been found guilty!" Leila retorted.

"That's our America," said Rosa resignedly, her explanation for the unexplainable.  "There are many things we cannot control. I count my blessings everyday that I made it home and went on to have two beautiful twin boys with my beloved – Aaron." She lingered on Aaron's memory longer than usual.

"Those men were greedy cowards," said Leila. *And murderers.*

At that moment, Rachel burst into the apartment, pigtails swinging.  "I hate him!  I hate him!" she cried, slamming her book bag onto the kitchen table.

Rosa coughed to suppress a laugh.  "Who do you hate, dear?  That Horowitz boy?"

"Who?"  Rachel looked confused.  "Oh, no, not him.  Gosh, Tanta, I haven't liked him in ages!  No, it's Danny.  Danny Rubin.  You know what he did?"

"Something terrible, I'm sure," Rosa grinned.

"He walked Jenny home from the library. Just 'cause she's so pretty.  I was sitting right next to her, too.  He knows I like him and doesn't even care.  I'm sooo miserable!" she cried.

"We can't have that," said Jonathan, striding in. "Besides, you're the prettiest girl in the world. How about I take you out for an ice cream? It'll make you feel better."

Rachel's coal eyes lit up at the sight of her favorite cousin. "Oh yes! Chocolate, please! Tanta, can I go before finishing my homework? Please? I bet Danny isn't buying Jenny an ice cream."

"Of course, you can. You know what else you can do – you can bring me one."

"Me too!" Leila added. She decided that she wasn't any better than Danny Rubin. She knew Nelson liked her – loved her – but still, she wanted to walk home with Roderick.

That night, Leila had familiar nightmares. She stood watching flaming bodies plunge from buildings, firemen and onlookers crowding the city sidewalks, doing nothing. The bodies fell around her, one after another, closer and closer, and yet she could not move. She awoke from that dream, as always, shaking with anger over her helplessness and trembling with terror over the instantaneous demise of so many people.

# 4.

# May 15, 1929

*Dear Mama,*

*I'm sorry I haven't written in so long. It has been a crazy spring. All the street vendors here are complaining more than usual, about the rising price of cotton to make dresses and pants, and how the pickpockets that used to just steal from the customers, now steal from them, too. There's this fight between the storefront shopkeepers and the pushcarts. The city may side with the storefronts and kick the street sellers out. Uncle Joseph is having a hard time. His landlord raised the office rent so his partner, Morris, wants them to move; but Uncle Joseph is having none of that, so they fight all the time.*

*At the Morning Spot, everyone is happy. The stock market keeps going up. One of my regulars, a guy named Sinclair who works at the Chase Bank, said the bankers are "raking it in." Mind you, no one tips Nan or me any better just because they are. Roderick is paying me more attention. He's an important man, but always explains things to me, and he listens to me, too. I told him the other*

*day that Standard Oil stock might have trouble,
and he told me I was right. He hasn't asked me
out on a date yet, but I keep wishing he would. I
know that's horrible. I should split with Nelson
before thinking such thoughts, but he's busy with
his union and we always argue when we do see
each other.*

 *I love you and miss you,*
*Leila*
*P.S. Uncle Joseph is trying to get you tickets on a
ship for Canada. In a few more months, we will
have enough money!*

* * *

The sun beat warm rays into the Morning Spot. Customers spoke giddily of record profits. Leila shared a smile with Roderick from behind the counter while cutting a slice of layer cake for the tailor. Still, not everyone was pleasant. A banker with heavy jowls shouted from one of the tables, "Hey – where's my eggs? What kind of lousy joint is this, anyway? Hey, Toots!"

"I'll be over in a jiffy, Hank," she told him. What she wanted to tell him was, "Mind your mouth, Hank. *And don't call me Toots.*"

"Why do you let them talk to you that way?" Roderick asked. "You deserve more respect than that. Don't they know you run this place?"

"How did you...?" she eyed him with a sheepish grin.

He motioned to the white aluminum sign hanging on the wall behind her.

"*Dear Customer: We appreciate your business! If anything is not to your liking, please feel free to speak to The Morning Spot Manager: Leila Kahn.*"

"Oh," she said. "Well, it's easier than creating ruckus. And, Hank's a regular."

"Hank needs a cuff to the side of his head," Roderick said, swiveling around.

Leila watched Roderick approach Hank. She had never seen him look anything but composed. Maybe he had too much to drink that morning.

"Hey, buddy," he said. "Why don't you apologize to the lady?"

Hank rose. "Who's gonna make me? A stinking silver-spoon pansy like you?"

Sinclair, the Chase banker, and Oliver, the muttonchops man, turned to watch the spectacle. So did everyone else. Walter, a skinny man with greasy hair whose background was a question mark, sneered, "Go on, Rod. Show him what you're made of."

Leila wasn't sure whether to break up a possible fight, watch Roderick defend her, or say something to keep the peace and placate Hank. Before she could decide, Roderick raised a fist and took a swing. Hank caught it in the air without flinching.

"Okay, okay," said Hank, "I wouldn't want you to dirty your gloves. Hey, Leila. I'm sorry. You know I love you. Just having a bad morning – boss up my ass and all."

Roderick repositioned himself at his stool, "We men can be such pigs." He reached for her hair. She thought she would have a nervous breakdown as he removed a crumb lodged in her strands. She also detected a heavy trace of whiskey on his breath.

"Thank you," she said, falling into his eyes.

He cocked his head, "Of course."

"Anyway," Leila turned to clear away Hank's plates, "pigs are neater."

Roderick sat quietly and read his newspaper, chuckling at her comment.

"What's so funny?" Leila asked.

"Nothing. Your work ethic is admirable. Where did you say you grew up again?"

"I didn't," she replied. *Damn accent.* "Back in Kiev, my parents – my mother – insisted we balance work and family. That – and respect for others."

"I can admire that," Roderick replied, polishing off his doctored coffee. "My family is quite well-known for our reputation of hard work. We…"

The sound of dishes crashing abruptly ended the conversation. Leila rushed to the kitchen to find the dishwasher on his hands and knees. The floor was a canvas of multi-colored liquids, food scraps and china. She decided it would be unwise to share this incident with Moishe, and began a worrisome mental tally of how much money it would take to replace everything.

"I'm sorry Miss Kahn, it was an accident," he pleaded. "I will clean it up, Miss."

Before Leila could say a word, she was interrupted by the arrival of one of her best customers.

"Leila! You got any of that fantastic coffee cake back there?" She recognized the booming voice of Officer Bryan O'Malley.

Returning from the kitchen to greet him, Leila noticed with a twinge of regret that Roderick had left without another word.

"Hello, Officer. You're here early this morning." Leila forced a smile.

"I couldn't stand listening to my stomach complain anymore!"

"It happens. What can I get you?" she asked.

"The usual, but make sure you bring me a slice of that coffee cake first!"

Leila laughed. "Coming right up."

She attended to his order, but her mind was racing. *Why had he left so suddenly? Why did his mention his family? Who is he?*

It didn't take much longer for Leila to figure it out.

"You look tired," she remarked when Roderick arrived the next day. In truth, he looked a wreck. Wisps of pink tinged the whites of his eyes, and the speckled green of his irises had darkened considerably.

"We're closing an important oil deal today," he told her, searching her eyes for a hint of admiration. The most she could offer was a face of bewilderment and questions.

"What kind of deal?" she asked.

"We bought a company last year and are putting on the finishing touches."

"What company?" she inquired, searching her brain for clues from her *Wall Street Journal* readings, wanting to provide him encouragement. "Marland Oil?" It was a guess.

He looked shocked. "How would you know that?"

She smiled. *Maybe I'm not just some dumb immigrant.* "I read also," she said, pointing at the stack of newspapers at the end of the counter.

"Well, yes, in fact. We merged it with Continental."

"I read that the former owner wasn't so happy about it, but he didn't have a choice. He was forced to resign – by some bank," she said.

"No, he had to resign because he wasn't very good at his job," said Roderick, squirming slightly. "We're spinning off their new company. It's going to go public early this fall." He leaned closer as she poured more coffee. She let her sleeve graze his.

"Public?" She couldn't believe he was sharing this with her, or the proximity of his face. *Or does he just think I'm too stupid to understand it?*

"Yes – start to trade on the New York Stock Exchange."

"Of course," she said, as if she knew the meaning of going public all along.

"I've been working hard on it," he added. "I was up all night ironing it out."

"What kind of deal, exactly?" she asked, twirling a strand of hair with her index finger, motioning for Nan to take care of one of the back booth orders.

"Hopefully the kind that'll make a lot of money," he answered, rubbing his blood-shot eyes.

Leila studied the man for a moment, the gears in her head moving faster than she could keep up with, when it dawned on her. Family, banks, oil... it couldn't be. *Could it?*

"Wait, are you related to—?" she hesitated.

Roderick interrupted, "It's not a top secret. I do work at that bank across from the stock exchange." He cocked his head in the direction of the Morgan building.

"But, is he...?" *Your father?*

"My uncle," he said, with a half-sneer, half-sigh.

*So that's why he acted so mysterious!* She was puzzled. He seemed not the least bit proud of his heritage. Most of the other men boasted about anything they could.

"I've got the scars to prove it." He removed his glove and extended the palm of his right hand toward her. A jagged line stretched from the tip of his thumb, across his palm, and to the left underside of his wrist. Leila felt almost embarrassed she hadn't noticed it before.

"Did he slice it because you lost money?" she asked.

"No," he grinned, "not quite. It was the bomb. Just my luck, too. First day as a partner and I'm the only one that got hurt."

She had a vague idea of the bomb to which he was referring. At noon on September 16, 1920, someone planted a bomb in a carriage across the street from the House of Morgan. Thirty-eight people were killed. Another four hundred, mostly office workers like typists and tellers, were injured. Only one of the partners was hurt, and she was looking right at him. Nelson had told her there had been a note placed at the scene, in a mailbox on the corner of Cedar Street and Broadway:

*Remember we will not tolerate any longer. Free the political prisoners or it will be sure death for all of you.*

*— American Anarchist Fighters.*

"They never found the guys who did it, did they?" she asked.

"No, though rumor had it that Jack, my Uncle, was the target of an assassination; in the name of revolutionary causes everywhere, or something like that."

"And that did not make you want to quit banking?"

"Nah, there's no better place to be right now," Roderick said, the green specks returning to his eyes. "You'll see, this market is going to explode bigger than any bomb."

"I thought there have been some recent problems," she said.

He looked quizzically at her.

"I read it in the *New York Times*. Something about an overdue correction?"

"That's just temporary. Markets correct all the time. They pull back and then head higher again. That's what they do. They always bounce back."

"But what if they don't?" she asked.

"They always do. Anyway, you've got me running late for the opening. See you tomorrow, Leila." Her insides warmed at the way he said her name.

"Yes. Tomorrow, Roderick."

He plopped a dollar on the counter and tipped his hat towards her on his way out. Leila felt the heat spread through her body. For the rest of that day, no matter how many snarling customers she waded through, she smiled at them like they were puppies.

\* \* \*

Back in his office, Roderick poured himself a tumbler of gin and took a seat in the high-backed armchair behind his mahogany desk. He stared at the steel Western Union ticker machine watching him from across the room atop a walnut stand with bronze-coated legs. The contraption resembled a crystal ball, only inside the glass dome, the metal device that could print out 500 characters a minute told financial fortunes. Every morning at ten o'clock, it would tell him what was happening on the floors of the New York Stock Exchange. For five hours it would revolve a coil of white paper imprinted with the changing black-inked values of the biggest stocks: AT&T, General Electric, United Steel. For most of 1928, and so far this year, the machine showed prices going up. The public, after all, wanted its chance to become as rich as – he was. This machine, with its language of abbreviations and numbers and jots and slashes, kept track of it all.

He glanced away from the ticker and out the window. Slightly to the right, stood the statue of George Washington in front of Federal Hall, and to the left, the Exchange. The American flag above its pillars whipped back and forth in the wind.

He pressed his nose on the window and peered further toward the right where he could barely make out the Morning Spot awning. He couldn't stop thinking about Leila. She was beautiful, far more so than she realized, which only enhanced her attractiveness. But he'd been with plenty of beautiful women. It was more than that. At a time when most women, or at least the ones that he associated with, sought the trappings of wealth, throwing themselves at him like pedigreed whores, she seemed indifferent to the money. There was this intensity in her. He always caught her reading newspapers between attending to customers. She had a way with her patrons, too. She made them feel comfortable. She made him feel comfortable.

She also took an interest in the details of his work. They weren't particularly compelling, he had to admit, but they were still important to him. As a young boy, he had a head for numbers. Numbers made more sense to him than people did, long lines of them spooling through his brain, falling into neat rows. He could manipulate them easily. He knew this was the only reason his Uncle Jack kept him at the bank, that and the fact that before he died, J.P. Morgan Senior made Jack promise to take care of his sister – Roderick's mother. Roderick quickly learned that the family business came with family secrets, and restrictions on behavior, on thoughts. He wondered what Leila's restrictions were like. What would the curves of her body feel like naked beneath him?

This pondering was far more satisfying than the task before him. On his desk lay two ledgers packaged between leather jackets. One book depicted the venerable institution's true condition, the other told a fabricated tale of exaggerated profits for the benefit of investors and customers. Creating the fake numbers, and making them as believable as the real ones, was his job, his duty.

It was never his intention to become embroiled in this fraud. But once he had stepped his toe in, there was no turning back. One day in 1927, Jack had barged into his office. Jack had never entered his office. He hated Roderick, and ignored him at all bank and family gatherings. Jack liked being in control; of which influential men were partners at the bank, of what time they met with him, of their external associations. He had handpicked each of the bank's 40 partners. Roderick was the 41st, and not his choice.

"Roderick, it has come to my attention that some of our real estate holdings in Florida have seen a rapid decline in value, would you agree?" As with all of Jack's utterances, this was more of a statement than a question.

Roderick knew all about the declining beachfront property values. The Morgan Bank had pressed many investors to purchase shiny new homes well above the price they should have sold for, under the promise they would resell easily for much more. It didn't turn out that way. No other investors appeared to buy the homes. Morgan's clients were stuck holding homes they didn't want. He knew what his uncle would say next, but braced himself for what he didn't want to hear.

"Yes, I would agree," said Roderick, his right lower cheek twitching.

"I can't have that," stated Jack, emotionless. "Our bank can't have that. Do something about it."

Roderick knew what he was expected to do without asking. He was expected to fake the value of those properties. The only thing that made the stuck buyers remotely happy was the fact that Morgan would overstate their home values. That way, they could be under the illusion that their investments weren't dropping, and the Morgan partners didn't have to acknowledge how wrong they had been about the entire venture.

That's how it began. But Jack didn't just want the values faked, he wanted to know by how much, and he wanted to know the real values and the fake ones at all times. So Roderick began producing two different sets of books.

It was wrong; it was unethical, illegal, and immoral. *It was what it meant to be a goddamn Morgan.* But there was nothing he could do to cross his uncle, who provided him his future, his status, his money. So he kept cooking the books.

When other deals or business ventures soured, he would do the same thing; the more an investment tanked for a client, or for the bank itself, the greater the difference between the fake and real books. Roderick and Jack knew just how much their books veered from reality. But if Jack cared, he didn't show it. He stopped coming to the bank for days at a time, citing other interests and travel, and leaving daily management to Tom Lamont, a blithering idiot that shared his disdain for Roderick.

Meanwhile, the burden of this truth weighed on Roderick's every moment. It drove him to drink a liter of whisky, or bourbon, or whatever elixir was handy, on any given day. It kept him from experiencing the slightest mirth. It made him stare for hours in his gild-framed bathroom mirror, repeatedly asking the questions that had no answers: *Who am I? What have I become?* He could never tell his uncle that he wanted out of the whole sad mess before it all blew up, and his utter powerlessness scared the hell out of him.

\* \* \*

Leila arrived home to a glorious May evening. Vibrant swaths of magenta, tangerine, and rose striped the blue dusk sky like the swirls around the candy canes at Cohen's sweet shop on Rivington Street. The air carried a gentle breeze throughout the Lower East Side. Leila was so gleefully distracted with thoughts of Roderick and the Morgan's that she circled her neighborhood several times before reaching her building.

Rachel was playing stoopball with a few of her friends. The brow under her raven ringlets was damp with the sweat of competition. Their building had the tallest stoop in the neighborhood, seven steps in all, so it was a magnet for kids. Children were laughing and scampering after every stray ball that bounced down the sidewalk.

The twins were unofficial neighborhood champs. Jonathan would wind his arm like a Yankee pitcher on opening night. He could go twenty points without missing a catch and finish a game with a hundred points. Joshua had stopped playing a few years ago.

"Hi, cuz!" Jonathan called to Leila, mid-pitch, his hay-blond hair a tousled mess, the sleeves of his work-shirt rolled to his elbows. "Your sister is gaining on me – she's out to take my title. It's war!"

"I bet on Rachel," Leila laughed.

"Is that all my talent means to you?" asked Jonathan, grinning.

"Sorry, Jonathan, but Rach is no slouch. We *all* better watch out for her. Now, would you mind making room for me to pass through the big game?"

"Do we have to stop now?" moaned Rachel, "I'm having my best run."

"Of course you don't," Rivkah answered, arriving breathless at their stoop. She hung onto the iron railing, her ample breasts heaving. "I haven't seen your sister in weeks; we're going to do a little catch-up, so keep beating Jonathan, okay?"

"Okay!" agreed Rachel, grabbing the ball, not needing the extra encouragement.

"Rivkah," Leila hugged her friend. "So good to see you, but I'm late for dinner. Rosa will be waiting for me to help with the finishing touches."

"Rosa definitely doesn't need *your* help in the cooking department," Rivkah chuckled. "Now tell me, what's new? Please. My life is one big bore right now. I need to come up with better fish stories for Joshua, or move on. It's tragic. How's your crush?"

Leila couldn't suppress a wide grin that unleashed her dimples.

"See, there's news!" exclaimed Rivkah. "Tell me!"

"Okay, but let's go over to Feinberg's Hardware, away from Miss Big-Ears over there," she gestured to Rachel.

The two walked a few buildings down the block. They strode passed Marcus's shoe store and Harold's Cigar shop, sniffing wafts of sweet tobacco. They passed another set of kids playing hopscotch, and a third playing stickball. Everybody was out tonight.

After they sat down on Feinberg's steps, Leila blurted out the latest development.

"Are you kidding me?!" Rivkah's emerald eyes nearly bulged out of their sockets. "He's a Morgan? Flesh and blood of the richest man in the world. And he talks to *you*?"

"His name is Roderick," she said proudly. "And he's Jack Morgan's nephew."

"I can't believe it – that's your crush? This calls for much shorter skirts!"

"Rivkah, calm down," hushed Leila. "The whole neighborhood doesn't have to know this. Besides, he is just a man."

"Who's just a man?" asked Rachel, who had appeared out of nowhere.

"Nobody," said Leila. "What are you doing here? Go back to your game."

Rachel stood, hands on hips, with an impish grin. "But I want to know who he is!"

"Rachel," admonished Leila.

"Fine," Rachel pouted, and stomped back to the stoopball contingent.

"I swear," said Leila, "that girl is everywhere. She's becoming like you!"

Rivkah laughed. "Forget about her, let's talk about Roderick. Is he Jewish?"

"How should I...? No, I don't think so."

"We'll deal with how you raise the children later. Jewish children take after the mother anyway. That's how I worked it out for you and Nelson, if it had to be that way."

"Rivkah, relax. I'm not having his children – I'm learning about the stock market and banking from him. That's all. It's a foreign world to me and I want to know more."

"Why? It's a world run by men," she replied, genuinely perplexed. "How much else do you need to know? Only enough to find a man."

"Honestly, Rivkah, it's 1929. There's more to life than finding a man."

"Sure there is," said Rivkah. "After you find a man."

Leila shook her head vehemently. "Why do women need men to live proper life? We work. We take care of ourselves. Why is it so crazy to learn about markets?"

"Because markets are tools of capitalist exploitation of the masses," declared Nelson, exiting the hardware store.

"You see," smiled Rivkah. "Thank you for straightening that out for us, Nelson."

At the sight of Nelson, Leila felt a slight panic. *What had he heard?* She wished the neighborhood wasn't so small, that her boyfriend didn't live a mere few buildings from her, and that he wasn't always appearing, though in the past she had welcomed this. She was in too good a mood to hear another tirade against bankers. Roderick was probably one of the richest men on Wall Street, and he still made time to talk to her. And even though most of the bankers were rude and arrogant, maybe they all weren't bad. At any rate, there had to be two sides to every story, and Nelson was only focused on one.

"Oh Nelson, don't you ever get tired of fighting?" she asked.

"I'll stop fighting when I'm dead," he replied. "Don't you get it? There's a change going on in this country. We workers can't afford to stop fighting for our rights."

She rose and studied him for a moment. He was searching for a very particular part of her. She didn't know if it existed. Of course she wanted fair treatment for everybody, but she didn't think it was wrong to want to make money either.

"Workers are striking because bosses don't have the slightest intention of sharing their wealth, even if it's made on our backs. The rich try to squash us at every opportunity. You know what happened at the Loray Mill in North Carolina last month?" Nelson inquired.

"They called in the National Guard," answered Rivkah, rising to join the conversation. Everybody in the neighborhood knew about that.

"Exactly," said Nelson. "First, the mill supervisors fired anyone they could, and when people kept striking, the mayor called in the National Guard to bust up the strikers. Never mind that they just wanted better wages and conditions. Imagine, women workers wanting shorter hours so they could raise their kids. How communist!" He began to shout. A small group of people gathered around him on the narrow sidewalk.

"I know, Nelson. I also want better conditions for workers," interjected Leila, taking his hand. She was so confused. She loved this man, didn't she? Yet, he irritated her so. He always had to talk as if he was delivering a speech.

"But how do you think that's going to happen?" asked Nelson. "There's still a war going on down there in Gastonia." He pulled his hand from Leila's in order to point towards wherever Gastonia was. "Owners don't share. They want to keep all the profits for themselves no matter what the cost to us. Something has to give."

"We're thinking of striking at the docks," said Joshua, appearing in his finest white shirt, black pants, and suspenders. There was a deep, earnest look in his gray eyes.

"Hi, Josh," Rivkah said with a flirty smile, adjusting her skirt and cloche.

He just tapped his cap with his fingers. His concentration was on Nelson.

"Smart lad," said Nelson. "If you want any organizing tips, I'll come down to the Fulton market." He turned to Leila. "See, even your cousin is joining the fight."

"You're my hero!" exclaimed Rivkah, squeezing Joshua's upper arm.

"And you're so subtle," said Leila.

"Subtle?' asked Joshua.

"Nothing," said Rivkah. "Ignore her."

"I think it's fantastic, Joshua," Nelson continued. "This is the time. These stock markets are rising every day because of our sweat, while our wages stagnate. It's insanity."

"But banks provide money to grow companies so they can hire more workers," said Leila, anxious to provide some balance on the topic, even though the words she had heard Roderick speak sounded hollow as she said them out loud.

"Bankers can pull their money out of the market whenever they want and leave ordinary people shafted. They are evil," said Nelson.

"Not all bankers," said Rivkah, coyly.

Nelson shot her a glare, as if she had murdered someone. "Why would you say that?"

"Leila works with bankers all the time. Roderick is—"

Now, it was Leila who shot Rivkah a glare. *What was wrong with her?*

"Who the hell is Roderick?" asked Nelson.

"Nobody, just a customer," said Leila. "He explains things about the markets."

"He's a Morgan," said Rivkah, in an inexplicable gesture of sabotage or stupidity.

Nelson glanced at Leila.

"He's one of Jack Morgan's nephews," she said. *Why did I tell Rivkah anything?*

"That explains it. Well, whoever this Roderick is," said Nelson, "he obviously knows nothing about struggle. Probably never had a callous on his hand."

Leila thought of Roderick's hand. Nelson was right; which only fueled her anger.

"There are battles going on everywhere between the working and ruling classes," Nelson carried on. "Just this month: the Rayon Mill strike in Tennessee, six weeks of the house wreckers' strike that brought higher wages here in New York, and a contractors' strike called by the Teamsters and garment industry. While your bankers are counting their money, we workers are doing something about it."

"They're not *my* bankers," retorted Leila.

Joshua added, "It's about time we fish handlers struck.

We're certainly not getting paid enough for the hard work and early hours we put in."

"Damn right!" affirmed Nelson.

Leila processed the fervor that overtook Nelson when he made these declarations. The gathering crowd was nodding in agreement with him, setting their packages down to listen. It was so difficult to reconcile all of this with the world downtown. The sharp suits, the gold watches, the cheery attitudes. She had never heard Roderick, or any of the customers, talk about unions or strikes, unless they affected stock prices.

"There are two Americas," said Nelson, addressing Joshua – with whom he was now allied – and the onlookers. "We must hope that ours wins, because otherwise America will become one big failed bank, with a lot of unhappy, jobless workers at its sidelines."

Nods traversed the circle of peddlers and laborers. She waited for them to dissipate to their evening routines. Rivkah and Joshua melted away, leaving Leila and Nelson together. Herb Feinberg slowly rolled down his dark-green awning for the day.

"Why are you always so pessimistic?" Leila demanded of Nelson.

"I'm just realistic," he responded. "Like you used to be."

All the joy Leila had carried home disappeared. Nelson had a way of sucking the air out of any celebration, a breath at a time, particularly when ranting about labor versus money. It seemed to her that it was easier to escape your surroundings than change them. It was simpler to deal with the world at the Morning Spot, even if she was only an observer, mainly because its struggles were too small and surreal to take seriously.

"Maybe I'm the one who's being realistic now!" she said, and stomped home.

When Leila reached the apartment, winded from the five flights of stairs and her argument with Nelson, Rosa was seated at the kitchen table, her hands in her lap. A copy of *The Jewish Woman's Home Journal* was spread before her, opened to a page advertising the kosher version of Crisco. None of the usual smells of boiling brisket or onion potatoes or garlic toast were present; no plates set. She blamed herself for holding up the evening meal, too fixated on her new infatuation and the frustration of her current relationship.

"How are you this evening, Tanta?" Leila asked, leaning down to kiss her aunt's forehead. "I'm sorry I'm late. Rivkah dropped by with her usual gossip. And, Joshua and Jonathan are playing stoopball with Rachel. Here, let me help with dinner."

"Don't worry, my Leila. Come, sit down," Rosa said softly, her eyes red.

"Oh my God – what is it?" Leila asked. "Are you okay?"

"Yes, my dear, I'm fine – well, as fine as I can be." She lifted a shaky arm to reveal an envelope between her fingers. "I got a letter today, from Russia."

Leila's stomach clenched. "What is it, Tanta?"

"It's your mother, Leila."

"Oh no!" said Leila, her nerves tightening. "Is she sick?"

"I'm afraid, she – she passed away. It was several weeks ago, a severe bout of influenza. The doctors did all they could, but…"

Leila could barely breathe. No. It couldn't be. It was some sort of mistake. "She was supposed to come here. We just didn't have enough money to sponsor her yet – but Uncle Joseph was trying so hard and I was saving everything I could from the diner…"

"We all wanted her here, my Leila," her aunt said softly.

"How come she never wrote that she was sick?" Leila felt her throat constrict.

"She didn't want to worry you, my dear."

"But she *should* have worried me," said Leila, raking her fingers through her hair. "I should have written her more. I was so caught up in my own life, in the coffee shop, with Nelson." *With Roderick.* Leila collapsed into a chair.

Rosa took Leila's hands in her own. "She knew about all these things and she was so very proud of you for making a place for yourself here. It's what she always wanted."

Leila could stand to hear no more. She fled the kitchen, flung herself on her bed, and cried. Burrowed under the covers, she didn't hear Rachel or the twins come home.

She had failed her mother in the worst way. Who was there when she died? Who stood by her bed while she burned with fever? Who went to her funeral? Her Mama died alone and here she was worried about men. Some daughter she was. Leila buried her head beneath the pillow and wept.

Hours later, Nelson was sitting beside her. "Your aunt said I might find you here – under the bed," he said, cupping her face with his calloused hand.

"Not quite under," she smiled, despite herself.

"Joshua told me," he said. "Had to bust up a Teamster's meeting to get to me."

"Better him than me," she said, resting her head on his chest. "Thank you for coming. I am sorry about before."

"Don't worry, my love," he brushed a teardrop from the corner of her eye. "When I lost my father, it was the worst day of my life – until my brother was shot anyway. No one knew he was sick. We couldn't prepare to say good-bye. I know how you feel."

"I didn't know Mama was sick either. I barely wrote her anymore," she moaned.

"You were busy. Working all week at the diner; weekends at Joseph's. She knew you thought about her," he said.

"But, I should have tried harder to get her here. We were so close. Uncle Joseph found a way to get her through Canada. She would not have died here. I know it," she cried.

Leila's body shook.  Nelson's arms tightened around her.  It was in these moments, where he was simply there for her, rather than addressing activists in Rutgers Square or pontificating about corporate evil or revolutions, that she remembered the sweetness of their love.  It was a shame he rarely showed her this side of him anymore.  She fell asleep as he held her until the early hours of the morning.

Leila remained home the next day, unable to shake the feeling of responsibility for her Mother's death. Her Mama had counted on her.  She tried to comfort her aunt to deflect her own sorrow.  Rosa had barely known her younger sister, but followed her life through two decades of letters. Together, Leila and her aunt read through the old letters, remembering a past they had both fled. Together, they cried for Esther's memory.

The following day, Leila dragged herself out of bed. Her aunt begged her to stay home, but she figured that the Morning Spot would assuage her. She hadn't thought about Roderick for a whole day.  She craved his presence, even as it had distracted her from focusing on her Mama.  The comfort Nelson had given her had melted into a prickle of anticipation.

At the diner, she found herself struggling to contain her tears.

"You look terrible," said Roderick, when he arrived.  He was wearing a fashionable brown suit and bowler, just a shade darker than his hair.

"Thank you," she replied flippantly, yet pleased he noticed.

"I mean, you look upset.  Anything I can help you with?"

She inspected his angular face, his jade-speckled eyes. *Did he really want to help or be polite?* Part of her wanted to tell him about her mother, and another part was angry with him for not knowing what she was going through.  If she hadn't been so wrapped up in fantasies of him, she might have paid more attention to her mother's plight.

"It's going to be a crazy day," he said, when she didn't answer him, "another oil deal – bigger than the last."

Her face fell further. *He doesn't care at all.* "You'd better be going then. Can't keep the markets waiting," she said, dashing to the register to make some change.

"Hey, wait a second," he jumped from his seat. The other customers stared at his abrupt gesture. "Leila, what's wrong?" He touched her shoulder.

She hesitated, ignoring the rest of the diner's curiosity. Why was it that the slightest bit of attention on his part made her want to dump out her soul to him? Nelson had left a Teamsters meeting and stayed with her an entire night, holding her as she cried. Yet it was to Roderick that she wanted to offer her deepest feelings, a man she barely knew.

She pursed her lips and swallowed. "The other night, I found out that my mother passed away. She died a few weeks ago."

"I'm sorry to hear that," he replied, somewhat awkwardly.

"I hadn't seen her in five years, but I always thought that I would be able to pay her way to come here," she continued, feeling defeated. "It's my fault she didn't come sooner!"

"Maybe, she didn't want to come," said Roderick.

"What are you saying? Of course, she wanted to come. She told me when I left Russia with my little sister, she would come," Leila lashed out, her voice rising.

"Okay, okay," he soothed, "I'm just saying, that you shouldn't be so hard on yourself, that's all. Maybe she had her reasons for staying behind longer."

"No!" Leila shook her head. What did he know anyway – about the pogroms, and her Mama working as a servant to the Lebedevs while Leila had to pretend not to notice the seeping away of her dignity, the sad droop of her shoulders, her unwillingness to ever talk about her Papa or Adam?

Why would her mother want to stay in Russia with all her painful memories? Why wouldn't she want to be with her daughters?

"My mother died when I was about ten," said Roderick. He presented her with a dollar bill and motioned to the register. She made change to quiet the stares of her customers. Just a normal transaction.

"How?" Leila asked, handing him some quarters. Her mind was in Kiev, at the entrance to her mother's bedroom at the Lebedevs, watching her sob, talking about the tickets for her daughters' voyage to America. Five years had passed since the Cossacks took the lives of her husband and son and she had become a house servant. Was she weeping because she knew she would never see her daughters again, either?

"It was never clear," he said, pocketing the quarters.

"Must have been difficult for you," said Leila, pleased he was sharing more of himself with her, but bothered by the thoughts he had unleashed about her mother.

"Not really. I suppose it's because I never knew her that well."

"I was fourteen the last time I saw my mother," Leila said. "Do you miss yours?"

"No, I have very few memories of her. Just that most of the Morgans paid her little attention, and she was always trying to be a part of their circle. Jack's father was the only one who cared about her. I think that's the only reason he took me in when she died, or rather placed me under a string of nannies in between boarding school."

*Nannies. Boarding school.* Leila stiffened. If she had his money, she would have sent for her mother years ago. Her Mama would have come – and still be alive today.

"Well, I miss my mother, and I will every day for the rest of my life," said Leila. She retreated behind the counter to assist her cook. She knew she sounded childish. She didn't care. When she returned, Roderick was back in his seat, buried in his paper, as if their conversation had never taken place. A few minutes later, he got up, settled his bill with extra cash, and left.

# 5.

# July to August, 1929

As the summer heat steamed the effervescent city streets, two items of interest captured everyone's attention. One was the stock market, and the other was the Yankees. Both blazed as hot as the summer sun. Any market hesitation in the first half of the year seemed to be replaced with certainty in the second. Babe Ruth would soon hit his 500th home run – the only thing that kept Nelson's spirits up, as work had dropped substantially.

Meanwhile, everyone around Wall Street kept talking about getting rich. So did the cabbies that drove bankers to their offices and the bootblacks that polished their shoes. Even the dishwasher at the Morning Spot had opened a brokerage account.

Leila heard men in the diner and on the Lower East Side lamenting about not getting in sooner. Words like "broker" and "margin" and "AT&T" and "General Motors" could be heard everywhere. Even the *Ladies Home Journal* promised everyone could be a millionaire in between photos of must-have silk summer dresses and Oscar Meyer Wieners ads.

Leila stored her sadness in an internal safe, throwing herself into work at the Morning Spot and with her uncle, as she had once done with her studies after her Papa died in Kiev. It was no longer the desire to pay her mother's way to America that fueled her, but something else; an uncomfortable longing to break free from family obligations.

Her conversations with Roderick had shifted from snippets about deals, to the books she was reading, and even to his uncle. He seemed more comfortable talking about work than his personal life, but Leila convinced herself that this had to be enough for the time being. Many of his problems revolved around money; making it, not making it fast enough, holding onto it. It was as if money was his air, his blood, and his manhood. She knew there had to be more to him than that. *What is he hiding?*

She longed for more time with him. Then, one mid-July Friday morning came the moment she'd been waiting for.

"I was wondering, Leila," he asked, after reading through the business page, "if you might possibly be free tomorrow evening?"

"Free?" she asked, a blush spreading across her cheeks. *Roderick Morgan is asking me on a date. Finally.*

"Yes well, Gershwin's *Show Girl* just opened last week to rave reviews at the Ziegfeld Theater and my wife and I—" he stopped mid-sentence. A hot drop of coffee had spilled onto the back of his hand, due to Leila's suddenly unsteady hands.

"Damn it!" he said, flicking the liquid away and shaking his wrist.

Leila's mind zoomed. The word "wife" ricocheted through her brain like a bullet. *He never told me that he had a wife. He isn't even wearing a ring.* She thought she'd die of embarrassment. Or throttle him. *Get a hold of yourself, Leila,* her mind warned. *Patrons are staring.*

"Here, let me get that for you," said Leila tightly, offering up a corner of the cloth napkin she was gripping with increasing intensity.

"Well?" he asked.

*Well, I hate you.* "I am going out with my boyfriend tomorrow night," she told him. It was the worst lie she could think of. She couldn't recall the last time she and Nelson had properly gone on a "date." She certainly didn't consider outings to his union meetings very romantic, and the sex afterwards had become almost perfunctory, like he reserved his passion for his fellow activists and not for her. *How can Roderick be married?*

"Oh, shame," said Roderick. "I was just wondering if perhaps you wouldn't mind watching Rodney, I mean, Roderick, Jr. – my wife hates when I call him Rodney – for the evening. I wouldn't ask, but our nanny is sick, and we have these tickets. And he's such a sweet little boy – just turned two years old."

She stared in disbelief. He had never mentioned a son before. He didn't even react to her mention of a boyfriend. "I'm not a nanny," she said.

"No, of course you're not," he said. "I was just thinking that you had mentioned extra money. I would pay you 90 cents an hour. A dollar, even. You said you were saving to move to Hollywood, one day."

She wanted to punch him, but tried to get a grip on her practical side. It was more than what Moishe paid her, and she did need the money. She told herself that she had been silly to think of him as anything more than a customer. He was someone with whom she exchanged periodic pleasantries while she served him coffee. No more. And yet as much as she felt insulted by his request, she was curious about his life. *Damn you, Roderick.*

"Maybe, if we change our plans, I could. Yes, I think I could," she said.

"Great," he said coolly, like he had just completed some business transaction. "It's 80 Park Avenue. Be there at seven."

After he left, she caught the bemused glance of Walter, the scrawny man that always wore black suits with his hair greased beneath his hat. He was one of her least-favorite customers. Unlike other regulars, he'd reserved comments about his background; someone had mentioned he was a bank clerk at Morgan. Someone else said he worked at National City Bank. She never got the straight story. She quickly averted her eyes and went to check on the lunchtime meat supply while she mulled over Roderick's request.

A babysitter. *I hate him.*

The next morning, as she did every Saturday, Leila made her way to Uncle Joseph's contracting office. Men sporting yarmulkes instead of bowler hats walked with their sons to the local synagogues, the most popular being the one with a multi-colored painted-glass Star of David, on Allen Street. Young women and their daughters strolled in the parks to catch up on the week's gossip and share distress stories about the rising cost of eggs and chicken and books for school. The pushcarts would return on Sunday.

When she arrived at the small office, furnished sparsely with two identical oak desks, matching chairs, and a row of aluminum file cabinets along the wall, Morris was already there. His religion was growing their business, whereas her uncle still maintained a weekly practice of his faith, and worked Sundays. As their bookkeeper, Leila usually wound up working both days. She handled the receipts and pending orders, and more recently, the latest Burroughs machine that allowed you to type out bills, calculate figures, and maintain records all on the same metal apparatus.

But today, she couldn't stop watching the Roman numeral clock above the filing cabinets, its hands barely registering the passage of minutes. She wished Morris would just leave so she could head out early herself, but with the exception of a brief lunch, he sat at his storefront desk, his white shirt-sleeves rolled up to his elbows, poring through the details of some job request. She couldn't stop thinking about what outfit she'd wear tonight, and what she would say when she met Roderick's wife. *His wife.* When the clock struck six, she still had several accounts to straighten out, but she would be late if she stayed to wrangle with the figures. Morris was still hunched over his desk, his fingers playing idly with the tabs of his new direct-dial AT&T phone. He hadn't spoken to her all day.

"Morris, I need to leave," she said, rising from the desk, her voice tight.

"Where are you rushing off to so early – hot date with Nelson?" he asked.

"Yes, a – date," she replied. "I'll finish up tomorrow morning, I promise."

"Alright my dear, have a wonderful time."

Ten minutes later, Leila sat at the white hand-painted vanity table that the twins had given her on her eighteenth birthday, which doubled as a lamp stand. As she examined her skin for blemishes, she replayed the situation in her mind: she had clearly misread Roderick's behavior. He *did* think she was just a waitress. He probably acted that charming with every girl he met. She had imagined she was special. *What an idiot I've been!* she thought to herself. He had a wife and a child. But that didn't mean she couldn't work for him, or get a glimpse at another way of life so different from her own.

She powdered herself with the soft bristle-brush that Rosa used when she expected company. Rachel watched.

"You look pretty," said Rachel. "Are you going to the movies with Nelson?"

"No, I'm going uptown, to babysit for a friend," answered Leila, as she primped her hair, alternately piling her dark-auburn mane in a twist behind her head, and letting it fall loose over her shoulders to determine the most flattering look.

"Down's nicest," advised Rachel, with an adult tone.

"Thank you," replied Leila, brushing it straight.

"You mean for that rich guy?" Rachel pressed.

"What rich —? How do you know about...?"

"I heard Tanta Rosa talking about him with Nelson last night. She says he's a shifty snake-cleaner salesman," Rachel answered.

"Snake-oil," Leila laughed, correcting her. "Rachel, you are such a big snoop."

"I just like to know what's going on," replied her wise-beyond-her-ten-years-old sister. She was growing up so fast. *She is your world*, Leila reminded herself. *He is not.*

"There's nothing to know. I'm watching his two year old son, that's all."

"In a grand mansion?" she enquired.

"A nice apartment." Leila wasn't sure why she felt compelled to defend his wealth.

"I heard Nelson tell Tanta Rosa that he lives in a penthouse on Park Avenue – that's where all the millionaires live, don't they?"

"Nelson talks too much," Leila retorted, applying a hint of blush to her cheeks.

"But, you don't like him, right?" she asked.

"He's paying me to watch his son – I like him because he helps me to buy us groceries," Leila said. She couldn't contain the self-righteousness in her voice, even though she knew her sister could care less about the groceries.

"So why did you put on lipstick?" Rachel persisted.

"Rach, go help Tanta Rosa with the dishes, and mind your own business."

"Fine," said Rachel, "I was just asking."

As Rachel stomped toward the kitchen, Leila inspected her face in the mirror. *Rachel is right. You are being ridiculous.* She reached for a cotton cloth to clean her lips and changed her mind. As she rose to finish dressing, she asked herself again why she felt so jittery. Yes, she had never stepped foot in a Park Avenue apartment, and a part of her felt anxious about looking out of place in such a setting, but there was also something about Roderick that made her nervous. *He is just a man*, she reminded herself. *With a wife.*

Her clothing choices were annoyingly simple. She owned two fashionable summer dresses. Leila chose the shorter one, a knee-cut, black-and-white daisy-printed dress Rosa had sewn for her. It wasn't silk, but it flattered her hips, as Nelson had told her. She grabbed her yellow hat from the brass hook on her wall, studied her face in the mirror once more, and walked to the kitchen.

Rosa was sitting on the hard-backed wooden chair that Nelson had recently repaired. Leila's mind raced to the evening ahead with a touch of guilt. She scanned the table in front of Rosa. A stack of letters from old friends and relatives who had not made it to America marked its center. She thought of the letter about her mother and, for the first time, what Rosa must have felt like losing her only sister. She thought of Rachel. She should be keeping her aunt company this evening, and yet, had no desire to do so. *What was wrong with her, that everything about her life made her want to escape it?*

"It's this cute bear that talks, Tanta!" Rachel beamed, jostling Leila from her guilt. "And he has a friend named Christopher Robin, and a tiger friend named Tigger who's always getting into messes. Everyone is talking about it at school."

"It sounds like a lovely story. Maybe you can take it out at the library," said Rosa. "I'm sure they must have a copy."

"But, I want my own copy," Rachel pleaded.

"We will see," said Rosa, as she suddenly gasped and clutched her right leg.

"Are you okay, Rosa?" Leila rushed to her side.

"I'm fine, dear," she inhaled sharply. "Don't you look lovely."

"Thank you, Tanta – I should be back around midnight. Are you sure everything is alright?" Leila knelt to massage her upper thigh.

"It's just the usual cramping; always gets worse at night, and a sure sign it's going to rain. I'm a regular weatherman that way. You might want to take a wrap just in case."

Leila grabbed her gray summer wrap, frowning to herself about its frayed state. Already a hand-me-down, she had worn it the past three years and hadn't been as careful at darning it as its previous owner. "Now I'm prepared. Are you sure you're alright?"

"Go ahead," she winced. "Rachel and I are discussing a strange bear named Winnie the Pooh."

Leila kissed Rosa's cheek. Her disease was worsening, despite Rosa's disclaimers. Last night, she could barely make it to the bedroom, a few feet from the kitchen, without nearly collapsing on the uneven floorboards. Leila couldn't bear the thought of her vibrant aunt immobile, and quickly brushed it away.

"Rachel, you better not give Tanta Rosa any trouble while I'm gone."

"I won't!" Rachel insisted.

"Goodnight, Tanta," Leila said and headed out.

Leila dashed to the El, reaching it a moment too late as its steel doors shut. It took another twenty minutes for the next one to arrive. Rosa's premonition was right. As she neared the stop closest to Roderick's building, the sky curdled and roared overhead. Within a minute she was drenched, running toward Park Avenue as sheets of rain slammed the city streets and bolts of lightning radiated electricity through the dark skies.

A brass plaque that read, "*Built in 1924 by the Mandel-Ehrich Corporation,*" marked the facade of his twelve-story building. The entrance was situated below a set of arched windows adorned by three terracotta figures; an immigrant, an Indian chief, and a frontiersman. It was an odd selection for such a grand building.

The doorman welcomed her warmly, as if she was an old family friend. "You must be Miss Leila Kahn," he said, tipping his scarlet hat in a distinguished fashion. "You are expected. Niles, the elevator man will take you to the tenth floor."

"Thank you," said Leila. She was impressed immediately by the building's majestic interior. The walls were ebony, decorated with a three-dimensional, rectangular indentation, and lined with a copper trim. The bas-relief bronze elevator doors were etched with lion heads. Her shoes sank into the plush, wine-colored carpet. *This elevator probably costs more than our whole building.* At the tenth floor, the elevator man opened the doors to reveal a hallway matted with navy blue-and-gold diamond-patterned carpeting. She spotted two doors, one on each side of a foyer centered about an arrangement of pink roses.

"To your left, Miss," said Niles.

"Thank you."

She reached for the brass ring drooping below an eagle head, and knocked twice. An earnest young man opened the door. He was dressed in a black jacket with perfectly ironed matching pants, shining leather shoes, and an accurately placed bow tie.

"Good evening," he said. "Please do come in."

"Good evening," she replied. "I am Leila. Sorry, I am late. I—"

"Don't worry, Miss. My name is Mr. Collins," he told her with a cultured accent that might or might not have been British. "You're sopping wet. Please, let me take your wrap. I'll put it over one of the kitchen heaters. The lady of the house is still getting dressed – never a brief happening. I'll tell Master Morgan you're here."

"Thank you," said Leila, removing her wrap, mortified as a sprinkle of drops loosened from its fabric onto the polished wood floor. She caught a reflection of herself in the entranceway mirror, an oval construction framed by thick waves of gold. The hair she had taken such care in brushing neatly down her back was a tangled wet mess.

At that moment, Roderick appeared in the foyer. Leila's breath caught in her throat. She had never seen him look so dapper, so handsome. He wore a short black tuxedo jacket and tails, black bow tie, and a crisp white shirt. His hair was slicked back around a perfect middle part. His skin was almost shining. She inhaled his scent of fresh pinewood and cinnamon, and felt heat run through her body. *Stop!* she scolded herself. *He is going out with his wife. You are babysitting his child. You have a boyfriend. You are not one of these people. You never will be.*

"Leila, so good of you to come," he said formally, lightly grasping her shoulders and kissing her cheek. "I trust Collins has given you a tour of the house?"

"Um," she glanced at Mr. Collins, not wanting to get him into trouble, "I just got here. The El was running a little behind."

"No matter," he said. "Please, come in, let me show you the library while my wife is getting ready. This way."

She grimaced at the thought of his wife as he escorted her through a long, dark hallway lined with squares of cherry wood. A decorative oriental rug stretched from one end to the other. There were four small end tables, two on each side of the rug, displaying potted plants and expensive-looking lamps. Gold- and bronze-framed photographs adorned every spot along the walls.

"Family," he told her, stopping in front of an octagon of elderly faces.

"You read my mind," she said, standing beside him.

"I don't know who half these people are, to be honest, but it's important that we Morgans show off our heritage at every possible moment, in every possible hallway," he laughed. His shoulder touched hers. She let it remain in place until he continued walking.

"Ah, here we are." He opened an ornate door and beckoned her to come in. "This is where I do all my work," he told her. "My sanctuary, if you will."

As she took in the grandeur of the place, her mouth dropped open. Heavy burgundy curtains tied with gold tassels hugged the sides of eight floor-to-ceiling windows. On one end of the room was a fireplace beneath a speckled black-and-white marble mantel carved with angels. On the other, behind an antique desk, was a wall of leather-bound books. "I do my work on a little cot in the room I share with my aunt and sister," she said.

"I'm – sorry," he said uncomfortably.

"No, I didn't mean to…" she said, not sure what she did mean. "Just, some of us make do with small spaces, but this room is wonderful. You must love it."

He beamed. The back of his hand brushed hers. She moved it away. Maybe his previous touch was an accident. *It had to be. We are in his home.*

"I'm glad you like it."

Leila stepped toward the library's centerpiece, a mahogany desk with an inlaid black band around its surface, on which stood a gleaming silver inkwell and feather quill, an engraved fountain pen on a gold stand, a modern typewriter, and several crisp white stacks of paperwork separated by thick yellow cards.

"Allegheny Corporation?" she asked observing the top set of papers and charts, recognizing the name of the important railroad company from her newspaper readings.

Ignoring her question, Roderick strode to a gild-framed portrait of a regal elderly woman. She followed him.

"She's beautiful," Leila remarked. She was astonished by the detail of the painting. The woman wore an elaborate white dress with fitted lace sleeves of a pastel-colored flower print, accented with scarlet seams. Her pewter hair was pinned up with a matching hair ribbon. On her wrist, she wore a diamond bracelet encrusted with rubies.

Beneath the painting was a small table with several crystal flasks of various colored liquids. He scooped some ice into a tumbler and covered it with a velvet-caramel shot. "Vermouth," he said, "best you can find. I'd offer you some, but…"

"But that might not be appropriate for the person responsible for your son tonight," Leila finished.

"Yes, precisely." He swallowed the contents of the tumbler, poured another, and gulped it down quicker than the first. Then, he poured a third.

Leila glanced towards the railroad papers again, but then caught sight of something more exciting. She recognized the ocean blue jacket protecting the hard cover book, with the white "Scribner's" lettering embossed on its spine.

"You have a copy of *The Great Gatsby*! It's my favorite book," she exclaimed, grabbing the book as if Roderick wasn't there. Her eye caught the title page. "Wow – that is not – that is his…?"

"Yes, it's Francis's autograph – but don't call him that," Roderick laughed.

"Francis? Wait, you *know* him?" Leila stared in disbelief. After she had taught herself from the more basic books, she devoured Fitzgerald's masterpiece. It toned her English phrases and her idea of what high society would be like.

"I wouldn't say 'know,' I'd say we travel in the same circles. Interesting fellow, even if he is a bit brooding compared to his wife, Zelda – who's livelier. We attended a party they threw at the Plaza upon returning from Paris. Althea's a fan and—"

"He does not like women very much, does he?" interrupted Leila.

"Why do you say that?" he said, amused.

"His women are all self-centered and boring. His men have more depth."

"I see, so you think Nick is deep?"

"He has thoughts, yes," she answered. It felt strange having a conversation about books, or anything else for that matter, here in his library; somehow it seemed more natural at the diner. Everything about this place was unsettling. She dreaded seeing his wife.

"I think he just seems to covet Gatsby's lifestyle, and Daisy and Tom's, too," debated Roderick, taking the book from her hands, his fingertips grazing hers.

*That can't be another accident.* "I think he likes observing it, it ees different world to him – one he does not belong in," she said, her accent getting the better of her.

"Then why does he insinuate himself so deeply into all their lives? He seems to have no life aside from how they defined it." She wasn't sure if he was mocking her.

"No," argued Leila. "He has no interest in being like them, he considers them careless. They don't care whose lives they wreck while amusing themselves."

"But *he* doesn't walk away from *them*, they leave *him* behind," he put down his tumbler and stood closer to her.

She pondered this, and his proximity, not sure what to do with either. "Maybe because he doesn't know what other kind of lives there are. He went to Princeton, yes?"

"I went to Princeton. Are you saying that if you go to Princeton, you're ignorant about the rest of the world?" His body was inches from hers.

"Yes," she said resolutely, nervously peering into his eyes, "you are."

"Maybe there are things I still need to learn then, about the rest of the world," his fingers sought her wrist. She felt a tingling in his grip. She couldn't move. She had imagined this moment, what his lips might feel like on hers, how their tongues would dance. It was wrong, impossible, and so unbearably enticing.

"Yes," she whispered, melting towards his body, forgetting where she was, who she was, as she felt his other hand on the small of her back. She tilted her head back slightly, arching her neck. She felt his fingers explore her hair. Her eyes half-closed as his face drew nearer. She wound her hand up his arm. She felt him harden against her.

Just then the grandfather clock chimed; it was half past seven o'clock. Leila heard heels tapping on the hardwood floors. She backed away from Roderick, colliding into the corner of the desk with a thud. She folded her hands together at her waist, looking down.

Althea floated through the doorway. Leila steered her mind to the truth of this night and felt an ache in her heart. A perfectly coiffed blonde bob framed Althea's perfect face. Her huge blue eyes and finely structured cheekbones were accentuated by burgundy rouge. *This is Roderick's wife, the woman who shares his bed, his home and his life. She's beautiful.*

Her dress was cornflower chiffon. It swished like a sea breeze as she waltzed in. She wore a strand of pearls draped towards her tiny waistline, and a stylish hat encircled with diamonds that matched the ones dangling from her ears. Her willowy arms ended in white silk gloves. In one hand, she held a long sparkling cigarette holder.

"Darling, I'm ready," Althea announced. "Oh, hello," she said to Leila, "you must be…"

"I'm Leila. Leila Kahn, Madam Morgan," said Leila, extending her gloveless hand, aware of her own shabby outfit and curves. "Pleased to meet you. Roderick has—"

"Oh, please," trilled Althea, in a breathy soprano, "call me Althea." She marched over to her husband and threaded her arm in his, as if to emphasize her ownership of him.

"Come darling," she ordered, stumbling ever so slightly in her silver satin heels.

They make a stunning pair, thought Leila with a hint of sadness and shame. The diamonds in his cufflinks matched the ones that sparkled in Althea's earlobes. Leila hated her.

"We will be back by midnight," said Roderick, stilted again. "My driver will take you home then."

"Thank you so much for watching our little angel," said Althea. "He's fast asleep so he won't be a bother at all. His room is the fifth door down, second hall to the right. Collins will show you."

"Yes, ma'am," said Leila.

"If he cries, just go in and comfort him," Althea continued. "Otherwise, make yourself at home in the parlor. Just be careful of the sofa covers."

Leila was puzzled.

"Althea has imported a set of embroidered Parisian sofa covers. Sitting would be offensive to them," said Roderick.

"No, darling," scorned Althea, "she can sit on them if she's careful. That's all."

"I will be careful," said Leila, thinking how illogical a sofa unfit for sitting was.

"Well, we really must leave now. Ta-ta, Leah!" warbled Althea.

"Leila," she corrected.

"Yes, of course, dear," said Althea. And with that the Morgans were off.

"Have lovely evening," Leila called to their backs, admonishing herself for wanting to be the one leaving with Roderick. Was Althea always that intoxicated, or that commanding? *Must be why Roderick drinks.* Then she had a more troubling thought: *Will he be kissing her tonight?* The idea was unimaginable.

As soon as the couple left, Leila tiptoed down the hallway with Mr. Collins and quietly pushed open Rodney's door. She tried to focus on the real reason she was here: to watch Roderick's son. How could she come into this home and act like she had? What would her mother think of her? What was Roderick thinking? She brought her hand to her cheek imagining it was his. Collins interrupted her brief reverie.

"Miss," he said.

"Oh, thank you," she replied. She turned her attention to Rodney.

There was just enough light from the hallway lamps to illuminate his room. She noted the luxuries sprawled throughout the space that was double the size of her apartment. There were three over-sized toy boxes with the Morgan name etched in script on the sides. Wooden alphabet blocks were tossed about the room, a baseball glove sat on top of a cerulean toy chest. Framed pictures of baseball players, cowboys, and clowns decorated the baby blue walls. The two bay windows, fitted with cushioned seats, looked south towards the twinkling grandeur of Park Avenue. Leaning on the wall beside them was a shiny blue tricycle, with something pinned under the front wheel. She stepped towards it, curious, and saw that it was a leather-bound copy of *Winnie the Pooh*.

Leila thought of Rachel. For the first time, she understood why her mother had been so adamant that she and her sister leave Russia for America. She wanted a better life for them. Leila knew that Rodney would never want for anything, even for something as seemingly trivial as a book, and hoped there would be a day when Rachel wouldn't either.

She gazed at the baby sleeping soundly, curled into a ball. His head was covered with unpeeled-almond-colored hair, a shade lighter than his father's. His body was sheltered by a heavily embroidered blanket; no doubt an import of Althea's. His hands were clasped together, making a pillow under his face; his breaths peaceful. Leila warmed to him immediately, pausing to glance back at him several times before leaving his room.

She was about to retreat to the parlor when she stopped to re-enter the library. The way to dismiss the forbidden thoughts running through her mind, as she sniffed the remnant of Roderick's cologne, was to concentrate on his business. Something about the way Roderick was so dismissive about the Allegheny deal intrigued her. But she wasn't comfortable enough to have Collins run in on her while she was leafing through papers. *Next time*, she told herself. Somehow, she knew there would be a next time.

Instead, she ran her fingers across the rows of leather-bound books. They luxuriated in custom-built bookshelves. She felt a bubble of shame, if only for a moment, as she thought of what a skilled carpenter Nelson was and how she had almost betrayed him; how she would have if Althea hadn't entered the room when she did. The noted authors of the day held court on these shelves; Robert Frost and Langston Hughes  sitting next to Edith Wharton, D.H. Lawrence, Ernest Hemingway, and Sinclair Lewis.

Leila extracted a Willa Cather book and made her way to the parlor. She arranged herself on the extravagant sofa and put her feet up on Althea's cushions. She contemplated putting a record on the Edison phonograph, but decided the silence of this home was all the background noise she needed. The peace was a stark contrast to the general racket that marked her evenings at home, with crying babies in the apartment below, old men arguing on the street, pipes leaking and floors creaking.

She lay back and tried to read, but her mind kept wandering. *I want to feel his hand on my waist again. I want him to kiss me.* She knew it was wrong, but while she was still connected to the moment, and in Roderick's home, she gave in to her imaginings. Before she knew it, she fell asleep somewhere in the pages of *My Mortal Enemy*.

She awoke to the touch of Mr. Collins tapping her shoulder.

"Oh my god, I am so sorry," she murmured. "Please, do not tell..."

He merely smiled and said, "I trust you were kind to Althea's cushions."

"I treated them with respect," she replied, eyeing the mantel clock. It was well past midnight.

Collins said, "The driver is waiting downstairs, so you won't have to take the train this time of night. The Morgans have retired. Let me help you with your wrap."

"Thank you," she said.

She was disappointed that she hadn't gotten the chance to see Roderick again. He had gone to sleep, next to his wife. *The way it was supposed to be.* She thought about his eyes holding hers before he bent to kiss her. *There was no way he could look at Althea like that.* She slinked away from the Morgan home and returned to her neighborhood, taken home by a driver for the first time in her life.

By spending Sunday finishing up Joseph's paperwork, nursing Rosa through a bad spell, and generally keeping as busy as possible, Leila attempted to skirt thoughts of the Morgans, Roderick's library, and the feel of his hands on her body – with little success. Now, back at the Morning Spot, Roderick was drinking his morning elixir and reading the papers like it was any other Monday morning.

"Thank you again for Saturday night," he said, tersely, as she poured his coffee.

"Not at all. How was the show?" she inquired, distantly. *If he's going to act like nothing happened, then so am I.*

"Lively," he replied. "I wanted to apologize for – my wife's behavior."

"None needed," said Leila. *Your wife's behavior?* "I was careful of the seat covers."

He shook his head. "She's a little preoccupied with minutia, my wife. She has all sorts of time for the finer elements of international needle-work, but if I try to discuss, say, just one of my bank deals, she couldn't be less bothered."

Leila didn't want to talk about Althea. She'd been happier before she even knew he was married, or felt his lips almost touch hers. "Maybe she just has other interests. You both like the theater, don't you?"

"I like serious plays, she likes bright-light musicals," he scowled like a child.

"Really, Roderick, a few musicals might do you good," responded Leila. She wasn't sure if she was flirting with him, or insulting him over this trivial problem. Was that a smile he gave her from the corner of his mouth, amidst his otherwise blank stare? Had he thought about their moment in his library? Was he sorry? Had he just been really drunk?

Leila took refuge in the morning rush of customers. She had to put Roderick, and especially Althea, out of her mind. She could still babysit – after all, his library was fantastic, and she wanted to know more about the Allegheny deal; but she would stay out of their marital squabbles over seat covers and show styles. She had to let this obsession stop. He was not good for her. It was probably best that he hadn't kissed her anyway.

Her resolution lasted exactly two weeks. With no mention of the library moment, Roderick asked Leila if she wouldn't mind watching his son again. She knew she should have said no, but agreed anyway. As wrong as it was, Leila couldn't help fantasizing about his lips, his touch, another opportunity. She borrowed one of Rivkah's dresses for the night – a plum frock with ivory stitched accents, and a neckline cut lower than any she had ever worn before. *What are you doing?* she asked her reflection as she inspected her appearance before leaving her apartment. *You can't encourage him. He's married. And he's a Morgan. But, you want him – more than you've wanted anything before – admit it.*

She arrived at the Morgan home, now familiar with its protocol. Collins greeted her at the door again. And as before, Althea was preparing for the evening in her dressing room. "Mr. Morgan is in the library," said Collins. "He suggested you meet him there."

Leila detected his raised eyebrow, and couldn't tell if Collins sounded judgmental or if that was her guilty conscience talking. "Thank you, I will see myself in then," she said, as primly as she could.

Roderick was standing by one of the floor-to-ceiling windows, the curtains opened to a view of the west side of New York, tumbler in hand. His expression was one of desire.

*I shouldn't be here,* thought Leila, one eye nervously watching the door, straining to hear the possible clipping of Althea's heels. *I should leave. I don't belong here.* To calm herself, she approached his desk. She noticed that the Allegheny deal, about which he had been so reticent that first night, still lay on its polished surface.

"How is the Allegheny deal going?" she asked him. "Any progress?"

"Yes, we are supposed to be financing this railroad holding company merger. Tomorrow we begin looking for investors. We are also lending them money to invest, depending on what kind of margin we offer them." He seemed happy to talk about work.

"Margin?" she asked; the word still puzzled her. "What do you mean by that, exactly?"

He huffed, "You never stop asking questions, do you?"

"I'm just curious," replied Leila. He was so hard to read. One minute, he was charming and holding her in his arms, and the next he treated her like a stupid child.

He explained curtly, "Yes, well, say you only have $100 to invest in the railroad, but you expect your $100 will be worth $1000 someday. We would lend you that extra $900 to invest."

"But, what if the railroad doesn't provide enough of a – what is word for it – profit? What if it only makes $200 or even loses money. Then what?" she asked.

"Then, you still owe me $900 and have to find it another way," he replied.

"But, what if I do not have it?" she persisted.

"You'd have it," he said, glancing at the library door and sighing.

"What if I do not?" she pressed again.

"This railroad company will make money, there's no doubt about it," he replied.

"Well, if you say so," said Leila. "Good luck with it, I suppose."

"No luck needed," Roderick snapped, "just a bunch of eager investors, and those are easy to find nowadays."

An uncomfortable silence fell upon them. Roderick placed a bronze lion paperweight over the Allegheny deal. Roderick always attempted to appear confident in his deals, but upon being pressed got defensive, so she supposed he wasn't really as confident as he tried to sound. While she was pondering the abruptness of his action and trying to engage his eyes to see if something more personal was going on, Althea had quietly entered the room and was now standing behind them.

She cleared her throat and said, "Really, Roderick, I'm sure Miss Kahn doesn't understand or care about your little deals. We should be going now, my darling."

"Yes, of course," he walked towards his wife. He did not turn back to Leila.

Leila watched Roderick place his arm around his wife's shoulders. *They deserve each other.* She pushed thoughts of the Morgan's to the back of her mind. For now, she would focus on the Allegheny deal. As soon as the couple left, she headed to Rodney's room to check on him. Hearing his peaceful snores, she returned to the library and the Allegheny documents. She read through them for hours. Most of them contained business jargon she didn't understand, but one particular set of contracts peeked her interest. All the words on them seemed to be identical, but the numbers were different. She couldn't understand why. She would ask Roderick about it, when the time was right.

When Roderick returned home later that night, he marched to the library while his wife drifted wordlessly to her bedroom and shut the door. His entrance startled Leila, who was poring over documents. She jumped away from them.

"Oh, sorry – I did not hear you come in."

"Yes, well, Collins is helping my wi—Althea, fix a wobbly something under her bed."

"Oh, why aren't...?" she stopped herself.

"Because Althea doesn't want me anywhere near her bed," he answered.

She didn't know what to say to that.

"I don't want to talk about Althea," he said.

*That makes two of us.* "I should be going," she said, her lips parting slightly.

"Of course. The driver is waiting for you in front of the building. Thank you again for coming here tonight – for watching Rodney," he said. He glanced at the documents on his desk. "I trust you kept yourself entertained."

"Yes, I did," she wanted to say more, ask him questions, feel his body pressed against hers, but she heard Collins' steps outside the room.

"All finished, sir. Is there anything else for this evening?" he asked brightly.

"No, thank you, nothing else," said Roderick. "Miss Kahn was just leaving."

"I see, sir – well, I will show her to the door then."

Leila approached Collins slowly, knowing that Roderick's eyes were following her, feeling a tiny amount of erotic power, in an otherwise powerless situation. Oh, how she wanted to stay instead. She pivoted at the door and waited for a moment.

"Oh, sorry," Roderick fumbled for his wallet as his eyes remained fixed on her. He extracted a ten-dollar bill and handed it to her. "Thank you for your services."

"You're most welcome, Mister Morgan," said Leila, slowly placing the bill into her purse. She left with her body erect, a pose she maintained until she entered the elevator, whereupon she allowed its soft walls to cushion her spirits.

\* \* \*

Roderick spent several hours in the library after Leila left. This was dangerous. It seemed like a good idea at first – he couldn't treat her like a cheap streetwalker and carry on a tryst in some hotel – but having her in his home wasn't going to work either. He didn't want to hurt her, but he couldn't give her up. His desire for her made him feel more alive than anything he'd ever known. He could never really have her, of course, because it would mean stepping out of himself and his world. He didn't have the strength.

He steered himself to another distressing thought: the Allegheny deal. The deal was perilous, and heading quickly to either demise or the biggest fraud that the Morgan bank would ever perpetuate against its clients. The two sets of books haunted him. He had noticed Leila's keen interest in the material on his desk. She sensed something was amiss, even without being aware of all the sordid details. He smiled to himself, certain that she had examined the Allegheny deal. It was part of the reason he had left it on his desk. Part of him needed her to know what he was doing, and part of him was afraid to tell her. Yet another part of him wanted her desperately, and hoped her interest in his deals would keep her interested in him. His head spun.

He poured himself a glass of bourbon and contemplated once again just how he had arrived at this entrapment of an existence. He could imagine the wife he'd never loved, and with whom he rarely communicated, drinking her own concoction in the bedroom they had only briefly shared. He thought of his Uncle Jack sleeping soundly as only those most secure in their power could. He thought of those two sets of books, and of Leila, the passion in her eyes and the desire for her that he couldn't shake; didn't want to shake.

He gulped another drink and considered that with all their differences, too obvious to count, she was similar to how he had once been, or wished himself to be. He had once suffocated under the pressure of his upbringing and longed to escape from the hierarchy of family authority, of living up to other people's standards, just as she surely did. But, he had succumbed absolutely to those pressures. He wanted the money, even if the name and the constant internal prison it represented was such a high price to pay for it – for being a Morgan. In another life, he might be with Leila somewhere in between their two worlds, but in this life, this world, that was simply not a possibility.

He paced his library. It was after his fourth drink that he decided he would share the books with Leila. He needed her to understand. He needed her to see why his part in this illusion was not his choice, but his punishment; his birthright. Maybe if she could sympathize with his plight, he could find a way out of it.

He emptied the tumbler. His thoughts were foggy; exhaustion set in. He would tell her. He would accept her response.

The next morning, he arrived early at the Morning Spot. The moments he spent there made him feel like a giddy boy. But today, he felt something else: apprehension.

"You are here early this morning," said Leila. He was glad that she noticed.

"Yes, well I was in the neighborhood…" he stopped at his poor attempt at humor and changed gears. "I needed to – tell you something."

He saw the anticipation in her chestnut eyes. He knew he could not tell her what she wanted to hear, how he felt about her. He cleared his throat, and took a sip of the coffee she had placed before him. He waited as she attended to some other customers, wishing it wasn't so crowded here this early. Every place was too crowded.

"Is it about the Allegheny deal?" she prompted quietly, when she returned. He surmised that for her, as for him, it was somehow easier to discuss finance matters, rather than longings. It was easier, and better, for both of them.

"Not exactly," he said. "It's about…"

"Yes?" she leaned in closer to him over the countertop. He wanted to touch her face, kiss her lips. He backed away.

"It's about – *all* the deals," he whispered. He swallowed to wet his dry throat. "Leila, I've been involved in…" there was no way to say it delicately.

"That's it. I'm quitting!" Nan stormed over to Leila, ripped off her apron, and slammed it on the counter, as much as a cotton apron could slam into anything. Her face was red. "I'm tired of that creep, Hank! I won't have his paws all over me! I won't!"

Leila eyed Hank, casually eating a helping of sausage. "I will take care of this," she soothed Nan, placing her hands on the younger girl's shoulders. "You stay right where you are." She turned to Roderick, "I'm sorry, I need to sort this out."

"Of course." Roderick watched Leila stand up to one of her most brutish customers. He admired her courage. He wished he could stand up to his uncle.

He was besotted with the sway of her hips. He had come to tell Leila the truth about the books. He just couldn't. He put on his hat and slinked out. He would tell her. Just not right now.

# 6.

# *September 2, 1929*

As Labor Day approached, the waning-summer scorch only intensified the putrid smells of rotting food and steaming sewage in the Lower East Side. The neighborhood was a cauldron of dying vegetables and spoiled meat. It was no better inside the cramped tenement buildings and crowded cafes than on the streets. What little cool was available came in the form of ice, or the latest refrigerator models that the local butchers and restaurants were using, which only further broiled the streets as they exhaled hot air.

The sticky humidity didn't help. Merchants, children, mothers, and laborers were forced to mingle their sweat and impatience. Leila detested the sleepless, sheet-soaked nights that came with this weather. The Lower East Side was a stew of trash and toxic fumes at the best of times, but now, it begged for a good scrubbing, or a cool, clean breeze.

She had been given two weeks off from the Morning Spot. Rather uncharacteristically, Moishe decided to close the diner for the end of August. He lamented that most of his wealthy banker patrons were off with their families in their West Egg estates along the coast of Long Island, counting their money anyway. He didn't need to be paying the electricity bills for that Frigidaire air conditioning unit some salesman had convinced him to buy on credit. Not in this heat.

"You think these people care about how I'm going to pay my rent?" he grumbled to Leila, stopping by the diner. "No, they take their afternoon swims in pools the size of my tenement, drink expensive bootleg, and drivel on about nothing on their fancy lawns."

Leila couldn't help but laugh at the absurdity of his caricatures, the sudden admission of the vast difference between him and his customers that she witnessed every day. She considered Roderick, Althea, and little Rodney luxuriating at the Morgan estate. What had he wanted to tell her that day before he left for his summer vacation – with his wife? Why did Nan have to pick that day to almost quit?

As for Leila, there wasn't really any place to go. She and Nelson, on better – or at least easier – terms with Roderick away, tried their luck at Brighton Beach, but the entire shore was like a scene from Ellis Island. It was as if every trans-Atlantic boat had docked simultaneously, packed with the worn and bedraggled, determined to start a magnificent new life, after they hit the beach. She recalled once believing in that elusive dream. She wondered if Roderick was right about her mother – had she given up on the dream?

A lack of money had shaped Leila's entire life. Not enough money had kept her mother from her and killed her. Not enough money defined Leila's life in America. It kept her from Roderick; from anyone like Roderick. She resolved to work harder. Instead of taking leisure time, Leila helped her Uncle Joseph during the weeks she had off. Mining paperwork kept her from her latest obsession. *All the deals. What did he mean?*

For the past two years, the market boom fueled Joseph's contracting business. The stock market kept minting new millionaires. And millionaires wanted to develop things, to use concrete and steel to show their wealth. Joseph could barely keep up with project demands. But in the past few months, projects had tapered off.

"Are you sure we dropped so much this month?" Joseph asked anxiously. He pressed his wire-rimmed spectacles into the bridge of his nose, as if his business problems could be corrected through sharpened eyesight.

Leila sat at Joseph's desk, the sleeves of her peach blouse hiked up her arms, adding up the August ledger on the Burroughs. He leaned over her shoulder. His breath heated her ear. She glanced up at him. He was tugging at his salt-and-pepper beard with one hand, and pushing his glasses with the other. He was a fit and vibrant man from all his walking around construction sites, but the worry over his finances had stretched his cheeks and infused the skin around his mouth and dark-brown eyes with a spray of thick lines.

"Yes, but it's probably just a summer slowdown," she replied, cautiously. "All the rich men are on vacation, so they cut back requests. Things will pick up after they return."

The explanation made perfect sense, but she was as worried as her uncle was about the declining receipts and rising bills.

"Last summer, my August picked up three-fold over my July, which was double May and June," he said. "Are you saying they didn't vacation then?"

"I guess they did," she said, unsure how to calm her usually implacable uncle.

"Something's wrong," he said, pacing. "Even Yossi's place is seeing a slowdown. And his jobs aren't paying on time like they used to." He smoothed his perspiring forehead and receding hairline. His armpits were wells.

"Maybe things will pick up this month. The stock market is having a good run; I'm sure that will help matters," said Leila, though as she examined the pile of uncollected bills, she couldn't suppress a frown.

"What is it, Leila?" he asked. "What's the state of our accounts receivable?"

"Accounts receivable? When did you become an accountant?" she ribbed him.

"When people stopped paying me," he said. "Now tell me, how are we doing?"

"Well," she swallowed, "the Compendium job is three months behind, the Aurora project two months behind, and the—"

"Oy-vey!" he raised his hand. "If that's how the biggest jobs stand, the other ones can't be better. This is not a good sign." He pulled over a chair and sat beside her.

Leila reflected on her conversation with Roderick about the Allegheny deal, and how there would always be eager investors. She thought about what he meant when he had mentioned *all the deals*. Were they all going bad? Did they relate to Joseph's clients? She peeled her hair from the nape of her neck to create a little movement, a little freedom.

"You look so beautiful, my dear," said Joseph, changing the subject. "Such a lovely young woman you're turning out to be. I'm very proud of you."

Leila averted her eyes. "Thank you, and I couldn't ask for a better uncle. You'll see, your clients will come back – they just need time off from the heat to think straight."

The crinkles in his forehead remained unconvinced.

"I'm starving – feel like getting a nice, hot knish?" she asked, mustering as much cheer as she could.

"With an ice-cold pickle. You go, I'll stay here and torture myself."

"Don't be upset. I'll resend invoices this afternoon, we'll get your books straightened out. You can count on me."

"Say hello to Yonah for me. He's a smart guy – people will always need to eat. His place will probably be around a hundred years from now," said Joseph.

Leila's head ached from Joseph's books as she wandered the few blocks to Yonah Schimmel's bakery on Houston Street, where Rivkah worked the counter.

"Hi!" greeted Rivkah. "Taking a break from the Wall Street boys for these guys?"

Leila tiptoed to kiss Rivkah on her cheek over the metal-framed glass counter. The bakery was packed with workers seated at long wooden tables complaining about their bosses or lack of work, with plates of knishes and pickles before them. *Baked, never fried,* as the window placard stated. Her stomach growled at the sweet onion aroma.

"You guessed it. I'm at the end of my vacation. Plus, I'm sick of rich men," Leila lamented.

"Exactly!" boomed a man with a bushy mustache and sizeable belly. "Who needs money when you can get a knish and a smile for 10 cents from your favorite baker."

"Hi, Yonah – Joseph sends his best." She thought about kissing him too, but decided her lips would only slide down his wet cheeks.

"Wonderful to see you, Leila," said Yonah, giving her a bear hug, erasing all her efforts to stay dry. "For you – two hot knishes with extra pickles for 20 cents!"

Rivkah laughed, "He means instead of for 10 cents apiece. Very generous, my boss is. How about you give me a few minutes for my lunch break, Yonah?"

"What, in the middle of the lunch rush? You want to make my customers angry enough to go over to that *gonif,* Moishe's place? No offense, Leila, since he's your boss."

"None taken," she replied. The neighborhood food rivalry amused her.

"I'll get customers from the sidewalk," said Rivkah. "Just five minutes, okay?"

"Fine. Go!" he agreed, shooing them with his hairy hands.

The girls assembled on a stoop around the corner, beyond the rush of Houston Street. Rivkah craved gossip. "So, what's new? How are things with you and Nelson? Is your Wall Street man away in Long Island for Labor Day – with his wife?"

"And you only got five minutes?" giggled Leila. "I'm fine. Rosa has been sick, the twins had no time off, and Rachel is as incorrigible as always. I cannot wait until she goes back to school. Nelson still wants to get married and is obsessed with the Yankees' chances in the World Series. And, Roderick is *not* my Wall Street man."

"Maybe give Nelson a chance. You would have beautiful children," said Rivkah.

"I don't want children," said Leila, with more ferocity than she expected. "Not yet anyway. And how come you are all of a sudden on Nelson's side? You always used to tell me I should find someone Jewish. And you were pretty keen on Roderick for awhile."

"Oh if you ask me, I still think you should marry Ira, the butcher's son, but seeing as he's short and cross-eyed... plus Roderick's married, and since I don't want to see you die an old maid, I'm coming around to the idea of Nelson."

"That's kind of you," said Leila, biting on a pickle. "I'll tell him you approve."

On her way back to Joseph's office, Leila mulled her friend's simple way of seeing the world. To Rivkah, the most important thing was to get married and have children. The notion of a woman making something more of herself was beyond her understanding. Leila wished she could see life as clearly – accept what was expected of her – but where had that gotten her aunt or her mother? They had both wound up alone through no fault of their own. She shivered at the thought of her dear Papa, shot by the Cossacks in Russia, and her brother, Adam, beaten to death. Her mother had never recovered. And Aunt Rosa, she had the twins, but would never find another husband.

What were her options? As dependable as Nelson could be, his first love was his cause, and as charming as Roderick could be – well, he was married. A wave of guilt slithered through her. What if Althea hadn't appeared when she did in Roderick's library?

When Leila finished making her way through the soap sellers, candy stands, and street artists on Houston Street, she saw that the entrance to Joseph's office was blocked by a group of workers.

"Hi, Leila," called Stan, a tall metalworker from the Ukraine, smoking a cigarette by the front entrance of the Farber & Abrams attorney's office next door. "I wouldn't go in there right now if I were you," he warned.

"I second that," said Jacek, the Polish electrician, tipping his cap.

"Why? What's going on?" she asked.

"It's not clear," explained Stan, "some fight between the two bosses, and you never want to get in the middle of those, that's for sure."

Leila pressed her nose against the corrugated glass at the top of the door. Joseph's arms were pumping. Morris's cheeks were red and scrunched. The two men had been best friends and contracting partners for over a decade. Together they attained plumbing licenses and turned their knack for fixing any problem with a pipe into a successful multi-scale contracting business. They even moved their families to the West Bronx together.

Joseph held up a handful of what looked like stock certificates and flung them across the room, shouting something she couldn't make out. Morris bent to pick them up and yelled something back. He stormed toward the door. Leila, Stan, and Jacek abruptly vacated their watch. Morris barged past and stomped down Houston Street, muttering loudly.

Leila rushed to confront her uncle. "What was that all about?"

"My partner," he tugged his beard in disbelief, "thinks money grows on trees." He returned to his desk, sat down, and buried his head in his hands.

Leila waited through a long silence for further explanation.

"How many times have I told him, you buy property, land – something you can stand on. You don't buy these – these pieces of paper!" his hand swiped another pile of certificates from Morris's desk to the floor. "And you certainly don't borrow to do it. I don't understand what he was thinking, betting in a rigged market."

Leila saw pain in her Uncle's eyes. He didn't take careless risks. But everywhere, people bragged about their "investments," how they would become millionaires. They just had to buy stock in RCA, or U.S. Steel, or Ford. If they didn't have enough money, now was the time to borrow it. It seemed that Morris had succumbed to the fervor. *What happens when people can't repay their debts?* Roderick scoffed at that question. She wanted to tell her uncle that he was worried over nothing, but she doubted that was true.

"He put up our business as margin, to buy shares in some railroad company. If things go wrong, we will be ruined," said Joseph.

Leila wanted to cry. Her uncle had built that business with Morris from the ground up. When they moved into this tiny office a few years ago, it felt like a palace. They had finally made it. They had their own successful business. The American dream.

"I'm the eldest son," sighed Joseph. "I came to this country, twelve-years-old, with your Aunt Rosa. I've considered it my duty to protect the family." Joseph slipped into the family saga, useful for any occasions that demanded inspiration. Leila could recite the tale in her sleep, and yet today Joseph's voice was tinged not with triumph but regret. "I went to night school for a plumbing license. I worked as an electrician's apprentice. When I left Naru, I promised your Aunt Miriam I would send for her when I could. It took eight years, but I did. We married and are blessed with four sons."

"I know, Joseph. You have a beautiful family," said Leila, to keep things positive.

"We just bought a brick house on Monroe Street next door to the one Morris bought. How he could be so stupid, if not thinking of me, then at least his family!"

"Maybe he hasn't told them. Maybe he doesn't understand the risk he's taking," she said, with a budding understanding about secrets.

"Of course he doesn't," Joseph raised his voice. "You know how I know?"

Leila shook her head.

"He also put up his family's home as margin. They could lose everything."

Labor Day carried an even stronger surge of heat into the city. The markets were closed, but newspapers ran stories about the country's top astrologer, Evangeline Adams, predicting stock prices would climb to heaven. The very next day they hit new records, which brought in the skeptics, or as Nelson preferred to call them, the realists.

The following night was Leila's twentieth birthday. To celebrate, Nelson organized an outing at Puglia, an Italian restaurant on Hester Street. The twins carried Rosa down the tenement steps so she could partake in the festivities. Nelson built her a makeshift wheelchair to undertake the half-mile journey to the Italian section of town.

Puglia's dining area was lined with exposed brick walls, covered with black-and-white photographs of Italian cities, and sprigs of ivy. A fresh garlic and basil aroma permeated the restaurant. As soon as they were seated at a corner table with a white-cotton tablecloth marred by an old tomato-sauce stain, two different conversations unfolded.

The more cheerful one, led by Rachel, was about Winnie the Pooh and the merits of living in the Hundred Acre Woods. Her excitement roped in Rosa, Jonathan and Joshua, and Rivkah, who was determined to be Joshua's girlfriend whether he was aware of this or not. Rachel concocted her own tales about Piglet with dialogue to surely give Milne a run for his money. The other conversation was about the markets and the economy. That was between Joseph, Nelson, and the more reluctant participant, Morris. Leila would have preferred Rachel's group, but happened to be seated between Nelson and Joseph.

"You heard what Roger Babson said yesterday. Sooner or later there's going to be a crash, and it's going to be terrific. I've been saying that for years," said Nelson.

"Don't remind me," said Joseph. "I'm a prisoner to the market, thanks to my brainless partner."

Morris retorted, "You're wrong, we will make a killing. Have some faith in me!"

"It's not you I need to have faith in," replied Joseph, gnashing his teeth, "it's those people Leila sees every day!" His palm struck the table, shaking the glasses.

"Stop! Stop right now!" The portly owner of Puglia, Gregorio Garofolo, appeared with a basket full of fresh bread. "All this talk of markets and money, it's no good for my food. Joseph, it's birthday of your beautiful niece, a festival, no? Why all this shouting?"

Joseph nodded an apology. "You are right, tonight is something to celebrate. We are in your hands, Gregorio, and we are very hungry."

"Now you're talking my language. You came here to build my restaurant 10 years ago. Today, look around you, we are filled with happy people eating capuzzello and pasta e fagioli – just like Mama used to cook in Naples."

"Then we eat!" declared Joseph.

"Gregorio." Nelson raised and pointed to his empty glass.

"Yes, my favorite Irishman," he replied.

"Could we have some of that cherry juice you're so famous for – to celebrate my love entering her twenties," he said, and flashed a wide smile at Leila.

"Excellent idea," Gregorio winked. "I made a fresh batch of juice last week. It will be perfect tonight. Miss Rosa, it's good to see you. This juice, it will cure you!"

Leila hadn't seen Rosa laugh so much in months. She leaned back in her chair, allowing the warmth and love to flow over her. Gregorio was right. Tonight was about eating, drinking and laughing, family and friends.

"Here's to the future!" she toasted.

"Here's to you – Happy Birthday Leila!" Glasses of wine clanked all around.

The twins took Rosa and Rachel home after a sumptuous feast. Joseph and Morris headed for the Bronx. Leila wasn't much for drink, she didn't even like the Kosher wine that dodged Prohibition, but tonight she'd had several glasses of Gregorio's concoction. Her insides were warm. She hadn't seen Roderick in nearly two weeks, and besides, he was married to a cold WASP bitch, as Nelson would say if he knew her.

Nelson took her hand in his. "Want to come over?" he asked.

"Yes, I'd love to," she answered, or maybe the cherry juice did. His hand felt rough in hers; working rough. Her feet were light. She snaked her arm around Nelson's waist, as he rested his around her shoulder. Together, they strolled towards Ludlow Street. Like Tanta Rosa said, Nelson was a good man, and he was here with her on her birthday. She shoved aside thoughts of Roderick and markets, and relaxed into her boyfriend. She didn't hear the men creeping from the alleyway.

"Hey! O'Leary! I thought I told you to stay outta my neighborhood!" shouted a man with a heavy Italian accent. Three men, one normal-sized and two hulking, in derbies and suits, blocked them. She recognized the scarves over their mouths. The Bugs and Meyer Mob. Why did they know Nelson? "Or I'm gonna do to you what I did to your brother."

Leila saw Nelson reach into his pocket. He had sworn he no longer kept a knife. Was he looking for a fight? She peered up and down the empty block. She whispered, "Nelson, let's just go," and grabbed his arm.

Nelson kept his hand where it was. "Lucky, relax – just walking my girl home. That's all. Not looking to start anything up."

"Didn't I make it clear to you and your mick family – to stay outta our streets. He don't hear too good, does he, Tony?"

"Yeah," Nelson weighed his words, in a way Leila hadn't seen before, "and I made it clear to you the White Hands got your number, so let's call it a day for now."

Tony, the giant by Lucky, inched forward. Leila gripped Nelson tighter. "That's a pretty girl you got there, O'Leary, wouldn't want anything to happen to her, would you?"

Nelson gave Leila a quick shove aside, clenched his fist, and nailed Tony in the gut. Lucky responded with a sharp cuff to Nelson's jaw that sent Nelson kneeling to the ground. "Stop it!" Leila cried. She jumped between Nelson and Lucky.

"Leila, get away from him!" yelled Nelson, rising back to his feet.

"You stop it, too!" she told him. She was mad at Nelson for knowing these people. She wasn't sure she had believed he had left the White Hand Irish gang, but that didn't matter. She was tired of men fighting, sick of their senseless aggression, and her memories of the Cossacks. She faced Lucky and steadied her tone, "Now, Lucky, we don't care about your bootleg. We are going home. You, all of you, should do the same."

Lucky took out a pistol and pointed it at Leila's nose. Tony simultaneously pointed his gun at Nelson. Leila stared at the black barrel, not flinching.

After a moment, Lucky burst into laughter. "You got quite a girl there. I should kill her, and then you. But me and my buddies are out for a bigger score tonight, so tell you what – I'm gonna let it slide. Don't let me see your mick face again, got it?"

Nelson nodded. Lucky and his two goons went back into the alley, hopped into a black Ford, and drove off.

As soon as they were gone, Leila said, "Please take me home."

"Leila, I swear, I'm not into that stuff anymore. I never would have been at all if it weren't for Pat. I had to try to stop him from getting shot that night. You know that."

"What I know is that I just want to go home," said Leila. She had been through this. His brother had been a hoodlum. It was Nelson that learned carpentry and worked hard to support his family when his dad died. She understood his resolve and loved him for it, but this violent undertone frightened her. Perhaps that was why his talk of union fights bothered her. It wasn't his cause that concerned her, but his method.

The next week, she was back at the Morning Spot. The markets zoomed up. She longed to see Roderick, but he had stopped coming in, leaving her to wonder just what it was he had wanted to tell her before he left on vacation.

Then, the world began to come apart.

# 7.

# October 24, 1929

Roderick sat behind his expansive desk, staring at nothing, thankful he was separated from the chaotic panorama of Wall Street by a window and three floors of limestone. His desk phone rattled. He lifted the receiver to hear the scratchy voice of the eldest Van Sweringen brother, the eccentric one, co-President of the Allegheny Corporation – one of his signature frauds.

"What the hell – you morons issued stock for my company earlier this year. Do I need to come over and sort it out? How much is it down?" yelled Van Sweringen.

Roderick was tempted to answer, "How do you think the market is affecting your damn company?" but restrained himself. Instead, he extended an outright lie: "This is just a temporary situation. It will pass."

He slammed the phone receiver onto its mount and poured a shot of whiskey. He glanced at the pile of papers before him, all of them transactions losing value by the second. He heard the muffled shouting of men swarming the streets, and police whistles, honking horns, and blaring sirens brooding below him. He leafed through the papers, took a healthy sip of his drink, stood up, and turned to face the window. Beneath him, men barked at one another like mad dogs. He could see the terror, despair, and rage from this height. He drained his glass, feeling the warm trickle of alcohol down his throat. He turned back to his desk, hoping that enough booze would calm his pounding headache.

He had spent a worrisome hour with the Morgan brokers on the ground floor, their desks lined up beneath the Louis Quinze chandelier hanging over the main hall. Their phones rang off the hooks. Their sweaty fingers struggled to hold onto the receivers as they fielded calls from frantic investors. Yesterday, absent a speck of actual bad news, the stock market had tumbled another 5 percent, losing an ungodly $4 billion in value. The numbers bounced so much these days that they meant almost nothing to Roderick. And yet, they meant everything; each percent, each dollar sign, meant everything to his family and to the health of the country, whether citizens knew it or not.

It was the fourth big wave of selling since the day after Labor Day, and the second biggest so far. Investors clamored to liquidate shares in order to raise enough cash to pay their margin calls. Bankers were increasingly exasperated by attempts to control a carnage that was beyond their control.

Roderick's fingertips bore into his temples as he rubbed circles into the sides of his head. No matter how hard he stared at the ledgers before him, it was clear that the Morgan Bank was running out of money; could go bankrupt, even. The real books would paint an even drearier picture. He shuddered at the prospect. Customers were running out of ways to repay margins and broker loans to the bank. His fragile nerves were further jarred by the booming voice of his boss, and uncle.

"Roderick, get in here!" Jack commanded from his office down the hall.

"Yes, sir," Roderick snatched up his reports. He squeezed the papers between his fingers, resisting the urge to tear them up, which would deter nothing.

Jack paced the Persian carpet in his office, smoking his pipe in exaggerated inhales. "Just tell it to me straight, without any of your maddening qualifiers. How many days like yesterday can our vaults withstand?"

Roderick cleared this throat and said quietly, "Two."

"No," Jack declared in disbelief.

"Maybe three – tops."

"No," Jack repeated.

"I'm afraid so," said Roderick. "I told you last month that we should try to call back some credit when things started getting shaky, just in case." He hesitated, studying his uncle like a chess piece, trying to feel out his position on the board. "If you recall."

"You know what the most irritating thing about you is?" asked Jack.

"No, sir," said Roderick. *But I'm sure you're going to tell me.*

"You're a pessimist. Now go back and do something with our numbers."

"But sir, there's really not that much I can do. Our customers are simply not – not in a position to – to make their payments to us. They keep selling at losses in order to try, but things are moving too fast."

"I don't want to hear this!" shouted Jack, before steadying his tone. "Look, last month, when I was getting my shoes buffed, I got a stock tip. That's how crazy things have become: a flier from my bootblack. When people who have no idea about the market are teeming with information about how to become millionaires from it – something is bound to go wrong. That's all this is, Roderick. A few morons getting scared – over nothing."

"A lot of them, though, sir," ventured Roderick.

"They are panicking for no reason!" Jack shouted.

Roderick replied quietly, "That's not true, you know they have a reason. We've been lying to them for months. So have all the banks."

"But, I don't know that," Jack said. "For the past decade, Americans have been able to buy things they never could before – cars, radios, refrigerators," his face began to flush, "even washing machines. That's what bank loans and layaway plans were for!"

Roderick felt nothing but disgust for this man who made his whole life possible.

"Don't you see Roderick? People couldn't get enough – they were like vultures to a kill, gobbling up the spoils they borrowed to get. And, you know what?" His tone dropped dramatically. "While they were buying, we were making a killing, funding the companies and products that would make this country even greater." His voice was riddled with conviction and self-importance.

"Well, that may be true, sir. But if the market doesn't stay up, people and companies will have to pull out, just to meet their margin calls. Stock prices will keep falling, as they keep selling to do that, and the more they fall, the faster they will keep falling. The market is dropping like a lead pipe thrown into a river, without any actual bad news being reported. Things are not good, sir. They're not good at all."

"You don't have to tell me how the markets work, Roderick." For a second, Jack looked like he might take a swipe at Roderick with his clenched fist. Then he calmed himself. "Look, the past six weeks have been a roller coaster. Some incomprehensible psychology has turned negative. Drastic moves are required. That's all. Things will be fine. I'll make them fine. I will not let this external noise destroy my – our – empire!"

"What do you propose to do then, sir?" asked Roderick.

"Lamont!" he bellowed to the man across the hall. "Get me the boys. Tell them to be here at noon." He turned to Roderick, "You'll see exactly what I propose to do."

Earlier in the week, Thomas Lamont, acting head of the bank, had written a letter to President Hoover claiming, "the future appears brilliant" and Morgan's "securities are the most desirable in the world." By Thursday, the markets opened with a huge tumble, and thousands of people couldn't sell shares at any price. Ugly crowds gathered outside the stock exchange and by the doors of the House of Morgan.

The "boys" didn't need to be prodded. That didn't surprise Roderick at all. Jack was the undisputed leader of the bankers. When he called, they came running. Plus, they were facing the possibility that their very lucrative ride through the 1920's might be coming to an end. Roderick knew that their banks only had so much money on hand, and if their customers weren't paying margin calls, and their investors were heading for the hills, they were in deep trouble. The inconvenience of an unscheduled meeting was nothing compared to the potential collapse of the entire banking system.

At precisely high noon, a harried group assembled in Jack's office. Four of Wall Street's most powerful bankers, sporting expensive navy blue suits, matching hats, and dark leather shoes, mumbled amongst themselves as they shifted nervously in finely carved wooden seats with soft leather cushions.

Jack Morgan was leaning back in a paisley covered armchair, like a sultan at his throne, examining his fellow bankers from behind his ebony desk. Just to the front of the desk, stood an antique globe from the early 1800s. It was encircled by a bronze equator, and resting in a marble arc, supported by a gold stand. Jack was fond of spinning the globe and considering what new business ventures lay on its painted continents. Today, he was worried about his current ones; so were the other men.

Roderick was in the office waiting for them with his uncle and Lamont. He knew that Lamont was little more than a figurehead. It was Jack that pulled all the important strings, but he preferred avoiding the limelight; and besides, Lamont was good with the media and bribing reporters, a necessary skill at the moment. Roderick was there, not because he was invited, but because he forced his presence upon them. He feared they would let their sizeable egos get in the way of more logical judgment and his would be the only voice of reason in the room. Jack barely glanced in his direction.

"We find ourselves, gentlemen, at a cross-road of sorts," Jack began. "This market correction – err, disruption – is scaring a lot of people, and a lot of companies. We must show them that we are *not* afraid."

There was a hush in the room, disturbed only by the ticking antique clock.

"What do you propose, Jack?" asked Charles Mitchell, chairman of one of the world's biggest banks, National City Bank. "Last time things got really bad, I added $25 million to the market, and things stabilized – for nearly seven months."

Roderick shook his head viciously, disgusted at these bankers for thinking that every problem could be fixed if you threw some money at it, before sheepishly recalling that he had said as much to Leila several months ago.

Jack said, "It might not be that cheap for you this time. We need another tactic."

"What are you suggesting, Jack?" asked Mitchell. Five days before the crash, he told his press friends that things had never been better, sucking more people in, playing them like fools, with the help of the *New York Times* and the *Wall Street Journal.*

"We pool together our leadership, and our capital. We will keep the markets from heading lower. People will take note and this – 'situation' – will be averted." Jack spoke calmly, and with utter assurance.

"And then," asked Mitchell, "we buy everything in sight?"

"Precisely," said Jack.

"How much do you think we'll need to pledge?" asked Albert Wiggin, Chairman of Chase National Bank, his voice strained. He adjusted his round glasses.

"Fifty million," said Jack, "split five ways equally. For now."

There was silence around the conference table. William Potter, president of the Guaranty Trust Company, chewed on his Waterman's fountain pen. Seward Prosser, of Bankers Trust, took several sips of water, meticulously setting his glass down and picking it up again to keep drinking. Wiggin twirled his mustache assiduously with his pinky finger. Mitchell sat unusually motionless.

"We're settled then," Jack said. "We all put up money to divert this – predicament."

"What if it doesn't work?" whispered Seward.

"Look, it *will* work. The markets have had a banner year, decade even. They are just suffering from a little loss of confidence. If investors know we are confident, they will become so as well. It's simple. It *will* work," insisted Jack.

Roderick shook his head and sniffed, clearing his nose.

"You have something to say?" asked Jack, sternly.

"We know that a lot of this growth we've seen has been based on sheer hype. People – whole *companies* – have been borrowing heavy to keep betting. What if that wheel has simply stopped turning?" questioned Roderick.

"You have always been a loser," said Jack angrily, ignoring the roomful of bankers. "No wheel will stop unless we allow it to. We will support the market. Period."

"But...we don't have that much cash, sir," said Roderick.

This factual statement was met with the most callous look imaginable from Jack Morgan, whose cheeks bulged like a blowfish. The other bankers looked into their laps, their documents, and the antique grandfather clock ticking in the corner of the room. Roderick knew he was right, and that none of the others had the guts to say anything because they were in the same boat. They all faced possible ruin if their money ran out, and there wasn't much time before that implausible scenario became their new reality.

"As I said before," continued Jack, "if we all pool our capital together, we all survive. If we don't, we will all fall." He paused. "Mr. Mitchell, I take it you are in?"

"Yes," he replied, stiffly.

"And you?" he nodded to Prosser across the table.

"Yes."

The other two bank heads, Wiggin and Potter, meekly agreed to put up whatever was needed. Roderick could barely hide his distaste for these sniveling men, bending so easily to the whim of his uncle. He thought the idea was terrible, dangerous; but nevertheless, the strategy was clever. A pool that would buy stock when it got too low, to keep it from going even lower, would give the markets confidence. Briefly anyway. After a solemn round of handshakes, the financiers all headed back to their respective firms and broke the news to their respective partners. Roderick hung around to speak to his uncle. Now that the cards were all on the table, he had nothing to lose. It was now or never.

"Sir?"

Jack was in no mood to listen, and hurried past his nephew with a sharp elbow to the ribs. Roderick followed, determined, and placed his hand on the giant's shoulder.

"You know this may be financial suicide, don't you?" He spoke slowly, with conviction, hoping his uncle would hear the truth in his words.

"You know what I know? That I curse the day I gave you a job here. If it weren't for your mother, I never would have considered it. You've always had a dark cloud around you, even as a child. Now, you're just being unpatriotic!"

Roderick could have taken the bait, again, but now was not the time. "This is not about the country, or me, Uncle Jack, it's about the bank."

"Are you daring to question *my* judgment, Roderick – our name?" exclaimed Jack, his hand smoothing back the hair he had left on his head.

"I'm just saying that I've looked at the numbers. Our trusts have been depleting precipitously for the past six weeks. We have no money coming in and many of the margins owed to us aren't coming in either. I just don't think it's a good idea to use up all our remaining capital to bet on the markets."

"I don't bet on the markets," stormed Jack. "I am the market!"

He began to stomp towards his office, and then turned back to Roderick, with rage-filled eyes.

"My father slaved for our family name, may he rest in peace, and I promoted his honor by making us the best international bank in the United States. If not for us, Britain and France wouldn't have had the billions they needed to finance the Great War. I lead the banks to help our country; don't ever forget that. And, as for putting in our own capital to help markets along, my father did the very same thing during the panic of 1907. It worked then, and damn it, it will work now."

Roderick knew to be delicate when conversation turned to the great J.P. Morgan.

"Things were different, then," he replied. "Yes, there were problems raising money, Wall Street was in a panic, and there were bank runs... but not nearly as many different classes of people were involved, and margins weren't as wide, and—"

"My father," interrupted Jack, "brought together the bank community and they bailed out the market, just like I'm doing right now."

"There was a severe recession following that panic," Roderick pointed out.

"There was a quicker recovery than there would have been otherwise," said Jack.

"Sir, please," Roderick pleaded, holding out a dossier of documents, "at least take a look at these figures, our *real* books. Because when the public – and more importantly, our clients – see how much we are exposed," he paused, unable to fully imagine the consequences of fraud and his role in it, "they may well stop doing business with us."

Jack turned around and snatched the papers from Roderick's hand. "Then I guess the public will never see these." He returned to his office and locked the door.

Several hours later, the bankers were back for a second meeting to commend themselves for having successfully averted a greater disaster. That Thursday afternoon, they saved the day. Tom Lamont told reporters that there was just a little distress selling on the Exchange, nothing to worry about. The newspapers would extol their heroism through the weekend. The lie would march on until greater forces stopped it.

Roderick left his office at ten that night, torn apart and unsatisfied. His uncle's arrogance was legendary, but his willingness to put the whole franchise, indeed the whole banking system and country at risk, was another matter. Once again, he wished he didn't have such a big part in all of it. He hated the fact that he lacked the courage to stand up for himself, and to his uncle. He wished he could just walk away from the Morgan name. But he knew that the only respite you got from being a Morgan was in your deathbed.

# 8.

# *October 25, 1929*

The next morning, headlines boasted of averted disaster. Roderick wasn't so optimistic. He knew the true state of Morgan's books, and assumed that other banks were in similar conditions. They might have lulled people into the markets, but many of their deals were nothing short of shams. He thought of Leila, as he did almost constantly. He had tried to stay away from her, from the complications his desire for her represented, but he had to see her – now. He appeared at the Morning Spot at eight o'clock, an hour before his usual – his old usual – time. He hoped she would be happy to see him.

* * *

Leila was serving Hank sausage and eggs. When the door jingled at Roderick's arrival, without looking, she somehow knew he had returned. She had tortured herself wondering where he was, what he was doing, what he'd meant to tell her before Labor Day. She'd worried about how the latest market turmoil was effecting him at the Morgan Bank. She wanted to throw Hank's breakfast at him.

"Mister Morgan," she said curtly. The sight of him rendered her short of breath.

"Hi, Leila," he said, sheepishly. "I – it's been a while."

"What do you want? To order, I mean?" she asked.

"The usual," he said, with a long look, broken by a smile.

That was all it took. Leila was struck with the longing she hadn't been able to shake. She brought him his black coffee. "No newspaper, today?"

"No," he said, "It's all lies. 'Bankers are saviors.' We're nothing of the sort."

Leila thought about the Allegheny deal documents she had seen on Roderick's desk. Again, she wondered what he had meant to tell her before Labor Day. She wanted to ask him why he had disappeared. She wanted to tell him she missed him. "Why?"

"All we did," he said, "was pay fifty million dollars to boost the markets, on the hopes that investors would rush back, because the bankers did. It's a foolhardy gamble."

Leila cleared her throat to speak. *This is what you came to say, after two months of avoiding the Morning Spot? Avoiding me? After telling me something was wrong with all the deals? While my uncle is frazzled from worry over his livelihood and family?*

Roderick kept going, "You should have seen him – like he was God almighty – the arrogance of that man!"

"That doesn't seem out of character for him," said Leila, trying to be reassuring; but inside she boiled. Roderick's frustration at his uncle was nothing new. Not a reason.

"What do you know about any of this anyway?" Roderick fumed, taking Leila by surprise. "You're just a—" he stopped himself.

"Just a what?" she raised her voice ever so slightly, so as not to alert all the other patrons to their conversation. "Just a stupid immigrant girl who couldn't possibly understand all the intricacies of finance?" She had never used the word intricacies. Suddenly, things were clearer to her. Not the details. But the big picture.

"I didn't say that," he said, "I didn't say you were stupid, Leila. I never thought that. I'm sorry."

"Well thank you, Roderick, that's comforting. But I'll tell *you* something, I was listening to you for all these months, and I know that you and the Morgan bank – hell, probably all the big banks – have been boosting up this market, gathering up ordinary people to keep it going, and lying about everything."

He gazed at her, wordless. She understood more than he thought.

She was surprised at how quickly her own words were coming out. "You have said it yourself, that you should do something – make public what a sham it is you're running behind those walls. Stand up to your uncle – because you know," she hesitated. "You know deep down he's wrong, and the market only went up because they bought some shares with their money, even while other people can't afford their margin calls!"

He fidgeted in his stool, wringing his hands. He hated the word margin. He hadn't meant to upset her. He reached for his flask in his breast pocket. It was already empty.

"Leila, listen to me, it's more than just – boosting the market – there has been a lot of lying going around. And I'm afraid. I..." he looked into her eyes, gulped a lungful of air and continued, "I've been involved in – more than I've told you."

"What do you mean?" her eyes widened.

"I mean, I – I've been doctoring our books."

"What do you mean?" she repeated. "The books of the Morgan bank?"

"Yes, our books. I've been keeping," he lowered his voice to a whisper and leaned toward her, "two sets of them. Only one is accurate and – well, you can imagine that's not the one the public knows about." He looked relieved.

She processed this information slowly, biting her lips, letting the poisonous ramification simmer. "So, you mean you have been – cheating the public?"

She looked at him with a chill in her eyes. Cheating the public seemed worse than betraying his wife.

He nodded slowly.

She attended to some other customers, collecting herself before responding to him. She thought she understood the importance of this admission, but was afraid she couldn't begin to comprehend its implications. When she finally returned to him, she asked simply, "What are you going to do about it?"

"I wish I had an answer to that question," he replied.

"You need to tell your uncle that you are not keeping those two books a secret anymore." She was convinced, for that moment, this was the only right thing to do.

"I can't tell him that. He doesn't care. This is the man who had Tom Lamont write a bald-faced lie to our president. I can't make him tell the truth. He'll —"

"He'll what – fire you? Disown you?" Leila snapped. "So what? You start over – you'll be in the same boat as rest of us, but at least your conscience will be clear."

"You really don't understand, Leila, it's not that simple," he lowered his voice so she had to lean in. "I faked these books too. Jack never touched them as far as he's concerned. I can't just tell the world. What am I supposed to say? The Morgan bank made billions of dollars on phony deals? Then just before the game was up, we suckered in more investors to flush down the drain? Am *I* supposed to write the President and tell him *that*? It doesn't work that way. They'll throw me in jail and throw away the key."

"My uncle is one of those investors, Roderick," said Leila. "And, he never wanted to be one – he never wanted to bet with borrowed money, but his partner did and he put up the business they had built together. It all may fall apart now." *Don't you care?*

She considered just telling him to leave. To never return. That instant, she saw him the way her family, and Nelson, did. It was one thing to obsess about wealth and luxury, but it was another to hurt or mislead people in order to be rich. She could see other customers straining to hear their conversation, and felt the heat in her face.

"Do you know how many others there are like that – people who do not have millions of dollars to fall back on – that feed families?" she demanded, hands on her hips.

"Leila," he pleaded, "yes – I just – maybe Jack's right. Investors see that the biggest banks are confident, and come back in, and this all blows over."

"You know you do not believe that," she said. "What, so Jack Morgan puts his money in to buy Standard Oil and Allegheny Corporation and whatever else – and everyone's going to follow him like lambs to slaughter?" She stopped. How could Roderick possibly understand this? He never had to fear where his next meal would come from. He got whatever he wanted whenever he wanted it. She shuddered. *Her affections were just like another deal to him.*

"I don't know. I guess I just need to hope, for all our sakes, that the markets snap back," he replied, his voice begging for understanding as he scrambled to pour a shot of whiskey into his coffee, angrily realizing that his flask was still empty. "I just – have a feeling, they won't." The tick in his cheek danced frantically.

"What are you going to do?" repeated Leila. A long pause settled between them.

He shook his head. "I'm sorry, Leila. I'm sorry about your uncle too, but mine is just too powerful to cross. I can't just turn my back on the entire family and destroy our name. We may not have to struggle financially, but we do care about loyalty."

She took a breath and inspected him. She saw a scared little boy, making excuses for the inexcusable. He hadn't answered her question. She wanted to help him, but more than that, she wanted him to see what he had done and fix it himself.

"Well, maybe you can talk to him again. If he sees that the pool isn't working, maybe he'll listen about the books," she said in a softer, measured tone, worried she had overstepped whatever role it was she had in his life.

"That's wishful thinking," Roderick grimaced. "He'd have to take losses that he's been faking he doesn't have. He's not going to do that. He'd have the company go down in flames before admitting he's a fraud." His nervous eyes fixated on Leila's, as if imploring her for a way out of this situation. But, she didn't know what else to say. He gulped down the rest of his coffee and left without saying a word.

Leila knew she crossed a boundary, but she had her own family to worry about. She couldn't be impartial; but she resolved to give Roderick some time to cool off, see reason. She felt a return of that pride in the way he confided in her.

By the end of the day, the efforts of the bankers and the media seemed to have worked on the worn psyche of investors. The markets recovered a little, yet despite all signs of outward bravado, no one was really sure what Monday would bring.

Leila dreaded returning home to her family's anxiety. She didn't think the markets would stay calm any more than Roderick did, especially after what she'd learned. *How could they?* She wondered if there was still some way to help Joseph, or if Morris was already selling stock to pay his margin, and losing money, in the process. She wondered what Roderick would decide to do. *Was there really a chance he could go to jail?* She was scared for him, too. Technically, he should go to jail. So should Jack.

Upon arriving uptown, Leila darted over to Joseph's office. He was buried in paperwork and documents, his head sunk into his hands.

"Uncle," she hugged him. "Are you okay?"

"Years we struggled, and for what, for this craziness to take it all away? I could kill Morris!"

"You don't mean that. He got in over his head, like a lot of people. I was talking to Roderick – the Morgan banker – today, and he thinks this might all blow over and become more stable on Monday," she said, desperately trying to reassure him.

"That son of a bitch!" Joseph's exclaimed.

She stiffened. "But, maybe he's right, maybe things will be fine," Leila proclaimed, though she wasn't convinced, and neither was her uncle.

"I wish I could believe that, Leila, but do you know why I can't?" asked Joseph.

"Why?"

"Because the market is just – people. And when people are scared, they run. I've seen this too many times. My Papa ran from Russia with Rosa and me. Even Aaron, Rosa's husband, ran; he couldn't make it here. After all the promises that America was the land of dreams, he couldn't handle the pressure anymore. Uncertainty creates panic."

Leila felt a knot in her throat and a pang of rage at Roderick's cowardice, even if Jack Morgan was the real villain. Hiding from the truth wasn't right. She was glad she yelled at him that morning. He deserved it. She peered into her uncle's gaunt face, his beard uncharacteristically unkempt, his eyes bloodshot from exhaustion and stress. Monday was years away.

"You know what you need, Uncle?" she asked.

"A new partner?" he joked. "Tell me."

"A hot, roast chicken and a fresh batch of noodle-kugel with those big, plump raisins that you like. There is much uncertainty in this world, but one thing that you can be sure of – Tanta Rosa will bake the most delicious meal for tonight's Sabbath. Please come join us," she extended her hand, beckoning him.

"I can't Leila, I should get back home. Miriam will have made a meal for the family there. Thank you, my dear – and give my best to my sister. I will visit her soon, I promise. Please be well." With that, he returned to the documents piled on his desk.

As the smell of garlic and rosemary floated through the stairwell, Leila knew she hadn't been wrong. Rosa outdid herself. The twins spruced themselves up with hints of lavender soap they borrowed from Leila to cover the fish smell that usually haunted them. Nelson stood there, yarmulke on his head. Rosa must have invited him, not knowing about the altercation with Lucky and his mobsters. Rachel mimicked Mary Pickford. *This was her life. Whatever she was looking for beyond this, it turned out was fake.*

Rosa lit the candles, administering a blessing over them. Joshua blessed the wine, and Jonathan, the homemade Challah bread. The family dug into the night's dinner with admiration for Rosa's skills and an insatiable hunger from the week's trying days. Leila was glad no one brought up the markets. The twins were in rare form.

"And then he threw the fish at him! Plastered on his nose. Funniest thing I've seen since I started working the docks. The only thing that could've been better was seeing that creep get smacked with a mackerel!" said Jonathan, before he exploded with laughter.

"Yeah, you should have seen the look on his face!" Joshua added.

"Mackerel shmackerel, you boys are lucky to have your job at the docks, earning an honest living with your hands, unlike so many people gambling their lives away in the stock market," Nelson interrupted. He shot Leila a frustrated, but eager glance. The anticipation of her joining the conversation was apparent in his eyes.

"Nelson, please," she said faintly. *Don't start again. Not tonight.*

"Everybody at the site is going haywire. Even our foreman is crazed. Nearly every electrician and plumber I know is worried about the stock market," said Nelson.

Leila studied Nelson's face. She wondered why he loved her so much. She wondered if his passion for her was actually about her, or just leftover passion from what he felt about so much else. Without being in the thick of it, Nelson had been right about the stock market. It was all a big scam. She replayed the conversation with Roderick about the doctored books. If Nelson only knew the truth of it, she thought, but she couldn't tell him. Such an admission would make her too close to the evil; tainted by association. And he would wonder why Roderick told her, and that was something she couldn't explain, even to herself.

She sighed softly. His heart was in the right place. This was one of the basic problems: it was always in the right place, just as it had been since the day they met on the street between their adjacent tenement buildings. She observed him across the table, nostalgic for that old heat between them. Instead, she only felt his fury at the world, eager to be drawn out, eager to be fanned. And then there was Roderick, who like his Uncle Jack, seemed to believe he could tinker with the whole world. Leila wished she knew which world she belonged in, and wondered when everything had become so perplexing. And in that confusion, she allowed Nelson to take her back to his place.

\* \* \*

Five miles uptown, Roderick's Friday night began with a fight with Althea. She was complaining about her travel plans to England, and wondering if they'd have to be postponed based on the market. Althea, an English aristocrat of sorts, traveled for "breaks" to London frequently. A distant niece of the countess of Buckinghamshire, her distain for Americans was surpassed only by her obsession with all the luxuries America could provide. In truth, she was as far removed from Queen Mary as he was from J.P. Morgan, but that didn't stop her from playing up her royal underpinnings.

Roderick detested this behavior, though her connection – however imagined – to the great lineage of her mother country had been thrilling when they first met. She had enchanted him with tales of her family, of endless cousins and aunts and uncles, of lavish family gatherings on the opulent lawns of grandiose country estates. Eventually he discovered that it was all a façade. Her family was really a washed up bunch of old royals, characterized more by constant fighting about their waning position in society, than companionship or support or love.

These days, he felt nothing but contempt for her. His only joy was his son, who he rarely had time to see. It had taken years for them to conceive a Morgan heir. While the months toiled on and her belly remained empty, her desire for a child grew clinical. Roderick wondered if she actually wanted a child, or just an object to bind her to the family fortune. During that time, he partook in numerous affairs to make him feel manlier, none of which did the trick. Once she gave birth to their only son, Althea ceased all pretense of love or warmth for his father – if it had ever been there to begin with.

"Can't you just do something about all of this mass hysteria?" she asked that abysmal Friday evening. She spoke in a low, almost guttural, clench.

"Sure! I'll just alert the *New York Times* that this is all a huge misunderstanding, and the market isn't going to hell ever again," he responded sarcastically. "Although with Jack's PR machine, that's probably what they're printing right now."

"But I don't understand. What's going on?" her voice screeched into hysteria.

"Althea, it's a complicated mess we're in. I can't just explain it to you. You wouldn't understand it anyway." Roderick was uninterested in his wife's pleas, particularly since she had never bothered to take an interest in his work in the past, and he was way beyond telling her the truth about his role in the current fiasco.

"But are we... poor, now?" she asked, her eyes filled with fear.

Roderick stormed out of the parlor, slamming the door behind him. Poor didn't begin to describe it. It would be a miracle if he weren't thrown in prison by federal authorities for misleading his investors. And that was only if his investors didn't lynch him first; and that was only if his uncle didn't kill him.

He wandered through his spacious apartment, bewildered as his wife. Yes, things had stabilized at the end of a hectic week, like his uncle insisted they would. The markets had taken a pounding like nothing Roderick had ever experienced – like nothing he had ever imagined – but he wasn't sure the bailout offered by his uncle's cronies would actually restore order. He coughed, as if trying to purge a sour taste from his mouth. Jack believed in his own prowess to control the universe. *What a sickening notion.*

He had to figure out what he would do if this really were the beginning of the end of the stock market, and the world, as he knew it. He stomped into the library and guzzled a glass of whiskey straight up, followed by another, and a third. He punched the wall above the bar, his fist sinking into the dark leather padding. When that ceased to alleviate his anxiety, he ambled to the portrait of his mother scowling at him, her lips perpetually pursed in an expression of disappointment. Pushing the painting aside, he knelt down. He checked that all of his books and documents were still in place.

# 9.

## *October 28, 1929*

On Monday morning, Leila read the papers with the intensity of a mother hen protecting her chicks. Front-page stories pressured people to buy stocks, declaring they were destined to rise again. How could they know? Leila wondered how long Roderick, Jack, and the rest of Wall Street would continue to claim things were fine, to fake not just books, but reality. How far would they go to protect the markets they held so dear?

Leila was surprised to see Roderick, mostly because of their recent conversation. But also because she assumed he'd be holed up in his office cooking the Morgan books. She felt disgust, and an annoying sense of concern, as he approached the counter.

"You are soused," she declared, immediately noticing his drunken state.

"I'm fine," he said, "a few early shots, that's all. This day is going to get ugly."

"I thought you said the pool would work, investors would regain calm, and all that," she replied, arching her back to avoid the stench of alcohol emitting from him.

"Well, I was wrong," he said loudly, apparently not caring who was listening.

"Keep your voice down," she hushed. "What is going on?"

"It's all over. That's what's going on. The markets are going to crash, because everyone will figure out how much they've been duped. And I, Roderick Morgan, helped dupe them." He spread his arms wide, like he was addressing a great hall.

"Roderick, calm down," she said firmly, "or get out. You are embarrassing me."

"Oh, you're embarrassed by me, little Leila. Lovely little Leila is embarrassed by me. I've been such a bad boy," he reached for her hand. She pulled it away.

"Stop it, Roderick. You've had too much to drink. I want you to leave, *now*." She felt the eyes of all her customers bearing down on her.

"But, I don't want to go in there. I don't want to see Jack. Come away with me, Leila. Let's get away."

"You're acting crazy, Roderick. Stop it." She reeled. She couldn't recall a time when she didn't want to run away. The thought of escaping with him was too much for her to imagine. She told herself he didn't mean it. She felt sorry for him; he was unstable, drunk, and pathetic. She wished with all her heart that she hadn't fallen in love with him.

"Roderick, you still have time to face your uncle," she encouraged.

Her words returned him to his composed self. "I'm sorry Leila, I don't even know what I'm doing. Althea's pulling me in one direction, Jack in the other. Please forgive me. I'll go now," he wobbled as he moved.

"Good," she said. "Do the right thing. Find a way to expose the truth."

"Sure," he said, slurring the "s." "I'll send a note to the President and skip the country."

"That's not what I meant and you know it," said Leila. She ached to grab his hand, to steady him, to hold him. She realized that with all his wealth, she had so much more than he did. She had people in her life that loved and supported her unequivocally. He had no such bedrock. But, wasn't that his choice?

His expression grew stern. He didn't want to disappoint her. He didn't want to keep disappointing himself. His thoughts were a jumble of "what-ifs" and "if-only's."

"I will do the right thing," he said. "You'll see."

With that, he stumbled out of the Morning Spot.

\* \* \*

Roderick bounded through the heavy doors of the House of Morgan, barely capable of walking a straight line. He had a massive headache from the almost lethal amount of whisky he imbibed the previous night, compounded by lack of sleep. Sunday had probably been the worst night of his life, topping off the worst weekend of his life.

Roderick knew his uncle didn't respect him. He also knew that Jack would have fired him years ago, if J.P. Senior hadn't guaranteed Roderick a position before he died. Jack never let Roderick forget that he was his mother's second-class bastard in a first-class family, a black sheep in a lily-white herd. Roderick hated his uncle.

It was that hatred that fueled him. He decided as a teenager, when he first walked into the House of Morgan, to become a better banker than his uncle. One day he would have a bank more successful than any other Morgan before him. And now everything was falling apart right before his eyes. For years, it seemed, no one had checked what banks did, or the validity of their investments, or the way they made money. Every driver, waiter, nurse, and teacher wanted to play the markets. They wanted to ride the wave of success – no questions asked; and if the markets buckled, it didn't matter. It was a better time to buy at lower prices and reap handsome returns later. Or so the twisted logic went.

When the market tanked last week, that success came into question. Jack blamed Roderick for not taking better care of the family franchise, as if somehow he willed the public's mistrust for Wall Street or its inability to pay margins. But Roderick knew there was nothing he could have done differently. His intuition told him that something would go terribly wrong. It was just a matter of time. The market wasn't even pushed up by real money; it was all either borrowed on margin, or worse, it was artificially inflated by groups of bankers who pushed prices as high as they could, enticed smaller investors in, and sold out at the top, leaving the smaller investors to lose their shirts.

He knew that real estate properties were hemorrhaging value. Florida had tanked years earlier because there weren't enough buyers to keep purchasing property at ever-higher prices. He told his uncle time and time again, but Jack ignored his warnings. Roderick insisted the bank couldn't keep stretching the same investors, stuffing them with broker loans for the Allegheny and other deals, but his uncle wasn't interested in listening about that either. Now everything was going to hell. Now, Jack was mad at him.

Leila's words berated him. *Just do something.* He wanted to do something, but his mind was a jumble. His head pounded. He had spent all weekend at the office, along with all the other partners, none of whom wanted to hear about the real state of their firm or of the collection of its shady deals that were falling apart.

The media boasted of recovery. Newspapers seemed criminal to Roderick, lapping up whatever his uncle – through the pouty lips of Tom Lamont – told them. And Roderick was part of the charade. The official story on Sunday was, "Traders busy preparing for a positive opening Monday." President Hoover reported, "Business is sound, trading is near normal." Unofficially, Roderick knew that every banker was petrified and at work to protect what he could before the storm.

Yet, against his conscience and every ounce of better judgment, Roderick worked to make the books look better. If investors pulled out of the market, at least they wouldn't pull out of Morgan. They would keep paying the margins they owed. Morgan would stay above the fray as best it could. He had resolved to protect his family, even if his family was a sham.

He had two documents with Jack's signature, one that pointed to the real book, the other, to the fake one. He took them home months ago, stolen from Lamont's office in a fit of righteous indignation. Lamont kept careful track of all paper that bore Jack's signature, but Roderick had slipped a replacement document into the files. If Lamont ever searched for Allegheny deal contracts, he wouldn't find either of them.

The two documents were a salve to Roderick. They helped ease the pain that he created each day. He had left them on his desk for Leila to see because he couldn't bear his own knowledge of them, alone. He knew he should use them to expose the truth, to expose the rotten way in which his uncle really did business. But, could he?

There was something he needed to do first.

* * *

Leila was concerned for her Uncle Joseph and what the stormy market might do to his business and his family. It didn't seem fair that he stood to lose so much on someone else's foolishness. She stayed later than usual at the Morning Spot after closing. She switched off all the lights except for the one that illuminated the coat rack at the back of the diner. She took a seat in the rear booth, her office. There, she spread out that day's newspapers. She read through them carefully, wanting to process their information, to figure out what was real, if anything, and what was a ruse. As she read, snatches of her fight with Roderick pelted her brain. Would he apologize tomorrow? Did he have the guts to face his uncle? She shook her head to refocus on the articles heaping praise on the bankers. She grew more and more frustrated at all the deception. What could she do?

She was startled to hear a tapping at the front door. She rose to answer it.

Her heart skipped several beats when she saw who it was. Quickly, she unlocked the door and let him in. She glanced to the left and to the right of the sidewalk outside. There was nobody around, except an old beggar at the far corner. She locked the door behind him, bolting it twice. She made sure she had fully lowered the window shades.

The booze on Roderick's breath permeated her nostrils as he approached her, but he seemed to be in full command of his movements, more than he had been this morning.

"What are you...?" she asked peering into his hazel eyes.

"I shouldn't be here tonight," he said. He seemed to be telling himself this more than her. He probed her face as he removed his hat, his coat, and then his suit jacket.

"No, you should not." Her breath came in short gasps. She took his hand in hers and brought it to her face.

"I don't know what's going to happen tomorrow," he said, the fingers of his other hand running through her hair, pulling her head back. "I just came here to..."

She didn't let him finish. She dug her fingers into his scalp and drew his face to hers. She parted her lips under the pressure of his and tasted cigars and whiskey. Their tongues touched. Leila moaned. He tightened one arm around her body, and cupped his other hand below the curve of her breast, then at her waist, and then her buttocks. She weaved an arm up his back, pulling him closer, and with the other, fumbled for the light switch.

She was wearing a blue blouse with a black skirt that fell below her knees. Roderick knelt to the floor. His hand trailed up the back of her skirt, finding the lip of her stockings. He pulled them down hard. She balanced herself on one leg and then the other as he slipped them off her feet. His hands were hot and clumsy and eager.

She shivered as his fingers slid across her ankles, her calves, and up her thighs. He stood up abruptly. Holding her with one arm around the small of her back, he hastily unbuttoned her blouse as she wriggled out of it. Finally freed, he flung the shirt at a counter stool. He unhooked the clasp of her lace bra, while still kissing her, and threw that away as well. His warm lips moved to travel the side of her neck, down toward her collarbone.

He paused to look at her. He gasped. She was now fully naked from the waist up. Her dark rose nipples hardened under his glance, as she briefly considered and then discarded the notion that her breasts were too small. He reached for them. Leila cried out softly as she felt the pressure of his fingers on her and the growing heat between her legs.

She had only ever been with Nelson, and he had never seared through her with just a look like Roderick had done. He had never made her feel like she could step out of herself. She opened her mouth to speak, but held her tongue. *Words would only ruin the thrill enveloping her.* With trembling fingers, she undid the buttons of his shirt, brushing her hand across the light-brown hairs on his chest, inhaling his cologne, traveling lower to the buckle of his belt. Her own eagerness surprised her.

"No, wait, wait," he whispered, gripping her hand. "Let me look at you."

His eyes lingered on her breasts as her excitement grew, then trailed the slope of her belly, moving from her tiny waist to the hips that she sometimes considered too curvaceous, but which under his stare felt just right.

He took her to the floor with him, both of them sinking onto the cold, hard, mosaic tiles. He hovered over her as he touched her, as gingerly as a blind man. He felt the tautness of her breasts, the soft silkiness of her belly, the dark triangle below her waist, the milky flesh of her upper thighs. Her panting intensified. She watched his every move and the pent-up longing in his face. His mouth closed around her nipple, sucking, as his hand trailed down between her legs, exploring her, feeling her tremble at his touch.

She shimmied out of her skirt. He quickly tugged off her panties. He unzipped himself, removing his pants, his tan shoes, and his socks in one motion. He lowered himself on top of her, inhaling the lavender sweetness of her scent.

Leila wrapped her legs around his body, binding him firmly. *How she had fantasized about this since she first saw him.* Even during her intimate moments with Nelson, she had thought of Roderick. *Roderick.* She ran her hands down his back, traveling over the cheeks of his buttocks, grabbing them as he slipped inside her, pressing her hips upward to take in more of him; to be as connected to him as she possibly could.

In the darkness, Leila gave into everything she had been fighting, relishing the weight of his body on hers. He buried himself within her. She felt the swell of her hips beneath his, the bowls of her breasts and tips of their buds pressing into his chest.

He moved inside her, slowly and then with increasing pace. She stopped caring about what would happen tomorrow. This sliver of now was all that mattered. Their bodies were united in frenzied passion, their heat making up for the coldness of the floor. The waves of her climax rippled from her center as she cried out his name. In that instant, in the joining of their impossible passion, in an impossible world, they were one. The pleasure obliterated all other thoughts and worries. It was everything she had dreamed it would be. He loved her. He needed her. She knew that now.

But, the afterglow of their lovemaking diminished all too quickly. Soon they returned to the coldness of the diner and the uncertainly of the night. As they lay entangled in each other's arms and legs, she worked up her courage.

"What now?" she asked.

"I wish I knew," he answered, his hands caressing her bare shoulder, his eyes sinking into hers, feeling himself rising again, but knowing what awaited him at the bank.

She lay with her head resting on his chest watching it rise and fall with his breath, content for a moment. She wanted to succumb to this wave of happiness. She didn't want it to ever end.

"I have to go," he said.

And in that announcement of his imminent departure, she was gripped by the agony of inexplicable loss and uneasy shame. The door shut behind Roderick Morgan as Leila quietly collected her tears.

An hour later, Leila was arguing with Nelson. She knew that her voice was too loud, that she might be waking her Aunt Rosa, that the whole neighborhood had nothing better to do than eavesdrop. This was not the time to be having this fight with Nelson. Her emotions shot out in every direction.

When she got off the El, all she had wanted to do was go home and replay the previous hours. Nelson wasn't supposed to have been waiting for her at her stoop. He wasn't supposed to remind her that she promised to be home much earlier, that they were supposed to visit Joseph.

"I just came back from Joseph's. He's beside himself with worry. I think I managed to calm him down enough to go home, but this mess will only get worse." He paused waiting for a response, and when none came asked, "What kept you so long?"

*I was in the arms of another man, one you hate. I would do it again in an instant.*

"Leila, I know things are crazy, but we haven't talked about us. Even after Friday night, you were silent. Do you still want to be my girl?"

She gazed at him. Had she promised him she would be? She couldn't recall. She had slept with Nelson out of guilt and Roderick's confession three nights ago, but everything had changed since then. Did she still smell of whiskey and cigars? Wood and cinnamon? Roderick had taken over all her other promises, and she didn't know if there was anything she could – or wanted to – do about it. Her mother would be ashamed at what she had become. "Everything's crazy right now. The markets, Uncle Joseph's business, Aunt Rosa's health… Just give me some time to think." She lied.

"But what's going to change?" he asked.

"I don't know. Nothing. Everything. I just know there's more to life than…"

"Me," he finished for her.

*Yes*, she thought, resigned in this resolution. What was she doing? Maybe she was no different from the bankers. She was anxious, furious, and at the whim of portentous, unnamable forces. She was in America, she had a job, and she had a boyfriend who wanted, more than anything in the world, to marry her. There was the promise of merriment all around her, and now it had given way to something darker. Maybe it wasn't even real to begin with. Maybe her relationship with Nelson wasn't real, either. He seemed too noble to be true. How could he still want her after what she did?

And then there was the restlessness inside her. The anxiety of the past week had sparked it further. Tonight sent it into a frenzy. Her desperation to fly away was a force, more potent than the flame she felt with Roderick. Something was happening around all of them. The world was shifting. The newspapers were giddy with tales of a booming stock market despite the bumps along the way. People were sinking their savings into the markets, living in the present, but paying for it with the unknown future. A loving family surrounded her, yet the very walls that embraced her were suffocating her. Would her love for Roderick suffocate her?

"It's not that, it's…" she started, knowing she would not be able to explain it to him.

"It's Roderick, isn't it?" he asked.

"What are you talking about?" she flashed. *He couldn't possibly know.*

"Do you really think he's so happy in his wealthy tomb? He looks down on you. You are just a servant to him. Everyone is," his voice grew louder.

"That is not true!" she said. "The wealthy give to charity, to the poor…"

"Leila, are you listening to yourself? They donate so they can see their name spread around like seed – look how great we are, we have our name on a damn plaque! They look down on the poor, and you know it. Six out of ten people in this country live in poverty, while idiots like Roderick worry about the number of karats in the diamond rings they give their wives."

"He does not —"

"Why are you so determined to defend those people?" Nelson snarled.

"I am not defending them. I am just saying that not all of them are evil."

"Leila," said Nelson. "This country has been undergoing massive problems while thieves like Roderick get fatter and richer, and it's coming to a halt. Wall Street's easy money is no substitute for hard work, for making things with your hands. Those people down where you work," he paused, "create nothing, and use everyone in the process."

"No, they do not…" She couldn't imagine Roderick had just used her. Had he?

"Leila, I love you. I will do everything I can to make you happy. Those people don't care about you. Marry me. Let me protect you from all of that. Just think about it."

Leila nodded. She was too drained to reply. But she didn't need Nelson to protect her, or Roderick – not that he ever would. Maybe tonight was a mistake. She could never have him, never fit into his world. He would always protect that world. No, she would find a way to protect herself, and Rachel, Rosa and even Joseph.

# 10.

# *October 29, 1929*

The next morning, Leila left early for work after a stressful night. She couldn't fall asleep with thoughts of her fight with Nelson and lovemaking with Roderick curdling in her head. It was always the same argument with Nelson. They had been together for three years. He wanted to get married. She couldn't live up to some ideal of what he wanted her to be. She wanted more than a crowded, noisy home that stunk of fish and mildew. And every time she saw Roderick, she felt further trapped. She was grateful to Rosa, and loved Rachel with all her might, but was drowning in their needs.

Nelson offered her more of the same impoverished living, the life of mobsters, union fights, and counting pennies. That wasn't what Mama envisioned when she sacrificed her future for her daughters, was it? Yet, how dare she complain when so many others had it so much worse? When her brother and Papa had died in poverty, for no reason other than being Jews, her Mama had never complained.

\* \* \*

Roderick had snuck away from the bank for the second time, at two in the morning, still aroused by his hours with Leila. His driver met him at the side entrance of the Morgan bank to avoid the crowds camped outside the main door. After a few hours of information checking and tumblers of whisky at home, Roderick's driver took him back early Tuesday morning. At six in the morning, it was already a madhouse. Piles of men, and a few women, lined the sidewalks and streets; investors poised to face their brokers, citizens to raid their bank accounts. They surrounded the cars that carried bankers to work. People wanted their money and wanted it now. They wanted blood. Shouts of "Death to bankers!" and "Hang Jack!" rang out in front of 23 Wall Street.

Roderick struggled to ignore their cries and hate, a hate that had intensified over the weekend, even as he felt some admiration for them. At least *they* were trying to do something. He puffed out his chest and tucked in his chin in a gesture of confidence, and walked with a purpose that belied his racing heart. He entered the House of Morgan, a folded newspaper in one hand, and his brown leather briefcase in the other.

Leila's advice – and Leila – haunted him. He recalled the firmness of her breasts, the sweetness of her breath, and the heat between her legs. She had wanted him as much as he had wanted her, even knowing about the books. But, doing anything meaningful meant confronting his uncle, holding nothing back. Was he even capable?

He sat at his desk for hours, drinking whisky and ignoring the incessant ringing of his phone. The sharp clipping noise from the ticker machine across his office sounded like it was coming from directly inside his brain. It spit out inked figures with a frenzy that he was certain was mocking him. The mechanic arms inside its protective glass bubble tapped out lower and lower stock prices. Roderick strode over to the ticker. He picked the machine up, lifted it over his head, and smashed it into the solid-oak wall.

"Blasted machine!" he shouted. Its glass fractured into a million pieces, but the arm at its center still fluttered. He raised his foot and stomped on it until it stopped.

Lamont bolted into his office. "What the hell are you doing, man?" he demanded.

Roderick eyed him with thick disdain. "Get the hell out, Lamont!"

"Pull yourself together," said Lamont. "Jack wants us to take a trip over to the Exchange. There's an important meeting going on at noon."

"About what?" Roderick asked.

"Closing the Exchange or some such nonsense. Come on."

The Exchange was the last place Roderick wanted to be. It was just like his uncle to stay away from the fray, always in the shadows. He grabbed his overcoat and hat, and followed Lamont. From across the lower lobby, Roderick saw a cluster of men before the bank's doors, yelling at the Morgan guards with fists clenching stock certificates.

Lamont said, "Not that way. Out the back."

The two men exited the bank through the same steel doors that normally opened for truckloads of gold bars. Once outside, they had no choice but to barge through the crowds to reach the back door of the Exchange across the narrow street. Fortunately, there were less people on this side of the Exchange than raging directly in front of it, but the task was still far from simple. Just when they reached the back of the Exchange, two guards told them to wait outside, so that people wouldn't spot two Morgan partners entering. "They might kill you," said an Exchange guard.

Roderick adjusted his hat to cover his eyes and waited by Lamont. He was looking down at his shoes when a man wearing a gray overcoat and matching bowler marched up to him and punched him in the stomach. Roderick doubled over.

"May you rot in hell," said the man, before he spit in Roderick's face and ran off.

Roderick wiped the spittle away. *I deserved that. The guy should have just shot me.*

Once inside the Exchange, the two men were instructed to wait in a marble stairwell until the forty Exchange leaders gathered in a conference room a floor above, two or three at a time, to avoid alerting the traders or the media.

On their way to the stairwell, Roderick caught a glimpse of the main Exchange trading floor. Fueled by alcohol, he braved the increasingly frantic crowd, and marched towards the heart of the panic: the big board of numbers that covered an entire wall of the massive room. He was shocked by what he saw.

Young boys, called runners, were slapping numbered tiles as fast as they could onto the board, replacing ones already there with new ones that showed lower prices. All the leading stocks were diving: GE, United Steel, Standard Oil, and Montgomery Ward. Floor traders trampled each other with handfuls of sell orders. They moved aggressively with one thing on their minds – selling. The Exchange was usually a sea of black sheets of paper signaling orders to buy, but now it was a massive red blur, indicating sells. Traders and investors were selling as many stocks as possible, and as fast as they could.

The hardwood trading-floor was covered with paper slips of hastily taken notes and crumpled pieces of stock ticker paper. Men scrambled to get to their respective trading posts, scuffing their normally polished leather shoes as they climbed on top of one another, screaming and panicking to sell anything and everything they could. No matter where he looked, he saw the same thing. Men wiped sweat off their brows, shoulders hunched. Men shouted at the top of their lungs, their ties loosened around their necks; hats and suit jackets lost in the chaos.

Roderick swallowed. The air hung heavy. He had seen enough. Leila was right. There was still a chance for him to do something. He knew things. He could expose the fraud, the inconsistency and the weakness holding up the market's entire foundation. Maybe if everyone knew how bad things really were, they could emerge from the depraved level to which they sunk. *Damn you, Jack.* His thoughts were racing, and his mind plotting. He needed to be sure of his plan. It couldn't be put off much longer.

He left Lamont at the Exchange and marched through the crowds once more, shielding his head with his briefcase. He would confront Jack, convince him that honesty was the right path; that deception only leads to further destruction. He had another, less noble thought: revenge against his tyrant uncle. He got as far as Jack's closed door, where he heard his uncle yelling into the phone. "Get out there again! Talk to Hoover! Call Bob at the *Times*, Larry at the *Wall Street Journal*! Tell 'em we'll put up as much money as we need to! We believe in the markets! That's the only thing that matters."

Confusion overtook Roderick. Was Leila right? What did this Jewish immigrant girl know of heritage and hierarchy? How could she know what was best for the markets or his family? What did she know about the pressure hanging over your head your entire life? To carry the bloodline through a son? To be nothing more than another cog in the great machine that is the Morgan Legacy? Leila knew *nothing*. His head ached like it would split apart. He hesitated at his uncle's office. Time to face his fate. He had to do this.

Black Tuesday

# PART II:

## *After the Crash*

# 11.

# *October 29, 1929*

It had been mere minutes since the fall, but it might as well have been a year, or a century. Leila remained rooted to the sidewalk, outside the fray of broken glass, filled with rawness. She stared at the tangle of policemen buzzing about his body. He was an anonymous victim to them. Yet she could close her eyes and imagine his eyes boring into her, the feel of his chest pressed to hers, the drops of his sweat on her skin, the connection of his body to hers. *This can't be happening.*

She stood alone in a mass of people, isolated not yet by the resolution of sadness, but by a loss she couldn't share, and an irrational hope she couldn't explain. *Let this be a nightmare. Let me wake up.* She raked her fingers through her hair. Once. Twice. *Why? Why didn't you come to the diner this morning? Why didn't you come talk to me?* She wished she could go back in time. She could have helped him more with words than sex. She had been too greedy for him.

The streetlights shined their beams through the darkness by the side of Morgan bank and down the narrow street that led to it. Her limbs, numb and cold, propelled her toward one of the police officers.

"Sir, please, is there anything I can do?" she asked, desperate to share a moment of proximity.

"This doesn't concern you, Miss," the man said. "Step aside!"

*But it does,* she thought, wishing she could explain. *This was my fault.*

She returned to her position, a sentry with nothing to guard. The policemen scoured the area, collecting bits of broken glass from the mangled car frame and scribbling on thick notepads. Reporters and photographers descended from nowhere and hovered around the body. Flash bulbs exploded from all directions as two medical attendants lifted the body and enclosed it in black burlap.

Leila stifled the urge to vomit at the sound of the zipper. Several men hoisted the bag onto a stretcher, the weight of the body evident in their strained shoulders and taut forearms. Once in place, the men secured the inert package with canvas straps and brass hooks, and rolled it into the waiting ambulance.

A few moments later, a well-dressed man with a thick coat exited the Morgan bank. He strode toward the center of the building's marble steps. A hum traversed the onlookers. The crowd seemed to turn on cue away from the body and toward the makeshift stage. The man waited for the vultures to gather before him. He had done this before.

His voice was steely and almost careless. "We are saddened by what has happened here this evening and, like all of you, await the police department's investigation into this tragedy." The reporters erupted with a barrage of questions.

"Hey, Lamont, who was he?" asked a tall journalist on the right side of the pack, sporting a plaid derby hat, a pencil stuck behind his ear.

"What did he do at the bank?" asked a shorter one on the left side.

"How much money did he lose?"

Leila's chest tightened. She flashed back to yesterday morning. He had been worried and drunk and scared.

But he had come to her last night. Had she overlooked his desperation because of her desire? What had happened since?

The man seemed almost amused at their eagerness. "We have no further comment at this time. Thank you, gentlemen, and good evening."

The reporters turned from the steps, as if chastened by the man. Another Morgan banker whispered something to the nearest policeman, who promptly ordered everyone to leave. The reporters scattered into the dispersing crowd. The tall one began asking people questions. One bystander angrily commented, "I'm surprised that *more* people didn't jump from that window."

Leila moved away from the reporter as he approached her. She had no wish to talk to anyone. She wasn't even sure she was capable of speaking.

The stragglers dissipated as night settled in. The bankers returned to their offices, to prepare for whatever tomorrow would bring. Windows all around Leila sparked with light. She looked away from them. All that brightness was an aching blur, a mockery of the darkness consuming her. She stared blankly at the street lanterns before her. She huddled on a sidewalk step, up the street from the Morgan building, her knees drawn close to her chest beneath her woolen skirt. The ambulance had departed but she couldn't leave.

"Leila." A thick Irish brogue sounded dimly from what seemed to be an immense distance. "Leila," repeated the voice, louder this time. She willed her eyes into focus and saw Officer Bryan O'Malley approaching her. She didn't bother to wipe her tears away. Her features were paralyzed. She found herself unable to speak.

"It's getting cold out, love," he said, kneeling beside her. "You shouldn't stay here. Let me have one of my guys drive you home." He offered his hand.

She shook her head, refusing to meet his eyes with her own. Her arms felt heavy and icy cold. She rubbed her hands back and forth over the tops of her arms halfheartedly, and then gave up the effort.

"I just don't understand," she whispered. In her mind she heard the horrific crunch of the body as it hit the car.

She vaguely noticed him studying her face. "You knew him, didn't you?"

She nodded. *I loved him.* "I – I think so. He – he used to come into diner," she replied. Her mind wandered back to their lovemaking, then to their earlier fight. Yesterday morning, he declared that he wanted to leave everything behind, for her. Surely he hadn't – couldn't have – actually meant that. A glimmer of anger traversed her limp body. At the time, she thought those were just the words of a scared little rich boy, whining about how hard the world is. But then, he came for her at night. Why? What had she meant to him? What if she had acted differently? What if she had agreed to run away with him in the morning? What if she had pressed him to stay last night? Made him promise to return this morning? She would never know.

"He was certainly a big man in these parts," said O'Malley. His voice was an amalgam of melancholy and respect, with a hint of the disgust that Nelson displayed.

*Was.* The word invoked a second onslaught of tears. A part of her hoped she had been mistaken. That it was someone else who had crashed to his death. Then she could ignore all the questions piling up in her head. Did this happen because of her? Should she have kept her hands to herself last night? Her thoughts became an incoherent jumble. Who had seen them? Who would blame her for his death? Would they be right to do so? Why didn't he come into the diner this morning?

"So – they know – who it was," she squeezed the words out.

"Yes. They wanted to keep it quiet – more than usual for these situations – until they've decided what to tell the press..." O'Malley stopped himself.

"Is that why he didn't answer questions – that man from Morgan?" she asked, her focus sharpening as she thought of his smug face.

"He's not really obligated to," said O'Malley, shrugging. "The police didn't bring anyone down to the station for a statement or questions either."

"Isn't that strange?" Leila asked. She replayed the man's actions in her mind. Her confusion began to numb the feeling of bottomless emptiness engulfing her.

"A little," he replied with some reluctance. "Usually, more statements are required, but it's a pretty open-and-shut case of suicide. Guy couldn't take the losses. Offed himself. He's not the only one – the phone at the station's been ringing all afternoon, mostly men. Train tracks. Guns."

"Dying," she grimaced. "Over money."

"Pride, too," said O'Malley. "You're rich one minute. Then, you're not."

"So the market crash pushed them," she said, slowly, knowing she would never be able to shake the images she had seen from her mind. Not knowing how she would remember to keep breathing.

"Yes," he sounded drained. "I've never seen anything like it. Twenty years on the force. Last night, this place was packed with frantic brokers and slum kids making mountain piles of all the thrown out stock tickers. Today it's a bloody war zone."

She nodded. "I got here at four this morning. Customers were waiting for me. They rushed into the diner like hungry animals." It was a relief to think about a moment that was not right now. A moment before everything went wrong.

"Something like this," O'Malley gestured to the spot where the body had lain, "was bound to happen."

Leila stiffened at O'Malley's words. How could he say something like this was inevitable? What if he was right? A shiver tore through her. What if this was the only way for Roderick to escape the burden of being a Morgan? She noticed O'Malley staring at her again. She couldn't let on how much she knew about Roderick.

"What about his – family?" she deflected. Her brain mercilessly flicked through the already ingrained images again. His body. Their fight. Her passion. His soft hair matted with blood. The tan shoes. The twisted legs.

O'Malley removed his overcoat and draped it across her shoulders. He peered into her reddened eyes. "The officers alerted his family," he said. "Standard protocol."

Thoughts of Althea and Rodney entered her mind. Althea had lost a husband, like her Mama had. Rodney, a father, like her. An ached rushed her head.

*You didn't think about them that last night. You just wanted him.*

"I don't understand – I saw him in the shop yesterday. He seemed fine," she said. She wasn't sure why she was lying to O'Malley. To protect Roderick? To protect herself?

"It's hard to tell what makes people snap," said O'Malley. "I've seen some crazy incidents on the beat. People murder their own kids when they are that far gone."

She winced at the thought of little Rodney, asleep in his gilded room, oblivious to the many monsters of this world; the many monsters in his own family.

"He didn't seem like the type to snap," Leila said, wanting to believe this, then suddenly doubting her own words, recalling his drunken loss of control. *Why hadn't he just come back this morning?* She could have calmed him. *She could have saved him.* But she was no good at saving anyone. She recalled how she and her older brother, Adam, fled their school; bolting through the sugar fields to their home. The Cossacks pounced on him, but she kept running. By the time she reached home, it was too late. She never saw him again.

"It's hard to know someone from a few coffees, Leila. Look, I know you're upset, but you should go home. Get some rest. If you want to talk about anything tomorrow, I'll be around. And here," he reached into his pocket and pulled out a small pad and a pen. "If you're too busy to talk to me at the shop – you can call me at the precinct. Anytime." He scribbled down a number and handed her the piece of paper.

She took it with shaky fingers and slipped it into the front pocket of her coat. What did he think she would want to talk about? She couldn't tell Bryan it was more than a few coffees. "Thank you, Bryan."

He kept starting at her. "Come on, I'll have someone take you home."

"I'm fine. It's kind of you to offer, but I think I'll take the El." She didn't want to spend time in a police car.

"Are you sure, Leila?" he pressed. There was something in his probing that made her uncomfortable. She preferred to be alone with her thoughts.

"Yes. Thank you." She didn't want to leave just yet. Leaving would make this moment end. She knew that once she left this horrible place, she would be leaving him behind, too. O'Malley stared at her.

"Okay, then." He hooked his hand under her arm to raise her up.

She retracted stubbornly and froze up. She knew she had to get this over with, to hear what she couldn't bear to hear. "Bryan," she said quietly.

"Yes," he replied.

"It was Roderick Morgan – wasn't it?" she asked. She needed to speak his name into the night air. From her lips, it felt so foreign and yet so intimate, an enormous secret that she had no one to tell. Bryan nodded with a question in his eyes.

On watery legs, Leila trudged down the steps of the El to Allen Street. She seemed to herself, vacant, as if she might melt away into the night. Yet her weakened body remained duty-bound. Her feet, disconnected from her head, guided her to her Uncle Joseph's office. She didn't have the strength to imagine what condition she would find him in. Just getting there was nearly more than she could bear.

The street beneath the El was less crowded than usual. Most of the peddlers had turned in for the night. Only the prostitutes milled about clustered in pairs, starting the night shift, hidden within the dark shadows below the train's iron girders. She was grateful there was no one to talk to. The people in her neighborhood wouldn't be empathetic to the news of a banker "offing himself." Certainly not for anyone carrying the Morgan name. No one could understand.

At the corner of Forsyth and Houston Street, she saw the flashing red and white lights of an ambulance. *What the hell?* She scrambled across the street. The lights threw the dirty red brick of the tenements into relief, and brought into highlight and then shadow a wall of distraught faces. People wailed. Leila spotted two police cars parked at the corner, one on each side of her uncle's office. She heard officers barking instructions.

*Could this day possibly get any worse?* As she approached her Uncle Joseph's office, the crowd thickened. These faces weren't strangers to her, like the ones downtown. Something was wrong. To her surprise, Leila noticed the black winter coat of Tanta Rosa. She was sitting in her wheelchair with her arms resting upon two children. Rachel stood beside her. Leila couldn't remember ever seeing her sister stand so still.

Leila scanned the crowd methodically for her uncle. She couldn't find him anywhere. *This can't be happening*, she thought. *Please, God. No.* She reached Rosa.

"What's going on?" she gasped. "Where's Uncle Joseph?"

Rosa pointed a slender finger to the office. "Inside," she said. She looked as if she had been battered by the world.

Several officers blocked the entrance. Leila pushed her way through and saw Morris' wife, Hannah, standing in front of them, her back to the street. One of the local doctors was speaking to her. The stout woman, with a bob of black hair, emitted a shriek as the doctor gripped her shoulders. Hannah broke from his grasp, let loose a terrible moan, and hunched over, bent at her middle.

With a wave of relief, Leila saw Joseph behind Morris' desk, his head down. A stack of documents hung precariously off the desk's corner. The phone receiver dangled from its cord to the floor, next to a scuffed black leather shoe.

Morris lay on the floor face up. His eyes were closed. A second doctor held his wrist with one hand and touched two fingers to the side of his neck with another. He released the wrist, gently placing it by Morris's hip.

Leila rushed over to Joseph. "What happened?" she whispered.

"Oh, Leila," he sighed, "Where to begin? He was shouting at his broker, the value of his shares had dropped so low. They wiped him out. They wiped us out."

"I'm so sorry, Uncle," soothed Leila, swinging her arm around his shoulder.

"I didn't understand why the broker would talk to him at this hour," Joseph went on. "Morris started trembling. He tore at his chest, then he doubled over."

Leila's body tensed up. For a split second, she was furious with Morris, for bringing this tragedy on himself with his risky decisions. She immediately chastised herself for thinking unkindly of the dead. This was the second market victim of the day. The only difference was that this time, it was God's will, not man's choice. Not that it mattered; both men had left loved ones behind to pick up the pieces.

"I tried to get him to breathe," continued Joseph. "I kept telling him to relax. I poured him a glass of water. I called Doctor Schulman."

"I should have come home sooner, Uncle Joseph," said Leila. Again, her second world had infringed on her first one. Again, the violence grew. "Maybe there would have been something I could have done to help him." *Why was she always too late?*

Joseph sighed. "No, my Leila. There was nothing you could have done. We talked about this, he and I, so many times. He made a mistake. I should have been more patient with him. Now, his family has lost him."

Leila contemplated Joseph's words. They were identical to the ones she had been telling herself on the way home. People make mistakes. They aren't always strong. They don't always, or can't always, do the right thing. Why wasn't she more patient with Roderick? Why couldn't she stop thinking about him, just for a second?

She forced her focus to this tiny, messy room where she had spent so many evenings and weekends. It had a look of constant struggle, of the perpetual threat of disaster. Now this. Her mind jumped ahead. Her uncle was probably ruined. His partner, and best friend, was dead. Morris was sure they could make more money investing in paper than pipes. She was mad at Morris for being stupid enough to thrust his life's work, and Joseph's, into the arbitrariness of the market. She was livid at Roderick. She wanted to tell him off tomorrow for being part of the fraud that killed Morris. But there would be no conversation with him tomorrow. Or ever.

Hannah draped herself over Morris's body, clutching his shirt, sobbing as she squeezed him tighter. The doctors melted into the periphery. One of her children, the youngest, broke through the policemen and came running toward her. "Mama, Mama!" he called.

"Get away, Benjamin!" she said, lifting her head from her husband's chest.

"No!" he stamped his foot. "I want to see Papa."

Leila thought of that moment in her life when she discovered she never would see her Papa again; when all she wanted to do was see him. Her heart ached for Benjamin. Everything changes in an instant.

Leila left Joseph's side and took the little boy's hand in hers. "Shh, Benjamin. Your papa needs to – rest now. Come, I will take you to Tanta Rosa." They walked outside to the waiting crowd. Rosa's eyes pined for information. Leila shook her head.

Aunt Rosa's body shuddered. She leaned forward to pick the boy up into her lap. Leila knew there would be a dull pain searing through her aunt's joints as she held Benjamin in her arms, and that right now, that pain was inconsequential. She stared in a daze at her tired old aunt, stronger than anyone she had ever known, supporting her adopted children. She wondered what Rosa was thinking deep down.

As she wondered whether she would ever have Rosa's strength, she thought about Joseph. How would he ever recover? How would he build his business again? *Damn Roderick. Damn Jack Morgan.* It was the callous ways of people like them that had struck the core of her family. She stared at the ambulance lights circling her neighborhood, illuminating the tired streets and broken faces. Who knew how long the damage would take to heal? Who knew how many other families would suffer?

Her heart felt like it would never be whole again.

# 12.

# *October 30, 1929*

Morris was laid to rest the next day. He was buried in a cemetery near his home in the West Bronx. With the family's money virtually wiped out, and the threat of a bank foreclosure looming in the future, Hannah turned to her extended family for assistance. The promises poured in. Cousins and friends pledged enough money to meet her mortgage for the next six months and cover the cost of the burial service and the tombstone. Even Joseph dipped into his meager savings to offer his charity to his best friend's widow.

Leila and the twins rode the uptown train to pay respects. Tanta Rosa couldn't come. Being outside in the cold for so many hours had been devastating, but she made up for her absence with food. Joshua and Jonathan carried a mountain of tin boxes of her homemade cakes, cookies, breads, soups and salads for after the burial.

For seven days, family and friends would visit Hannah and her children. The gathering prayed sporadically and chattered constantly. No one asked Hannah questions about the nature of Morris's losses, but it was all anyone talked about as they stood outside smoking or in transit from their homes.

Leila's boss, Moishe, surprised her by giving her the rest of the week off. He too, had known Morris for years. For four days, she went dutifully to the West Bronx, along with her Uncle Joseph. She didn't say much during those days. Everyone assumed her blank stares and faltering efforts at conversation were just sadness about Morris. But no matter what was put before her, her mind flipped back to Roderick. She felt a profound sense of helplessness. She missed him. She couldn't comprehend the notion that she would never see him again. She couldn't imagine what it would be like to return to the Morning Spot and go on with her routine there, when his presence would be forever absent.

As she rode the subway each day with Uncle Joseph, she felt a growing bond between them. Both of them wanted things to turn out differently. Both of them failed in their quest to change the outcome. Both of them grieved as a result.

After the first evening, she contemplated telling her Tanta Rosa about Roderick, but held herself back. She thought about talking to Rivkah, but decided that Rivkah wouldn't understand. She didn't feel comfortable talking to *anyone* about Roderick. She sunk into the solitude of her loss as events around her swirled on.

After several days, Leila noticed a change in Hannah's spirits. She seemed to take some pleasure in the laughter of her children. Hannah's sorrow had transformed into quiet acceptance. Leila caught herself staring at Hannah, astonished by how this woman was able to function. She found herself wondering what Althea was doing during these terrible days. Was she devastated at the loss of her husband? Was she struggling to come to terms with raising her son without his father? Was she falling apart or remaining resolute?

And Leila found herself increasingly angry with Roderick again. How could he have taken the easy way out, when his life was so much easier to begin with? Why did he participate in Morgan's fraud instead of just walking away?

On Friday morning, she arrived at Hannah's, surprised to see Nelson sitting in the living room. He was immersed in conversation with one of the old women from down the block. Leila's heart stuttered, then warmed. That was the wonderful thing about Nelson. Even with so much tension between them, he would always do the right thing. She watched him keep the children occupied, telling stories and playing hand games with them. She was grateful for his presence but acutely aware of her betrayal.

A few minutes later she felt him standing behind her.

"Leila," he turned her around and wrapped her in his arms. "How are you?"

"I am doing alright," she answered, oddly comforted by his embrace. She hadn't told Nelson about Roderick's death. Yet, she was fairly certain that Roderick's suicide would be common knowledge already in Nelson's circles. It had only taken a day before details about his life, along with pictures of Althea and little Rodney hit the papers. Still, it was not a conversation topic she wanted to engage him in. As for her relationship with Roderick, her feelings, those were secrets that she could never share with him.

"Everyone has been so generous," Nelson commented, making small talk to bridge the distance between them. "The kids are missing their Halloween parties."

"Yes," agreed Leila, vaguely, "we always stick together, especially in these saddest times." She sounded stilted, but couldn't help it. "It's good of you to come." She was still sore from their fight earlier in the week. *Was it really less than a week ago?* She remained hurt when she thought about Nelson's critical words of Roderick. His accusations stoked her defensiveness that night. She knew he was right, and she detested him for it. She could allow herself to be mad at Roderick for what he did, but she wasn't ready to allow anyone else to hurl insults at him.

"You know I'll always be there for you, Leila," Nelson replied, leaving it at that.

Benjamin arrived with pound cake. He was dressed in his finest clothes.

"Here," he said, holding out the plate. "This is Papa's favorite."

"Well, then, I shall have a big piece," said Nelson, with a grin.

"Aunt Leila, do you want a piece, too?" Benjamin asked.

"No my sweet, I will have one later," said Leila. Her appetite had disappeared during the past few days.

Benjamin scurried away to offer cake to other relatives.

Nelson watched him plaintively. "I don't think he understands why everyone is here. It must seem like a party to him."

Leila shrugged. She was looking at Benjamin but thinking about Rodney, too young to be aware of what happened to his father. "I think he knows this isn't a party."

"I didn't mean..." he began.

"It's fine," she stopped him. They stared at the room in an uncomfortable silence.

A minute later, Nelson's voice had a sharp edge. "At any rate, this isn't as grand as the Morgan wake is going to be."

"What?"

"I thought you might have been invited. Tomorrow night," he said.

She felt like she'd been punched in the stomach. She was furious. Why would he care about the loss of a man he detested the very idea of? Was he testing her?

"So, I guess you do know what happened," she said.

"His death was all over the papers," said Nelson. "The Herald reported that the creeps at Morgan wanted to keep it a secret. Some junior clerk spilled it when he got fired that night. Goes to show, you can't ever get the truth from the big boys."

Leila looked away, first through the window, then to the brick buildings across the street. She had read that as well.

She hadn't thought it seemed out of character for the great Jack Morgan. He probably didn't want the troubles of his least favorite nephew to taint his precious image. And he certainly wouldn't want anyone digging into the circumstances that led to those choices. *Two books. All the deals. Why Roderick, why?*

"Leila—" He pursed his lips. "Why didn't you tell me about it? It happened around six o'clock, right? You must have been around there."

"Yes, Nelson. I was around. His body smashed into a car and then splattered on the ground like a griddle cake," she said coldly. *Is that what you want to hear?*

"That must have been hard for you," he offered, his voice even.

"Yes, it was," she said dully.

"So are you going to his wake?"

"I don't know," answered Leila. She hadn't been invited. She didn't even know what time it was being held. Until Nelson told her about it, she hadn't considered its existence. What should she expect? *It isn't surprising that Althea didn't invite me.*

"Well, it's going to be at eight o'clock tomorrow night, at their home," he said.

"I don't know," she repeated. She wasn't sure if he was being mean or somehow helping her. She didn't understand why he would want her to go. But nothing made much sense to her. She straightened her skirt to steady her hands. "How did you...?"

"I was flooring the new Hoffman place. They were invited. It seems that it's quite the event in those circles. It's not every day a Morgan dies and all that – though if it happened more often, the world would be a better place."

"Honestly, Nelson – you are impossible!" declared Leila. She noticed Joseph raise his eyebrows at them. This was not the place to fight. Embarrassed at her outburst, she left

Nelson standing at the window. A few minutes later, she saw him leave. She waited until she was sure he had left the area and excused herself. She was furious at Nelson. And yet his casual mention of Roderick's wake filled her with anxiety and excitement. Like there was still a part of him she was going to see there.

The next morning, she went to visit Rivkah. "I need your advice," Leila said, peering over the counter.

"I'm all yours," said Rivkah, ever eager to be consulted for her opinion. "Yonah," she called over her shoulder, "I'm taking a break. Can you watch the register?"

"All you do is take breaks," he replied. "Who's supposed to be the worker here?"

"Yonah," she said scornfully. "Leila is in mourning. Her uncle's partner just passed. You should be ashamed of yourself."

"I'm trying to make enough money to avoid my own heart attack," he said, eyeing Leila. "Fine. Go. Five minutes though, that's all."

"Thanks, Yonah." Rivkah flew from her spot behind the counter, grabbed her wrap from the door hook, and put her arm around Leila's shoulders. She guided her out the door. "What do you need to know?" she asked.

Leila measured her words. "Nelson told me something last night at the Shiva."

"He came up to the Bronx for that? What a guy," she commented.

"Yes, it was very sweet of him," Leila grumbled, already annoyed at how Rivkah took Nelson's side. "But – then we got into this big fight..."

"Alright," Rivkah interrupted, "My advice is to wait a few days, you both have kind of a temper sometimes, I've been meaning to mention it, and then you can—"

Leila raised her palm. "No, it's not about Nelson. It's about Roderick…"

"But, he's dead," Rivkah replied, "They're having a wake for him tom—" she covered her mouth with her hand.

"How do you know these things?" demanded Leila.

"Nelson told me yesterday evening. He stopped by for a knish. I had to ask him what was new. One thing led to another and…"

"So, you know about the wake?" Leila confirmed.

"The one tonight at his home on Park Avenue?" asked Rivkah. "Yes, I do. Again, Nelson – I was going to…"

*Why did they have to keep talking about Nelson?*

Leila interrupted, "Anyway, I am wondering if I should—"

"Go? Yes, I think you should," Rivkah advised emphatically.

"But, I wasn't invited," said Leila. "And, I don't know if it's appropriate."

"Listen, I know you carried a torch for him, and I'm not going to ask what else. But if you don't go, you'll always wish you had."

"I'm not sure his wife will be pleased at my showing up."

"His wife has other things to worry about. Like who she's going to marry next."

"Rivkah!" Leila admonished.

"All I'm saying is that you should do what's in your heart. You've been a wreck this whole week, and it can't be about Morris, or your ongoing fights with Nelson, bless his muscular soul. You were playing with fire, but now… well, you should go."

Leila hugged her. "Thank you, you're a dear friend."

Rivkah grinned, "If you don't want to go alone, I could be your chaperone. Maybe Roderick has a cute cousin? I mean, had."

Leila couldn't resist smiling for the first time in days. It felt good.

As soon as she left Rivkah, though, the sadness returned. It was mixed with dread. She was going to Roderick's home and there would be no Roderick there. She shuddered at the thought of facing Althea. She had been intimate with her husband the night before he died. She considered not going; but there was no way she could stay away.

# 13.

# *November 2, 1929*

Leila had never attended a Christian wake. There were probably a million pieces of protocol she could get wrong, and she had no idea how she would react to Althea. The precious moments she had spent with Roderick the night before he died were moments she had taken away from his wife. But the potential for embarrassment was overwhelmed by Roderick's constant presence. He shadowed her. She lingered on the memory of his body covering hers. Snippets of their past conversations interrupted her thoughts. Every word replayed like a talkie film in her mind.

*"What happens now?"*

*"I wish I knew."*

When she arrived at the Morgan home, she was struck by an intense floral fragrance. In the entranceway stood a bronze alter with lion heads sculpted into its four sides, topped by a lavish bouquet of white lilies. It was surrounded by six silver candelabras, three on each side, containing slender ivory candles. A well-appointed crowd mingled in the foyer, their crystal glasses clanking. Murmurs of conversation and spills of soft laughter were punctuated by whispers of "how could he?" and "isn't she holding up well – poor thing?" Even in mourning, the high-society types dressed to the nines, as if they could never stop showing off to each other.

Past the foyer stood a long wooden table, heavy with silver platters of fruit and cheese, a glittering row of crystal tumblers, and a shocking amount of illegal alcohol in decorative bottles. The atmosphere was so different from the warm tone at Hannah's. There, children laughed and played on the sidelines. Here, it was just the adults reveling. There was no sign of children anywhere. She figured that Rodney must be asleep in his room. She longed to check in on him, hug him, and tell him he would be okay. *Your Papa is dead now, but he will always be part of you.* Then, she realized that was silly. Rodney was two-years-old. He would never remember his Papa. She wondered how much of that was her fault.

Collins greeted her with a grim nod. "Miss Leila. How kind of you to stop by at a time like this. Let me take your coat."

"No, that's not necessary," said Leila. *I'm still not sure I should be here. No, that's not true – I know I shouldn't. But I need to be.*

"As you wish," Collins replied.

"How is she holding up?" asked Leila, noticing Althea across the room. She wore a charcoal-colored silk flapper dress, its beading sparkling in the light and its hemline cut provocatively above her knees. She twirled her fingers around her strands of pearls, and bent her head back in an exaggerated laugh. *I haven't laughed all week.*

"You'd think she was throwing a dinner party," said Collins.

Leila noticed a tall, elderly gentleman walk over and grip Althea's shoulders. He appeared to be lecturing Althea more than consoling her. His face was shadowed partially by his top hat; his stance erect. He was flanked by two younger men, glued to his every word and movement. Collins saw the direction of her glance.

"Yes. That's him. *The* J.P. Morgan, Jr. *Jack* himself. It's the second time he's been here this week – the second time ever."

Leila watched Althea bury her face in his chest, her manicured nails digging into the sides of his lapels, as if he and he alone could provide her solace. The gesture of her emotion seemed unnatural, thought Leila, not so much because it was dramatic, but because it seemed so intimate. Jack appeared to be almost bothered by her display, his feet shifting slightly back and forth. His head raised away from hers, turning sideways every so often, as if he was looking for somebody. *So this is the man Roderick hated.*

"She wants to ensure she's in his good graces," remarked Collins. "This is the first time she's shown any feelings all day."

"Maybe that's her way of coping," said Leila. *If Roderick were watching, would he be amused or repulsed?*

"No," he said, "that's her way of keeping the family fortune. Roderick didn't have his own will, you know."

That surprised her. She thought all the rich had wills. "Wouldn't his fortune go to Rodney, then? I mean, Roderick, Jr." *This was Althea's main concern? And why was Collins sharing it with her?*

"Well, technically," said Collins quietly. "But word is, he has no more fortune."

"You mean – he was completely wiped out, in just the past week?" She assumed Roderick was savvier than Morris and the others swallowed by the market. Things were bad for everyone, but for Roderick Morgan? Surely, he would have kept something aside.

"No, beforehand. This past week just cemented his downfall... so to speak," he caught himself. "I overheard Jack talk to Althea about it, how careless Roderick was with the family money. She didn't take the news very well."

Leila assumed the bank was having trouble because of Roderick's confession about the two sets of books, and of course, there were the market problems. It made sense that Roderick's fortune was tied up in the bank, as a partner, but would he have been that careless? *Could Jack be mistaken? Or lying?*

She eyed Althea, attached to Jack like a child hungry for security, and tried to suppress her disgust. What did she know about what Althea was feeling? And what would Althea be thinking if she knew about her relationship with Roderick?

"At least she has a son," Collins continued. "That should help protect her. But the old man, he decides about the family fortune. He controls everything that happens."

Althea lifted her head off Jack's chest to glance toward the front entrance. Their eyes met. Leila wanted to flee or pretend she hadn't noticed. How often had she dreamed of having Roderick to herself, taking him away from Althea?

"So nice of you to come, Miss Kahn," said Althea stiffly, approaching her. Jack appeared to have recognized a long lost friend across the sitting room. Leila recognized the object of his attention: the portly man that delivered the statement to the press last Tuesday night.

Althea didn't wait for Leila's response. "Would you mind helping the guests with their coats? Collins is overwhelmed and we're expecting more visitors within the hour."

Althea's eyes were blue ice. Leila felt them sear her own. *I should go. Right now. But I can't. I can't.*

"Yes, Madam Morgan," Leila said with equal formality. "I will put the rest of the coats and hats in the library."

"Thank you, Leah." Althea left to pounce upon one of the Rothschilds.

Leila glanced through the salon's double doors. A gleaming hardwood coffin with golden, eagle-head handles occupied center stage. More guests chatted away, sipping whiskey and swaying their heads with laughter, as if the coffin was an awkwardly placed piece of furniture, not containing the body of a man they knew. No one seemed particularly sad. Leila had been the only one near his body after he died. She couldn't imagine its state, underneath that intricately carved lid. Althea, or perhaps Collins, had placed a silver-framed photograph of Roderick on a cherry-wood stand by the side of the coffin. She couldn't bear the sight of it. If she lingered too long she would burst into tears and cause a scene.

When the next guests arrived, she gathered their coats, like just another part of the help, and headed to Roderick's library. At first glance, the library appeared just as she had last seen it when Roderick had given her money and sent her on her way. On second glance, the fan-shaped lampshades were the same, but the lights shone dimmer. The room carried an unusual, faint lemon scent. The table beneath his mother's painting carried Roderick's glasses and liquor bottles as if waiting for him to partake. It seemed as if at any moment she might turn to see him behind his desk, talking about a deal, discussing a book, or watching the way she moved – but it remained empty. She ran her fingers over the ebony wood of his desk. Althea must have cleared everything away, except for Roderick's fountain pen and ink well.

Beyond the door, she heard snatches of chatter, much of it about the stock market. One man said, "Things will be back to normal soon; time to pile into AT&T and General Electric." Another lamented about selling his West Egg vacation home to make ends meet. A cultured female voice asked, "What will become of his lovely wife?" Another answered, "Althea will have her share of suitors." No one talked about Roderick at all.

She understood him more at that moment than ever before. Roderick strived for acceptance from these people. Why else had he married Althea? In his death, he was the reason for this gathering, but not its focus. Leila placed the coats on Roderick's velvet couch. She had never known anyone to take his own life. The stock market crash had taken his wealth, but was the loss of money worth dying over? Or was it loss of pride, like Officer O'Malley had said? Or maybe fear? What if people discovered the two books?

He *was* responsible for brewing a cauldron of economic lies. But what had caused him to think it was all too much? She couldn't make sense of it all.

The din of the guests' voices in the hallway blended into one. She leaned closer to the steel radiator, warmed by its faint hiss. Leila thought of Nelson, how hard he worked as a carpenter; and of her cousins toiling at the Fulton Street docks every morning, barely able to afford bleacher seats to a baseball game; and of Hannah and her children. They would never see a fraction of the extravagances Roderick took for granted. *How could he be so weak? Why didn't he own up to his actions? Why didn't he fight his uncle?*

She eyed the pile of sumptuous coats she had placed on Roderick's couch and felt a swell of anger. She had to get out of here and away from these loathsome people. Nelson was right. She was just a servant here, an outsider. Where she was once envious of their endless luxuries and fancy clothes and possibilities, she was glad she grew up as humble as she did. She would make something of herself, but never be like the Morgans.

Leila longed to return to the Lower East Side. She headed to the door.

She was blocked by the dark figure of Jack Morgan.

"Sorry, Sir," she said, backing away, "I didn't see you coming in."

"Evidently," he said, walking right past her.

Leila watched the old man step toward the middle of the room, scouring the portraits. He stepped toward Roderick's desk and then returned to the portraits.

"I thought you were leaving, Miss."

"I am. I mean, I was," said Leila. "I mean – I am so sorry for your terrible loss. Can I get you anything before I go?"

"No," said Jack. He took a sip from his brandy snifter. His brow wrinkled at Roderick's mother. The whites of his knuckles encircled his glass.

"I can't imagine how she would be feeling," said Leila.

"Who?"

"Roderick's mother," she answered with a quiver. "He was her only child, no?"

Jack turned. His eyes bored into her. She felt small before this commanding man.

"He was a disappointment in life, and died a lousy coward," he grunted. "She would be well rid of him if she was alive. We are all better off."

Leila was speechless. She knew that there was no love lost between Roderick and his uncle, but was stunned at the man's arrogance. His nephew's corpse lay cold in the next room.

"But, he took his own life, sir," she said. *Because of you.*

His grey eyes chilled her blood. "That was his choice," he said. Then, he turned back to the portrait, picked up his glass, and took another slow sip of brandy.

Leila stood in disbelief. He didn't care about any of this – Roderick's death, Althea, little Rodney. She understood why Roderick disliked him so. But she knew about those two sets of books. She had to say something in Roderick's defense, in his honor.

"But, he did so much work for you, you don't feel *any* responsibility for – what he did?" she asked.

Jack's eyes now filled with what could only be interpreted as hate. She stepped back. His gaze alone could knock her to her knees. Roderick had once told her that Jack didn't like to be questioned. She saw that now. He scared her – to the bone.

"He suffered the consequences of his choices, *his* wrong decisions, Miss."

Something about his unyielding, almost brutal, tone peaked Leila's curiosity.

"You mean the wrong decisions before his death?" she asked.

"Young lady," said Jack Morgan. "My glass is empty."

"Yes, sir," said Leila taking the snifter. She wanted to ask him more, but his manner closed the conversation. "I will be right back."

On her way out, she bumped into Jack's valet, one of the two men she had seen standing next to him earlier. As Leila slid by, he locked the door behind her. She wondered if that would be the last she saw of Jack Morgan.

Later that night, Leila found no comfort in sleep. All she could do was toss and turn on her cot. Try as she might, she couldn't exorcise the image of Roderick's limp corpse bleeding onto Wall Street. Jack's squinty eyes seemed to be watching. What had he wanted from Roderick's library? Certainly it wasn't a moment of peace and a quiet from the rest of the guests. And it wasn't to gaze at Roderick's mother's portrait. She recalled how his eyes lingered on Roderick's desk. *Why?*

She shivered in her nightgown. He gave her the creeps. What was he looking for? Did he find it? Her mind zoomed back to the night she had examined the Allegheny deal papers that Roderick left lying on his desk.

She recalled a document signed by Jack Morgan. It was a contract of some sort, marked "For Investors." She hadn't thought anything of it until she flipped to the next document. It was identical. Except it cited the value of the Allegheny Corporation as several million dollars lower than on the first. She thought about the two sets of books. Roderick said his fingerprints were all over them, not Jack's. But what about the Allegheny documents? Could one of them be real and one fake – both with Jack's signature?

Something stirred within her, slowly at first, then with alarming acceleration. *Roderick had information that pointed to Jack.* Why didn't he use it? Why give up, rather than fight? Her mind raced. How long had Roderick been keeping both sets of books? Was everything about the Morgan bank suspect? Was that why Jack was so interested in Roderick's library? Did he think Roderick was hiding anything else? *Was he?* Or was it just those Allegheny documents?

A terrifying question burst forth. *Had Roderick left them for her to see that night? If so, why? In case something – happened to him?*

She heard a loud knock at the front door. She leapt out of bed, her heart pounding.

"Leila? Leila Kahn? Are you in there? I need to speak with you!" a female voice cried from the hall. The sounds of neighbors shuffling followed.

Leila wrapped her robe around her. Rachel sat upright in her bed.

"Who is that, Leila?" she asked.

"Shhh," Leila placed her index finger over her lips, "go back to sleep. I'll go see."

"Can I come with you?" asked Rachel, moving to a stand.

"No, you stay here with Tanta Rosa."

She stepped gingerly to the door, trying to avoid the squeaky floorboards. She pressed her eye to the peephole. "Althea?" she said, almost to herself. She saw the widow's streaked and messy face. Eye-powder caked below her sagging and watery eyes.

"Leila, I need to talk to you." Her whisper was frantic. *Had she found out?*

"Is everything okay?" Joshua's sleepy voice asked from the salon.

"Yes, Joshua, you can go back to sleep."

"Wait a moment," said Leila to Althea. She didn't want everyone in the house hearing whatever she had come to say. She unlatched the lock, peering through a crack.

"I know you'll think I'm crazy," said Althea, her voice hushed but shrill. "I probably am. But – you're the only person I can talk to about this."

"My family's sleeping," said Leila. *Had Althea gone mad? How had she found her way to the Lower East Side? Oh, the driver.* Leila opened the door all the way. Althea wore one of Roderick's coats. Leila's nose twitched at the scent of his cologne on his wife.

"Come," said Leila, covering her robe with one of the twin's heavy coats, and slipping into her shoes, "let's go downstairs and talk outside."

Althea followed Leila quietly. The two women descended the creaky steps. Neighbors' doors cracked open as they passed. At the front stoop, Leila noticed the Morgans' red Rolls Royce parked across the street. The driver's head rolled back. He looked either asleep or dead. A lavish vehicle parked in front of a butcher shop offering round beefsteak at 51 cents a pound; she could imagine tomorrow's gossip.

Leila noticed Althea shivering and gestured to the car. "Should we go in there?"

"No!" Althea's exclaimed, "Don't you understand? I don't know if I can trust him!"

Leila stood dumb struck. Althea was before her, in the middle of the night, freezing and frantic on Orchard Street. Didn't she have other people to comfort her besides the woman who had slept with her husband? Leila felt responsible for her pain.

"Althea, why are you here?"

"He wants everything," she said, trembling.

"Who wants everything?" Leila asked, scanning the nearly empty streets for any observers. She saw one couple ducking into an alleyway, and a few homeless men huddled together around a small pile of burning fruit crates down the street.

"Jack does."

"What do you mean, 'everything'?" Leila asked, thinking back to Jack's terrifying appearance in Roderick's library.

Althea's breath came in shallow spurts. "He said something about an oil deal, or maybe a railroad. I'm not sure. Kept asking about papers. I don't know what he was talking about. Something about his signature. His empire."

Althea was babbling. She seemed as lost as her husband had been. Yet, her words made awful sense to Leila. An unexpected twinge of sympathy hit her. Did Althea know how much he had shared with her about his life? How well did she know him?

"Althea, you should go home. Get some rest. You're upset. I can't imagine what you must be feeling – with Roderick..."

"Don't talk to me about Roderick," she snapped. "He was *my* husband!"

Her words stung worse than a slap.

"Okay, let's concentrate on Jack, then," said Leila meekly.

"Yes." Althea's mood flipped again. "Jack wants some documents. He made it clear that if he doesn't get them, he's going to take my son."

"I don't think he would do that," assured Leila, though she was fairly certain Jack could do anything he wanted.

Althea continued, "And, if he takes my son, I will be left a pauper."

Now Leila understood. The sympathy vanished. This woman didn't care about her son, or Roderick, just the money.

"Althea, there's nothing I can do for you, I'm sorry," said Leila. "Maybe you should go back uptown now, talk to Jack when you are feeling more—" she wanted to say *stable*, but decided upon, "up to it."

Althea's eyes flashed. "Leila, I'm not here for you to condescend to me. You're nothing but a poor little waitress. I'm sorry I ever let you into our home. I knew there was something going on between you and my husband, but I couldn't believe he was stupid enough to care about, let alone share secrets with, someone like – *you*."

Leila's heart stopped. What did she know? "Althea, nothing happened, really. I'm sorry if..." Her voice trailed. She had slept with her husband. No lie would change that.

"I don't need your apologies!" hissed Althea. "I saw you that night in our library, and I said nothing. I thought Roderick would tire of you, like all the rest. I'm sure he would have. But now, you are the only one who may know what Jack wants. As much as I hate to say this – I need your help to keep my son and fortune. You owe me that."

Leila saw the contempt in Althea's eyes. Didn't she deserve her scorn? She saw something else in Althea's face: lines of desperation. She thought of Rodney. He would grow up without his father, like she had. Leila couldn't help Roderick anymore, but maybe she could help the family he had left behind; maybe that would be a way to help him, too. For the moment, she tucked away her own grief.

"I will do what I can," she promised.

Althea's features relaxed. "Good. Please come to my home Monday night. I will gather all the documents I can find, and you can help me go through them."

Leila wasn't sure what she would find within the Morgans' home, but she had as many questions as Althea. "I'll be there."

Althea slipped into her Rolls Royce without another word. Leila remained outside for long minutes in the cold. *What have you gotten yourself into?*

\* \* \*

Althea awoke late the next morning. Pulling back her satin sheets, she stretched her legs and sat up in bed. The maid had arranged an elaborate spread of breakfast foods on a silver platter in her sitting area. A note next to the platter read, "Madam, you really must eat." She had barely touched food during the past week.

Today, she was famished.

She put on her silk robe and arranged herself on her sofa. She uncovered a plate of poached eggs with Parmesan cheese. A basket of warm croissants emitted a waft of steam. She reached for the coffee pot and poured a cup. She added a sugar cube and drop of milk, watching it swirl. She felt remarkably at peace after having enlisted Leila's help.

She couldn't trust Jack's people to help her make sense of Roderick's documents, and she knew Roderick shared more work information with Leila than with her. She was surprised at how little it had bothered her to see them in the library. She didn't know what he saw in Leila, but his interest had lasted longer than with any of the others. She had to be pragmatic. This immigrant girl could be of use to her.

The past six days had been a haze. She found it hard to believe her husband was dead, or that he'd had the courage to take his own life. She was sad that it had come to that, of course, and sorry that her son would never know his father, but she was relieved, too. She would find another husband in time, after she secured her fortune.

She sipped her coffee. She would find a way to placate Jack.

"Madam Morgan!" called Collins. "You have a —"

"Get out of my way, lad!" Jack appeared at Althea's bedroom door.

She spoke with composure. "Jack, I told you last night, I would find them."

He marched towards her. "Althea, I don't have time for this. All I found in your husband's library was a nosy immigrant girl. I thought I made myself clear. I want whatever he had. Do you understand?"

"I do, Jack," she said. "I have kept up my side of our bargain for years. I keep an eye on Roderick. You treat me like a proper Morgan, with a proper heir."

Jack eyed her. "You surprise me, Althea. I remember our bargain. It seems you lost control of him. Do not play me for a fool."

"I would never do that, Jack," said Althea. "You can trust me."

"Is that why you spent the middle of last night with that same girl?" he asked.

"You – you followed me?" Althea said, incensed and frightened.

"This isn't a game. Get me the documents," he ordered.

"I'll get you what you need. But give me some time. I just lost my husband."

He stifled a laugh. "It's a bit late to play the lovesick wife. You have a week."

"Or what?" She was surprised at her boldness, but as long as he didn't have what he wanted, she had the upper hand. He underestimated her.

"Do not try my patience. Good day, Althea."

He strode past Collins, who was dusting frames in the hallway.

"Is everything alright, Madam?" he asked.

"Yes, Collins. Thank you. Everything will be," said Althea.

# 14.

## November 4, 1929

The notion of returning to the Morning Spot filled Leila with apprehension. She hoped her customers wouldn't ask any questions. She didn't think she could answer any.

Buried in thoughts of Roderick and Althea, she hadn't even glanced at the newspapers. After a week away, it almost felt like the market didn't matter. But then, Monday morning came. She was on the El and everyone was reading the newspaper with worried faces. She picked up a copy of the *Times* left on the seat beside her.

The Rockefellers had bought a large amount of stock in Standard Oil a few days earlier. The editorial page praised the Morgan bank and Federal Reserve for putting even more cash into the market. She wondered if that was in addition to the money they discussed at the meeting Roderick had told her about five days before he died. She remembered his anger. And hers. He had avoided her for nearly two months. *Why?*

The headlines talked about "prosperity" and how things would soon be back to normal. Her past week had been anything but normal. She took a deep breath. She unlocked the door to find the tiny world that had become her second home looked exactly the same. There were no dead bodies on the ground. The eggs were aligned in neat rows in the refrigerator. Each table had a salt- and pepper-shaker. Normal.

Nan arrived and greeted her with a huge hug. "Thank God you're back and I don't have to deal with Moishe following my every move!"

Soon, her customers streamed in for their breakfasts. It was all like last Tuesday never happened. Oliver, the man with the muttonchops, said, "Glad to see you, Leila. I heard you had a harder week than some of the rest of us. I hope you're holding up okay."

She wasn't sure what he meant by that. *He couldn't know about her and Roderick, could he?* She observed the pack of men eating and drinking at her counter. *What had they been saying about her all week? What had they said about Roderick?*

"Moishe said your uncle passed. I'm sorry for your loss," Oliver continued.

Leila exhaled in relief. "My uncle's partner. Thank you. Yes. He was like family."

She straightened silverware behind the counter, grateful that her patrons seemed mindful of her week. She began to relax. But as she rang up some orders at the cash register, two customers interrupted her return to routine from the back booths.

"Hey, Leila!" shouted Sinclair, the Chase banker.

"Yes?" she said, walking over with a coffee pot.

"We wanted you to settle a bet for us."

"If I can. You want to know if the market's going to go up or down?" she smiled, trying to regain some of the lightness that she used with her customers.

"See, Walter over here says he heard it from a guy on the inside that the Morgan guy was involved in some shady stuff. But I think he just lost a ton of money for the bank and couldn't take it. You used to talk to him a lot – what's your opinion?"

*Keep breathing,* she told herself. She observed the two men waiting for her response. Were they there the morning she and

Roderick had fought? She couldn't remember. She recalled another time she had seen Walter – the morning Roderick had asked her to babysit, and before that, when Roderick had stood up for her and almost punched Hank. A sixth sense sparked her suspicions. His slits for eyes made her skin crawl.

"Come on, Leila," urged Walter, "We got today's breakfast riding on it."

"I don't know," she said. "I suppose we need to wait to see if the police come up with anything."

"This ain't no matter for the police," said George, a customer with a white handlebar mustache from across the room. "This thing's got federal written all over it."

"Nah," said Sinclair, waving his hand. "The guy went nuts. It happened to my neighbor, too, may he rest in peace. The Fed's have got better things to do."

"Or maybe the guy was hiding something and then went nuts," surmised Walter, peering at Leila intently.

"The whole country's going nuts," added a face Leila didn't recognize, joining the debate. "Guy probably thought his old man would come down on him hard – whatever he was doing – and jumped."

They looked at Leila. She swallowed nervously. Did they expect her to really know what went on, or was this just part of idle morning chatter?

"It was his uncle, not his old man," she corrected them softly. "Excuse me boys… got to go seat that crowd over there." She hurried away. She realized she was sweating.

She had no idea what had transpired between Roderick and Jack before he died. She wished she did. She feared the more people gossiped, or reporters investigated, the more likely Roderick would come out looking bad. Did Jack want it that way? He would do whatever he could to hide those two books; and even if something did come out, he could blame everything on Roderick. Wait a minute. *Jack would do whatever he could.*

"Hey Leila," called Walter, "You didn't settle our bet!"

"Let me get back to you on that, Walter." She shifted her voice into one of confidence to motivate him to leave the diner, "Go out and make some money!"

"Yeah, I wish," said Walter, grabbing his hat and heading toward the exit.

"Me, too," said Sinclair following him.

Leila watched them leave. Walter had revived her initial dread. Navigating the diner wasn't going to be easy. She considered quitting. Moishe would find someone else. Maybe she could work for him uptown. Then it dawned on her – perhaps there was something she could learn from her customers.

At eight o'clock, Leila arrived at the Morgans' home. Her nerves were a tangle at the thought of being alone in the apartment with Althea, without guests, without Roderick. She considered what they might discover together. The thought titillated her. She would preserve the mask of pleasantry she had carefully constructed on her walk from the El. The mask she'd seen Althea use and discard at will.

"Hello," she said, surprised to find Althea open the door herself.

"Good evening, Leila," Althea said formally. Leila again found herself embarrassed over the contrast in their wardrobes. Even tonight, Althea wore the most fashionable of garments: a short, peach-colored dress with a hint of gold trimming. Pearl earrings dangled from her lobes. Her bobbed hair was impeccably neat. It all felt wrong.

Leila was relieved to hear Rodney scamper toward her. He toddled out of the salon, his feet covered by the flannel pads of his pajamas. They were decorated with little sailboats. He waddled over holding out a ship. She scooped him up.

"Hi there, little guy," she smiled. She lifted him up to face-level. He had his father's hazel eyes. He revealed a row of baby teeth and cried, "Ley-Ley!"

"What a pretty boat!" she cooed.

"I thought you might want to say, hello," said Althea. "It's past his bedtime, but things haven't exactly been on schedule around here."

"It's good to see him," said Leila, "How's he coping?"

"Fine," replied Althea. She sighed. "He does perk up every time somebody comes through the front door. Maybe he's waiting for his father to arrive, but he's too young to really know. I suppose one day, I'll have to explain to him what – what happened."

As Leila held the woman's son, she wondered what Althea could possibly say. How could she ever explain what happened to his father? That his father had chosen to take his own life? Her Mama had never spoken to her about her Papa after he died. It was a sorrowful secret she locked away.

"May I put him in for the night?" she asked.

Althea paused. "Certainly. Yes, thank you. I gave the staff the night off – who knows if any of them are working for Jack? I took the liberty of gathering Roderick's materials in the dining room. I will be there when you return."

Leila dipped Rodney towards Althea for a goodnight kiss. Althea merely spun around and headed towards the dining room.

As she carried Rodney past the photographs of various Morgans, the great loneliness of the apartment weighed on her. It wasn't just heavy with sorrow over Roderick's death either. The Morgan home was infused with sadness before, an absence of warmth, of love. She hadn't really thought much of it then; her visits were always painted with the excitement of seeing Roderick, and comparisons of his luxuries to her lack of them.

If Althea and Roderick had shared the same kind of love her parents had, would he have betrayed his wife with her? To alleviate her guilt, she decided the answer was no.

She lay Rodney down, and kissed his forehead. "Good night, sweet boy."

Leila returned to the dining room to find Althea seated at an ivory chair stitched with deep burgundy velvet, its legs carved with elaborate vines. She held a glass of wine in her hand. Leila glanced at the gold plated pens and papers strewn across the grand marble table awaiting a purpose. She sunk into the plush seat beside Althea.

"Shall we begin?" Althea asked. She still wore her diamond engagement ring and matching wedding band. Leila felt a twinge of jealousy.

She pulled her chair closer to the table. Althea appeared to be awaiting instructions from her, like a frightened child lost in a mass of documents. It occurred to her that Althea hadn't looked through any of these papers by herself.

"That's a lot of material," Leila said.

"I gathered everything I could from around the house," Althea explained, a nervous strain in her voice. Under any other circumstance, Leila would be the last person she should confide anything in. *She's desperate.*

"That was very smart of you. So Jack hasn't seen any of them?"

"No," she said with a finality that aroused more questions.

Leila cleared her throat, unsure of how Althea would react to the news that her husband had been faking Morgan's books. *Could she tell her? What help could she be if she didn't? Would she be betraying Roderick?* She was the only one that knew Jack was engaged in faking the books, even if Roderick was the one who kept both ledgers. *Should she – could she – be the one that told people?*

"Althea, there's something I need to tell you about Roderick."

Althea's posture straightened, but her eyes looked distinctly bored.

"Before he died, he – Roderick – told me about two sets of books he was keeping for the Morgan bank." Leila searched through the piles for something to help her explain.

"What does that mean, exactly?" Althea said dully.

Leila realized she would have to educate Althea with her limited knowledge.

She answered, "Every bank, every company – even my diner – keeps a set of books that show the incoming and outgoing money. In the case of the Morgan bank, Roderick kept one set that showed the real figures, and another that made it seem like more money was coming in than there actually was."

Althea processed this for a moment. "My husband was a crook?"

"Well, no. I mean, I think Jack forced him to fake the books." She hated the way Althea kept referring to Roderick as her husband. But he was, wasn't he?

Leila grew nervous. Why should she defend Roderick to his own wife? Yet Althea had cut to the core of the matter. Roderick's actions weren't merely deceitful, they were illegal. But her heart told her she needed to prove that Jack forced him to do what he did. Jack was the true crook. *Shouldn't Jack face the consequences?*

"Yes, Jack has a way of getting people to do what he wants," replied Althea.

Leila rummaged through the documents. She navigated a sea of receipts and signatures, documents printed on different colors of paper, and hand-written notes with random figures. Then she discovered exactly what she was looking for. At the bottom of the biggest mound of paper, there were two brown, hard-backed, leather-bound ledgers.

Just like that. *Why would he have left them so easy to find?* She set them before her, momentarily oblivious to Althea's presence. She lifted the front cover of each. They were indeed official records of some sort. She noted the scrupulously inked rows of dates and numbers and listings of company names like Pennsylvania Railroad and New Haven Railroad. The elegance of the figures and Roderick's meticulous writing style mesmerized her. Leila understood what these numbers represented.

Althea leaned in. "What are you looking at?" she asked. "Is it what Jack wanted?"

"I don't know," replied Leila. "I can't see why Jack wouldn't already have his own copies of these two sets of books. He likes to control *everything*, no?"

"Everything," agreed Althea. "Do you think Roderick kept these here and Jack has another set at the bank? Then what does he want from me?"

"I'm not sure. You said it was something about a railroad or oil deal, right?"

"Yes, that's what he said. Please – what can I give him?" Althea squeaked.

Leila saw Althea's desperation. This woman had no interest in protecting Roderick's name or going after Jack. But was it Leila's place to judge her? What did she really know about Althea or their marriage? Wasn't she ultimately just an intruder here? Was any of this any of her business?

She would help Althea and be done with it.

Leila reflected upon the signed Alleghany documents in Roderick's library. She hadn't known about the two sets of books when she came across them, but the contract marked "For Investors" showed a higher value than the other one. She wracked her brain, trying to recall what those two numbers were.

"I'm not sure," she told Althea. She leafed through the books again. She focused on the numbers. Something jolted her memory. In the first book, on the top left corner of page 127, she saw the word "Alleghany," and on the column over, a date: February 3, 1929. In the next column, there was a value: $31.5 million. She flipped through the other book to page 127; it appeared exactly the same, except that in the third column, the number was higher: $35 million. She looked back and forth several times to make sure.

"What? What is it?" asked Althea, placing her hand over Leila's wrist. This hand had touched Roderick. Her fingers were soft like Roderick's, a life without work. There was urgency in the grip of this hand.

Leila took a deep breath. She considered withholding information from Althea, just as Roderick had. She wasn't certain she wanted to tell Althea about the existence of the two signed Allegheny documents. She extracted her hand from Althea's grasp and pointed to the spot in each book. "See these two numbers, $31.5 and $35 million?"

"Yes." Althea suddenly seemed very interested.

"One – the higher one – is the value that investors would have seen."

Leila sorted through the pile of documents again, flipping over items marked "deal," until she reached the one she was searching for.

"See, this is the Alleghany deal; the value investors see is here." She pointed halfway down the page.

Althea's delicate brows crinkled. She tugged at her earring vigorously. "I don't understand. That's what they think they bought – a deal worth $35 million – but it really wasn't?"

"Yes," said Leila. She tried to hide her fascination. It could all be so simple. "They thought it was worth something that it was not."

Althea peered over the second book, scrutinized page 127, and said slowly, "Here it says the deal is worth less, only $31.5 million – that's the real value?"

"I think so," nodded Leila.

"So this entire book," Althea pointed to the one with the higher values, "is fake?"

Leila gulped as the enormity of this situation sunk in, of what Roderick had been doing, since – she flipped to the first entry – April 17, 1927.

"Yes." She watched Althea's face cycle through a variety of contortions.

"But, Jack didn't mention any books, he mentioned some document!"

Leila was still searching for the documents she had seen that night in the library, with Jack Morgan's signature. She couldn't find them. She asked, "Is this all you have of Roderick's? Are you sure there are no other documents anywhere?"

"I don't think so," answered Althea. "Why, what are you looking for?"

Leila weighed her response. She needed the document with Jack's signature on it that matched the number in the real book. That must be what he was looking for.

"I'm not sure," she said. Althea would have no idea what to look for herself, she thought with a degree of superiority that surprised her.

She raked through the stack of documents again. They seemed to be copies of Morgan deal documents for investors. Jack Morgan had signed them all. She assumed that way investors would consider them legitimate. They all matched the numbers in the fake book, but she couldn't find any double document for the Allegheny deal that would tie the fakes to Jack. Where could it be?

Leila's brain throbbed. She collapsed her head in her hands.

"Would you like a cup of hot tea?" Althea surprised her by asking.

Leila raised her head. The search had drained her; not because she couldn't find the document she wanted, but because she knew it existed. She saw it in her mind clearly now. "Yes, thank you. That would be lovely."

"I think we both may need some," said Althea, almost warmly.

While Althea was in the kitchen, Leila tried to recall the document's shape, its texture, the way the words were written and where the numbers were located. It appeared no different than any of the other ones covering the table. Slightly thick stock, crème colored paper, bold black ink, Jack's signature a hasty line. She couldn't find it. She rose from her chair in frustration and paced the room. Roderick had to have it somewhere. It must be in the library. She had to see for herself.

She wandered into the room and toward the desk. She opened each of the ebony drawers on its right side. Empty. She opened the left door to reveal four more pullout drawers. Leila opened each one carefully. They were emptied too – she assumed by Althea – the contents now lying in a pile on the dining room table. She knelt to open the small drawer under the liquor table.

Nothing.

She stood in the room's center as Jack had. She surveyed the cases of books, their beige, blue, and red cloth covers aligned perfectly on the shelves. *Perhaps he had hidden the documents in one of them?* Althea appeared with a china tray on which was a teapot, two tulip-shaped cups on saucers, a creamer, a sugar bowl, and a plate of shortbread.

"Here, sorry it took so long. I couldn't find everything," said Althea, setting the platter down on Roderick's empty desk. "Do you think the document Jack wants is still in here? I went through everything already."

"It must be," said Leila. "Unless Jack has it." *Could there be more than one?*

"He sent his valet over here again today," said Althea. "I honestly thought he was going to choke me, the way he backed me into that wall." She pointed toward the hallway, as her hands massaged her neck. "He doesn't have what he wants."

Leila eyed the portrait of Roderick's mother, as Jack had done. Nelson told her that sometimes the wealthy concealed valuables in hidden wall safes behind pictures. She moved the painting sideways, peaking behind it. The wall appeared flat.

"Maybe he'd have hidden something behind her," she said. Althea sat on Roderick's couch, sipping tea and watching Leila.

"I searched behind the portraits here. That's where I found your two books," said Althea coldly. "I also searched behind the ones in my bedroom. And his bedroom."

Leila's face fell. Again, she was reminded of how much she hadn't shared with Roderick. "It's got to be here somewhere. Help me," she said to Althea.

Althea rose. "Help you?"

Leila corrected herself. "I mean – you want to find what Jack is looking for."

They unhooked the heavy portrait and set it on the floor. They tapped their hands over every inch of the wall, pressing their ears to listen for hollow areas. They found none. Leila was about to give up when she remembered something else Nelson had said – about floorboards.

"Wait a minute," she said. She never thought Nelson's paranoid tales of the rich would be so useful. She pushed a heavy chair out of her way and knelt down. A palm-sized section of rug had been flattened beneath its center. She slipped her hand beneath the spot, searching blindly while Althea stared at her quizzically.

"There!" she exclaimed. She flipped up the rug to produce a section of loose floorboard. She scooped her fingers beneath the groove by one of the wood panels.

"What on earth are you—?" Althea started.

Leila upended a second section of flooring. She touched the cold edge of what felt like a steel box with her fingertips.

"Althea, this must be where it is!"

Their eyes lit up with relief, both women happy for different reasons.

Leila extended her arm further beneath the floorboards. She extracted a rectangular lockbox. A layer of dust coated its surface. Leila placed the box on the rug.

"Just open it!" Althea snapped.

"I don't think I can, it has a key—" Leila stopped herself mid-sentence as her fingers easily pried the lid open. Something wasn't right. Althea began to sob.

"It's gone... isn't it? What Jack wants – it's not there," she moaned with rising hysteria. "The books aren't enough if he has copies. They can't be. Jack will kill me!"

Leila stared at the empty box. Despair overwhelmed her. Those documents had to be somewhere. *Oh Roderick, where did you put them?*

# 15.

# *November 5, 1929*

The next morning, Walter and Sinclair returned to the diner. They entered, squabbling about what the Rockefellers' stock purchase meant for the future of the market. As soon as they were seated, Leila poured them coffee, avoiding eye contact. After last night with Althea, and her failure to find anything useful to implicate Jack, she had no desire to talk about Roderick with these men.

They had opposite thoughts in mind. "So Leila, simple question: was he a dumb bastard or a guilty bastard? You must have an opinion," Walter pressed.

"I'm busy this morning," she responded. "Nan will take care of you, ask her."

"But I'm asking you," said Walter, aggressively. He grabbed her shoulder, pinching through the material of her dress with his fingers.

"I don't know!" she said impatiently, trying to shake loose.

"I think the lady gave you all the response you need," said a familiar Irish voice.

Walter released his grip. "Sure thing, officer. No harm intended."

"I think you best be going," said Officer O'Malley.

"Course. Have a wonderful day, Leila," he tipped his hat and left. Leila glanced at Sinclair, who shrugged, his palms facing upward.

"Thank you, Officer O'Malley – Bryan," she said. "People can be pretty insistent about things around here."

"I can see that," he said.

"Can I get you some coffee cake?" she asked. Her last conversation with him seemed like a distant nightmare. She hoped he wouldn't bring it up.

"Absolutely."

She returned, plate of cake in hand.

"So, how are you holding up?" he asked.

"Why, I'm fine," she averted her eyes. "It was a hard night after Morris's heart attack. Family and friends gathered together all week. But I'm glad to be back here."

His eyes scrunched. "I meant, how are you holding up after what happened here last Tuesday?"

"Oh," she sighed, "I can't shake it from my mind. It was so *awful.*"

"Anything else?" he asked gently. "Is there anything specific you want to talk about – about that night?"

She peered into his eyes. They appeared honest. He was a policeman after all. But so were the men who shooed the crowd away from Roderick's body after someone from Morgan asked them to. Could policemen be trusted? Could anyone? Doubts swelled in her mind. She wanted so badly to talk to someone. Bryan had always been friendly. He had offered to take her home that night. He had given her his phone number. It was still in her coat pocket. Something about him reminded her of Nelson. It wasn't just the Irish brogue, it was something that seemed to want to make things right.

Maybe he could help. Maybe he would be interested in finding out the truth about the Morgan bank. Or maybe he just wanted to know what she knew, like Walter.

She set the plate of coffee cake before him. "No, there's nothing else."

For the rest of the week, she mulled her options. She had to tell someone about the two books and the missing document that connected them to Jack Morgan. If she told Nelson, or anyone in her family, they might blame her for not telling them sooner; before Joseph lost his business, and Morris lost his life. Plus, any revelations might unleash a scandal. Besides, she didn't know where the document was anyway. Maybe she should just drop the matter. But that was impossible. The notion of some horrible wrong going not just unpunished but unnoticed, was unbearable. She began to understand Nelson's need – ever urgent, always inconvenient, but honest – to fight the wrongs of the world.

After the Friday lunch rush, she excused herself to make a phone call. She walked away from Wall Street, up Broad Street until she reached Stone Street. She entered a wooden phone booth. She extracted the piece of paper from her jacket pocket, dropped a coin in the slot and with a shaky voice, gave the number to the operator.

A gruff male voice answered, "First Precinct, what's the crime?"

"I would like to speak with – Officer Bryan O'Malley, please," she said.

"Who wants him?" said the man.

"Uh, just a friend of his," she replied, nervously.

"Yeah, lemme get him for you."

She waited for several minutes, her stomach in knots.

"O'Malley," he picked up.

"Hi, Bryan – it's Leila. You said to call anytime, and I – I need to talk to you."

"Leila – I'll be right over, just gotta finish up some paperwork."

"I'd rather not speak at the Morning Spot. Is there somewhere else we can meet?"

"Of course," he said, "There's a deli over on 120 Broadway. No one ever goes there this time of day. Would that be okay for you?"

She hesitated about leaving the Morning Spot for too long, but answered, "Certainly. I'll see you there."

"I'll be there in ten minutes," he said. She didn't inquire about his paperwork.


The Broadway deli was deserted. Its thick air, circulated by two slow moving fans, reeked of cigarette smoke and grease. Bryan sat at a back table. He had already ordered two mugs of coffee. He beckoned to her. "Leila, I'm glad you called."

"What would happen if a bank like, like Morgan, was involved in – some shady dealings?" she spurted.

His eyes widened. "What kind of dealings? What do you know, Leila?"

"I don't know anything. But if I did, what would I do?" His tone had frightened her.

He studied her for a moment, then leaned in. "You would be very careful, Leila."

"Of course," she replied. She winced. His urgent manner troubled her.

"No, Leila, you need to understand this," he said sternly. "The people that run places like that – they're different from you and me."

"I know that," she said. She recalled the darkness in Jack's eyes.

"I don't mean because they have money either," he continued, "but because they are very powerful. They are remorseless. Promise me, you will be very careful."

Leila's palms began to sweat. He sounded like Nelson. She wondered what Nelson would say if he knew about the books and Jack's signature on some missing document. Would he be careful with that information? No. Nelson wouldn't think twice.

"I promise," she assured Bryan.

# 16.

# *December 5, 1929*

Over a month had passed since Roderick's death. Leila stayed true to her promise, but only in her actions. She could not turn her mind away from the other Allegheny document. During those snowy early December days, talk at the Morning Spot centered on President Herbert Hoover. He delivered his first State of the Union speech before Congress. Bankers took comfort in his suggestion that business was sound. There might be some banking law revisions, but nothing major to worry about.

The stock market rose daily, proving that Wall Street had averted a crisis. The Morgan bank would survive intact. Leila's sorrow over Roderick turned into a dull familiar ache. He was gone. The world, outwardly anyway, went on as before.

Walter goaded her whenever he could. "Jack Morgan should be happy. He can keep merging railroads and making money."

"I suppose," she answered. Had Jack shifted his focus away from the documents? Did he have someone else keeping double books? She realized it had been a month since she had last seen Althea and little Rodney. She ached to stop by. She wondered if Althea was getting on with her life, while Jack was getting on with his mergers.

"It would be a shame if anything went wrong with the mergers, right?" Walter added.

"It seems to me that if anything goes wrong with them, it would be the bank's fault, now wouldn't it?" Leila countered. She didn't know what Walter was driving at, but she was glad she put him in his place. She wished he'd just find another diner to frequent.

"Maybe, maybe not," he replied. He swigged the rest of his coffee.

The rest of her customers aligned themselves, depending on their vocation, on various sides of the debate over Hoover's message. Leopold, the tailor, remarked to Howard, one of the younger bankers, "I don't care what you or President Hoover says about the economy. I just want to get out of this turmoil with the shirt on my back!"

"You're a fool, Leopold, that's why you sew buttons for a living, while the rest of us are going to get rich! He's our *president!* Why would he lie? Where's your sense of patriotism?" Howard retorted.

"If things are so good, how come my customers stopped paying for suits?" Leopold snapped back.

"No one told you to become a businessman," said George, from down the counter.

"Hey, cheer up," said Walter, regaining his earlier swagger, "Hoover said the bankers and the Federal Reserve put enough money in the market to keep things moving. And he's going to cut taxes for businesses. He's got a plan. Everything will be fine."

For a second, Walter's words reminded Leila of the quiet confidence Roderick exuded when they first met. But his edge was sharp. *Things always bounce back.* She half-expected Roderick to bound through the door and lend his opinion like he used to. She caught herself watching the door; its stillness tortured her insides.

"Yeah," agreed Howard, "and he said that all the money used for market speculation would now be going into normal channels of business."

"See," said Walter, "everything is going to be fine. The Morgan bank really did save the day, right?" He looked again at Leila.

At that moment, the door swung open in a fit of bells.

Rivkah flounced into the diner. "So, *this* is what all the fuss is about?" she said. Every customer turned to stare at her. She reveled in their attention.

"What on earth are you doing here?" asked Leila. "Is everything okay, uptown?"

"Uptown, yes. Here, no," she replied, still panting. "It seems your boyfriend and my – well, whatever he is, let's just say your cousin, Joshua, have been arrested in some ruckus by the docks. I came by to take you with me so we can sort it out."

"What happened exactly?" asked Leila. What had Nelson gone and done now?

"Something about firing them before Christmas. Joshua and Jonathan asked Nelson to be there early this morning to help out. They knew there'd be trouble. We should get over there." She winked at Howard.

Leila called over to Nan to watch the place. She grabbed her coat and hat. "Let's go," she told Rivkah.

Rivkah seemed immobile all of a sudden. She was catching glances from men around the diner and smiling back at as many as she could.

"Rivkah!" exclaimed Leila, tugging at her friend's coat. "Joshua. Remember?"

"Oh, right," answered Rivkah. The two exited the diner. "You know, there are some real dreamboats in there. Maybe I should switch jobs with you."

They reached the Fulton Fish Market docks minutes later. One of the fishermen paused from spraying down his boat to tell them the rioters had been taken to the Tombs.

"The Tombs?" asked Leila.

"Yeah, the joint down on White Street. They'll be in central booking for awhile," said the man. His face was weathered. He stunk of fish. "Wasn't their fault either."

"What wasn't?" asked Rivkah. "What happened?"

"There was this rumor going around yesterday," he explained, switching off his water hose, "they were gonna be cutting jobs and wages to make up for some debts the bosses owed. The boys down here, they didn't take it that well."

"Was there a fight?" asked Leila.

"This Irish guy – he's not a fisherman, not sure where he came from, but he was doing all the talking. He said that if the President could meet with hundreds of businessmen in Washington to talk about helping them and get a standing ovation for it, then the guys who worked their tails off down here deserved better. That Irishman, he was a sight, he was," the man smiled.

"His name's Nelson O'Leary," said Leila. She blushed.

"You know him?" asked the man.

"They're getting married," offered Rivkah.

"Really? Congratulations! Got yourself a real man there," said the fisherman.

"We're not – oh, never mind So what did he do?"

"As soon as he got here, three, maybe four in the morning, he marched up to the boss's office, banging on the door. All the other guys followed him. He was shouting, demanding the workers' voices be heard."

Leila could imagine Nelson leading the other men. Part of her was angry with him for causing a fight, but deep inside, she was proud of him for taking a stand. It was something she struggled to do. It was exactly the behavior that got her back up, too.

"Go on," prompted Rivkah.

"Well, the boss, this German fellow – he's run the docks for decades – he called your Nelson a lousy mick and slammed his door shut. Then, they beat the door down. Someone called the cops. A few minutes later, there was a sea of policemen here waving batons like the guys had just massacred a small city." He pointed to a dilapidated brick office building marked Fulton Co. Fisheries across the street from the water. "Nelson and the boys were arrested for destruction of property and disturbing the peace."

"So there wasn't really a fight?" asked Leila, "just a lot of shouting?"

"Yeah, but try telling *them* that. Those guys over there," he pointed towards Wall Street, "they shout and it's a crisis that the President needs to remedy! Around here, it's a disturbance that the cops come to break up and no one else cares."

He saw the sad look in Leila's eyes. "Don't worry – they didn't really do anything wrong. Worst case, they'll be in the pen a couple days and everything will go back to normal." He laughed softly and shook his head. "Normal, whatever that is."

The old fisherman was right about the Tombs. When the girls arrived at the White Street station, they were told new prisoners were held in the general cell, the "pen," awaiting further booking instructions.

She wandered into a room lined with pine benches. It was full of chatter and shouting against the whir of ceiling fans. Dark-blue uniformed policemen sat at desks piled high with papers. Beside each desk, a man was seated in a bare wooden chair, talking to the officer taking his information. More men were seated on the pine benches waiting their turn to recount their side of the story. The room smelled of tin, peppered with sweat, even in December. None of the seated men wore suits. They sported the woolen pants, frayed shirts, and caps of laborers. Some were black. Some were white. Some were Asian. All were young. She scanned the room.

She spotted Nelson and the twins behind an internal cell with iron bars.

"There they are!" exclaimed Rivkah. She bounded for the cell.

Leila held her back. "Wait a moment," said Leila, grabbing her by the coat.

From the far side of the room, she observed the men in the cell. They were glued to Nelson's words. His back faced the outer room. Leila winced at the sight of his arms restrained behind his back in cuffs. His head bobbed with animation from beneath his dark-gray cap. Even the policemen at their desks paused from paperwork to listen. Pride displaced the last remnants of her anger. *He'll stop when he's dead.*

She spotted Officer O'Malley entering the main room from a side hallway. He was carrying a bunch of folders.

"Leila," he called out, "what brings you here?"

"One of your – prisoners," she said, "Nelson O'Leary – over there," she pointed.

O'Malley cracked a smile. "That guy? He's captured himself quite an audience."

"They're getting married," blurted Rivkah.

"Oh?" he raised an eyebrow. He probed Leila's face with curiosity. She averted her gaze. If he had a hundred questions, he kept them to himself.

"Bryan, how long do you think it will be before they are released – Nelson and those two – my two cousins in there?" she pointed to the fair-haired men standing in front of Nelson, as a burst of applause traversed the cell. "And all the rest."

"Hmmm, well, they're not my case – shouldn't be more than a few days, but I'll see what I can to do speed things up, okay?"

"They didn't hurt anybody," she said.

"I know that. This is all part of the mixed-up system we call justice around here," he cocked his head toward the cell. "Go over there, I'm sure he'd be happy to see you."

She approached the cell. She heard the passion in Nelson's voice, tired but fierce.

"We have to win this fight – for the good of our country, our children, and our future!" he proclaimed.

His words were potent, but she thought something troubling laced his tone; the glimmerings of resignation, the feeling that the deck was stacked against you. *No. Nelson would never succumb to that feeling.*

She and Rivkah waved to the twins, silently waiting for Nelson to finish.

"And that's why, my dear friends, we cannot stop our quest. Those men on Wall Street have committed a great crime against our country. Yet here we sit. It is our duty, as men and as proud, hard-working Americans, to keep fighting."

"Hear! Hear!" called the prisoners. Leila looked at the policemen, expecting someone to quiet them. But they were nodding their agreement.

"Hear! Hear!" she echoed, clapping.

Nelson turned around. He beamed a grin from behind the bars.

"Leila!"

She blushed. "You just can't stay out of trouble, can you?" she allowed herself to tease him. He was unharmed; even better, he was in his element.

"True, I'm no stranger to these roundups – but I had some help this time," he said, gesturing to the twins.

"I see that," she said.

"Hi, Leila," said Jonathan, sheepishly. "Tell Mom I'll be home as soon as I can."

"Hi, Rivkah," said Joshua. "Don't worry, they're treating us pretty well, except for a bruise or two."

"I'll be your nurse when you get out," said Rivkah.

"I heard you caused quite a ruckus at the docks," said Leila.

"Somebody has to," said Nelson. He turned sideways so that he could wrap one of his shackled hands around the bars; she placed her hand over his. "I'm glad you came. I've been wondering what happened to you."

Leila released her hand. She hadn't been able to confront Nelson the past month. She couldn't tell him she was obsessed with a dead man, his family, and their crimes.

A cell guard stood to break up their affection. Bryan motioned him back down.

"You were right – about so many things," she said.

He looked puzzled. "So, when I get out of here, how about a nice dinner somewhere?" said Nelson.

"That would be wonderful," she lied. Shame over her betrayal would keep them apart. She wished she could explain it to him. But she feared destroying the respect he had for her. She missed his outbursts more than she cared to admit. Loneliness consumed her. Roderick was gone and Nelson was beyond reach. And she was to blame.

She had assumed that underneath the bustle and fight, the lament of the Lower East Side was its destiny. Maybe that was wrong. Maybe there was something she could do about it. *Somebody has to.*

She smiled inwardly. She was thinking like Nelson. It terrified her.

# 17.
# New Year's Eve, 1929

As the winter grew colder, she realized that she didn't miss Roderick as much. His strong smile, his thick hair, his erotic touch; they didn't tug on her with the same desperate ache. Yet that damn piece of paper; it haunted her like a ghost stuck in her soul.

The more she read about things snapping back to normal in the papers, the angrier she got. People were struggling more than ever. They were scared of the future. That was her reality. Things weren't normal. Two books existed for the biggest bank in the country. One document connected them to the world's most powerful banker.

*Where was it?*

Leila spent the last morning of 1929 buying Tanta Rosa's groceries at the Hester Street market. Christmas sales had been awful. Many peddlers were closing pushcarts for good, their hunched backs tired and sad. Yet, all along the Lower East Side streets, Leila saw people wishing each other a better New Year. *We always hope.*

She caught herself searching for Nelson in the crowds. They hadn't spoken much since his arrest. She was so proud of him, but she was afraid if they spent time together, he would find out about her indiscretion. She couldn't hurt him that way. She had caused too many others hurt.

Later that evening, Leila brushed her hair with terse strokes. She sat alone at her vanity table, preparing herself for what would surely be a strange night ahead.

She could still back out. But how would she ever be able to return to her life then?

Rachel was playing with her new Chanukah dolls in the salon. The labored breathing of Tanta Rosa emanated from the kitchen, slower than ever.

*How much longer did her aunt have?*

Her mood turned morose as she gripped her hairbrush harder. She was overtaken by tortuous speculation. How might things have been different if she had never taken the Morning Spot job? Maybe she still would have read about the market and formed her own conclusions. Maybe she could have kept Morris from investing and he would still be alive. Would Roderick still be alive if they hadn't met – if she hadn't pushed him to confront Jack? Would she have betrayed Nelson? Would she be paralyzed by documents?

She eyed herself in the mirror with derision.

How much had she unintentionally impacted other people's lives for the worse?

Since the night she had tried to help Althea after Roderick's death, she had heard nothing from her. She assumed Jack had dropped the notion of documents, since the markets were going up anyway. She was shocked when Althea's driver appeared at her tenement with a note asking her to watch Rodney for New Year's Eve.

Leila had other plans for the evening. Rivkah and the twins were dressing up and going out. But she found herself unable to say no to Althea.

Rivkah was exasperated. "Leila – are you seriously going to miss a fun New Year's Eve bash with your family and friends to spend the night in that boring place watching a baby? After all they put you through?"

"I just need to do this. Althea deserves to get out, and she gave a lot of the staff off, and she trusts me with Rodney." Her explanation sounded ridiculous, even to her.

"She has plenty of money, more than all of us will have in a million lifetimes. She can find someone else to watch her son. Let it go."

"I will," said Leila. "After tonight."

"Fine – you'll be alone on New Year's Eve while I'm kissing your cousin at the stroke of midnight. That better be one darn cute baby," said Rivkah.


The wintery night sky was a deep navy blue. The stars shone brightly. The cold air on the El pierced through Leila's heavy coat like it was a flimsy silk dress, chilling her bones. By the time she arrived uptown, she had lost sensation in her fingers and toes.

She walked to Park Avenue, wiggling her extremities to restore feeling. All around her, on the sparkling Upper East Side streets, couples were draped in the finest coats, floating along in their finest boots, laughing gaily. As they walked through icy patches on the streets, the women flirtatiously clung to their men for security, their high-heels slipping and sliding on the sidewalks, their heads thrown back in fits of giggles. One woman bent at her middle, her boyfriend's arm around her shoulders, and vomited into a gutter. The New Year's Eve festivities were in full force.

Althea wasn't home. Collins told her that she had left with some Rothschilds to a swanky party at the Algonquin Hotel. She really couldn't keep them waiting, could she? She had said that Leila should make herself feel at home. She was thrilled and very grateful Leila could watch Rodney for the night. She didn't know what time she'd be returning, but Leila could have the use of the driver to take her home, and the extra cot in the kitchen if she chose to stay over and leave in the morning – early in the morning. Collins relayed all of this to Leila, sniffing to punctuate the intonations of Althea's voice.

"She gave me the rest of the night off, as well. I hope you don't mind being alone here. The driver's supposed to be back by midnight."

"No, not at all," Leila assured him. "Rodney and I will be fine."

Collins stood for a moment. "Why, if you don't mind my asking, are you here?"

His question took her aback. Was he accusing her of something or just curious? *Why? Because she couldn't stay away. Because there was work here left undone.*

"Because Rodney needed a babysitter."

"Miss Leila, you're young, smart, and beautiful. You don't need these people. You're better than them. You're better than him."

She wasn't sure of that. Aside from having had an affair with him, she still hadn't told authorities about the fraud. Her lip quivered. "I don't know, Collins. Why do you stay here?"

"They pay me, Miss. But you didn't get paid anything near enough," he answered.

*This isn't about money, not really.*

"I'm going to go check in on Rodney. Happy New Year, Collins." She kissed his cheek and headed down the hallway.

Leila peaked through the door crack. Rodney was curled up in a ball, fidgeting with a toy pirate in his crib. His room was filled with presents. On one of his toy chests, she saw a wooden popgun. A shiny, red metal top lay on the floor, amongst a pile of green, wrinkled tissue paper. Leila heard more boxes being pushed aside as she opened the door.

She spotted an extravagant train set and model Great War airplanes. They had been placed next to an oversized teddy bear wearing a black cowboy hat with white trim.

She wondered if Althea had bestowed more presents upon her son than during any other Christmas, to make up for her husband's absence. She pitied Roderick; maybe the abundance of toys for Rodney was a way to make up for other absences.

She remained with Rodney until he was sound asleep. On her way to the library, she was drawn like a child to the magnificent Christmas tree that stood in the very spot where Roderick's coffin had been just two months ago.

She had never seen anything like it. Twinkling light bulbs circled their way to a gold star at the top. Green and red ornaments hung off the branches by hooks. Leila noticed her reflection in one of them. She barely recognized her strained cheekbones and creased forehead. She had aged ten years. She should be laughing tonight with everyone else, celebrating at Puglia's. Instead, she was here babysitting Roderick and Althea's son.

She had irrevocably altered his life through her attachment to his father. A sorrow swept over her. Roderick should be alive for this Christmas. He should have watched his son open presents. He shouldn't have given up. She turned her back to the tree, away from the overpowering scent of pine. She headed for the library.

Alone in the apartment, maybe she would be able to find some hiding place that eluded Jack and Althea. Even if she never found that document, she would figure out a way to implicate Jack. She had to keep promising this to herself rather than backing away. This was the cause her Tanta Rosa said would find her. She couldn't turn away.

*Especially now.*

She rubbed her hand over her belly, feeling for the swell she knew would come.

She heard footsteps in the hallway. A shiver ran through her spine. She thought the apartment was empty. The steps were heavy, not the tapping of Althea's heels. She could hear them approaching the library.

She reached for the poker standing by the brick fireplace.

"Leila."

She exhaled a sigh of relief. It was Collins.

"Yes."

"There's something I need to give you," he said.

He held out a book. "Here... Roderick, he – kept this notebook. Every night when he wasn't too drunk, he'd write something in it. I should probably be giving this to Althea, but I think you might know better what to do with it."

"How did you get this?" she asked, taking the book.

"I was here when Jack and his cronies went rummaging around Roderick's things, while his body wasn't even in the ground yet. He was up to no good. I don't understand what he was doing and I don't want to. But I've known Roderick for years. He wasn't perfect, by any means, but he's not like Jack either."

"So, it was you," she realized with a thrill, "that emptied the metal box?"

"Yes, Miss Leila," he grinned.

"When?"

"After you left the wake, I approached the library. The door was locked, but," he motioned to his breast pocket, "I've got the skeleton key. It opens all the rooms around here, and the box – it was pretty easy to pick open."

"You must have stopped his heart for a moment," she said, gleefully.

"Let's just say, he wasn't very pleased to be disturbed. I saw how his stooge shoved you, too, Leila. I'm no hero, but that's no way to treat a lady."

She blushed at his compliment. "I can take care of myself," she said.

"I'm sure," said Collins. "Anyway, having barged in on the old man, I apologized, of course, and told him that the missus sought his presence in the salon; they were about to do the eulogies for Roderick. I said it might be a good idea for him to attend."

"Of course, he had to go. Family and all that..." Leila grinned. "And then you removed the floor boards and took this out?" she asked. She leafed through the black-leather diary with its green outline. There was no title on the cover.

She could tell that letters represented first names:

"J" for Jack, "A" for Althea. And "L" for *Leila.*

The entries seemed to go back a few years, but there were more of them in the weeks leading up to Roderick's death. One particular entry stopped her blood flow:

*"With such turbulent times, it is my fear that 'J' will stop at nothing."*

It was dated October 28, 1929.

The words sparked a jolt of fear in her. She recalled the ferocity in Jack's eyes when he barged into Roderick's library. She thought about Althea's extreme fear when they discovered the empty box. *Could Jack kill if he had to?* She shivered.

Maybe Roderick didn't commit suicide.

"Well," Collins continued, "The old man – he had already moved the furniture. I think he was searching for something under the rug. I got there in the nick of time."

"Was this diary the only thing in there?" she asked.

"Yes," answered Collins, "I found it in the corner of the box. I must confess, I was surprised there was anything in it."

"There was nothing else, then – nothing at all – besides this diary?" she asked.

"No, Miss – I was only there for a moment, but I had enough time to look very carefully into it. This was the only thing I found."

Her heart sank. She flipped through the pages of the diary. Once. Twice.

"What's the matter?" asked Collins.

Leila shook her head. She would go through the rest of the diary when she was alone, but it wouldn't be enough. It contained Roderick's words, the last thoughts of a troubled man. There was no document in it; nothing tying Jack Morgan to any crime.

# PART III:

## The Discovery

# 18.

# *January 1, 1930*

The radiator in Leila's bedroom chose New Year's Eve to give out. That left the iron stove as the only source of heat in the apartment. Tanta Rosa had to break out the extra quilts she kept stowed under the wire beds. The twins piled into the apartment several hours into the new decade, drunk and laughing. They lay snoring in the salon. It was unlikely something as natural as cold temperature would wake them anytime soon.

Leila spent the night at the kitchen table by the stove. In the soft, butter glow of the old gas lamp, she pored through Roderick's diary, trying to make sense of his cryptic words. If she could understand the abbreviated mess in his mind, maybe it would clarify her own muddled thoughts. But it jumbled them further.

She wished Collins had burned the damn thing.

Periodically, waves of exhaustion engulfed her body, but her mind fought them back. She remained alert as she studied the enigmatic entries. She began to commit every entry to memory, from cover to cover. There were the ones that referenced Jack and the bank:

*"April 30, 1927: Met with 'J' on Eastern. Wants another 10 mil."*

*"September 20, 1927: 'J' thinks $50 mil isn't enough for Pacific."*

*"March 5, 1929: Hate 'J.' He will ruin us all. He will blame me."*

*"September 30, 1929: "Things will only get worse. Need a way out."*

Other entries ranged from scrawled notes about bank meetings to when his bootlegger would share the latest selections of whiskey. But it was the references to her that were most infuriating. They sounded more like the conflicted musings of a schoolboy, than a man of his stature.

*"July 8, 1929: Held 'L,' her hair smelled like lavender. I must stop this."*

*"July 15, 1929: Wanted 'L' so."*

*"October 28, 1929: Is 'L' right? Will 'J' listen? Should I turn myself in?"*

She couldn't bear being referenced in his diary in such staccato. It reminded her of her loss. Not of what she had, but of what she would never have, a closeness that would never be. She forced herself to concentrate on Jack. The more she thought about her encounter with him the night of the wake – his steely, inhuman eyes, and the disdain for Roderick in his voice – the more she questioned where he was when Roderick fell.

She reread the October 28th entries, etching them into her mind like a scar. There were two. The first one was impeccably rendered by Roderick's fine penmanship.

*"October 28, 1929: Must confront 'J' for bank's sake. This has gone on too long."*

The other one was incoherently scrawled. The words were unaligned fragments of emotion meeting ink. They were about her.

*"October 28, 1929: Was intimate with 'L.'"*

She clutched her stomach to soothe the swirl of discomfort. That night was a jumble for her too; the moments with Roderick, the late night fight with Nelson.

She had never felt so utterly confined and confused at once. She wished it never happened.

She ripped out the page. She crunched it into a ball and hurled it into the corner of the kitchen. She didn't want to be reminded. Not like this. Not by a few words in a diary about Jack and deals and whiskey. She rubbed her hands together. A dull queasiness settled in her stomach. She needed a cup of tea.

With the whir of Roderick's brevity in her head, she filled the teapot with water. The pot whistled steam for minutes as her thoughts whipped about. She had reveled in sharing secrets with Roderick; but now those secrets would never let go of her. They were there, but not fully there, in his diary. All she could do to loosen their grip on her mind was attend to the unfinished business he had left behind. The question was – *how?*

Without the two different Allegheny documents suggesting Jack Morgan's participation in his bank's fraud, what could she do? Who would listen to the crazy accusations of a waitress? She remained certain if the books were made public, without Jack's signed documents, only Roderick would be tainted, not Jack. The thought infuriated her. Jack had bested them all. He had orchestrated everything perfectly.

She sipped the tea slowly, allowing its heat to calm her insides. She willed herself to return to the next page in the diary. October 29th. It was the day that would be etched into the history books and in her soul as Black Tuesday. The day of Roderick's death.

*"October 29, 1929: 'J' will stop at nothing."*

The words haunted like a premonition. The ones that followed left her numb:

*"October 29, 1929: I wish I had never met 'L,' she pulls me."*

It was his last entry. He must have entered it the morning of his death, or very late the night before. He was probably drunk, though that didn't help her understand it any better.

It angered her more than the lack of evidence against his uncle. *Pulls you where? What do you mean?* The interpretations were too numerous and painful. *Pulls me away? Pulls me to kill myself? Pulls me to confront Jack? Pulls me to my death?*

She flipped through the empty pages that followed, hoping that she had missed something – knowing she hadn't. They remained blank. She dragged her fingers through her hair from the temples upward, tugging at the roots. Her core ached.

*I wish I had never met you either.*

Her body shook. She slammed the diary shut and flung it at the same corner of the kitchen. It landed behind an opened sack of potatoes with a sharp thud. Paint chips from the cracked plaster of the wall fell upon it.

Rosa called out from the bedroom, her pitch scratchy, "Leila, are you okay?"

"Fine," replied Leila, startled. "I'm sorry I woke you, Tanta."

She pressed her fingers against her temples to stop them from throbbing. She stood up. The floorboards creaked beneath her as she walked to the bedroom.

"No, it's not fine. Nothing is fine."

Rosa sat up in bed, "Is it something you want to talk about?" She coughed. "Could you bring me a glass of water, dear?"

"Of course, Tanta," Leila rushed to the pitcher by the kitchen sink, knocking over a stack of tin spice boxes. As she cleaned up the mess of herbs and powders, Rachel wandered into the kitchen in bare feet, rubbing her eyes awake.

"Is everything okay?" she asked.

Leila knelt to hug her sister, "Yes, everything is fine. Go back to sleep."

"Can I have some milk?" asked Rachel. "I'm really thirsty."

"Certainly." Leila extracted the glass bottle from the metal icebox.

"I'm afraid there's not much left. I forgot to restock on my way home earlier." She peered at Rachel, half-expecting a fuss. She deserved it. But her sister gulped the quarter cup of milk, returned the glass, and wiped her mouth with her nightshirt sleeve.

"Rachel!" Leila admonished, stifling a giggle.

"That hit the spot!" she smiled.

Leila never understood where Rachel picked up her phrases. It occurred to her that her sister was growing up.

"Now, you can go back to bed," Leila said. "I'll tuck you in."

Rachel dove beneath the covers. "I'm cold," she said, her voice a tiny tremor. "Is Nelson going to come fix the heater?"

"I'll ask him tomorrow," said Leila. She hadn't thought about Nelson since Collins gave her the diary.

"Okay," said Rachel. Leila watched her sister's dark curls flow over the cotton pillow, her small head sinking into the folds. She seemed to fall asleep immediately.

Rosa's coughed deepened. Leila rushed back to the kitchen for the pitcher. "Sorry about the delay," she said, handing Rosa the drink. "Here you are."

"Thank you," said Rosa. She steadied the cup between her hands and sipped. "Now, come here, sit by me. Tell me what's on your mind."

Leila sank into a floor cushion that doubled as a bed pillow. Snow fell steadily past the window behind her aunt. She was glad Nelson had replaced its worn rubber insulation to keep out the draft. She trembled even though she wasn't cold anymore.

"What if you knew something, and didn't know if you should share it?" she asked.

"That depends," answered Rosa, "on why you wanted to share it."

"To help people," Leila replied. "But I might be hurting people in the process."

Rosa nodded, "And would one of the people you might hurt be you?"

Leila was taken aback by the question. She had only contemplated what might happen to Roderick's reputation if she told the authorities about the books. Her aunt's question raised a more unpleasant thought. Was she somehow complicit in his crimes as long as she didn't make them known? How could she live with that?

She responded with effort, dispensing each word slowly, reluctant to release the whole thought. "I'm afraid that if I told the truth – people would think I was a part of the lie."

She was shocked at how selfish her words sounded. Wasn't everything Jack had done bigger than her pride? Wasn't it bigger than her relationship with Roderick?

"I see," said Rosa, wincing in pain as she adjusted her body on the thin mattress. "Leila, no matter what you do, there will be people who take it the wrong way or don't believe you. What would be worse: holding back what you know or sharing it?"

"I wish I knew. I don't think I have enough information to make people believe me. Not only might they think I was a part of this – this – *crime*, but I can't even prove a crime happened. Do I share what little I know or do I wait until I know more?"

"I can't answer that for you. But if you're feeling so torn up now, it won't get easier until you make a decision. Life is like that. We often regret what we don't do more than what we do."

"I suppose so," Leila sighed, though she wasn't so sure she agreed with her aunt. "But sometimes I wish I had never gotten involved at all."

"Fate has a funny way of making that decision for us," said Rosa, yawning. "Maybe we both need to sleep on it."

Leila reached for the shawl that had dropped to the floor and draped it around her aunt's meager frame. She took the quilt from her cot and added it to the pile already on Rosa. She tucked her aunt into bed, making sure that she was snug for the night.

"I'll be in soon," whispered Leila, kissing Rosa's forehead. "Thank you, Tanta."

"You're most welcome, my child," replied Rosa.

Leila returned to the kitchen with a clearer head. She knelt down to the corner by the stove. She retrieved Roderick's diary, brushed the dust off its jacket, took it back to the table and sat down.

This time, as she thumbed through its pages, she marked each one that referred to Jack Morgan with a tiny piece of newspaper, though she remained more drawn to the pages that referred to her. Her instincts about him, in the beginning, had not been wrong.

*"March, 30, 1929: Found out 'L's' name today."*

*"May 5, 1929: Happy to get coffee before work early, to see 'L.'"*

*"June 6, 1929: 'L' looked sad. Her mother passed."*

Leila hadn't thought about her mother much since Roderick's death. She didn't even know where they had buried her. *Some daughter you are.*

Her mind flashed back to a day in third grade. A classmate had stolen her mathematics assignment and handed it in as her own. Her mother consoled her and told her to start the assignment over. Leila had insisted that it was due *today*. "Tomorrow is only another today," her mother had replied. "Finish your milk, and do it again. You will know the lesson that much better."

Leila ripped a sheet of paper from the ledger she kept for household expenses. She laid it flat on the table. Propelled by a rush of giddiness, Leila began to fill the sheet, scribbling slowly at first, and then with more speed and purpose as the night evolved into dawn. She started on page one. She wrote down every date and phrase from the diary's pages relevant to Jack Morgan. Sometime around four in the morning, as the twins were getting up to go to work, her plan took a more concrete shape. She barely noticed them crowding around the kitchen to pack the dinner's leftovers for their morning meal.

"Hey, you keeping fisherman's hours?" joked Joshua, grabbing his wool hat.

"You're welcome to go down to the docks in my place," teased Jonathan.

"Yes," she said absently as they shuffled out the door.

She hoped that when she was done, if she stared at the dates, names, and figures long enough, they would provide more evidence against Jack. She could accomplish what Roderick wasn't able to. This thought kept her awake throughout the night. She would show everyone that a Russian immigrant girl could make a difference. She would make sure that the truth was told – not with fists and shouts, but with words and numbers.

All the next day, she kept going. And well into the second night.

# 19.

# January 2, 1930

"Wake up, silly sleepyhead!" shouted Rachel in Leila's ear.

Leila squinted her eyes open. She pressed her back upright and lifted her head from the pile of Roderick's diary and ledger papers. Rachel tugged at her shoulders.

With a shock, she realized that she had overslept.

"Rachel! What time is it?" Leila asked, stretching her arms. She sprung to her feet. "I've got to get to the Morning Spot!"

"It's almost nine o'clock, time for school. You never came to bed last night," Rachel said. She ruffled through the sheets of figures Leila had been working on. Each was a mess of lines and numbers. "Did you have homework, too?"

Leila reached for the sheet Rachel was holding. She plucked it from her fingers and placed it on the pile of papers she had created. She smoothed the stack and inhaled a heavy breath, gazing at her mental handiwork.

"You could say that," she grinned.

"Yours must have been really hard," Rachel exclaimed. "I'm going to get an 'A' on mine." She opened the door to greet a friend waiting in the hallway. "Bye, Leila!"

"I'm sure you are," said Leila, feeling the kind of pride for her sister she was sure her mother must have felt for her. "Bye, Rach."

Rachel was about to leave when she swung around to face her older sister. "Leila, it's nice to see you before I go to school."

Before Leila could reply, Rachel whirled about once more and skipped off, shutting the door behind her. Rosa hobbled into the kitchen.

"You seem to have come to a decision," said Rosa. "You look much better."

"You know… I think I did."

Leila raced up the iron steps to the El. A derailment on the ride gave her more time to contemplate the situation at hand. She couldn't wait to get down to the Morning Spot. With her brown leather satchel full of last night's notes, and Roderick's diary in hand, she inhaled a lungful of the frozen morning air.

Leila smiled as she strolled towards the diner, pleased with her detective work. She hummed the tune to "Honey," one of her favorite songs from Rudy Vallée and his Connecticut Yankees. She arrived at the diner at ten o'clock, after the morning rush hour. There were a few customers lingering over their breakfasts, but none of her regulars.

"I am so sorry, I'm late, Nan," she said. "I guess I overslept."

Nan shot her a gaze of curiosity. "It looks like you didn't get any sleep at all."

"How was the morning rush?" Leila asked. "Any mess-ups I should know about?"

"No, everything was perfectly smooth, except for the piles of snow these guys tracked in," she said, mopping up the muddy slush by the door.

"I did put a second mat at the entrance for a reason," said Leila.

"I know – that's what I kept telling them," she said. "Men."

"Yes. Men," Leila agreed. "If it wasn't for us cleaning up after them…" she trailed off. The front door opened with a burst of snow and a swish of frosty air.

"Good morning to you, Leila! Happy New Year!" boomed Officer O'Malley. He stamped his boots, releasing a fresh batch of snow, and removed his coat.

Leila wanted to throw her arms around him. "It certainly is, Bryan. Have a seat." She dried off one of the counter stools. "Nan, can you cut Bryan an extra-large piece of coffee cake – on the house."

"You're certainly chipper on this blustery day," he beamed.

"I guess I am," she replied, pouring him some steaming coffee.

"It's a wonderful sight," said Bryan, bringing the cup to his mouth.

"Will you be working later tonight at the precinct?" she asked him.

"Depends what you mean by 'later,'" he replied. He removed his gloves and rubbed his hands together over the coffee mug. "After you close up for the evening?"

"Yes," said Leila. "There's something I want to show you."

"Alright, then," he said, "let's meet at the deli on Broadway after you're done here. But whatever you do, don't tell anyone and please be careful."


Leila started arranging condiments in an orderly fashion at the booth tables half an hour before closing time. She began wiping down the counter tops while her final customers finished their warm drinks in preparation for wintry journeys home. She scarcely paid attention to their yammering about the market making a sizeable comeback to kick off the New Year. Her heart was beating so loud, she was sure they could hear it.

As she prepared to leave the diner, she had to steady the jumble of knots in her stomach with a bottle of Coca-Cola. She rarely drank the beverage that everyone was crazy about. It made her head spin. But she heard it did wonders for soothing your stomach. She locked the door and stepped onto the cobblestones outside. The cold breeze felt refreshing on her face. She inhaled and headed towards Broadway.

Bryan was waiting for her at the same back table they had met at before. He held out a cup of coffee. She caught a whiff of the caffeine. Dizziness overcame her. Her knees buckled slightly. She steadied herself and took a seat opposite him. *I must do this.*

"Are you okay?" he asked, reaching out his arm to steady her. "You look pale."

"I'm fine," she replied. *Why does everyone keeping asking me that?* "I think it's just the cold, and I didn't – I didn't get much sleep last night. My aunt was sick."

"I'm sorry to hear that," he said. "You should be taking better care of yourself."

Leila swallowed against the dryness in her throat. She didn't want to talk about her health. "Bryan, I do know something. I'm not sure I can prove it, but I know something – and, it's big." She waited for him to ask a question, but Bryan just nodded and leaned forward across the table between them.

"Go on," he encouraged. He lit a cigarette.

Leila took a breath. "The Morgan bank – it's – in lot of trouble," she began.

"All banks are," said Bryan, "aren't they?"

"Yes, probably, but I don't mean normal trouble. I mean, I think – I know – they're covering their troubles."

She relayed to him the parts of the story that she decided she could discuss. She didn't tell him about the extent of her relationship with Roderick, only that the two had met at the Morning Spot, and that she sometimes worked for him and his wife as a babysitter for their son, Rodney. On one of the nights, she said, she happened upon the two books, while she was, she had to admit, snooping around Roderick's library.

"So, these two books, with different representations of the bank's finances, were just laying there on his desk, out in the open like that?" he asked incredulously.

"Uh, not exactly, they – they were in a pile on side of his desk," she stretched the truth. "I was curious. I looked through them and noticed there were different numbers for the same dates, and they matched company names being written about in the papers."

"Just like that – you *noticed* different numbers and those company names."

"Yes," she said looking down at her shoulder, then up at him, "Just like that."

Bryan looked utterly baffled. "So you're saying you just *found* these two sets of books, poking around the Morgans' library, Roderick Morgan's library – the Morgan partner who committed suicide, is that right?"

"Yes, that's about right," she answered meekly.

"Did you ever – talk to Roderick Morgan – about what you found?" Bryan asked.

Leila's insides clenched. *Why did it matter if she talked to Roderick about the books or not? Why did it matter if she hadn't really seen those books until the night she was there with Althea, and that it was Roderick who had told her about them in person? She was giving Bryan information; wasn't that enough?*

"No. I – I did not," she lied.

She averted her gaze toward the coffee-stained tabletop. She fidgeted with the ashtray. Then she shifted her eyes back to Bryan. "I didn't know what to do about them, or who to talk to, so I – I didn't tell anyone. I didn't say anything," she said.

She reclined in her chair, inspecting Bryan's face. Beside them, the janitor mopped the black-and-white floor tiles. She listened to her stomach rumble.

Bryan twisted his mouth and smoked his cigarette to its butt. Finally he said, "Then, you know Roderick was faking Morgan's books, is that correct?"

She nodded her head and sighed, "I guess so."

"Leila, do you have any idea how big that is?" he asked. Smoke escaped his mouth and billowed into her face. The smoke made her gag.

"I think so, but I – I think that Jack Morgan put him up to it."

Bryan's eyes bulged. "Can you prove that?"

She began to remove the diary from her bag. She took out her notes instead.

"These are the dates where I think certain figures were faked," she handed him the sheets of paper.

"And, how did you come to pick these dates?" Bryan asked, leafing through her numbers. "Just from looking through the two sets of books themselves?"

"Yes," she said quietly, before adding, "I have a head for numbers."

"So, you mentioned," said Bryan, with a hint of skepticism. "Well, if we're going to prove Jack was involved with these numbers, we're going to need those books. We'll also need something to link him to them. If Roderick created them and kept them in his library, maybe he was just trying to make himself look better by faking these books."

"No!" Leila insisted, "It had to have come from Jack."

"How do you know that?" he asked with a puzzled look on his face.

He crushed his cigarette butt out in the ashtray.

"I don't, it just – makes sense," she paused. She had to stretch the truth further. "You see, about a week after Roderick died, I – I was invited – to his wake."

One of Bryan's eyebrows raised.

"I saw him there – Jack Morgan – in the library. He was looking for something."

"The two books?" asked Bryan.

"Maybe, but I think he was looking for something else, too," she said. "He probably has his own copies of the books, or maybe he was surprised that Roderick created his own copies and wanted them. Althea told me he controls everything."

"Althea?"

"Yes, Roderick's wife. She – she was upset so, I tried to comfort her. She said Jack wanted something, but she didn't know what. That's all."

Both of Bryan's eyebrows raised in unison.

"And do you know what it is he wanted?"

"I saw something else there, one night while I was babysitting – and – snooping."

"Go on," said Bryan. He reached into his pocket for his notepad.

"Please," said Leila, "let's just talk first okay?"

"Certainly," replied Bryan, putting the notepad away.

"I saw – a document; two actually, and they were both signed by Jack – for a deal for the Allegheny railroad. They were identical except they had different numbers on them. One went to investors – the higher one. The other was in the real book – the lower one."

"So, you have some evidence," Bryan's face lit up considerably.

"No, I don't," she admitted. "I went back there last week again, to babysit. I couldn't find it anywhere."

"Did you tell Althea about it?" Bryan asked. The glow in his face disappeared.

"Not exactly. I told her we needed something, but – well, maybe I did tell her that we needed something Jack signed, but – I don't think she had it."

"Listen to me," said Bryan, with a rising urgency in his tone. "Don't trust her."

"But—" began Leila.

"Don't. Don't trust her. I mean it."

Leila's pulse sped up. "Why Bryan? What aren't you telling me?"

"Leila, the night Roderick died, my team was called to investigate his office. I wasn't involved, I was on the ground, but – they were turned away."

"Turned away?"

"Yes, they were told to go back down to ground level. The chief of police, my boss, was waiting in the lobby. He said the matter would be dealt with internally. A guy on my team asked him 'what gives?' He wouldn't answer. We just assumed that was how the big banks operated now, and there was nothing we could do about it."

"But that man who spoke to the crowd – from Morgan – he said the police would be investigating," she said. She shuddered at recalling a detail from that night.

"He was lying," said Bryan. "The whole night bothers me every time I think about it. Call me crazy, but when my guys don't get a look-see, something shady is going on. Now you're telling me Morgan's faking the books. Whole thing makes more sense."

"Then, what do you think happened?" asked Leila, her heart pumping wildly.

"Open-and-shut case of suicide, my backside!" Bryan pounded the table.

"So," she hardly dared say the words, "you think someone *killed* him?"

"I don't know for sure, but you see why it's important to be very careful, Leila," said Bryan. "These people will stop at nothing. Leila… Leila…"

She was no longer paying attention. Her mind raced back to the diary entry:

"*'J' will stop at nothing.*" She had urged him to confront Jack.

Her body shivered. *Oh my god, Roderick. What have I done to you?*

She sprang to her feet. She brought a hand to her belly to stave another wave of queasiness. Bryan pushed his chair away. He stood up. He gripped her shoulders tightly.

"You must get those books from Althea Morgan. And you must be extremely cautious about it. I would say you should bide your time and find the right moment, but this shouldn't wait. There's no telling what may become of those books. At this point, they are all we have. Can you get to them?"

Leila swallowed, "Yes, I can go over there."

"When?" Bryan pressed.

She sensed a rise of urgency in him. "Tonight, I suppose."

"Tonight then," agreed Bryan. "Just don't do anything to arouse her suspicions."

"But I don't think she even knows what to do with those books," said Leila.

"Don't underestimate her," said Bryan. "Will you be okay going up there alone?"

"Oh yes, of course, I will," replied Leila. "I've been—" she stopped herself. "I've babysat there several times recently. It won't seem strange for me to stop by and say 'hello' to Rodney." As soon as she said this, she realized how strange it would be.

"Alright," said Bryan. "I'll come by the diner tomorrow morning. You can let me know how things went. Two pieces of cake if you have the books. One if you don't."

"I'll get the books," she replied. Bryan opened the door to the sidewalk.

"My car is parked over there," he pointed. "I could drive you uptown."

"No, I'm fine. I need the air," she said. "Goodnight, Bryan."

She headed in the direction of the El. Before she reached the train, she stopped in an alley full of trash bins marked "City Property." She fell to her knees and vomited on the icy ground. Her body heaved until there was nothing left. Then she wiped her face with a handful of snow. She felt a bit better. She was relieved she had shared some secrets with Bryan. The burden of holding them had sat heavy in her stomach.

Leila took the El up to Park Avenue and 80th street. It was too cold, she reasoned on the way, for Althea to be out and about. Besides, it was the middle of the week and the holiday party season was over. If she called first, Althea could give her an excuse not to come. She rushed past the doorman before he could ask if she was expected and jumped into the gilded elevator. Niles welcomed her with a friendly smile as he slid the heavy brass gate closed and prepared their ascent to the 10th floor.

Collins greeted her knock. "You really can't stay away, can you?"

"Neither can you, so we're even," Leila stormed in.

"I came to talk to Althea; is she around?" she asked.

"She should be back in an hour or so," said Collins. "She wasn't very clear on where she was going, but said she'd return before nine. Do you want a cup of tea?"

"No, thank you." Leila's stomach was doing somersaults. She stepped into the foyer. It was full of crates and boxes. "What's – what's going on here?"

"The word is that Althea and Roderick, Jr. are leaving," Collins explained. "One of Jack's nieces is moving in with her family. The movers have been packing all day."

Leila couldn't keep her nerves steady. "When did this happen?"

"Last night, I think, though I can't be sure. Jack made another appearance, alone this time. I tried to eavesdrop but the two of them went into the parlor and shut the door. Early this morning, those," he pointed to the stack of crates, "appeared. The movers are returning tomorrow to pack more things up and stick them on a ship bound for England."

"I don't understand," said Leila, "I was just here. It seemed like Althea would be staying indefinitely – I thought at least through the winter."

"So did I," agreed Collins, scratching his ear. "But apparently they're off to London. I'm pretty sure the old man gave her a generous go-away present. He was carrying quite a thick envelope when he arrived."

Leila shifted her weight from one foot to the other. She scanned the foyer as if somehow she could make the boxes disappear.

"Things change, Miss Leila," said Collins gently.

"They certainly do." *Now what would she do?*

"Where will you go?" she asked.

"Oh, I'm a pretty flexible fellow," said Collins. "I'll find some other wealthy family to look after. The missus gave me three months pay as a good-bye gift – in gold coins no less. In these times, that's a small fortune. It'll last me at least four."

"So it's really over," Leila whispered.

"Miss?"

"Nothing," she shook her head.

"Did you find what you needed in Roderick's diary?" Collins asked gently.

Leila stiffened for an instant. "I don't know," she replied.

"I see," he nodded. "Well, maybe it's time to let it go. Whatever it is."

"I wish I could," she said. *You have no idea how much.* "Do you mind if I – take one last look at the place?"

"Of course not. I'll give you a sign when I hear the elevator crank," said Collins.

"Thank you. I'm glad – he had you."

"I'd say the same about you, Leila. I hope it brings you some peace."

Collins returned to his post by the kitchen. Leila was tempted to check on Rodney, but she didn't know how long she had until Althea returned. She was torn between him and the books. She chose to head towards the dining room.

The dining table was clear. Only a tall, sterling silver candelabra adorned its polished wood surface. The drapes behind it were closed, drawn together by golden-rod-colored tassels. She didn't have to spend any more time in this room – there were no sets of books to be found here.

She considered searching Althea's room. The thought made her feel like a common thief. Was this really what her mother had sent her to America for? Her feet chose a path back to Roderick's library. She lingered in the doorway. It didn't appear like anything else had been touched since last time, but it no longer smelled like lemons or memories. The desk was still empty except for the antique pen and ink well. His mother's portrait still hung in the center of the wall. The drapes were drawn closed.

It struck Leila that she had never seen the Morgan's home in the daylight. Everything that transpired happened during hours of darkness. Even the first time she came here to babysit – a lifetime ago – the sliver of sun gave way to the rise of the moon. She stepped to the spot where Roderick had held her for the first time, where she had felt his breath on her face, his grip on her wrist. At that moment, nothing had mattered except the two of them. *Had she ever really belonged in his arms? In his world?*

She glanced up at his bookshelves. She wondered if any of those books would be read, or if they would simply be boxed up and re-shelved in some fine English home. Maybe Rodney would read them when he got older. The thought made her smile. She allowed her fingers to traverse the spines of fine, hard-leather-covered books as if to comfort them in their time of upheaval. They stopped at *The Great Gatsby*.

She recalled Roderick's voice discussing the character of Nick as if it were yesterday: *"But he doesn't walk away from them, they leave him behind."*

*Yes, they do. The rich get to walk away leaving everyone else behind.*

Leila removed the blue book from beside its companions. She brought her nose to its cover and inhaled. She allowed its aroma to embrace her. She savored the familiar tock of the clock. She placed the book on Roderick's desk. She lifted its cover.

"Oh, Miss!" called Collins.

She shut the book. She had every intention of returning it to its former spot, but something inside her made her hold it to her stomach, then behind her back. She rushed to the foyer. She reached for her bag and slid the book inside. She looked up to notice Collins watching her.

"I…" she began.

"It's okay," he said. "I've got quite a collection myself, not books exactly – but other pleasurable items."

She smiled and smoothed out her dress. "How do I look?" she asked Collins.

"Like someone who's about to begin the rest of her life."

"That sounds corny," she smiled, "but thank you."

"What can I say, Miss Leila?" he replied, "I'm a cock-eyed optimist. Only way to work for these people day in and day out."

The door swung open. A red-cheeked Althea swooped into the foyer.

"Collins, take my coat and bring me a hot toddy. It's positively awful outside."

"Certainly, Madam," he said. "And Madam, Leila stopped by to say goodbye to little Roderick, Jr."

Althea wiped away some errant strands of hair stuck to her forehead by the snowflakes. "Leila, how did you ever know we were leaving?"

"I didn't. I was just – I was babysitting for the Hoffman's and finished early. I thought I'd come see if Rodney was still awake. Silly of me." *What are you talking about?* she asked herself of her lie.

"I guess Collins told you our wonderful news?" Althea chirped.

"Yes. London – it must be nice to return to your family," Leila enthused back.

"Not really," she said with sadness. Then slowly, she smiled from ear to ear, shaking her hair as she removed her peacock-feathered cloche.

"Oh, what am I talking about, of course, it will be utterly fabulous, and of course, if you ever find yourself there, you must stop by and say hello to us."

Collins expelled a noise that sounded somewhere between a chortle and a snort.

"That's a wonderful offer, Althea, thank you," replied Leila, knowing there could be no possible way she would want her to visit – not that she could afford a trip to London.

"I will leave a forwarding address for my cousin's. He lives in Mayfair. We will be staying there until we find our own *suitable* home."

"Thank you," said Leila, noting that Althea didn't appear to be moving towards writing down her cousin's address.

"A pen and paper, Madam?" Collins suggested, with a slight grin.

"Excuse me?" replied Althea.

"Althea, would you mind terribly if I said goodbye to Roderick, Jr.?" asked Leila.

"Of course not," Althea gestured toward the hallway, "you know the way. Collins, where is my toddy?"

"Coming right up, Madam. You may find having it in the sitting room to your liking; it's the warmest room in the apartment. I'll bring it there for you," Leila heard him say as she walked down the hallway.

She observed that the walls were stripped of the family portraits that had once lined them; where they had once seemed pompous, they now seemed merely forlorn. When she turned into Rodney's room, she saw that most of his toys had been packed away already. Only his crib with its overhead mobile of ships gave any indication that this was a child's room. He was fast asleep. Leila bent over the top rim of his crib to pick him up. He emitted a tiny cry and snuggled in her arms. She luxuriated in his warmth against her chest, giving him a kiss on his head. She was torn. She couldn't help but compare the uncertainty of her family's future with that of this little boy.

He would want for nothing. Except a father. *I'm so sorry, Rodney.*

A tear crept down her cheek. He was so much more innocent than the adults in his world. Much more than she was. For she could no longer deny what her body screamed at her with growing conviction each day. She had missed not one, but two periods.

She traced her hand over Rodney's shiny hair. *Will he ever come to know that he might have another brother or sister sharing his father's bloodline?*

She uncurled his fingers from around her hair and placed him back in his crib. She covered him with his blue flannel blanket, then tiptoed out of the room. She paused at the doorway to look at him once more. *Will I ever see him again?*

Across the hall, the door to Althea's bedroom beckoned. It was opened a crack. Lights glowed from the inside. Leila stepped into the room, her heart beating wildly. She inhaled a musty perfume, a pungent scent that almost made her retch. She was stunned by the sheer whiteness of the room. An enormous ivory canopy bed, adorned with flowing vanilla veils and stacked with crème-colored throw pillows, stood guard in the center. Beyond it, a sitting area semi-circled a grandiose white brick fireplace. Its pristine appearance reflected none of the warmth of her cramped bedroom. It was only the crystal figurine of a ballerina atop the fireplace's slate shelf that sat beside a black marble ashtray of half smoked cigarettes that captured any hint of human emotion.

She scanned the room quickly, fearing Althea would enter at any moment. She tried to imagine where Althea might have placed the set of books. She saw a small white desk with gold trim by one of the windows. She walked a foot in its direction. There were stacks of papers on top of it. She could see numbers on them, but their overall appearance wasn't familiar. They were receipts of some sort, probably for Althea's clothing and jewelry. She darted towards a small trunk by the fireplace, made of stained wood and circled with leather strips. She opened the lid of the trunk and peered inside.

The only thing she saw were three neat piles of folded dresses in silks of vibrant crimson, violet, and turquoise. She shut the lid and stood up. The room was spinning.

She paused to consider her predicament. If there were any books here, how on earth would she be able to take them without alerting Althea? Once they were missing, how would Althea not suspect her immediately? Her heart sunk at the hopelessness of the situation. She had come to retrieve evidence, but had no idea how to get it or where it was. Her plan was turning to nothing, like the snowflakes melting on Althea's face.

"What are you doing in here?" interrupted a high-pitched voice.

Leila turned to find Althea glaring at her.

"Nothing. I was – I was just – I saw the light and—"

"Get out of my room," ordered Althea.

"Yes, ma'am," replied Leila. "I'm sorry. I – the truth is – I was looking for those two books. I had another idea how we might be able to prove that Jack was involved."

"Why didn't you just say that?" Althea asked.

"I don't know," said Leila, trying to read her face. "I wanted to see for myself before bothering you with it. I know how much you've been through. I shouldn't have been in here." *I shouldn't have done a lot of things.*

"Why is it so important to make a connection between Jack and my husband?" Althea asked.

"Because," Leila paused, "I don't think – that Roderick killed himself."

"What do you mean?" Althea frowned.

"I think he was going to confront Jack the day he died, maybe get him to come clean before things got worse for the bank, and something happened to him."

Althea planted her hands on her hips. "So you think Jack killed him?"

Leila nodded. "Yes, or someone working for him did."

"That – is – the – most – preposterous thing I've ever heard of," Althea said between clenched teeth. "How could you even think of something like that?"

Leila took a step back.

She couldn't mention the diary, so she said, "It's the books. I mean if Jack didn't want anyone to know about them, and Roderick was going to tell people, that might be worth killing someone over."

"Listen carefully to me, Leila," said Althea, "Roderick was a very depressed man. For years, he drank himself into oblivion every night. He hated his work, his uncle, and – me. He had no other way out. The bravest thing he ever did was kill himself."

"But surely, you must consider that maybe he was going to do the right thing."

"What? Turn himself in? Spend the rest of his days in prison? Leila, you don't know Roderick. You don't know anything about us. I think you should leave my home."

"Yes, ma'am. I'll be going."

As Leila approached the front door, she saw Collins watch her from the kitchen, rooted to his spot.

Althea followed close behind her.

Leila knew this was the last time she would be in the Morgan's home. She had failed to get those books. She had done wrong by Althea and Roderick and Rodney. Her lips trembled. She had the diary, but without the books, how could she share it? Even if she wanted to expose everything in it; even if she had the courage to admit her own involvement – how could she? What would it mean?

She reached for her coat. She turned to Althea with a final effort.

"Althea, just one more thing. If you do change your mind – if there's anything I can do to help with any of Jack's demands – I'll go through those books again with you. If you want to tell the truth to the world, please, contact me."

"I won't be needing anything from you," she said. "Jack and I have come to an understanding."

Leila glanced at her. She had nothing to lose, "Which is?"

"It doesn't concern you, Leila," Althea said coldly.

She stood erect and motioned for Collins to open the door, which he did with exaggerated slowness. As Leila took her first step into the hallway, she turned around once more.

"Good luck to you, Althea." She opened her mouth to say more.

"Leila," said Althea. She placed her slender fingers softly on Leila's.

"Yes?" Leila prompted, perplexed by the tenderness of her gesture.

"And, to you." She removed her hand.

"Thank you."

"Believe me, I did what I had to do," Althea remarked as if looking for approval.

"I suppose you did," Leila replied.

"I gave Jack the books and all the documents. I had to."

There was nothing Leila could do but gape. She felt the weight of impossibility bear down on her soul as the heavy door closed behind her. Althea's words lingered in the air while the elevator car carried Leila to the lobby of 80th Street and Park Avenue.

On the way down, Leila tried to imagine what she would do in the same circumstance. Would she choose to protect her son over anything else? As much as she had entertained noble thoughts of alerting the world to Jack's crimes, in Althea's place, wouldn't she do exactly the same thing? Protect her own?

She rubbed her belly, still undetectable beneath her shirt. How could she have been so careless? So stupid? So wrapped up in her passion?

Yet in the midst of her mortification rose a flicker of duty. Another part of Roderick was living. Their secret was growing inside her. She could not be angry about Althea's decision. In a way, she had to admire Althea for her resolve. No, she was mad at herself.

Leila journeyed back to the Lower East Side, battle-scarred as if returning from the Great War. What would she say to Bryan the next day? She had tried the best she could. She hoped he would understand. She felt useless.

# 20.

# January 3, 1930

The city awoke beneath a heavy blanket of powdery snow. Because of the weather, Leila left home at half past five in the morning. She didn't want to be late for work two days in a row. Extra time was required to traverse the covered streets.

The sidewalks lay buried under two feet of white cotton. The streets were empty. In the distance, she saw a few people trudging, their lower legs invisible beneath the piles of snow. There were no vendors setting up their pushcarts and advertising the day's specials. She paused. Her neighborhood glistened in pure transformation. Every tree branch was magically decorated. Every streetlight shone elegantly. Every building, no matter how dilapidated, appeared stately in the muffled silence of glimmering, fresh snow.

When she finally reached the El, she discovered it wasn't going to be operating. The excuse relieved her. She would have an extra day to avoid telling Bryan she had failed to get the books. She was exhausted. She had slept fitfully last night, barraged by her restless mind no matter how badly her body begged for rest.

Back at her tenement, she crawled into bed and immediately fell asleep. Soon after, a pouncing Rachel shook her awake.

"Leila, come downstairs – there's no school today. We're going to have a huge snowball fight! It'll be swell!"

"Thanks, Rach," Leila sat up, rubbing her eyes and forehead, "but I think I'll sit this one out. I'm not feeling very good this morning."

She got out of bed and went to the kitchen. Rosa had a cup of tea waiting for her at the table.

"Okay, but if you change your mind, you can be on my team with Jonathan. He and Josh didn't go to work either; they're waiting for me by the stoop on Ludlow."

Rosa limped around the kitchen.

"So, I guess I'm stuck with all of you today," she said, sporting a grin that reminded Leila of how she used to be.

"It seems so," replied Leila. "I can't remember the last time the twins skipped a work day – the city really is at a standstill."

"It had to happen sometime," said Rosa. "Joshua brought me some extra bottles of milk yesterday, and some cocoa powder along with my medicine. I think I'll brew up a nice pot of hot chocolate for when they return."

"No, now!" exclaimed Rachel, jumping up and down, her dark curls bouncing.

"Later," said Rosa. "Go make snow angels and leave me and Leila in peace."

"Nah – snowball fight!" said Rachel, wrapping her woolen scarf several times around her neck. "We're going to win!"

"I'm sure you are," grinned Leila.

When Rachel was gone, Rosa shuffled to the seat by Leila. She slowly lowered herself down. "You came home late last night. I was worried," she said.

"I was taking care of some things after work. I think they're behind me now."

"Are they really?" her aunt asked, cupping Leila's chin with her hand.

"Yes, why – what do you mean?" asked Leila. She took a sip of tea, savoring the hint of mint and honey her aunt had added to the brew. Its warmth trickled through her.

Her aunt stared at her.

"It's been a hard couple of months, that's all. They made me more tired than usual," Leila went on.

"Leila, you know you can tell me anything, don't you?" said Rosa.

"You have enough on your mind, Tanta."

"Believe me, my dear, I would love to have my mind occupied – anything to stop focusing on this old body!" bemoaned Rosa. One of her legs seized up as if on cue. Once the discomfort stopped, she continued. "Just remember, I am here for you."

Leila saw a look of pain in her aunt's eyes that reflected her own, not from her body, but from inside her heart. She could no longer keep the secret from her aunt.

Leila swallowed hard. "Tanta Rosa, I don't know how to say this. You – you have been so good to me and to Rachel. Since the first day."

"My dear," soothed Rosa, "nothing you could do would make me love you less."

Leila sniffled to clear her nose. She had to inhale several times before she could speak. "Oh Tanta, there are so many reasons I haven't been myself lately, but – but – the biggest one is that – I'm – I'm – pregnant."

She waited to be told that she had brought dishonor to the family, that she had been selfish, and had never stopped to consider the consequences – of loving Roderick, of wanting him so much that the wanting displaced all other loyalties. She waited to be told to find another place to live so Rachel and the twins wouldn't see her in this state.

Rosa cleared her throat. "I know," she said.

Leila stared in shock at her aunt.

"How? It was all those trips to the bathroom, wasn't it? I tried not to wake you..."

"It wasn't that," her aunt said gently, "it was everything else – you were so tired and pale. You haven't eaten anything in weeks."

Leila gazed at her. Could she spill the other secrets, the other reasons that she was exhausted and had no appetite?

Her aunt continued. "You have been so sad. It was your inner pain that told me."

Rosa had read through her mask. She suffered Leila's deception in silence and wasn't even angry. Leila found a new respect for her, and a deeper love.

"It's – the baby isn't – Nelson's," she whispered.

For a second, she thought about how much easier things would be if it were. Nelson would marry her. He would protect this child with his life. Roderick had taken her love and left her alone. A part of her would always hate him for that.

Rosa wet her parched lips and said, "Are you absolutely sure of that?"

"Yes," gasped Leila. *Of course I am.*

"Leila, I know you think of me as an old woman. But I'm not so feeble as to forget. I will tell you my secret because you are telling me yours."

Leila was confused. Her aunt had only ever been open with her. *Hadn't she?*

"You see, I felt that same sadness and fear – for the same reasons."

Leila shifted in her chair.

"The way you have been acting, Leila – it is not out of being pregnant with Nelson's child. You haven't wanted Nelson in, oh I'd say, almost a year, am I right?"

Leila nodded meekly. She hadn't seen Nelson in the same light since that brisk March day at the Morning Spot.

That one simple order. *"One coffee. Black."* Those three simple words had irrevocably altered her life.

"Who is he, my Leila?"

A great white shame engulfed her, as if she was being judged by all of her descendents. She couldn't look at her aunt.

"Leila, it's okay. I understand." Rosa paused. She seemed to be having trouble expelling the words. "I was in your shoes, eighteen years ago."

Leila's mind involuntarily did the math. Eighteen years ago, just after the Triangle Shirtwaist Factory fire. Rosa escaped with her life, and became pregnant with the twins. Her husband left her shortly afterwards, because he couldn't make it in this strange land and support a wife and two young boys. That was also family folklore. Wasn't it? *Wasn't it?*

"But…"

"You see my dear, things haven't changed too much since those days, not for us women anyway. We may have gotten the chance to vote, our skirts may be shorter, but the price we pay for our silence remains the same – and it's the cruelest burden of them all."

"You mean Joshua and Jonathan?" *That's why they have such fair hair.*

"I was not always this ancient looking," said Tanta Rosa. "Before they were born, I was quite the looker. Like you, I wanted to make something of my life, be free, independent," she took a breath, "make it in America."

Through the floors of their apartment, Leila heard strains of arguments coming from the neighbor's place. Since the economy had worsened, their fights had intensified. They had four small children. The baby was always contracting influenza and they did not have money for doctors. As their rampage paused, Rosa continued.

"He was older than me, a very rich man – out of my league, as you'd say. I used to see him on my way home from the factory at a little beer garden on Broadway. Oh, he was so handsome. I began stopping there after work, before returning here. At the time, your Uncle Joseph lived here as well, along with several boarders. Anyway, he was married and I was – well, there's no real excuse for it, but I was madly in love."

Leila covered her opened mouth with her hand. She had never looked at her aunt as a woman before, as someone with a body that passionately hungered for another.

"Did you?"

"It was only once," she answered. "That's all it takes, doesn't it? Men move on with their lives as if nothing happened, but we women live with our actions forever. I was lucky I had a big brother who cared about me. And never asked a single question."

"What did Uncle Joseph do, Tanta?"

"He had a friend named Aaron Finkelstein, a German Jew that worked in plumbing with him."

"But, I always thought, Aaron – he ran off because he couldn't support you and the twins, and was ashamed of that," Leila tried to piece this revelation together, to rewrite her own understanding of Tanta Rosa's history.

"He did leave," said Rosa, "but that was part of the bargain Joseph struck with him. You see, my lover was married, established, and a Gentile. Also…"

Tears formed in Rosa's eyes. Leila wanted to grab her aunt's hand, but kept still. She was witnessing the release of something her aunt had long ago locked away.

"Yes?" Leila prompted gently.

"Also, he wouldn't accept that he was the father. He turned on me, as swiftly as he had once wooed me. He denied he had ever met me. The lives growing inside me deserved more than an anonymous father. Aaron gave me the most amazing gift a friend could give – the protection of his name."

Leila flinched at the word "name." She hadn't thought about that. What would Roderick have done if he had lived? She would never know the pain of the rejection her aunt experienced. Her pain was a pain of loss. It was a pain that was pure and safe.

"Oh Tanta Rosa, what a horrible secret you have had to keep."

"Not so horrible," her aunt replied, smiling softly. "I have two beautiful sons, and I wouldn't change that for anything in the world. Only Joseph knows the truth."

"So – they don't know?"

Rosa shook her head. "It's better this way – better to believe their father left them, rather than denied their existence; better to believe I wasn't careless about conceiving them. I made peace with my decision. You must keep my secret too, my Leila."

"Of course I will," Leila replied. "And you must keep mine."

Her aunt nodded. "Who is he? The father?" she asked.

"Someone who will never be able to deny he is the father," she said grimly, "but whose family would never accept it. Someone I love – loved, very much."

"Your banker," her aunt stated.

*How did she know that?* Who else knew?

"Yes, Roderick Morgan." A strange liberating relief bubbled over her. She could utter his name aloud before her aunt. "I wish I knew what to do. I've – I've thought about just – getting rid of it." As soon as she spoke the words, she realized how harsh they sounded. Could she really? If she did – could she live with herself?

"I see," said Rosa. "That is one difference between my time and yours. For me, it was never a question. My best friend had died that way. I wasn't willing to die for James. But times change. You must do what you feel is right for you."

"I wish I knew what that was," said Leila, more to herself than to her aunt.

"Whatever you decide, my dear, I'll be there for you – as much as this old decaying body will let me. God punished me for what I did – he gave me two beautiful sons, but he took away my womanhood. But, when I see my boys, I know the struggle is worth it."

All throughout the day, Leila reflected on her aunt's story. How could the twins not be constant reminders of how deeply her aunt was betrayed? What if James had another family – well cared for while her aunt darned garments until her fingers could no longer function, to keep her young boys fed? She couldn't wind up in the same situation.

The next day, Leila told Rivkah about the pregnancy, and also a terrible lie.

"Are you going to tell him?" asked Rivkah.

"I can't. And you must swear on your own grave you won't tell a soul."

"I promise, Leila. I know things weren't great between you and Nelson – I understand why you wouldn't want him to know."

Leila looked at her blankly, searching for a hint of irony in her face. There was none. Rivkah believed this was Nelson's child. It was better this way.

"There's this spot on Allen Street. The street girls use it. It's not pretty, but this doctor has a reputation for very good work," said Rivkah.

Leila's heart ached. How had she sunk to such a low that she was contemplating destroying Roderick's baby? What else was there to do? Her heart flamed at Roderick. It's always easier for men, yet we women blame ourselves. *I don't have a choice, do I?*

"I'm so sorry," Leila cried. She didn't know who she was apologizing to. She felt as though she would be apologizing for the rest of her life.

"I will sort out the details," said Rivkah.

# 21.

# January 4, 1930

The next morning, Leila left at the usual time for work. She hoped Rosa wouldn't notice her shaking hands. The snow was now piled high on the sidewalks, the whiteness replaced with a dirt-lined grunge. The prospect of confronting the Morgans weighed heavily on Leila's mind. There was no friend, no Aaron Finkelstein, to be a salve for her mistake. How could she ever let Nelson know how deeply she had betrayed him?

She was thankful for Rivkah. She could not do this alone.

The clinic was housed in a dark brown tenement off Allen Street. It lay tucked on the other side of the El girders, by a small synagogue where the girls took their johns for brief interludes. As they approached its unmarked door, a woman in her late twenties exited with her arms wrapped around a girl who appeared no older than fifteen. They held each other, weeping. Leila overheard them talking about how they would make the money back soon enough. Her eyes watered.

"Are you sure you want to go through with this?" asked Rivkah.

"I can't be a mother right now, not like this."

"Okay," said Rivkah, squeezing her cold hand. "It's for the best then."

Leila gulped, her eyes red. "Let's go."

Inside, they were directed to a set of steps leading to the basement. The clinic was packed. A bunch of young women sat in the tiny room, looks of guilt, terror, and shame painted in their eyes. Most of the girls had come alone. Only one of them seemed to be accompanied by her boyfriend, and she appeared more terrified than the rest. He sat beside her with his arms folded, as his smoky eyes scanned the women in the clinic with undisguised disgust. Leila felt terrible for the young woman who sat with him. She was glad she could grab Rivkah's hand for the support this man deprived his woman.

"Rivkah, I… I—" She was interrupted by the nasal voice of an entering nurse.

"Leila. I'm looking for a Leila Kahn. The doctor will see you now." She exhaled a long drag of her cigarette and spilled its ash on the grimy floor.

Leila eyed the nurse. She noted her cool apathy, her absence of caring. She was just another name on this woman's tongue. Her body – all of the bodies in the waiting room – meant nothing to her. Leila grabbed her satchel. She dashed out. She stood in the street, bent at her middle, exhaling every bit of oxygen within her in short spurts.

Rivkah maintained her grip. "Leila, are you okay?"

"I don't know," moaned Leila. "I just – I can't do this. Let's get out of here."

Leila was pulled to the diner more than ever. She couldn't put off speaking to Bryan any longer. There was no time to waste. When she arrived at the Morning Spot, it was well past lunchtime. She asked Nan if Bryan had been looking for her earlier.

"No, I haven't seen him at all today," she replied, clearing some plates.

Leila excused herself for some air. She walked to the phone booth on Stone Street. She waited, shivering, for the operator to connect her.

"First Precinct, what's the crime?"

"I would like to speak with Officer Bryan O'Malley please," Leila answered.

"O'Malley didn't come in today," said the gruff voice. "Who's calling?"

"A – friend of his," she said. "Do you know if he'll be in later?"

"Uh, just a moment," said the man, "would you mind holding on, Miss?"

She waited with the phone receiver pressed to her ear, shivering in the icy booth.

Another man picked up.

"Miss?"

"Yes, sir?"

"Sergeant Henderson, here. You said you're after O'Malley?"

"Yes, that's right," she replied. She was growing impatient in the cold.

"Officer O'Malley didn't come in today."

"Oh," she said. "Did he come in yesterday?"

"No, he didn't," said the Sergeant.

Leila couldn't recall Bryan talking about time off. He seemed just as eager to move forward with the investigation of Jack Morgan as she did. He probably didn't come in yesterday because of the snow, she reasoned.

"Miss, do you know Officer O'Malley?" asked the Sergeant.

"Yes, I – he's a customer of mine at my diner."

"I see. And has there been any foul play there recently?" he asked.

"At the diner?"

"Yes." He sounded annoyed.

"Why, no. None at all," she replied. She wasn't exactly sure what he meant, but was acutely conscious of her Russian accent, as if it could identify her.

"I see. Miss, would you mind coming down to the station to help us out a bit?"

She suddenly felt like she had committed a crime. She wanted to do anything but be in a police station. "Uh, yes. Yes, I could. Why? What's the matter, Sergeant?"

"Officer O'Malley was shot early this morning, near the Morning Spot diner."

Leila felt like she was knifed in the stomach.

"What? Is he...?"

"He died instantly."

That knife twisted inside her.

Silence.

"Miss, are you still there?"

She gulped. She could emit no words. It took all her concentration to keep from crashing to the hard floor of the booth. The phone receiver flew from her grip, as it rammed against the glass. She could hear the Sergeant's voice calling out to her.

"What did you say your name was, Miss? Miss?"

Leila braced herself against the booth. She reached for the receiver and hung it up. She staggered through the packed snow back to the Morning Spot, using one arm to maintain her balance, the other placed firmly at her mid-section.

She arrived back at the diner barely recalling how she had gotten there. She scanned the piles of snow for signs of blood, but the only colors she saw were muddy brown and sooty black. She supposed that the door jangled as she pushed it open, but the sound didn't register. A few customers at the counter watched her come in, but she didn't greet any of them. Wordlessly, she hung up her coat and hat.

Nan approached her. "Leila, are you okay?" she asked. "You look terrible!"

"What?" she asked, blankly.

"You look white," Nan repeated. "Come sit down in a booth. I'll get you a pop."

Leila allowed herself to be escorted to a back table. She sunk into the leather of the booth, and scanned the diner. Her confidence in her plan had been destroyed. First by Althea's admission that she had given all the books and documents to Jack, and now because the one man she thought could help her had been murdered. She longed to return to the day before she had ever set foot on Wall Street, had ever met any of the Morgans, had ever known about the markets, or crashes, or fake books.

Bile rose in her throat. Bryan's death had something to do with Jack, as did Roderick's. How on earth could she prove it? She leaped up and dashed to the toilet.

When she returned, the soda Nan brought awaited her. Everyone stared. Nan and the cook appeared concerned. Customers chatted amongst themselves. She could barely hear what they were saying, nor did she try to listen. Were they talking about her? Suddenly, everything about the Morning Spot felt hostile. She took a sip from the bottle, hoping to calm the renewed urge to retch. She would have to compose herself; walk behind the counter, greet her customers, and pretend everything was fine. She just didn't know how she was going to manage that, because all she wanted to do was crawl away.

At that moment, the door sprang open in a fit of bells.

Walter barreled in, stomping snow from his boots. She caught his gaze and straightened her back. She walked behind the counter. He sat down on a middle stool.

"Can I get you anything?" she asked.

"Just a coffee," he replied, his eyes sullen slats.

"There you go," she said, pouring the hot liquid into his cup, staring him down.

"You look upset, Leila," he said.

"Now, why would I look upset, Walter?" she retorted, uncomfortable with his penetrating comment, wondering why he always seemed to be around at the most devastating of times. *Who is he?*

"You tell me," he replied, eager to engage her in this cat-and-mouse game.

"I have nothing to tell you," she said coldly.

"I heard your officer friend had some bad luck this morning," Walter jeered.

Leila fists clenched as her arms rose. "Get out!" she screamed.

"Aw Leila, I'm just drinking coffee, that's all," he said. "I'll be leaving in a jiffy."

Nan and the cook hovered nearby. The rest of the patrons focused on the two of them. Leila didn't care. "I said get out!" she repeated more loudly.

"As you wish," he said pleasantly. He reached into his pocket and flicked a dollar coin onto the counter. "Keep the change. Invest it in the stock market."

Leila trailed him to the exit. "Do *not* come back here."

"Then don't try to be something you're not," he warned. He grabbed her arm and brought his face close. The smell of his garlic breath brought a vomit taste to her mouth. "No one likes a hero."

Leila shoved Walter out the door and slammed it shut. She spun around to find everyone's eyes were on her. She wished they would all just go away and leave her alone. She tied her apron around her waist, reached for a cloth towel from behind the counter, and wiped down the countertop. The rasp of Walter's words repeated in her mind's ear. *No one likes a hero.* The more she replayed his words, the more her hands shook.

For the rest of the afternoon, Leila weighed the notion of going to Bryan's precinct to talk to his boss. But she didn't know whether she could trust him. Bryan said that on the night of Roderick's death, his boss made everyone leave the bank before conducting an investigation. She had no evidence to give him, just her suspicions; a crazy immigrant girl poking her nose in other people's business. *Who would believe her?*

Once outside, she locked the diner doors. She stood on the front sidewalk. It was nearly deserted. There were only a few cars by the Exchange up the road. She turned towards the station. The shock of Bryan's death had become a biting fear. She had to see his boss.

Leila buttoned her coat, and wrapped her scarf several times around her neck. She trudged through the snow and ice to the corner of Stone Street. The thin side street was empty in the frigid evening darkness.

Halfway down the block, she heard footsteps behind her. Someone was following her. She quickened her pace. The footsteps grew louder. She spun around.

"Who's there?" she called out.

She saw a tall man rushing towards her. He wore a dark overcoat and a hat pulled down to his eyes. She sped towards the north corner. He chased her. Her heart pumped wildly. She broke into a run. *She had to run.*

Another man with a scarf tied around his mouth stopped her.

"Hold it!"

He grabbed her elbow with one hand. She saw the shiny blade of a knife in the other. She started to scream but the man behind her cupped her mouth with his gloved hand. She bit down on it as hard as she could through the cold leather.

He let go with a growl and shoved her to the ground.

"Bitch!" he yelled.

She landed hard on her right side. Her forehead hit the curb and her vision blurred. She tasted drops of blood forming in her mouth. She tried to prop herself back up.

The man with the knife hovered over her, his arm raised, his fist wrapped around the handle of the blade. She inched back. She struggled to lift herself off the icy street. The other man pushed her back down. He slammed her face into the dirty slush. She could taste the mud and blood. She sputtered to breathe.

She thought about her aunt, Rachel, Joseph, and Nelson. She struggled to raise her head again. She lifted her face from the snow, and turned to see her assailant.

His dark eyes narrowed. Hot breath poured from his face.

"Forget about the books!" he snarled.

She pulled herself into a fetal position. She saw his body pause. Then she felt the full force of his boot, kicking her squarely in the ribs.

Before she could regain her breath, the two men raced off.

Leila lay winded on the ground, her lips and forehead bleeding. She was unable to lift herself for what seemed like hours. She wished she could recognize one of their voices, but couldn't. Finally, an old man passed by. He helped her to her feet, and gave her a handkerchief to clean the blood and dirt from her face.

"You took quite a tumble there," he said kindly. "This ice will kill you."

"Thank you for your help, sir," she said weakly. "I'm okay now."

"Are you sure?" he said.

Leila brought a hand to her ribs as a jolt of pain gushed up her right side.

"I just need to get home," she told him, struggling to remain balanced on her feet. She brushed the dirt from her coat, noticing that it was now torn in several spots. She searched for her satchel, frantically inspecting the icy sidewalk. It was gone.

"Can you please just help me to the El?"

She wrapped her scarf around her head. She didn't want anyone to see her. She wanted to slip away. She had been careless. She was angry with herself, too embarrassed to notice that she couldn't stop shaking.

By the time Leila reached the Lower East Side, she could hardly move. She also couldn't shake the feeling someone was following her. She imagined that if she let down her guard, the two men would appear again. She kept casting furtive glances over her shoulder. When she crossed Allen Street, she could sense the hairs on her skin standing. There were so few people out on the dark streets. Who would hear her if she screamed? She couldn't go home though; she couldn't let Tanta Rosa see her like this.

There was only one person she could turn to. She had been fighting him for so long. But she needed Nelson. She shuddered to consider what her fate might have been if the two men hadn't run off. She held her belly tightly through her coat. What would have happened to her baby?

She pressed on past Orchard Street. She was headed toward the East Broadway offices of the *Forward Newspaper*. But when she reached Delancey, she noticed light still shining through the windows of the Mona Lisa cosmetics shop. The glow was inviting. It promised a temporary respite from her anxious walk. Plus, she didn't want to confront Nelson in this state. No telling how he'd respond. She ducked into the store.

"Can I help you, Miss?" asked the cheery salesgirl behind the glass counter. Her lips reminded Leila of dark cranberries against her pale cream skin.

"I'm just looking for some lipstick, like the shade you are wearing. It's lovely," said Leila, her head down. She adjusted her scarf to cover a larger portion of her face.

"Thank you," the animated girl beamed a smile to reveal a row of angelic white teeth, "I'm glad you like it. I have a new order in the back. I'll go get it for you."

While she dashed to the storage area, Leila lowered her scarf and peered into the gem-studded counter mirror that customers used to test the latest beauty products. She looked a fright. There was dried blood caked to the corner of her lip. Her right eyelid was chafed and accented by a spreading fan of bruises. She removed her glove and dabbed some of the blood away with her spit.

"Oh my, what happened to you?" the shop girl inquired when she reappeared with a fistful of metal-encased lipsticks.

"I – fell on the ice," said Leila.

With a worried look, the shopkeeper fetched some cotton and dipped it in rubbing alcohol to disinfect her wounds. Leila flinched as she brought the swab to her swollen lip.

"Thank you," she told the girl abruptly. "I'll take this one, please," she pointed to the brightest color in the array of Tangee lipsticks. *That should cover my lip.*

"That'll be $1 dollar for the gunmetal case and $2.50 if you want the gold case."

"For lipstick?!" Leila nearly choked. It had been a while since she had spent any money on cosmetics. Any extra money went to food or Rosa's medicines. "How about I give you 70 cents?" she said.

"Deal. It's been a slow start to the year. You've been my only customer all day."

"Thank you," Leila forced a painful smile. "It'll only get slower, I'm afraid."

"What do you mean by that, Miss?" she asked.

*Was I that naive when I first started at the Morning Spot?* There was a safety in that ignorance. *What did knowledge get you?* she asked herself. *A swollen lip, a black eye, and a lifetime of guilt.* Including O'Malley, three people had died because of her in the past few months.

"Nothing," she said kindly. "I've just had a long day too. Um – do you – have anything that might be able to cover this up?" she pointed to her eyebrow.

"Tangee makes this wonderful cream-colored foundation. It's only two dollars..." the shop girl said eagerly, before she lowered her tone. "But here, let me apply it for you, free of charge – because you're my best customer of the day."

The glitter of the cosmetics shop made Leila feel more normal. Almost as if she hadn't just been attacked. Now it came rushing back to her. *Forget about the books!*

Leila continued her sojourn toward East Broadway. She thought about Nelson finishing up his weekly column. He was the only Irishman welcomed at the Yiddish paper, and had his columns on labor translated for inclusion. She moved slowly, balancing on the ice patches, trying to keep her boots from getting sopping wet in the slushy puddles. She breathed through the surges of pain throbbing at her middle.

The *Forward* building was one of the most majestic in the neighborhood. In the dark night, its ten stories stretched upwards forever. As she neared its stately doors, the stone heads of Karl Marx, Friedrich Engels, and Ferdinand Lassalle – men Nelson routinely quoted – guarded the entrance and promised safety.

She scanned the crowd of beggars gathered to receive food for the night. Huddled beneath a streetlamp was a woman about her age, nestled with two small children. The little boys cried softly. She hushed them with a lullaby, holding them close. Nelson brought canned goods and leftover food from local restaurants to these people.

"Miss?" pleaded an old woman from behind her, leaning against one of the barren trees in the triangle's center. Leila could make out every vein in her bony face, her cheeks were so withdrawn and hollow. She reached into her coat pocket and pulled out all her change: 48 cents. She placed it into the woman's palm. *Less than the price of a lipstick.*

"God bless you and your children," the old woman mumbled.

Leila forgot about the attack. She felt a rage burst within her. She stomped through the oversized, double glass doors of the *Forward* building. On the far side of the lobby, she entered an austere elevator of simple bronze and iron and asked the bald elevator man to take her to the sixth floor. The clunky metal box opened to a huge loft, with a sea of desks filled with sweaty reporters melodically tapping typewriter keys.

"Hey Leila!" called Nelson from behind one of the Underwood typewriters. His sleeves were rolled up past his elbows, like it was the middle of a balmy summer day.

"Oh my god – I'm so glad to see you!" she exclaimed. The feeling was genuine. She darted toward him, trying to ignore the simultaneous swell of nausea in her belly and pain in her ribs. She swung her arms around him.

"Leila – Jesus Christ – what happened to you?!"

"Nothing. And everything." She buried her head in the crook of his shoulder, as every emotion poured out of her. "Oh, Nelson. I haven't been upfront with you all these months. I'm so sorry about all of it."

"Are you okay?" his voice was drenched with concern as he held her.

"I'm okay," she said into his shoulder.

"Leila. What happened to your eye? Who the hell hurt you?!" he raised his voice.

"I need – I need to tell you," she said with effort. Then she squeezed him tight, "I've been so horrible to you and all you've ever wanted to do was help me."

"It's okay, it's okay," he said, calming his tone.

"Can we go somewhere – alone – to talk?" she asked between shakes. She could feel the stares of reporters upon her back. She wished they would go back to their writing.

"Sure. Let's go over there." He pointed to a large office encased within glass windows. "Abe's out." He swung his arm around her waist as she leaned into his body for support, and made her way to the office of the most important socialist in New York City.

She sat on one of the hardwood chairs. She attempted to remove her coat, but had to contort her body to avoid aggravating her side. Nelson closed the door behind him and held her in his arms. She nestled her head against his chest.

"You're shaking. What happened?" he said with worry. "Who did this?"

"It was two men," she replied, "down by the Morning Spot, while I was on my way to the police precinct."

"What two men?" asked Nelson. "Here, have a few sips of water."

She took the cup and drank quickly.

"Why were you going to the precinct?" asked Nelson.

"You know that policeman I said hello to, while you were at the Tombs?"

"Irish guy, O'Malley. Cousin of my buddy, Shamus. He's an upstanding guy."

"Was," she corrected quietly.

"What do you mean, was?" he stood up. "Leila, Jesus – what's going on?"

"He's dead. He was shot this morning, in front of my shop."

"What? You saw that?" Nelson asked incredulously.

"No, before I arrived. But, I think it was – I think he was waiting to see me."

"Why?"

His suppressed alarm made her nervous. "Then I called the precinct today and they told me; they didn't seem to know who shot him. But – Nelson – I think I know."

"Was there some sort of a fight?" he asked.

"No," she said. "He was investigating some shady dealings at the Morgan bank."

As he paused to digest this, Nelson offered her a second glass of water.

"Did it have anything to do with that – that Roderick guy?" he asked.

She couldn't mask the stunned look on her face. "Why would you ask that?"

"I got a chance to speak to O'Malley when I was at the joint."

Leila took a deep breath. *He can't know.*

"I told him that you were my girl after you came to bust us out, and he said he knew you. One thing led to another, and before you know it we're talking about Roderick, how his death was more suspicious than anything else."

"What else did he tell you?" asked Leila, a panic in her chest.

"That he thinks bankers are pigs. The poor, poor bastard," Nelson sighed.

"He reminded me of you," said Leila softly.

"Yeah?" Nelson's cheeks blushed. He wiped a drop of blood from her lips that had escaped from beneath the Tangee. "Was it the brogue?"

She laughed. It hurt her lip. "No," she paused. "His heart."

"Oh," he said softly. He reached to touch the bruise around her eye.

Leila turned from his hand. "Nelson, you must promise if I tell you everything, not to get all hot-headed. I don't want to have to bail you out of jail again," she said.

"I can't promise, but I'll try to control myself," asked Nelson. "You don't have to talk about this now though. I should get you home; call the police about those men."

"No, I want to talk about it," Leila insisted. "When the stock market went up so fast early last year, the Morgan bank put together all of these deals – railroads mostly."

He nodded, "Trusts and such."

"Yes, I suppose," she said. "But, for some time, the value of those deals, as far as investors and the public knew, appeared much higher than what they were really worth."

"So, the bank was swindling people? Sounds about right," said Nelson.

"When things got really bad in the fall, around the crash, I – I – found out that the bank was actually keeping two sets of books." She paused.

"How did you find out about them?" he asked. There was hurt in his eyes.

She sat silently.

"Never mind," said Nelson, "Roderick told you. He—"

Leila cut him off. "Yes, Roderick told me – at the diner. He was trying to find a way to tell Jack Morgan that it was time to tell the public the truth. That's what Officer O'Malley believed – so he was killed."

"Morgan's a lying thief and a murderer, and tonight, he came after you!"

His anger, once so frightening, now barely fazed Leila. She faced very real threats: O'Malley's death, her attackers, the tumult in her belly. *Jack.*

"I can't say for sure," she said, "But two large men did. They told me to forget about the books. One had a knife—" her voice faltered. Her calm dissolved. She could have died.

"I will kill him! I swear to God I will, Leila. I will kill him!" Nelson ranted.

"You can't," she said. "You will never get near him."

"Look at you, Leila," Nelson retorted. "He can't get away with this."

"But he's covered himself so well. Roderick is dead. No one else has the books. O'Malley is dead just for asking questions. And someone's after me... If I had proof of anything that could be traced back to him, that would be one thing, but I don't."

*The only reason I'm alive is because I don't have enough evidence against Jack.*

"Are you sure?" asked Nelson. "Is there anything that Roderick ever said to you, ever showed you, ever gave you, that could help?"

Leila thought about the diary. "No, there isn't."

He took her hands in his, rubbing them with his thumbs. "I'm glad you came to tell me all of this. The man's a criminal. I want to see his bank burn to the ground!"

"Nelson!"

"Don't worry, I'll try to restrain myself. But notifying the police isn't enough."

"I feel exactly the same way," said Leila.

"Really? You do?" he asked with the same hopefulness with which he had once tried to get her to come to union meetings.

"Of course. And I intend to do something about it. But tonight I need to rest."

"Let me take you home then," said Nelson.

She hesitated. Now that she had told him her story, she felt even worse for having betrayed him. But she also knew it would be futile to resist his offer. "I would like that."

She wasn't sure what hurt more, her heart or her ribs. Both pains lingered as she walked alongside Nelson. She was grateful that he was beside her. The night seemed darker than usual. The cold was bone chilling. Everything was grey. It was as if she and the night sky had chosen to share the same somber mood.

At her building, she told Nelson she would be okay. Reluctantly, he promised to make his own inquiries into the two men that attacked her. She sensed he was holding something back, but a jolt of pain in her lower abdomen kept her from asking him.

As she entered her foyer, she could barely see the outline of the wooden staircase. The only light in the hallway had burned out and the inside was nearly pitch black. She patted the walls as she climbed the five flights of stairs, inhaling the familiar yet unsettling smell of onions, urine, and kasha on her ascent.

Her aunt waited for her at the kitchen table. Rosa's face fell to the floor when she saw Leila. "My dear, what happened to you?" she asked with concern.

"Nothing," said Leila. "I fell on the ice, that's all. Then I had to go see Nelson."

Her aunt eyed her expectantly.

"I just need to lie down for a bit." She flinched as she removed her coat.

Leila sidled past Rosa and crawled onto the bed without washing her face. Pain shot up and down the right side of her body, then like daggers, focused its attention toward her belly. She cradled her head on her upper arm and lay on her left side, her legs tucked in a ball at her chest like she was an infant. She gritted her teeth and tensed her body.

After everyone else had gone to sleep, Leila hobbled to the toilet in the tenement hallway. She lay doubled over on the bathroom floor, trying to alleviate the cramping. She slowly pulled her dress up past her thighs. What was she hoping for? What would be the worst possibility? That she would lose this baby that she herself had considered destroying? She found traces of blood between her legs, but not too much.

She felt horrible, but her baby was safe. Her baby was a fighter.

She burst into tears. Her stomach convulsed as if she was going to vomit. But she didn't. Instead, the tears seemed to cleanse her. She didn't know how long she lay on the tile floor, sobbing. Eventually the tears stopped. Her body felt numb and empty, and yet, clarified. She left the toilet. She walked slowly down the hall. She resolved to fight like hell to keep Roderick's baby. She would fight to bring Jack to justice for everything he had done. But she was scared out of her mind. She was going to be a mother. Like her aunt, she would raise her child without a father, But she would love it with all her heart.

About two weeks later, the newspapers reported that the entrance to the Morgan bank had been vandalized late at night. The glass on the doors had been smashed, and a fire had been set in the back of the building. According to reports, a gang of men – possibly the White Hand Gang but no one was sure, it happened so fast – beat up Thomas Lamont, just after he exited the building and before he reached his driver.

Lamont was left bloodied on the street. He had a broken arm, two broken legs, and several broken ribs. There was a note pinned to him. "Next time, it'll be you, Jack."

The men were not apprehended.

The same night, a few blocks away, a man was found beaten to death. His body was tossed in a back-alley city dumpster. There was a note pinned to him too.

"Justice is served."

According to reports from the area homeless, the man cried for his life to be spared while being pounded. Two cops on the beat stopped and stared down the alley. They kept on walking. No suspects were ever found.

The following night, Nelson came to visit Leila.

"Leila, there's something I need to tell you, too," he said, as they stood on her front stoop. He leaned against one of the iron railings and held her wrists.

"What is it?" she asked with concern.

"I'm leaving," he replied softly. "I don't want to, but I'm afraid – I have no choice. Believe me, I can help you more if I'm not here."

He looked away from her.

"Leaving?" she felt her heart sink. "What do you mean? For where? When?"

"I'm heading out to California. Leila, I'm glad you told me about what's going on with Jack Morgan and the bank. I – I had some of friends look into it. I promise you – you'll be safe. As for me, I need to leave New York."

She sensed he was hiding something else from her. "But why now?"

He looked down at his feet. Nelson never looked down.

"The job situation here will only get worse. As it is, there are too many people in our city and too little work. I met a contractor who's starting a business working for some of the Hollywood studios."

"Hollywood," she repeated.

"Yeah – of all the places." He smiled at Leila, reached for her hair, and then dropped his arm. "You remember how much we used to love going to see the pictures?"

Tears welled in her eyes. She thought of those easy days of seeing a Douglas Fairbanks film and sharing a smoke afterwards, walking arm in arm together on the boardwalks. They felt a lifetime away. *She* had thrown them away.

"I didn't know you were thinking of leaving."

"It's time for a change," he said. "I hear the weather's terrific out there – the sun shines all year around. You can save a fortune on winter clothes alone."

His effort at humor was admirable, but useless.

She licked a salty teardrop from the top of her lip.

"Rivkah once told me you could be a movie star." She forced a smile.

"I don't know about that," he grinned sheepishly, "Can you imagine me parroting lines that somebody else wrote?"

"No," she laughed softly, as more tears cascaded down her cheeks. She was surprised by the outpour of her emotions. "Not at all. I just never thought that you'd…"

"Move away," he finished her sentence. "I figure – there've got to be a lot of set designers out in L.A. who need organizing. And maybe it's time to stop…"

"Stop what?" she asked, softly.

"Stop hoping we can be something we're not meant to be," he said. "I know this is probably the wrong time to bring it up again, but there was a time when I always thought we'd be together. You know, raise some anarchists of our own."

"There was a time I thought that too," she said. "I don't know what happened either. But you are the kindest, sweetest man I've ever known."

"I could say the same about you. You are a brave and amazing woman."

"I'm neither. I always wished I could be the person you saw in me."

"You got involved with all this banker turmoil when you didn't have to; you put your life at risk. Leila, you *are* the person I see in you," he replied.

"No, I'm not," she wrapped her arms around him and held him tightly.

After a few moments, he gently loosened her embrace.

Her heart sunk. Yet she knew that if he stuck around, there would be no way to explain the bump in her belly, the child that was not his.

"I've always wanted to go to Hollywood. I hope you meet – that you…" her voice was trembling so much that she couldn't finish her sentence.

"Leila, I'm sure we'll see each other there," said Nelson, tenderly. "Meanwhile, do what you need to do here. And remember, I will always love you."

She wasn't sure about that. *How could he if he knew the truth?* The two clung to each other in a bind of good-bye. After several long moments, Leila quietly removed herself from their embrace. She watched Nelson leave the stoop of her Orchard Street tenement for the last time.

# 22.
## March 1, 1930

It was almost Spring again, yet the barren tree branches still hung melancholy and mournful. The brutal winter had not yet relinquished its grasp of the weather or Leila's heart. Both of the men she loved were gone. Even her Uncle Joseph had relocated his office to the basement of his West Bronx home – like all the other shopkeepers closing their doors around Orchard Street – the drop in business rendering it impossible to pay the rent.

Leila threw herself into the Morning Spot with outward abandon. She kept the diner more spotless than usual, and the orders current. But she felt no desire to interact with her customers beyond surface pleasantries. The lines between them were too wide.

Something else fueled her. She had almost lost her baby during the attack; now she took better care of herself. She noticed her body more, not the nausea, but other changes. Her belly grew larger. She let out the waistlines on her skirts. Her ankles swelled with each cup of coffee she poured. Her breasts spilled out of her bra. Through the dull aches, she was amazed by what was happening inside of her; things she could not even fathom. Every once and a while, amidst all of the devastation, the world seemed a wondrous place. Leila walked tall.

As she took care of her body, she could no longer ignore the nagging in her mind. This thought grew in her as the baby did. She'd pinned so much hope on Officer O'Malley. He was going to be the one to know the secrets of the books. He would help her understand what happened. He would use the law against Jack Morgan. She would help him right all of the wrongs that had been committed.

But O'Malley was dead. There was no one to rely on but herself. So one Friday, in the middle of March, Leila took off from work early. She put on her hat and marched over to the New York District Attorney's office on Worth Street, a fifteen-minute walk from the Morning Spot. She told her story to some assistant to an assistant of the assistant D.A. The man listened politely, jotted a few notes, and thanked her for her time.

Leila was not satisfied, but she was hopeful. She began waiting for a reply.

Each evening when she returned home, she sprinted up the stoop, her door key poised in hand. She checked the frayed metal letterbox in the front foyer. Each night she went to sleep willing the new day to come faster.

Finally, after three weeks, the response arrived. It came in the form of an official letter stamped with the maroon wax seal of the New York County Court. It was addressed to Miss Leila Kahn. She opened the letter with trepidation. Her fingers trembled. She was certain it would be a cursory *thank you, but no* type of letter.

Instead, it was a copy of an indictment again the great Jack Morgan, brought about by the People of the United States of America. A judge and jury would listen to the facts. Everyone would hear her story. They would decide the outcome of her fight against Jack and the House of Morgan. A wave of excitement and apprehension fought for control of her. She would make a difference.

The following Monday, as instructed in the note that came with the indictment, she was to return to Worth Street.

She gathered her notes from the diary. She walked through the Lower East Side, each step ominous. She began looking over her shoulder again. She was terrified of being attacked any minute, yet strangely secure that she had knowledge that would change the world.

Assistant District Attorney, Anthony Borteli, was a dashing young Italian man with thick ebony hair and sharp black eyes, a second generation American. At first, as he told Leila, he hadn't believed her story, but as more complaints funneled in from the shareholders of the Morgan trusts who had lost their shirts, he changed his mind. He refined his case. Leila's information was central to it.

To build up public support, Borteli tactically leaked information to the press. It took no time for news of the impending case to command the headlines and conversations of New York City:

*"Russian Girl Takes on Bank Titan"*

*"Leila vs. Goliath"*

*"Jack Attack: the House of Morgan vs. the Lower East Side Tenements"*

The swell of media attention unnerved her. She found it hard to believe that suddenly she was part of the headlines. It also brought a slew of new customers to the diner, eager to meet the great Leila Kahn. Moishe was ecstatic. The world was fast sinking into economic depression, but the Morning Spot on Wall Street was thriving.

With preparations for the trial underway, Borteli coached Leila to act as normal as possible. "Don't answer any questions. Don't give anything away. Just smile."

That was much easier said than done. She couldn't wait for the trial to start.

Each day she would stare at the small, wooden clock that hung above the diner's door, willing its iron hands to speed towards six o'clock. She thought of Los Angeles. She wondered how Nelson was settling in on the West Coast. She also couldn't help but wonder how Althea and little Rodney were faring in England.

But mostly she thought about the trial. How would it go? Would it be over before she became a mother? Right now, she barely registered a small paunch in her belly, but soon it would be impossible to keep her pregnancy away from the world.

While Leila contemplated the course of the people in her life, tiny buds appeared on the young sycamores that lined the streets of the Lower East Side. One morning, as she left for work, she realized with a glimmer of excitement that the coldness of winter had melted away. It had been a full year since her fateful first day at the diner. To commemorate the occasion, she celebrated with a chocolate cake and some candles with Nan and the cook. Her customers seemed unaware of the anniversary.

Most of the old regulars were focused on the rally in the stock market and making back the money they had lost in the fall. Others had simply disappeared. Leopold, the tailor, had gone out of business, so he no longer came down to Wall Street to measure the men during their busy work day. Oliver, the muttonchops man, had moved away to Louisiana to start a new life with a small shrimp boat, after he sold his remaining shares in the market. Even Sinclair, the avid Chase banker, had departed for Florida to try his luck opening a motel near Orlando. She hadn't seen Walter since the night of his warning, not in the diner and not on the streets. *It was if he had vanished into thin air,* she thought with a shudder.

One night in late March, she felt the first fluttering of her baby, like a swirling inside of her. She was giddy and terrified. She couldn't sleep. She scoured her meager bookshelf for something to distract her. She hadn't opened Roderick's diary since O'Malley's death. It maintained its hiding spot within a stack of worn books beside her bed. It lay beneath his copy of *The Great Gatsby*.

Being careful not to disturb anyone's sleep, she dug into the stack and reached for *The Great Gatsby*. Even sitting amongst the mildewed, second-hand copies from local booksellers, it maintained the scent of fresh leather. She sniffed its leather binding, preserved like a memory. She lit one of the gas lamps, setting it to its dimmest setting. She took the book to the kitchen and placed it on the table.

Leaning into the hard wood of the kitchen chair, she closed her eyes loosely. She allowed herself to be carried back to that night of passion. Everything since had become hopelessly complicated. But she could still resurrect the deliciousness of every touch, every breath, as if it had just occurred. In her mind's film, she recalled the hungry ache in his speckled eyes when he first gazed upon her breasts. She recalled the feel of his hands as they cupped over her breasts, how his fingers spread out as they slipped down her waist and found that spot of heat between her legs. She remembered how he called out her name when he climaxed. She reflected on how they wordlessly gathered their clothing before he had to return to the bank. How he stopped to hold her one last time. How he squeezed her as tightly as if she was the last life raft of the ill-fated *Titanic*. How the scent of wood and cinnamon lingered as she sunk to the floor and sobbed.

As these thoughts flushed her heart, she ran her fingers over the gold-engraved title on the book. She caressed its letters.

She opened the Gatsby book and leafed through its thick, textured parchment, page by page, not so much to read them, but in an attempt to understand why she had been so drawn to their story, and to Roderick. About mid-way through the book, she noticed that a few of the pages lay less flat than the others. She flipped towards them, puzzled.

She found two small envelopes stuffed into the inner creases of the pages.

One was marked, "Allegheny"; the other was marked, "Leila."

She felt her heart stop. Slowly, she set the one with her name on it off to the side of the table. She stared at the curves of her name, written in his hand. How had he known she would return for this book? She was afraid to find out.

Instead, she slid her finger under the waxy seal of the envelope marked "Allegheny." It opened easily.

The interior of the envelope was shiny pewter. Inside, there were two single sheets of thick paper. Each of them was folded many times over. She removed each one separately, unfolded it, and gently placed it upon the table.

She took a deep breath when she realized what lay before her.

They were the identical first pages of the Alleghany deal document she had seen on Roderick's desk. They both had Jack's original signature at the bottom. They each had different figures for the value of the deal.

Her heartbeat returned, now thumping wildly. Roderick had trusted her with the missing piece. The two pieces of paper now lay before her. Yet, she was not surprised. A part of her knew Roderick believed in her, even as she constantly questioned herself. He saw in her what she hadn't yet been able to see in herself. Like Nelson. Roderick and Nelson, from opposite places, found the same thing in her.

She stared at the Allegheny documents. She memorized Jack's arrogant signature. She repeated the conflicting numbers over and over in her mind.

It took her another hour before she could bring herself to open the second envelope. Inside, she found another folded note. It was written on ivory parchment paper in dark red ink with impeccable flourish:

*Dear Leila,*

*If you are reading this letter, I fear the worst has happened. Jack threatened my life on numerous occasions, every time I have brought up the idea of going public with the bank's fake books. I took precautions, but I fear it may only be a matter of time.*

*Know that because of you, only because of you, I had the strength to confront Jack. You gave me a courage that I never thought existed within me and for that, I am profoundly grateful. I apologize that I never expressed this to you. I have done wrong, and I am prepared to pay for it, even if it means being parted from my son, and from you, and spending the rest of my days locked in a cell. In many ways, I was already living in a cell. Because of you, I am no longer scared. Because of you, I became a better man.*

*I am sorry I brought you into all of this. But I am not sorry I met you or that I had the chance to hold you in my arms. I have no doubt that you will go on to do all of the great things you desire. You must seek them out. You must move on.*

*My love forever,*
*Roderick*

Tears rolled down her cheek. She only read through the note once. Then Leila sat for a long time watching the flicker of the lamp. She held the letter in her trembling hand. She caressed her stomach with pressure. She understood and the questions were calm.

*Had he really loved her, or was he merely 'grateful' to her?*
*Was she really his love or just a moral muse?*

She wondered about these two extremes, her thoughts pitching back and forth between the possibilities. Gradually she realized that they weren't such extremes at all. She, after all, felt the same way about him. She needed him to see in her something greater than her surroundings, something greater than what she saw in herself. With his note, he confirmed that he had. Maybe that's what their love was – a weaving of two personal half-complete stories, stories too detached from their real worlds to exist for more than one brief connected interlude.

But she was going to have his baby. That made their connection permanent.

A part of her would never relinquish the despair that engulfed her on the street of the financial district that fateful Tuesday night in October. But she was glad that he had discovered some peace with his life and a purpose that he had strived to find.

She refolded both of the notes, the one that calmed her head and the one that pierced her heart. She returned them to their respective envelopes, and returned the envelopes to their pages within *The Great Gatsby*. She returned the book to the middle of her pile. She watched her aunt and sister's chests rising and falling with their sleeping breaths. She'd found her peace. It was a richer feeling than any external trappings of wealth could ever provide. It was contentment. She smiled as she switched off the lamp.

Roderick was right, it was time for her to move on. That meant facing Jack. She had given the timelines and deal lists from the diary to the district attorney. Now she had more proof of the connection between Jack and the fraud. She had the ammunition to win this case. She and Roderick would fight Jack together. The thought gave her comfort. He would want her to do this.

She sighed. She released him.

# 23.

# April 1, 1930

Anthony Borteli worked the justice system with lightening speed and prowess. As ambitious as he was strategic, he took advantage of a couple of bad stock market days and a few well-placed bribes through the Italian mob network to secure a trial date.

His efforts were rewarded. The official trial date, April 5, 1930 splashed bold across all the newspaper front pages. The country careened toward a Depression like it had never seen before; businesses – large and small – kept closing, people lost their jobs at an alarming pace, and others were evicted from their homes with nowhere to go but the streets. The possibility of retribution for all this pain brought a buzz to the streets of Manhattan. People needed a focus for their anger.

That focus was Jack Morgan. He was the man that did this to them. The villain that lied and manipulated a nation would be facing justice – and all because of a young immigrant girl. The mere possibility was reason enough for hope in these dark days.

As the day of the trial neared, more details were leaked about the prosecution's evidence against Jack Morgan and his bank president, Thomas Lamont. Debate in the media reached a frenzied pitch.

On one hand, there was the *Wall Street Journal.* It sought to sooth the public with promises by bankers and politicians that the country was back on track. Everything would be fine by the end of the year, if not sooner, and blaming the nation's greatest banker – and a great American to boot – for a crash that occurred, through no fault of his own, was "sour grapes." Investors should have known better than to bet their shirts in the market anyway.

The *Forward,* fast becoming the largest newspaper of labor, in no small part because of the trial and its most unlikely of instigators, told a different story. It wrote of a country mired deep in a Depression that was the direct result of the "great banker" lying to, and stealing from, the public. If Prohibition bootlegging was a crime, rigging the entire stock market and by extension, the whole of the American economy, was treason of the highest order.

In turn, other investors, the poor and the middle-class ones, added their complaints to the charges that the district attorney would be levying on Jack Morgan and his bank. They were grateful for the possibility of having their day in court, and maybe of getting a few dollars back for their financial woes.

But it was Leila that was situated smack in the center of the trial of the century.

Photographers followed her every movement. She had to have one of the twins accompany her to and from work to avoid their hustling her. Moishe hired a guard for the diner to keep them from disrupting her during the day. This, he paid for out of his own pocket. Though he grumbled about the expense, he insisted it was his obligation. As he told her, more than once, and with a measure of pride, "I got you into this mess, Leila – and I'm not going to leave you in the lurch."

Journalists waited for her at the stoop of 99 Orchard Street and at the Morning Spot every day, angling for a "scoop," hungry for some slice of sensationalism to transfix an ailing, media-obsessed nation, searching for heroes.

The pressure was mounting inside her as well, like a constant drumming in her bones. Borteli reassured her that he had verified the documents she presented to him. They did indeed carry the true signature of Jack Morgan. He was less certain that he would be able to enter the premises of the bank to retrieve the alleged fake books.

"Why do you keep using the term 'alleged'?" Leila had asked him nervously at one of their meetings in his stark Worth Street office. "There are two sets of books, I've seen them. Althea Morgan has seen them. Roderick told me about them."

"Yes," he had agreed, "but unless I have them in my hands and the jury can see them, I'm afraid it's your word against Althea's."

She felt her lungs deflate.

"But, the two documents relate to those fake books."

"Yes, and they will be crucial to our case," he said. "Look, Leila, our strategy is simple: we must lead the jury to believe that Jack knowingly doctored that Allegheny deal. From there we need to convince them that this was just the tip of the iceberg, and that the bank isn't, and wasn't, what it represented itself to be. We must prove that all the shadiness and book-cooking was ordered by Jack and that it brought the market down."

"And what about Roderick?" she asked, her stomach in knots. Borteli's strategy seemed at once both logical and impossible to her.

"Roderick is an unknown at this point," he answered.

"An unknown? What do you mean – an unknown?"

"The jury may conclude that Roderick alone committed and conceived of the fraud, and well – you can't hang a dead man. They may conclude that his guilty conscience pushed him out that window, and his punishment has thus been duly delivered. They may decide there was no murder at all. Case closed. I've got no real proof to go on."

Leila's face fell. Her heart sank further when she received the news from the District Attorney's office that the judge hearing the case had indeed rejected his request to search the premises of the House of Morgan. The judge let the murder charge remain, but Borteli had his doubts.

"I'm telling you, Leila," explained Borteli, "it's not that I don't believe you, but I need real evidence. I've canvassed everyone at the police precincts. I've interviewed every guard at the Morgan bank, and every employee I could get a hold of leaving the building. No one saw anything. Or if they did, no one's talking. It's a tough sell."

"But, the diary entries – from Roderick. Roderick felt his life was threatened."

"That may be so, but I'm afraid it just doesn't constitute real evidence," he replied.

"But what about Officer O'Malley's death?" she cried.

"I checked with his boss. It was filed as a gang related homicide – bootleggers."

"I don't understand. He's guilty!" she exclaimed.

"That's what we need to prove," said Borteli. "I did get something interesting in the post today that may be helpful. In an envelope addressed to you."

"Who sent it?" she asked.

"I don't know," he said. He directed her at some stills. "Here, take a look."

She bent her head over a photograph on his desk. It showed Roderick's lifeless body, lying in a dark pool of blood. Her eyes widened as she lifted her head towards Borteli. "It's Roderick Morgan, just after he – after he hit the ground," she murmured.

"Look at his head. Look closely," instructed Borteli.

She squinted to examine the image. At the side of his head there was a mark, a darker hole by his right temple, almost smooth with the cobblestone ground.

"Oh my God!" she gasped. "Is that…?"

"No other way to read it," he said. "Roderick Morgan was shot before he came out of that window."

She inhaled sharply. "So this proves he was killed, doesn't it?"

"Well, it's hard to jump out of a window after you've shot yourself," said Borteli, "but a number of things could have happened. Roderick could have shot himself and then jumped because it didn't do the trick. He could have shot himself by the glass window and the force of the bullet exiting his head shattered it, before he fell."

"But that doesn't make any sense," said Leila.

"No," agreed Borteli, "but in a courtroom, it's not always the sensible story that people believe."

Leila shook her head from side to side. It was too much. She returned home that night in a haze of despair. *Jack Morgan was winning before the trial even began. How could the judge deny them the right to investigate Roderick's office.*

Leila spoke at length with her Uncle Joseph about the trial. Morris's wife, Hannah, had added her name, at his urging, to the list of investors duped by the Morgan deals; in particular the Allegheny deal. Joseph even tried to get a related manslaughter charge added to the laundry list of charges the D.A. had compiled – due to Morris's heart attack – but was told that it was too much of a stretch.

The night before the trial, Joseph, Hannah, Rivkah, and a group of other Lower East Siders gathered at Moishe's local establishment. Rosa begged to be taken. She sat quietly and observed as conversations got heated and strategies were discussed.

"Leila," Joseph began, standing tall by his table at the front of the restaurant, "you are at the center of all that has gone wrong in this country. You brought the truth into the light, and opened the door for the rest of us to see into the practices of the powerful, secretive banks that are destroying the very fabric of America. The people of this country knew J.P. Morgan to be a business titan, but also a man of charitable pursuits who built libraries and funded hospitals. His son Jack has shown himself to be a common thief."

Leila's stomach was doing somersaults as her uncle spoke. He sounded more like a revolutionary, than a contractor. The baby kicked steadily within her belly, as if he – for Leila had decided she was carrying a boy – was determined to be a part of the fanfare. Ever since Rosa told her about her uncle's role in her pregnancy eighteen years ago, Leila viewed him with greater admiration. Tonight, he was in his element.

Shouts of "Hear! Hear!" reverberated through the diner. More people piled in, packing it beyond capacity. Moishe uncharacteristically served free coffee to everyone.

"Kill the bastard!" yelled Stan, the metal worker.

"Throw 'em all in jail and throw away the key!" said Joshua, his fist high in the air as Rivkah watched him, smiling.

"Wipe 'em off the face of the earth!" cried Nelson's friend, Shamus.

She knew Nelson would be here if he hadn't left for California so abruptly. She had her suspicions about why he did. They had never found the Morgan vandals. *But it's better he's not here,* she thought as she patted her abdomen.

Leila surveyed the room. She stared at the drawn faces with sunken cheeks, and the homemade clothes darned by dim light in airless living rooms. She inhaled the smell of cheap tobacco coating their garments. She realized that tomorrow's trial was about more than fraud; it was about the equal ability to pursue the American dream, the thing that tied all her fellow immigrants together. All they knew of Jack Morgan, they had read in the papers. She was the only human link.

The weight of their futures bore down on her shoulders. She had wanted to make a difference. She had wanted people to approve of her, to see her as more than just a

Russian immigrant. Now, she sat at the crossroads of that desire. Yet, their hope wasn't an inspiration to her, as it should have been; it was an anvil tied to her feet. Her aunt was right – sometimes the cause finds you. But, if she were a true revolutionary, that cause should inspire a vengeance within. Yet, a fear had crept into her resolve once she learned about the gunshot to Roderick's head.

She knew too much and it didn't matter. She wanted to disappear.

Her eyes caught Joseph's from across the room.

"This is not a battle that will be easy," he continued. "Tomorrow's trial will be the start of a long war, but what we must remember is that we are not turning away from it. We are heading toward it, and we have Leila Kahn, my precious niece, to thank."

"Hear! Hear!" erupted the room.

"Ahem!" Moishe cleared his throat with a sound that echoed in his diner.

"My apologies," said Joseph with a smile, "we also have our host of the evening – Moishe – to thank, for hiring Leila to work at the Morning Spot on Wall Street, where she came into contact with its corruption and manipulation."

"To Moishe!" everyone shouted.

"Leila," asked Joseph, his eyes shining, "is there anything you'd like to say?"

All eyes fell on her. The desperate looks made her feel uncomfortable. She didn't know what to say. She gulped so loudly she was sure everyone heard her.

"I just want to say," she began, a waver in her voice, first facing her uncle, then awkwardly turning toward the rest of the diner, "that I – I really hope I don't let you down." She sat down immediately, conscious of her growing belly.

Joseph retook command. "We hope we don't let you down either. You are doing a great mitzvah for your people. I could not be prouder. To Leila!" He began to clap.

One by one, the now-substantial audience broke into a shared applause before Joseph called the evening to an end. He urged them all to come to the courthouse the next morning to support Leila and the call to justice she had sounded.

"Remember, my comrades," he said, still using the language of revolution, "we must be present when that jury takes its seats, in great number. We must show them their decision isn't just about what they hear in that courtroom, but about the kind of America they want our country to be. If ever there was a reason to take off work, and I know that many of you are struggling to find work – as am I – this is it. They have money and fancy lawyers. We have our voices. May God bless each and every one of you."

Her uncle sounded as if he was running for office. Leila wondered if in fact he had considered it. He didn't speak with the gruffness of Nelson, but with a measured, rational strength that moved and comforted her.

After everyone left the diner, Leila sat alone with Joseph, Rosa, and Moishe.

"I'm so afraid," she admitted. "Jack Morgan, he's a very scary man."

"Not for nothing," said Moishe. "But he doesn't know who he's dealing with."

"You mean, me?" said Leila, her confidence non-existent.

"I mean, all of us – we immigrants – we know how to fight!" he proclaimed. Then with a softer voice he added, "And you, Leila, of course you."

Leila said nothing more for the evening. Joseph and Moishe ushered Rosa out to the street, pushing the wheelchair she once fought so hard to avoid. They spoke of legal strategies, their voices brimming with confidence.

Meanwhile, she was tied up in knots inside, and her baby kicked vigorously. She wanted the trial to be over. She caught Rosa's glance as her aunt sat, arms folded at her lap.

Rosa knew that whatever happened at the trial, the real fight had only begun. Leila thanked her for understanding with her eyes. She wondered if everyone would be so admiring of her if they knew what she had done, how she had gotten the information she passed to the D.A. They might think she was a bigger fraud than Jack Morgan himself. The thought settled in her head and would not go away.

As Leila prepared Rosa's bed for the night, she overhead Joseph speaking in tense tones.

"Is there anything else I can do before tomorrow?" Joseph asked pensively.

"No, my dear brother," said Rosa, "you have done more than enough."

"Are you sure?" he pressed.

"Well, there is one thing," said Rosa, "promise that whatever happens, you will be there for Leila."

He paused. "Of course, I will, Rosa. That goes without saying."

"Good," said Rosa, "because I don't think she knows what she's up against and she will need you – more than I ever did."

Leila wondered with alarm and shame, if her aunt had just subtly told Joseph about her secret; in that way that brothers and sisters communicate without using all the words. She was ashamed of what Joseph would think, but she couldn't worry about that tonight. She had to be alert for whatever the Morgans threw at her.

Her journey to sleep was disrupted by a shock. It started in her mind and found its way to her gut. She recalled the outcome of the Triangle Shirtwaist Factory fire: the bosses got off – scot-free.

She hoped this time would be different.

# 24.

## *April 5, 1930*

Leila awoke before dawn to see Aunt Rosa sitting at the fire escape window. She was overlooking the street below and biting her nails. Leila stepped to the window and examined the scene. There were at least a dozen reporters camped out on the stoop, spilling over onto Orchard Street. They were drinking coffee and jotting in their notepads. She recognized one man. He wore a crumpled brown-plaid derby hat. He was the reporter that had been asking the most questions the night of Roderick's death. A chill traversed her body – this time, he was here for her story, and there were no policemen or guards around to keep him away from her.

The circus had begun.

Suddenly, the idea of being in the papers was the last thing in the world she wanted. She watched the group of reporters continue to grow, but had no wish to speak to them. The district attorney had warned her to keep her thoughts to herself, so as not to give them anything that could be twisted against her. As if she would be the one on trial.

She was a bundle of nerves. She selected a simple white blouse and black skirt. She brushed her hair vigorously and thought about seeing Jack Morgan again, this time, with the entire Morgan name on trial. It is because of him, not me, she reminded herself, trying to steady her trembling hands.

When the time came to leave the tenement, she walked quietly out the back entrance. She strolled through the small courtyard that had once contained a single water pump and four outhouses for use by the entire building; now, women gathered there to gossip and hang laundry. There she met Joseph, Moishe, Hannah, and Rivkah, and together they set off to the courthouse on Centre Street.

The majestic steps in front of the New York County Court building teemed with citizens, reporters, photographers, and paperboys when Leila arrived. The sharp beam of a camera light blinded her as she walked up the stone stairs to the grand entrance. It took a moment for her to register these people were here as much for her as for the trial itself.

"Hey Leila, Leila Kahn – show us those pearly whites for the *Daily News!*" called a scruffy man wearing a gray jacket and sporting a polka-dot bowtie.

"Leila, over here – let's get a swell shot for *Time Magazine!*" shouted another young man, kneeling before her on one knee as he angled his camera.

She bobbed through the gauntlet of reporters. She tucked her chin to her chest and held her new satchel over her protruding belly. It was one thing for these journalists to twist anything she might say to them against her, as Borteli warned; it would be a million times worse to plaster a picture of her six-month-pregnant stomach over the front pages. She stuck close behind her Uncle Joseph using his tall frame as a shield.

The courthouse at 60 Centre Street had been completed four years earlier after a decade of planning and construction. It was the cornerstone of the legal system of New York, and this would be the first trial against a prominent – perhaps the most prominent – Wall Street banker. She caught her breath, grateful to be flanked by Joseph and Moishe. She ascended the limestone steps toward the front doors. Pausing to glance up at the massive 24-story building before her, its ten enormous pillars as imposing as the ones at the New York Stock Exchange, a succession of flashbulbs captured her gaze. The following week, the *Life Magazine* headline of her profiled face would read:

*"Moments of Wonder: Leila Kahn embarking on her fight against the bankers."*

It would picture her head tilted backward and mouth opened in awe.

She stepped into the lobby. White marble floors and wood-paneled walls marked the interior. Assistant District Attorney Anthony Borteli stood waiting, briefcase in hand. He was the picture of sharp-suited earnest, sporting a lets-get-down-to-business look.

"Good morning, Leila," he said, with a short grin. "How are you feeling?"

"Nervous," she replied. She wrapped an arm beneath her belly, then quickly placed it by her side.

"Perfectly normal," he said. "Try to relax, not too much will happen today. The judge will state the charges and we will go from there, okay?"

She nodded. "Okay."

At that moment, she heard a thunderous roar from outside. She was glad she was inside, away from the fray, but she could hear shouts of "Hang the bankers!" and "Hang Jack Morgan," even from behind the solid oak doors of the courthouse.

Jack Morgan and his entourage were marching up the courthouse steps. They wore their finest suits and hats. Jack entered the building with an air of calm Leila wished she felt. His head was held high. The men surrounding him stood erect and silent.

"Defense lawyers," Borteli whispered in her ear. "Those guys in the black designer suits will be representing Jack and the bank."

"There are – seven of them," counted Leila.

"Yes, well, money will buy you that sort of thing."

Jack and his team sauntered past her like they were late to a trivial meeting they had to endure before heading to a more important one. Thomas Lamont walked with a pronounced limp, a cast on his arm and leg, and a bruised eye beneath his puffy brows. None of them gave her so much as a passing glance, except for Jack. He looked at her with a hate that made her want to sink through the cement floors. She felt her uncle squeeze one hand, and Moishe squeeze the other.

She released her hands from their grips and said to Borteli, "I'm ready."

"This way," he said. He ushered her to the elevators. They ascended to the main courtroom on the fifth floor. She was thankful they did not share the elevator with Jack.

"The other plaintiffs should be meeting us on the fifth floor," Borteli said, noticing her eyes search the corridors of the lobby.

The elevator opened to a stark hallway of pristine silver-specked marble, and solid oak, high-backed benches. Large bay windows framed both ends of the hallway. Borteli walked with purpose directly to a set of austere carved doors. He held them open for Leila and her family and friends.

It was all done to maximize the theatrical. Borteli wanted their side of the courtroom stacked full of plaintiffs and supporters. The more the merrier to influence the jury. Leila would be seated in the front row, along with Joseph, Hannah, Moishe, Rivkah and the twins. She would face the judge from the right side of the courtroom benches, just behind a wooden divider that separated the onlookers from the two lawyers' tables. The judge's box was raised higher than the witness box toward its left. On the left side of the courtroom, Leila spotted a group of suited men marching in.

Jack's team had also decided to stack its side.

Walter entered with them. He sneered at her. He mouthed the word "Bitch."

Leila reflected back on the night of her attack. She hadn't seen the men's faces. Was one of them Walter? Was he a slimy spy on Jack's payroll or more violent? That's why he was always showing up and watching things at the Morning Spot. His presence strengthened her resolve to put Jack in his place. *I'll teach you to scare me.* But she would probably never know for sure who had attacked her the night Bryan was murdered.

*Stay focused.*

Her pulse quickened when she spotted Jack's profile in the front row. Althea was beside him. *She wasn't in England.* Rodney was seated on her lap, directing a baby smile at his great-uncle's legal team. She was dismayed to see that Collins sat beside her. *What is he doing there?* Althea turned her head around. The two women exchanged stares. Althea's expressionless face sent shivers up Leila's spine. And yet Leila felt a pang of remorse. She had never wanted to hurt Althea or drag her into this. At the same time, it seemed the inevitable result of so much set in motion, of having shared the same man.

"Don't look at her," whispered Borteli. He signaled for her to be seated. "Don't look at any of them. The jury shouldn't be able to read your thoughts."

"Will she be – speaking?" Leila asked.

"She's on the list for the defense, yes," he answered, "but not today. And only if they decide to mount a defense. They are not obligated to."

"I see," said Leila, unnerved by the thought of seeing Althea more than once.

"I'm going to be up there," said Borteli, pointing to the prosecutor's table, where his legal assistant was already seated amidst a pile of papers. "I will call you after building our case with some of the other plaintiffs. It may be a few days. It's important you remain composed. Juries watch everything, even when you think they aren't," he said.

"Alright," she agreed.

A few moments later, a dark-hair middle-aged man with a slight hunch entered from a door behind the judge's box.

"All rise for His Honor, Wilfred Grayson," the bailiff pronounced.

Everyone in the courtroom sprang up.

The judge entered with the manner of a great emperor about to address his kingdom of subjects. He wore a robe of black silk that billowed as he quietly took his seat within the box. He was a slender man with a well-kept mustache that twisted slightly at the ends. His blue-gray eyes roamed the gathering behind their gold spectacles. They rested briefly on Jack Morgan, with what appeared to be a look of cordial recognition.

Judge Grayson lifted his gavel with his right hand and said, "You may be seated." He lowered it with a sharp bang on a cherry wood block.

The trial clerk cleared his throat and announced, "The trial of the United States vs. John Pierpont Morgan, Jr., Thomas Lamont, and the Morgan bank will commence."

A muffled chatter spread across the room. Against her instructions, Leila leaned forward to cast a glance on Jack. His face was as implacable as it had been the night she bumped into him in Roderick's library. It was as if he was accustomed to stepping into courtrooms every day. He appeared bored.

The judge faced the defense table of lawyers and bankers and said, "Misters Morgan and Lamont, you stand accused of fraud in the matter of the Allegheny Railroad Trust, conspiracy to commit fraud regarding the state of the bank's financial health, and conspiracy to commit grand larceny. How do you plead?"

"Not guilty, your Honor," stated Jack.

"Not guilty, your Honor," echoed Thomas.

"So noted," said the judge. "The prosecution and defense will present their opening arguments. Mr. Borteli, you may begin."

As much as she tried to listen to the assistant district attorney's argument, Leila was lost in thought. She stared at the American flag hanging from behind the judge's pulpit, a reminder of the dream that attracted and mocked so many. This room wasn't about that promise – it was supposed to be about justice no matter who you were. Yet she couldn't escape the feeling that this room felt like power. It had the polished wood smell of the Morgan's apartment. The entrance resembled that of the Morgan bank. The judge sat as if on a throne. How could it represent "the people"? She then had a more troubling recollection. She had seen Judge Grayson before – at Roderick's wake.

"And to conclude, your Honor," said Borteli, "we will prove, beyond a reasonable doubt, that Jack Morgan and Thomas Lamont did knowingly and willingly conspire to defraud the American people."

Borteli returned to his table.

Loud murmurs of support emanated from Leila's side of the room.

"Order, order in the court. One more outbreak and I will clear the room," proclaimed Grayson, striking his gavel.

"Mr. Anderson, you may proceed," he said to the lead counsel for Jack's defense.

"Thank you, your Honor," Anderson said, with a dulcet tone. "Members of the jury, I will be brief. We are here today to defend the reputation of two great Americans, Jack Morgan and Thomas Lamont, from the ridiculous accusations of a collection of frustrated investors and a disgruntled, unstable former employee of Roderick and Althea Morgan. During the course of this trial, we will prove that these accusations are unfounded, and restore to good graces the reputation of these fine men. Thank you."

He nodded to the judge, to Borteli, and to the jury, before taking his seat.

The only words that Leila heard were "disgruntled and unstable employee." They stung like a hornets' nest. She was not their employee. Her love affair with Roderick began before he hired her to watch Rodney. It began when her heart would flutter as he entered the diner, when his eyes warmed at the sight of hers. Through all of his sadness and frustration, she coaxed from him his better self. *Didn't she?* He had written that in his letter to her. *So what was she?* A little leg pushed against her insides. *Let them say what they want.* It didn't matter anyway. She was carrying his child. Just like Althea had.

Borteli began his case just as he said he would. He called the first investor that lost money in the Allegheny deal, a Mr. Gerald Apfel.

"Were you led to believe this was a solid investment?" asked Borteli.

"Yes," said Apfel, resolutely.

"Once you purchased your shares in the Allegheny trust, did their value plummet substantially and immediately?"

"Yes."

"Thank you. And would you have invested in the Allegheny deal if you knew that its true value was being misrepresented?"

"Objection," proclaimed Anderson, remaining in his chair. "Leading the witness."

"Your Honor," said Borteli, "I am trying to illustrate a pattern of being – mislead."

"Your Honor," Anderson retorted, "we have not even determined that the value of these deals was misrepresented. I move to strike the question."

"Objection, sustained," declared the judge. He turned to the jury, "You may disregard that last question."

"But, your Honor…" said Borteli. He looked helplessly at the judge's bench.

"Please rephrase your question, Mr. Borteli."

"If the value of the Allegheny deal had turned out to be lower than what you paid for it, like an old horse someone told you was a foal, would you still have invested in it?"

"Objection," said Anderson.

"Overruled," said the judge, "you may answer the question."

Again the answer was yes.

Borteli repeated this three-question strategy with twenty different witnesses, each of whom provided the exact same response. After each one, Judge Grayson asked Mr. Anderson if he wanted to ask any subsequent question for his cross-examination. In each case, Anderson responded serenely, "Not at this time. Thank you, your Honor."

This pattern continued for two days of testimony. The monotony frustrated the media with very little new information to go on, other than surmising that "the Morgan camp seems to be saving a trick up its sleeve," as the *Daily News* put it.

The agony of waiting kept Leila and her supporters awake each night. Leila wondered what the punishment would be for not showing up to trial. What if she just disappeared before everyone could discover her secrets? She decided to ask Borteli.

"They'd find you and put you in jail," he replied.

He looked her in the eye and said, "That is also the penalty for perjury."

"Perjury?" she asked.

"Lying under oath."

Hannah was the last of Borteli's claimants to testify. She was dressed in black to remind people of her widow's status. She walked to the witness box and sat down. She folded her hands on her lap, another trick Borteli suggested, to restrain her shaky nerves.

"Raise your right hand," said the clerk, "and put your left one on this bible. Do you swear to tell the truth, the whole truth, and nothing but the truth, so help you God?"

"I do," she said quietly.

Hannah proceeded to answer, "yes" to all three of Borteli's questions.

Then, Borteli added some new ones.

"How much of your money did your husband invest in the Allegheny deal?"

"All he had," she whispered, lowering her head, "and more."

"More? How so?" prompted Borteli.

"He borrowed – ten times what we had – against his business and our home, and invested that too," she explained.

"Madam, I apologize for this intrusion into your sorrow, but when did your husband pass away?"

"He had a heart attack the night of the big crash," she replied, wiping away a tear.

Leila's side of the courtroom erupted with sympathetic cries. Her heart ached anew for Hannah's loss that night. And her own.

"Order!" proclaimed the judge.

"Do you think," started Borteli, "that the heart attack was brought on by his shock at the manner in which his shares in the Alleghany trust plummeted?"

"Objection. Calls for speculation," Anderson announced. "She's not a doctor."

"Let me rephrase," said Borteli. "Was your husband healthy before that night?"

"Objection," repeated Anderson.

The judge looked down at Borteli with scrunched eyebrows.

"Borteli, you will rephrase the question. Don't push this court."

"I'm sorry your Honor, members of the jury," said Borteli, nodding towards the judge's box and then the jury box. He marched up to the witness box. "Madam, when Morris passed, who received ownership of the Allegheny shares he held?"

"I did, sir," she replied.

Leila felt a rush of satisfaction as the defense lawyers squirmed and checked their notepads.

"Did you also receive all records regarding those shares?"

"Yes, sir."

"Then would you please tell the court, Madam, what you noticed when you examined those documents?"

"That he paid for a thousand shares with his money – and the money he borrowed."

"And how many shares did your last statement say you own?"

"Four hundred," she answered.

Leila watched the jury lean forward. This was a kind of fraud even she didn't know about. Was Roderick involved in that too? He never mentioned it. The Morgan bank had lied about how many shares they would be giving out to investors after taking their money, before the value of the trust even dropped.

*Bravo Borteli.*

"I see," said Borteli, "and did you ever sell any of those shares?"

"No," she said. She added, "No one would have bought them."

Leila's side of the room burst into chuckles.

"Order!" yelled the judge.

"Nothing further for this witness," said Borteli. He cast a subtle wink at Leila.

"Mr. Anderson? Cross?" prompted the judge.

"Thank you, your Honor," said Mr. Anderson. He strode toward the jury box, capturing the gaze of each juror slowly. He then turned to Hannah.

"I'm very sorry for your loss, Madam," he said politely.

She nodded wordlessly.

"Was your husband, a betting man?" he asked.

She looked puzzled. "What do you mean?"

"Let me rephrase: did your husband invest in other trusts, besides those of my client's bank?"

She shook her head, "I don't think so."

"You don't think so," he said with a sneer. "Yes or no, Madam."

"No, I don't think he did."

Anderson marched forward. He handed her a stack of papers.

"Madam, can you please read the top line of each of these documents."

Joseph's eyes fell into his lap. He sucked in his breath.

Hannah's eyes began to water. "I – I can't."

"You can't – what – Madam?" Anderson continued, "Read?"

"Objection! Badgering!" shouted Borteli.

"Objection sustained. Mr. Anderson, you may read this information for the court," said Judge Grayson, with what Leila considered his first act of human kindness.

Anderson read through a litany of trusts in which Morris invested and lost money, making a grand show of leafing through the parchment pages after each one.

When he was done, he asked Hannah, "Now, let me repeat the question. Do you think your husband was a betting man?"

Borteli listened helplessly as she said in a tiny voice, "Yes, maybe he was."

"No further questions, your Honor," said Anderson.

"Re-direct?" the judge asked Borteli.

"Just one question, your Honor. Madam, referring back to just the Alleghany deal, what did your banker tell you when you tried to sell the remaining shares you had in this trust?"

"He said, they're not worth the paper they are printed on," she replied.

"Thank you, Madam. No further questions."

The judge checked his pocket watch and the roman-numeral octagonal clock hanging above the wood paneled wall behind the witness box.

"I am calling an adjournment to today's proceedings. We will meet here again tomorrow morning at precisely ten o'clock in the morning. Court is dismissed." He punctuated his statement with another bang of his gavel, rose, and left the room as everyone stood. As soon as the door closed behind him, mayhem returned to the courtroom.

Leila and her team exited the building to a deluge of reporters and, it seemed, every photographer in the city. To Leila's relief, they were looking for Hannah.

"Hannah! Did the Morgan bank kill your husband?" called the same reporter that Leila had recognized from her window and from the night of Roderick's death. She heard someone say that his name was Tyler Rand. He worked for the *Tribune.*

"Hannah! Hannah! Hannah!" the blaze of voices swarmed around her. Joseph and Moishe nearly beat them off. They escorted Hannah and Leila to the Ford that Borteli had waiting for them on Worth Street. Once they assembled, Leila asked the question that had plagued her since the trail began.

"Mr. Borteli, why didn't the defense lawyers ask any questions of all the other witnesses who had bought into the Allegheny deal? Why just Hannah?"

"Hannah threw them for a loop, that's why," he replied. "They had to be more careful with her because of Morris's death."

"But you were prepared," she said with hope.

"I do my job," he said. "I use whatever evidence is available to make my case. You know something Leila, if it was up to me, I'd hang the bastard by his toenails."

"Will you be prepared when I testify?" asked Leila.

His face sagged with worry, "You will be harder, Leila."

"Because of the double books? But we have the documents that Jack signed, and the shares that Morris paid for but never received – surely that will be enough?"

"The judge denied our request to search for those books, Leila," he reminded her. "All we have is what I've managed to accumulate for the market prices of the deals your notes pointed me to – that's not really evidence of fakery. I will of course, use the two different signed Allegheny contracts to shed doubt as to the integrity of Morgan's deals, but only if I can get them past the judge, who happens to be a friend of Jack's."

"I knew I'd seen him before. At Roderick's wake," declared Leila. "Is that legal?"

"That's our America," replied Borteli, "but something else worries me."

"What is it?" asked Joseph.

"They will ask Leila how she got this information. And then I'm afraid," said Borteli, with an anguished furrow streaking across his forehead, "they will crucify her."

# 25.

# *April 8, 1930*

Borteli's words lingered like rotting meat as Leila took the stand the next morning. Borteli had instructed her to take slow, deep breaths when she wasn't speaking, and before she answered each question, to keep her voice calm. He kept his questions short and simple. She found herself relaxing. She reminded herself that no matter what happened, this would come to an end soon.

"Miss Kahn, would you please tell the court what these two documents are about?" he directed her. "Your Honor, I am referring to Exhibit B1."

"Yes," she said. "Both are contracts relating to a deal for the Allegheny Rail and Trust company."

"Thank you. And whose signature is on both of them?"

"Jack Morgan's," she replied.

"Objection! She's not a handwriting expert," said Anderson.

"Your Honor," said Borteli, "Mr. Anderson knows full well that we both had these documents analyzed by experts. They are indeed both signed by Jack Morgan. I refer you to Exhibits B2 and B3, their conclusions. May I proceed?"

The judge nodded. Borteli prompted Leila through the explanation of what each document represented, and how the values went into fake and real books.

"Objection!" cried Anderson. "There is no evidence of any faked books."

"Yes, there is," Leila told him.

"Your Honor, may I continue with my witness?" Borteli jumped in.

"You may proceed."

"How do you have this knowledge of fake books, Miss Kahn?"

"Objection!" exclaimed Anderson.

"Alleged faked books," Borteli corrected himself.

"Because he told me about them."

"Who told you?" prompted Borteli.

"Roderick Morgan." Her eyes traveled to Althea, who turned away.

"When did he tell you this?"

"Just before he was killed."

"Objection! There is no evidence he was killed!" roared Anderson.

"You will disregard that last statement," the judge instructed the jury.

"About when did he tell you this?" asked Borteli.

"At the end of October, last year," she said.

"Objection," Anderson said, returning to his steely calm manner. "No one has any knowledge of any such conversation taking place, beyond what this – witness – alleges."

"Objection overruled. You may continue Mr. Borteli," said the judge.

"Did you ever see these books yourself, Miss Kahn?"

She took two deep breaths. "Yes, sir."

The jury and the rest of the room exuded a collective murmur.

"Where?" he asked.

"In Roderick's home," she said.

"When?"

"After his death. I saw them with Althea, his wife," she said.

She looked up to the domed ceiling. She prayed to Bryan O'Malley to forgive her for lying to him about how she first came to know about those two books.

"Objection!" Anderson shot to his feet. "Your Honor, I have an affidavit here, signed by Althea Morgan, stating that she has no idea about any dual sets of books; that if her husband had them, she was completely unaware."

"She's lying!" exclaimed Leila, speaking out of turn.

"You bitch!" yelled Althea, leaping to her feet.

"Hey! Watch it!" Moishe stood up and shouted at her.

"Order in the court!" cried the judge. "Mr. Borteli, control your witness."

Borteli had Leila explain the night at the Morgan's with Althea. She stopped short of saying that Althea had given those books to Jack. She wanted to protect Rodney from any future shame about his mother's actions. She had already said too much.

Her reluctance didn't matter.

As soon as Borteli was done, Anderson came at her with full force.

"Why don't you admit it, Miss Kahn, you are lying about these alleged books, you are lying about Roderick's death, and you are lying about the Allegheny deal. You want to muddy the good Morgan name because you are a poor, ungrateful, servant."

"Objection!" cried Borteli.

"Employee."

"Objection!"

"Miss Kahn, exactly what was the nature of your relationship to Roderick Morgan?"

"Objection – relevance!" proclaimed Borteli.

"Goes to the motive for her charges against my client, your Honor," said Borteli.

Leila felt the crush of all eyes on her. Everyone waited for her to share her secret. Anderson approached the rim of the witness box. She could see the hairs in his nose.

"Objection. Your Honor, Roderick Morgan is not on trial here," said Borteli.

The two lawyers faced each other as if about to draw pistols and dual to the death.

The judge peered at Jack. Leila followed his gaze to see Jack blink back.

"Objection sustained. Please keep your questions to the evidence at hand."

Leila exhaled a quiet sigh of relief. *He doesn't want any focus on Roderick.*

"No further questions for this – witness," said Anderson.

Leila could barely hold back her tears. She had begged Borteli not to use the diary unless he had to. She shot him a pleading glance. *Don't make me do this.*

He nodded his head once.

"Re-direct?" asked the judge.

"Thank you, your Honor." Borteli sprang to his feet again.

"Miss Kahn, is there any other information you have that would indicate the existence of these 'alleged' fake books?"

"Yes," she said, sucking in her stomach.

"And what would that be?" he asked.

"Roderick's diary," she answered, quietly.

The courtroom became a field of whispers. She closed her eyes. There would be nowhere to hide after this. She would not be the city's heroine.

"Your Honor, I have in my hand a diary in the name of one Roderick Morgan, which I present as Exhibit D," said Borteli.

"Objection! I was not made aware of this diary," said Anderson.

"Approach the bench," said Judge Grayson.

The judge examined the diary. He returned it to Borteli. "You may use this as evidence." Anderson's face reddened as he searched the judge for a different response. Leila could have sworn the judge nodded ever so slightly, as if he was sorry.

"Where did you get this diary?" asked Borteli.

"From the Morgan's home," she said.

"Did you steal it?" he asked.

"No," she replied. She saw Collins watching her from his seat. "I mean – I was going to return it, when I realized that it contained information about these – deals. So I took it home and copied the dates that were noted as fake."

"Noted by whom?"

"Roderick Morgan, sir."

The next day, Anderson got another chance at questions due to the new evidence. He approached the witness box, paused for a long moment to stroke his beard, and asked:

"Miss Kahn, were you having an affair with Roderick Morgan?"

"Objection! Relevance!" shouted Borteli.

"Calls to motive – to seduce and destroy Roderick Morgan and otherwise hold a dangerous grudge against this fine family, culminating in this spectacle," explained Anderson. He could barely contain a smug grin.

"Objection!" repeated Borteli.

"Overruled. Please answer the question," said the judge.

She couldn't open her mouth. She thought she had evaded detection earlier.

"It's a simple question," said Anderson. "Yes or no, Miss Kahn. Here, let me refresh your memory." He turned to the page from October 28th and said with a flourish, "'Was intimate with L.' Miss Kahn, would that 'L' stand for Leila?"

Every nerve in her body turned to cement. She couldn't respond.

"Please answer the question," said the judge. "You are under oath."

*From responsibility comes possibility. I'm so sorry Mama.*

"Yes," she lowered her eyes, "I was."

The audience emitted a collective gasp, followed by a gush of whispers, before the judge could restore order. Rodney chose that moment to burst into tears. Althea sat stone-faced. Leila glanced at the faces of her family and friends, trying to gauge their reaction. Reporters were furiously scribbling notes. Leila felt palpable shame overtake her. She sought the reaction of Joseph. He nodded his support. She was glad that Rachel had not attended today's proceedings, did not know who her older sister really was.

"Miss Kahn, you claim that Roderick didn't kill himself, that somehow – my client was involved in his death, is that correct?"

"Yes, sir," she replied.

"And you make this claim because of a few diary entries, from a man you were carrying on an illicit affair with, and who was so disturbed as to take his own life?"

"No!"

"You mean there was no diary entry that said, 'Jack threatened to kill me'?"

"Yes, I mean, no – not specifically," she eyed the jury box. Did they know how much Anderson was twisting her thoughts?

"Please," she begged the judge, "let me explain."

Judge Grayson nodded. "You may explain what you saw in that diary that lead you to believe that Roderick feared for his life."

"Thank you, your Honor," she whispered. She turned to the jury and took a deep breath. "There was an entry – it said – 'J will stop at nothing.' The 'J' referred to Jack."

"How do you know that, Miss Kahn?" asked Anderson.

"All the entries that had to do with the bank also referred to 'J.' He ran the bank."

"Miss Kahn, isn't it possible that your affair with Roderick Morgan clouded your judgment about his actions? About your interpretation of his dairy?"

"Objection! Calls for self-examination," exclaimed Borteli.

"Let me rephrase. Isn't it possible that your feelings for Roderick Morgan caused you to ignore the man he truly was? A man capable of keeping double books at his bank, and a double life and affair from his loving wife? A man that couldn't take any more of his own deceitful ways and decided to end it all?"

"Objection," said Borteli.

"Sustained," said the judge.

"Why would my client have had anything to do with taking Roderick's life, when – by everything we have learned here – Roderick was a man destined to commit suicide?"

Leila didn't know why Borteli hadn't brought up the photographs yet, but she decided that now was as good a time as any.

"Because he was shot before he was pushed out of the window."

Anderson's nose twitched. He inspected the jury, a collection of open-mouthed citizens, and then turned back to her.

"And how do you know this?" he asked.

"Because of the photographs," she replied.

He marched up to the witness box with a folder, extracted its contents, and placed a set of photos in front of her. "Are you referring to these photos that are Exhibit C?"

"Yes, sir," she answered confidently.

"You mean, this photograph that shows a tiny discoloration, a smudge, by Roderick's head?" he asked. He held it up for the jury to see, but did not hand it to them.

"Objection!" cried Borteli.

"Sustained," said the judge.

"Your Honor, please let the record show that we have had three inspectors proclaim this smudge nothing more than a photographic error," said Anderson.

"And we have three that say it could have been a bullet hole," Borteli retorted.

"*Could have been?*" sneered Anderson.

"Mr. Anderson, please direct your questions at the witness," said Judge Grayson.

"Miss Kahn, where did you get those photographs?" asked Anderson.

Leila saw Borteli's eyes close. "Someone dropped them off at Mr. Borteli's office."

"Who, Miss Kahn? Who dropped them off?"

She swallowed and shook her head in defeat, "I don't know."

"No further questions," said Anderson.

He sauntered to his seat at the defense lawyers' table, but just before taking it, he pivoted toward the judge. "Actually, sir, if I may – just one more question?"

"Proceed," instructed Judge Grayson.

"Exactly whose baby is it you are carrying?"

"Objection! Your Honor!" yelled Borteli, as he leapt to his feet.

The courtroom erupted into a cacophony of voices from both sides of the aisle. The judge attempted to restore order to no avail. Finally he declared a recess for the day, and instructed everyone to return the following morning at 9 o'clock.

The rest of the afternoon passed by in a blur. Leila felt like she had been beaten from limb to limb. Every time she thought about his characterization of her, it sent shivers through her body. As they left the courtroom, she couldn't look at, let alone speak to, her family and friends, nor Borteli. She was surprised that Joseph and Moishe positioned themselves protectively at her sides as they had each morning and evening.

Only tonight they did so in silence.

As they left the Centre Street building, reporters bombarded her with a torrent of questions about Roderick, the diary, and her baby. Leila did her best to ignore them, but the ache of her humility soaked her to the core. She couldn't face another barrage of Anderson's questions.

Only the supportive arms of her uncle and Moishe kept her from collapsing on the street. They led her to a waiting car surrounded by a second lot of reporters.

The following morning, it took every ounce of resolve for Leila to leave her tenement. When she arrived at the courthouse, all talk had turned from Jack Morgan to vicious speculation about the baby she was carrying.

She slinked up the front steps of the courthouse building, hunched over and protecting her unborn child, mortified by prospects of what the day would bring. She had wanted this trial to be over before anyone knew – before anyone could think ill – of this innocent life inside her. All her hoping was for naught.

The walk from her seat to the witness box felt impossibly long. She averted her eyes from the jurors, despite Borteli's instruction to always look at them and carry her head high. She had brought shame to everyone she knew, to all the supporters who had counted on her. There was nothing she could do about it.

Anderson wasted no time.

"Miss Kahn, whose baby are you carrying?"

"Objection! Relevance!" shouted Borteli.

"I'm merely trying to establish the depravity of this woman, to show a pattern of lying and covering up the truth," Anderson told the judge.

"You may proceed," said Judge Grayson, "but with caution; and bring it back to the charges at hand."

"Thank you, your Honor," said Anderson. "Miss Kahn, are you currently – with child? I remind you that you are under oath."

"Yes," she said, barely audible.

"Pardon me?"

"Yes," she said, more clearly this time.

"I see, and how long have you been keeping this secret?"

"Objection! That has no relevance whatsoever to this case," said Borteli.

"Mr. Anderson," the judge said sternly.

"Miss Kahn, are you in fact carrying the child of Roderick Morgan?"

Leila looked over at Althea. She was holding Rodney, but otherwise registered no emotional reaction. Leila looked to Borteli for any kind of aid. It did not come.

"Miss Kahn, please answer the question – whose baby are you carrying?"

"Objection!" yelled Borteli, rushing toward Anderson like he was going to punch him. "Your Honor!"

"I am trying to show the jury that this – woman – stooped to conniving her way into Roderick's life. She seduced him as part of a larger scheme to bring harm to the Morgan family. The only foil in her plan was that Roderick, the poor man, wasn't mentally stable enough to withstand her poisonous ways, and in a fit of intense anguish, was driven to take his own life."

"Objection!" called Borteli again, "Your Honor, that is ridiculous!"

"Your Honor," said Anderson, "please direct the witness to answer my question."

"Miss Kahn," said the judge, "I'm inclined to give Anderson some latitude here. Would you please tell the court – whose child are you carrying?"

*It was over.* She had wanted more than anything to protect this child from the harm that the Morgans could cause, and now, even before it was born, it was embroiled in a scandal. The courtroom waited in total silence. She couldn't move her mouth.

"I repeat," said the judge, "whose child are you carrying?"

Everyone in the courtroom held their breath awaiting the answer – from her friends, to the reporters, to the Morgan bankers. There was nowhere to hide, nothing she could do. In her witness box, before this full courtroom, she had never felt so isolated. She considered lying under oath, betraying Roderick's love. Would that be best for her child? She had already given him more anguish than any baby deserved before he was even born. He needed a name. How could it be Morgan?

"Miss Kahn?" she heard the judge's voice echoing in her ear. "Miss Kahn?"

She steered her gaze back to him. He was asking her a question. She had to make a decision. She had to protect her son. She now knew why Roderick had lied about the books as long as he did, because sometimes a lie is better than facing the truth, and sometimes that lie protects people you love.

She looked at Jack, as expressionless as always. She had come so far.

"Miss Kahn. Who is the father of your child?" asked the judge. "I remind you, that you are under oath."

"Roderick," she whispered. *God help me.* "Morgan."

"No further questions," said Anderson, throwing up his hands.

Leila realized at that moment, that all her thoughts of being a heroine, of doing the right thing, of exposing Jack, of carrying on some fight that she believed Roderick had begun, were grand delusions. She had failed. She had failed everyone.

"Re-direct, please," said Borteli.

Leila waited anxiously for anything Borteli could ask to salvage the situation. She was glad to see him approach the witness box. She exhaled a soft sigh.

"Miss Kahn, please tell the members of the jury why they should believe you," asked Borteli, eyeing the jury and her simultaneously.

"Pardon?" she was sure that she hadn't heard him right.

"Why should we believe you – an immigrant who saw a ticket out of her poverty by seducing Roderick Morgan, by stealing him from his wife and son? Why should anyone believe anything you say?" Borteli's voice grew gruffer with each insult.

The jury members sat at the edges of their seats, their mouths open. Leila's chest tightened. What the hell was he doing? Why was Borteli turning on her like this? He was supposed to be on her side.

"Maybe Mr. Anderson is right," said Borteli. "Maybe you are no better than a common prostitute trying to take what doesn't belong to her. You couldn't afford Althea's life, so you decided to steal her husband. Isn't that it?"

"No!" said Leila. She was mortified. Borteli's accusations had come out of nowhere. She crossed her arms over her chest to protect herself from his words. This line of questioning was like nothing they had practiced all those days in his office.

"You got into his head like a poison and turned him against his beloved wife."

"No – that wasn't it." She thought she could die from the shame eating at her insides. *Why is he doing this to me?*

"You killed Roderick, didn't you Leila – as sure as I'm standing before this court – as sure as if you'd pushed him out the Morgan window yourself. You – killed – him!"

"No! Why are you...?" Her eyes darted around the stunned room, finding the intent faces of the jurors, of Anderson. She felt like she was being choked.

*Was Borteli working for Jack?* This couldn't be happening.

"No?" said Borteli, his voice rising. "No? Why? Because you loved him? What would someone like you," he said, "know about the love between a man and his wife?"

"Stop!" yelled Joseph, leaping to his feet. He leaned across the divider between the audience and inner court. "Stop it! You bastard! Leave her alone."

"Order in the court!" declared the judge loudly. "Mr. Borteli, is there a point you are trying to make? This is your witness, remember."

*Yes,* thought Leila. *Yes, thank you, your Honor.*

"My point," he said in an measured tone, "is that this woman isn't fit to shine the shoes of that man" – he gestured to Jack – "or that woman," – he gestured to Althea, who had returned to the courtroom without Rodney. "My only remaining question is: Why didn't she just take the money?"

"Do you have a question for your witness?" asked the judge.

"Maybe you can tell me, and the jury, Miss Kahn," said Borteli, his hands on his hips, "whether you're carrying Roderick's baby or not. But frankly who the hell cares whose baby you are carrying? Why didn't you just take all of this – evidence – to Jack Morgan? You would have received a pretty penny in return for your silence, I'm sure." He hurled this new accusation at her in one breath.

Leila shook her head. She couldn't help but glance at Althea, who again, looked immediately away. She peered helplessly at the judge for assistance, but none came.

"Objection!" shouted Anderson, though he had no grounds. He was not her lawyer. Her lawyer was destroying every ounce of dignity she had left.

"Borteli, you are on a thin rope," said Judge Grayson.

"I'll rephrase. Did it not occur to you, that instead of wasting all of our time with these allegations, you could have just blackmailed Jack Morgan?"

At this point, Hannah was weeping, and Joseph's brow was glistening.

Moishe's head had collapsed into his hands. Rivkah and the twins looked perplexed.

"Answer the question, please. Miss Kahn," said Borteli with a malice Leila would never have considered him capable of producing. "And remember, you are under oath."

Leila didn't need his prompting. *The hell with you, Anthony Borteli. The hell with this court.* She leapt to her feet and blurted out what was in her heart.

"Because it wouldn't have been right! That's why. Because I don't need his stupid money! What I did was wrong, so very wrong, but I did it out of love. Without considering the consequences, yes. And I am so sorry for all the pain I caused you, Althea. That I caused everyone," she gazed at the audience. "But I never meant to hurt anyone – no matter what you think of me, at least know that. What Jack did, though, he did with intent – out of pure greed."

"Nothing further, your Honor. The prosecution rests its case."

Borteli shrugged his shoulders and returned to his seat.

"Mr. Anderson," beckoned the judge. "Any further questions for this witness?"

"Defense rests too." Anderson nodded courteously to Borteli. He nodded back.

"You may step down, Miss Kahn," said Judge Grayson.

Leila peeled herself from the witness box, hanging her head. She returned to her spot beside Joseph. He wrapped his arm around her shaking shoulders.

"Will you be starting the case for the defense tomorrow?" Judge Grayson asked Anderson and the rest of the Morgan team.

"The defense will take advantage of the Fifth Amendment, your Honor, and decline to take the stand. Further, we respectively feel that the prosecution's case is so lacking of merit that the jury will find little substance to consider through deliberation. Thus, the defense rests."

"So noted," said Judge Grayson. "Before I call these proceedings to an end and have the jury convene to discuss its verdict, is there anything either of you wish to say?"

Anderson responded with an even tone, "Yes, we move for a motion to dismiss on the grounds that the prosecution did not present any credible evidence for a jury to decide guilt beyond a reasonable doubt."

The judge appeared to consider Anderson's request.

*No*, thought Leila wildly. *No*. This can't be for nothing. The jury has to have its say, even if – she felt her heart sink – even if they hate me and acquit Jack because of me. They have to have their say. She eyed Borteli. He appeared utterly placid, as if he hadn't even heard Anderson's remarks.

Judge Grayson replied, "Thank you, Mr. Anderson. But, the court will let the jury decide." He turned to the jury, "Kind members of the jury, your work has now begun. Please return to your chambers to deliberate your verdict. Thank you."

"All rise," said the clerk.

Outside on the courthouse steps, Leila couldn't bear being near Borteli. But there was something else she had to know. While she searched for him, Collins ran up to her.

"You were great in there," he said, tipping his hat.

"What are you talking about? Everything went wrong," she cried. "And why were you sitting with – them?"

"Well, they kept badgering me about you, so finally I decided I might as well pretend I'm on their side, in case you ever needed some inside help. Thank you for not giving me away on the diary."

"It was the least I could do," she said. "Without that diary – well, none of this would have even been possible. It's odd, though, that they didn't call Jack to the stand."

"Not really," said Collins. "I heard them talking. They decided to paint you as an unreliable a witness so they wouldn't have to testify. Jack's ego is massive. He doesn't believe a jury would consider anyone as reliable a person as he is. Plus, I don't think he ever anticipated such a – scandal. He just wants it all to go away."

"Well, my own lawyer helped their case," lamented Leila.

She still couldn't understand why Borteli had turned on her. She wanted to ask Joseph about it, but was too embarrassed to broach the topic. It was like Nelson always said, the powerful stick together. She thought Borteli was different, that he was on her side. But it turned out, she was wrong. He was on the side of money, like Althea.

"Yes, that did seem strange," said Collins. "I wanted to jump up and throttle him, and you know, I'm not inclined to outbursts."

She processed this and smiled. "Thank you, Collins – for everything. And good luck to you."

"And you, Miss," he said. He disappeared into the crowd.

She spotted Borteli standing by the far pillar of the courthouse, near Anderson and his team. They were laughing like old friends. *This was all a big show. Everything was a big show. All the shame, all the hope – it was all for nothing.*

She walked towards them, then decided against it.

She felt her baby kick wildly, like he wanted to get out and fight his own battle. No matter what verdict was returned, she needed to get them away from the darkness of these city streets and the depths of their shadows.

She owed him that much.

# 26.

# April 10, 1930

The morning papers were ablaze with proclamations, none of them kind to Leila. *"Lady Leila's Lover – a Dead Man?" "The Kahn Job – What You Don't Know About the Morgan Child" "Immigrant Girl Deceives Her Way to the American Dream" "Go Back to Russia!"*

It was too painful to read the articles beneath them. Only the *Forward* was sympathetic, and the *Tribune*. They both declared the justice system was as corrupt as the banking system. They considered Borteli a discredit to the legal profession. They declared his bullying tactics an effort to throw the trial, and called for his disbarment.

Leila was just tired. She had no interest in attending another day in court, or being there when the verdict was delivered – which according to Borteli could be any day. She had no desire to be judged anymore. She couldn't imagine what her family and friends were really thinking of her.

When Joseph arrived to pick her up for court, Leila asked him to sit down first.

"I wanted to apologize for everything," she said. "I've been a disappointment to the whole family. I never meant to bring shame to—"

"Leila, none of us come into our lives knowing exactly what to do," interrupted Joseph. "We make do with what

God throws at us. There will be time to worry about how you bring up your child, but as far as the courts go – whatever happens, it will be over."

"Exactly," said Rosa. "Moishe is waiting for us outside. Now, let's go."

Leila didn't believe it would ever be over. At the courtroom, she dutifully took her seat for the last time in the audience box. She awaited the jury's decision along with the reporters and supporters. She tried to melt into the hard, unforgiving wood of the court's benches.

Hours went by. Still there was no verdict. At one point, the judge entered, called the jury in, and read a note from the head juror out loud.

"We have failed to reach a verdict yet. We have one member of the jury who remains in opposition to the rest. We need more time."

"You may return to your deliberation," said the judge. "If this remains the case, and you see no change for a decision, I will have no choice but to declare this a mistrial."

Anderson looked pleased with himself, as did everyone on the Morgan team. Althea had not come to court; for that Leila was grateful.

Borteli's face was unreadable.

The room broke for a brief lunch and returned at one o'clock to await the verdict. The clock ticked slowly. Two o'clock eventually came. Then three o'clock. The room felt stifling. The frustration, the anger, the anxiety – all seemed ready to burst at any moment. The tiny being inside of her determined she should move. She exited the courtroom.

She paced the hall, end to end, hoping to quell him, and herself. At four o'clock Borteli came to get her. With no emotion in his voice, he said, "The jury has reached a decision."

She took a deep breath and wordlessly followed him inside.

Once the jury piled back into their seats, Judge Grayson faced the head juror, and asked, "Have you reached a unanimous verdict?"

"We have, your Honor," said the foreman.

He handed a piece of paper to the clerk, who handed it to the judge. Judge Grayson opened it and returned it to the clerk, who gave it back to the foreman.

"In the United States vs. Jack Morgan, Tom Lamont, and the Morgan bank on the charge of conspiracy to commit bank fraud, how do you find?"

"We find the defendants," he said, as the room stopped moving entirely, "not guilty."

Leila and the rest of the audience on her side released a collective sigh of defeat. Rivkah coughed loudly. Leila was almost relieved. This would almost be over.

She knew that there would be no justice for Jack Morgan.

"In the United States vs. Jack Morgan, Tom Lamont, and the Morgan bank on the charge of grand larceny, what say you?" asked the judge.

"We find the defendants," said the foreman, "not guilty."

Leila's stomach caved in as much as the baby would allow. It was truly over. Roderick's death would go down as a suicide. The photo of the bullet at the side of his head would make its way through the tabloids. It would be the subject of idle gossip, but it would not bring any justice.

"And on the charge of conspiracy to commit fraud in the case of the Alleghany Railroad Trust, what say you?"

Leila stopped listening. There didn't seem to be any point. She had entered a fog of despair. It was the smallest charge anyway.

"We find the defendants—"

She sunk her head into her hands. She couldn't even watch anymore.

"Guilty."

The room was stunned silent for a second. Then, it broke into a chorus of applause. Leila couldn't believe her ears. A burst of joy whirled through her body.

"Order! Order!" yelled the judge, madly striking his gavel.

Jack Morgan looked stunned. So did his legal team. So did Borteli. *Serves him right.* Glee curled through her body – an unrestrained, exhausted joy. Joseph's arms wrapped around her, followed by Moishe's.

"You did it! We did it!" Her whole body tingled. She barely noticed the decline in Jack Morgan's face and stance, as Anderson requested that he be held on his own reconnaissance before sentencing. *Sentencing! For Jack Morgan. This was impossible.*

Outside the courthouse steps, the media circus reached its peak. Leila was momentarily blinded by lights and nearly deafened by shouts. She was still reeling from the verdict. The whole scene felt void of reality. *Had it all come down to this?*

How could the media love her one second, vilify her the next, and then love her once more? She spotted Borteli talking to a group of reporters, like a Hollywood actor on the red carpet. As he answered a question, he noticed Leila. He beamed, motioning her over to him. His eyes looked thrilled and proud. She was totally confused.

He brought her towards the cameras, and threw his arms around her. She realized he had positioned their embrace for the reporters. She started to wriggle away from him, but he held her tight.

"I'm sorry, Leila. I'm sorry I had to do that." He whispered in her ear.

She stopped moving. *What could he possibly have to say to her?*

"I knew you wouldn't let me down," he said.

"But I don't understand," she said. "I thought – you were working for Jack."

"So did the jury, or at least, they weren't sure," he said.

He grinned from ear to ear.

"Wait – you – that was an act? You knew they would convict Jack?"

"I wouldn't say, I knew. I hoped of course – but – we really didn't have enough evidence for the larger crimes, so it all came down to those two documents and the Allegheny deal. But then all the diversions – the affair, the baby – made everything you said suspect. It clouded the issues. I didn't want the jury to acquit Morgan because they thought you were a… a—"

"A whore," she finished for him.

"Exactly," he said, proud and a little sheepish. "The moment they perceived you were being attacked by *everyone* – they came to your aid – by looking at the evidence."

"Pretty smart, counselor," she said.

"Well," said Borteli, "it worked to confuse the jury even more, which helped us in the end."

"Their confusion allowed them to be clear," she concluded.

"You could say that," he replied, and smiled.

So did she.

*That's our America.*

# 27.

# *May 1, 1930*

One evening, when the spring showers ceased long enough to reveal a magnificent rainbow arching over the girders of the El, Leila waddled home from grocery shopping to find Rivkah waiting for her on the front stoop.

"Where have you been hiding?" Rivkah said, rising to give her a big hug.

"I needed a break after the trial. Moishe gave me some time off and—"

"Since he did get you into all of this," her friend teased.

Leila shook her head. "I really made a big mess of things," she said.

"Love will do that to you," said Rivkah.

"I suppose," Leila grinned, softly.

"You know, you didn't have to listen to me when I told you to flirt with Roderick," said Rivkah, her eyes twinkling.

"So it is all your fault, then," Leila joked.

"Guilty, your Honor," smiled Rivkah. "Smoke?" She extracted a thin pink cigarette from her purse.

"Thanks," said Leila. She placed the cigarette in her mouth. "Light?"

"Yes, but..." Rivkah stopped mid-sentence to gape at two young men walking by, arguing about prohibition. She took a long toke of nicotine and blew a series of smoke rings at them. The rings danced above the sidewalk, slowly evaporating in the evening air. The fellows tipped their hats at her.

"Hey girls!" they said in unison.

Leila spotted Ira, the butcher's son, walking toward them from across the street. Rivkah turned to wink at him. The girls burst out laughing.

"Hey! What's so funny?" asked Ira, his cheeks turning red.

"Nothing," said Leila. "Rivkah is matchmaking – in her head. As always."

"I am not!" Rivkah retorted with mocked scorn.

"I came to bring your aunt some fresh ground chuck," he said. "Uh, here," he handed Leila a brown paper package. "My father thought she might like it. He's going to be closing shop over here; he can't afford the rent anymore, so he's moving to Queens. He hadn't seen her for awhile and wanted her to have this."

"Thank you, Ira," said Leila. "I'll make sure she knows where it came from."

"Uh, you're welcome," Ira turned on his heels and departed hastily up the block.

"You are incorrigible!" Leila told Rivkah. "I thought you liked Joshua."

"Joshua – seems to have lost interest in women," said Rivkah.

"What?"

"You heard it here first," she laughed.

"I'm thinking of moving away." Leila liked the way those words sounded.

"What? Not you too. What will I do without you? And where would you move?"

"I'm not sure yet. I don't think I can handle Wall Street anymore. I need some peace for my baby, and space to think clearly. I'm giving Moishe my notice tomorrow."

"Wait a minute, not so fast," said Rivkah. "You've been here for the past six years. You fought a huge battle against the biggest banker in the world. Your family is here. I'm here. How could you just – get up and leave?"

Leila paused. She saw the anguish in her friend's eyes. Rivkah couldn't understand the importance of this move. Her life was about holding onto the heritage of her past; shorter skirts and darker eye shadow were just minor distractions along the way. But Leila couldn't stay in her past, as much as she had grown to appreciate the love around her more than she would have imagined possible a year ago. That love that once seemed so confining was the bedrock of all she was, but also of all she would become.

"Rivkah, I love you. And my family. I think I even love the Lower East Side. It took me awhile to realize that. But, it's time for me to move on. I can't explain it – but I must."

Rivkah's lips trembled as she processed Leila's words. Then a smile spread across her face. "Okay, if you must, you must. But, if there's one single, dreamy man out there that likes red-heads, you write and tell me right way. Deal?"

Leila embraced her best friend. This was a deal she could live with.

The next morning, Leila confronted Moishe when he came down to the diner.

"Moishe," she said, "first, I wanted to thank you for all your faith in me, and for being there in the courtroom every day. You are a very kind man. And second, I was thinking of moving on – from the diner. From this area." *From New York City.*

His faced dropped. "I was afraid you might tell me something like that."

"I'm thinking of the baby, that's all. It's too – hard here. Too many memories."

"It's hard everywhere my dear. I know. I'm closing the Houston Street Morning Spot at the end of the month. There's only so many coffees a man can offer on credit," he said, pressing his palm to his forehead. "People are leaving the neighborhood. The tailors are moving to the factories, and the ones staying don't have enough garments to sew. The builders have nothing to build. The city has new health orders I can't afford to pay for."

Leila nodded. "The Houston Street diner was your favorite."

"I know, but times are hard. I can't afford to keep two places open."

"But you will keep the Wall Street Morning Spot opened?" she asked.

"Right now, yes. These bastards are the only ones paying any real money, and even they're not eating as much as they used to."

"They don't stay around as long either." She gestured to the counter, empty except for one man hunched over a ham sandwich. "Last year – they were happier. Now, they chat a little bit and leave, but nothing's like it was." *Nothing will ever be like it was.*

He rested one doughy hand on her upper arm and tugged at his graying beard with the fingers of the other. "I would have to fire Nan if you stayed on," he said, as he watched her polish silverware behind the counter. "I couldn't afford both of you here."

"But, Nan has three children and an unemployed husband," she declared, keeping her voice to a hush. "There must be another way."

He looked at her with a long, sad gaze. "There's only one other way," he said, "and it wouldn't be much better for her, I'm afraid."

"What is it?" she asked.

"I've been thinking about moving out of this city, while it gets back on its feet."

"You're kidding," she said. She watched a strange transformation come over him. That resignation that had pressed into his shoulders seemed replaced by a faint glimpse of hope bubbling from somewhere inside of him, propping them up. She knew that feeling, the weight of the past giving space to the lightness of the future. "But you *are* this city."

He chuckled, softly at first, and then he burst out into deep belly laughter. He pounded his fist on the counter. Nan glanced up from her polishing with a curious look.

"What is it?" asked Leila. "Let me in on the joke!"

"That does it!" he exclaimed, a broad smile lit his face. "Now that I say it out loud, it almost makes sense. I'm packing up! I'm heading west. I'll open a place on Fairfax Avenue where rents are nothing and I can serve all the Hollywood movie stars their coffee." His face dropped again.

"Are you serious?" she asked. She was having trouble following the swirl of his thoughts. Was he doing what she dreamed of doing?

"But that means I'm going to have to close the Morning Spot downtown, too."

Moishe's enthusiasm, even while delivering bad news, was infectious.

"You won't believe it, but I've been thinking about that for awhile – giving this baby a fresh start, away from all the madness." *Away from Jack Morgan and his bank.*

"Well then what are you waiting for?" he beamed at her.

"What do you mean?" she asked.

"You're coming to California with me. I have family there. The baby will grow up a Stern. That's it, case closed. That beautiful long hair and—"

"So you've told me before," she stopped him. She eyed her belly, growing bigger and harder every day. Her baby surged inside of her. He seemed to be doing a somersault. A wide grin spread across her face.

"So you'll come?" Moishe asked.

"I'm sure Rachel would love it there – she'd be a female Jackie Coogan. And the weather – it would do Tanta Rosa good. And even the twins – they have plenty of docks in California and a wide open sea for fishing!"

Her head spun as she mapped out the futures of her loved ones.

"Exactly!" encouraged Moishe. "And you could manage my shop there. It'll be like you're me, but—"

"But I'll be me," finished Leila.

For the first time in a year, she had a clear sense of who that was. The year had beaten her up beyond belief, and through it all, she had questioned and berated herself at every fateful juncture. She had lost her Mama and her lover. She had betrayed her boyfriend. People had died because of her, and no amount of geographical distance would bring them back. She had faced an evil man head on, and even if she didn't put him in jail where he belonged, she chipped a tiny bit off his steely veneer.

She had discovered that the power of Wall Street was no less than that of the Cossacks. The violence of her childhood was random and immediate. Here in America, the powerful evoked grinding poverty and a slower death. It was time to put that behind her, for herself and for her baby. She knew where she was going. Life would begin again.

# EPILOGUE:

# HOLLYWOOD

## January 29, 1931

Leila stood on the sidewalk of Hollywood Boulevard, her pulse quickening. Across the street, the blue neon sign of the Pantages Theatre gleamed a welcoming light to the audiences gathering for the evening performance. Before her, the dark glass entrance of Musso and Frank's Grill beckoned. She hesitated, adjusting then readjusting her cloche. She had avoided this moment for months, but couldn't hold it off any longer. She entered through the glazed door. She was greeted by a rotund maître d' wearing a fire-engine red tuxedo jacket, a stark white shirt, and a black bow tie.

"Greetings Miss, are you meeting someone here?"

"Why yes, I—"

"Leila!" called an Irish voice from one of the inside booths.

"I see you've located your party," said the red-jacketed man. "This way please."

Leila nervously slid into a scarlet-leather semi-circular booth. How could she begin to close the eight-month gap in conversation, during which so much had changed for both of them? Mostly because of her. Light chatter seemed the easiest way.

"Nice place," said Leila. "Hollywood sets must be in demand."

"Well, John's a buddy of mine," Nelson replied with some tension, equally disposed to accentuate the impersonal. He gestured toward the wood carving under the murals of pine forests and ponds that spanned the length of the restaurant. "I did some work for him here."

Leila looked around. The restaurant was a haven for starlets and film producers, even as the Great Depression rampaged the country. The ceilings were higher than at any other restaurant. The air was crisp with an aroma of coal-infused, smoky wood, more like winter in New York than the endless summer of Los Angeles.

"It's lovely," she remarked.

"After dinner, I'll introduce you to the best chef in the world, the great Jean Rue, creator of his legendary pork chop. But enough about food. How are you? How's…?"

"Adam. Adam Kahn. He's a lovely boy. Born right here at Cedar Sinai."

He looked at her wistfully. "I'm sure. He's got a beautiful mother and—"

"Moishe has been so helpful," Leila added.

"Why didn't you ask me for anything when you got out here?"

"I betrayed everything about us – I couldn't ask you. I didn't even ask him."

"I know that," he cut her off.

A long silence settled at the table between them.

"Besides, you had run off to Hollywood – so quickly, too – like you were running away from something…"

"It takes a lot to make me run," said Nelson, "but it was necessary given the circumstances."

"So, it was all your doing – the Morgan vandalism, beating up Lamont, the man in the dumpster?"

"Let's just say, I had help from a couple of boys at the precinct. They were angry about O'Malley. Said they'd turn the other cheek if I got out of town; left no ties."

"I wish I could have been there," she said. *Where did that come from?*

"It wasn't pretty," he said. "But the bastard had it coming. I just wish I had a chance to see Jack that night. You did well with the old fashioned day-in-court thing. I followed the trial day by day out here. Everyone did."

"I don't know about that," she said. "He got away with murder and I came off as..."

"Umberto!" Nelson called to the waiter. Umberto was also dressed in neatly pressed blank pants, a red tuxedo jacket, and a white pressed shirt with black bow tie. "Could you bring us two glasses of your finest brew?"

"You mean, our finest apple ale?" he corrected, an eyebrow raised.

"Yes, of course," said Nelson.

Leila chuckled softly.

"What's so funny?" he teased.

"Nothing. What about prohibition?"

"Good point. We should toast to that too," he said. "But, first – to Adam!" He leaned back and fixed his eyes upon her. "You look beautiful tonight. It's been too long."

She felt her cheeks grow warm and tucked several strands of hair behind her ear. She had worn it loose and flowing over her shoulders tonight.

"Here you go, Sir!" said Umberto, bringing their drinks. He set them down on the white tablecloth, making room by the ivory and maroon china bread plates.

"Thank you," said Nelson. He raised his glass. "To Adam – and – to friendship!"

"I'm sorry I didn't reach out to you when I first got here," said Leila, raising hers and meeting his stare. She gazed up to the high ceilings secured by heavy oak beams, then behind her, noting the fine detail in the dark wood trimming above their booth. "I just – had some things to work out for myself and Adam, and getting Rachel settled… And Moishe, he's been like a mother hen. He and his new wife have been wonderful and— oh Nelson, I'm so sorry, for everything!"

"Shhh," he put his finger to his lips. "You're here now. I'm glad we finally ran into each other at Moishe's wedding." Nelson paused as he swirled his ale in his glass.

"I'm glad too," she said softly. "To friendship."

They clinked their glasses together.

"To friendship," he echoed, a distant look returning to his eyes.

"Delicious," she said, taking a dainty sip. She scanned the booths in front of them. She spotted Mary Pickford, Rachel's favorite actress, drinking a dirty martini. Her face fell. She tried to distract herself by browsing the menu.

"You're thinking about Tanta Rosa, aren't you?" he asked gently.

"I miss her," said Leila, pleased that Nelson still knew her so well, or parts of her anyway. She had taken that closeness for granted. "I wish she would have come to California, but she insisted on staying with Uncle Joseph. Did you hear that Jonathan moved in with them? He met a nice Irish girl, you'll be happy to know. They're getting married this summer."

"Those Irish come from good stock," he smiled, relaxing. "What about Joshua?"

"He picked up and moved to San Francisco. Didn't tell anyone, just left a note. Which reminds me, I have other news – Rivkah may be moving out here!"

"Really – you think Hollywood is ready for her?"

"I got her letter today and no, hardly," replied Leila, with a giggle, "but she says she's not going to spend one more winter freezing and—"

"And it never snows in Hollywood," Nelson finished.

"No, it never does," she agreed. She leaned back in the soft leather cushion of the booth and studied his face. It had changed during the past few years. There was more salt in his jet-black hair. His features seemed more angular. His bright blue eyes were sharper and wiser. She had once loved those eyes, before she became intoxicated with Roderick, and fraud, and the Morgans. She saw a pain in them. She was sure she had caused it.

"Nelson," she said, "I never meant to hurt you."

"I know that, Leila. I…"

"I hope you can forgive me," she said. "It was all so – complicated."

"I can try – but I hate the Morgans. I think I knew that I'd lost you when you started at the diner; I just told myself I was imagining things," he replied. "Maybe we can start to be friends again. It's a crazy town, Hollywood. It's hard to trust anyone."

"We both kept too many secrets from each other," she said.

"Yes, we did," he agreed.

"So I guess we move toward the future and see what it brings."

"To the future, then!" he exclaimed, lifting his glass.

She raised hers again to meet his. "To the future."

Leila leaned back and sighed. She was in Hollywood. A world away from Wall Street. Many worlds away from Kiev. She had given birth to a wonderful boy whose whole life lay ahead of him. Everything was different. Each day brought a new adventure and a fresh chance.

Thoughts of New York drifted into her head. Jack was fined one million dollars after many appeals. It was nothing compared to the money he made during the boom times, and he did not spend a moment in jail. He remained at the helm of the Morgan bank, and Lamont continued to be quoted in the papers, promising a turnaround as the country suffered. Althea finally moved back to London for good.

Leila was happy the ordeal was over, that she had spoken her piece and brought at least some of Jack's actions to light. From time to time, she thought of Roderick, his tragic death and how he had tried to do the right thing but was too weak to accomplish it. She had done what she could in that regard. It was harder than she would have imagined.

She stared at the man before her. This man she knew so well and yet had left for someone she would never truly know. She didn't know what would happen between her and Nelson, but she saw him in a clearer light finally. There was nothing she could do to change her past. Every time she looked into the eyes of her son, she realized she wouldn't want to. She had made mistakes but could regret none of them. All she could do was make the best of what she had.

She recalled her mother's words from a lifetime ago in Russia.

*Tomorrow is only another today.* She looked forward to that new today.

# ACKNOWLEDGMENTS

*Black Tuesday* went through tons of revisions in the process of becoming the book you have in your hands – or on your electronic reading device. Any imperfections or mistakes remaining are mine and mine alone. But really, isn't perfection overrated?

I am profoundly grateful for the editorial suggestions and mental encouragement of friend and author, Morris Berman, who kindly and patiently improved the content of this novel, and kept me sane through the myriad of rejections it received, and subsequent revisions it endured. Thanks also to David Lobenstine, my structural editor now for four books, fiction and non-fiction. His abilities are substantial. Thanks to Allison Kemp for her copy-editing expertise and for locating the photo I fell in love with that resides on the cover. Thanks to my researcher, Krisztina Ugrin, with whom I've now worked on two books, for her attention to historical and fictional detail, and to Clark Merrefield, for his reads and comments. Thanks to my publicist, Celeste Balducci, for all her enthusiasm for this project. Thanks to Lukas for everything.

I feel blessed to have the support of so many people in my life; family and friends and colleagues, far too numerous to mention here. I hope you know who you are.

Please accept my heartfelt gratitude and love.

Made in the USA
Lexington, KY
25 November 2011